New Zealand Sh
Second S

Other titles in this series

New Zealand Short Stories First Series
Selected with an introduction by D. M. Davin

New Zealand Short Stories Third Series
Selected with an introduction by Vincent O'Sullivan

New Zealand Short Stories Fourth Series
Selected with an introduction by Lydia Wevers

New Zealand Short Stories
Second Series

Selected with an introduction by
C. K. Stead

Auckland
Oxford University Press
Melbourne Oxford New York

Oxford University Press

Oxford University Press, Walton Street, Oxford OX2 6DP

OXFORD   NEW YORK   TORONTO
DELHI   BOMBAY   CALCUTTA   MADRAS   KARACHI
PETALING JAYA   SINGAPORE   HONG KONG   TOKYO
NAIROBI   DAR ES SALAAM   CAPE TOWN
MELBOURNE   AUCKLAND
and associated companies in
BERLIN and IBADAN

Oxford is a trademark of Oxford University Press

First published 1966
Reprinted 1976, 1977, 1985, 1989 in this format
Introduction and selection © Oxford University Press 1966, 1976

ISBN 0 19 558014 1

Printed in Hong Kong
Published by Oxford University Press
1A Matai Road, Greenlane, Auckland 3, New Zealand

Contents

Acknowledgements

The Editor is grateful to the following for permission to use copyright material: to MacGibbon and Kee for Frank Sargeson's 'The Undertaker's Story' from *Collected Stories* (first published in *Landfall,* June 1954), and to Mr. Sargeson for 'City ' and Suburban' (first published in *Landfall,* March 1965); to Roderick Finlayson for 'The Bulls' (first published in *Landfall,* March 1956); to James Courage's executors for 'No Man is an Island, (first published in the *London Magazine,* December 1958); to Minerva Bookshop Ltd. for Olaf Ruhen's 'My First Whale' from *Lively Ghosts* (1964); to Helen Shaw for 'The Bull' (first published in the New Zealand *Listener,* 30 April 1954); to Blackwood and Janet Paul Ltd. for Amelia Batistich's 'The Gusla' from *An Olive Tree in Dalmatia*; to E. S. Grenfell for 'Old Tolly' (first published in *Landfall,* June 1953); to Maurice Duggan for 'In Youth is Pleasure' from *Immanuel's Land* (1956), and to Blackwood & Janet Paul and Victor Gollancz Ltd. for Maurice Duggan's 'Along Rideout Road that Summer' from *Summer in the Gravel Pit* (first published in *Landfall,* March 1963); to W. H. Pearson for 'At the Leicesters' ' (first published in *Canterbury Lambs,* No. 3, 1948); to Phillip Wilson and Denis Glover for 'It was Easter' and 'End of the River' from *Some are Lucky* (1960); to Robert Hale Ltd. for David Ballantyne's 'Other Gardens' and 'A Leopard Yarn' from *And the Glory* (1963); to Janet Frame and W. H. Allen for 'The Reservoir'; to O. E. Middleton for 'Saving the Breed' for *Short Stories* (1953), and to Mr. Middleton and Michael Joseph for 'The Doss-House and the Duchess' from *A Walk on the Beach* (1964); to Jacqueline Sturm for 'For all the Saints' (first published in *Te Ao Hou* December 1965); to Mrs. Amato for 'Perspective' by Renato Amato (first published in *Landfall,* September 1961); to Noel Hilliard and Robert Hale for 'A Piece of Land' from *A Piece of Land* (first published in *Mate,* June 1960); to the Hutchinson Publishing Group for Maurice Gee's 'The Losers' from *Short Story One* (first published in *Landfall,* 1959); to Eyre & Spottiswoode for Maurice Shadbolt's 'The People Before' from *Summer Fires and Winter Country* (1963); to Alexander Guyan for 'An Opinion of the Ballet' (first published in *Mate,* June 1960); to Marilyn Duckworth for 'Loops of her Hair' (first published in *Mate,* December 1962). C. K. Stead's 'A Fitting Tribute' was first published in *The Kenyon Review,* April 1965.

Introduction

This anthology has been made to supplement the first World's Classics *New Zealand Short Stories*, edited by D. M. Davin, published in 1953, and since reprinted many times. That collection covered the whole span of New Zealand writing, though it is worth noting that two-thirds of its stories belonged to the fifteen years from 1937 to 1951, when the form in New Zealand assumed stature and importance in the hands of ten or a dozen writers. The emphasis of the present volume is on new developments. Where a writer included in the previous anthology has gone on writing short stories, but has added nothing which seems a development in form or in substance, his recent work has not been represented here. Such writers are not strictly speaking 'absent', since the intention is that the two volumes should together represent the New Zealand short story. On the other hand, writers like Maurice Duggan, O.E. Middleton, and David Ballantyne, with only single and brief stories in the first volume, now, by virtue of their recent work, assume something like central importance in the second.

Twenty-one writers, twenty-six stories, from a period of thirteen years: the anthologist is bound to think statistically. Can so many from so few, in so short a time, deserve this status? Alternatively, is an average of two stories per year enough? My answers to these questions can only be—yes, to the first; to the second, no. The short story in New Zealand has had for a long time a special place. It has been recognized, not as a novelist's by-product, or as the promise of a novel, but as a form in its own right by which a talent may fully declare itself. The best of our short stories, though seldom in wide circulation, have had a way of persisting and being talked about. Often they have proved more durable than novels. This is a situation in which the form has flourished, and my difficulty has been, not how to find stories worthy of inclusion, but rather, which among many are most worthy, and further, how to represent in the space available at once the chief strengths of recent short-story writing, and its breadth among widely varying talents.

No anthologist expects, or hopes, to satisfy all those who know the field in which he is working; but he may feel it right that he should say something of the method by which he has arrived at his decisions. Like anyone else, I have had to take it on trust that I have an ear for the true notes in fiction, and for the false ones. I have read passively, waiting to be gripped by something, waiting for the story to make the first move. No formal theory has governed this procedure—only the feeling that to look conscientiously for 'significance' would be to look for one, or at best a limited number of significances, and never for the unpredictable one that makes the work of fiction distinct. What I have sought might be described simply as pleasure, if that did not seem to put too common-place a value on the qualities which achieve it. One looks of course for formal competence; or rather, one is distracted when it is absent. But no amount of competence will alone achieve the moment, or moments, of illumination (in a short story there may be no more than one) which, on the other hand, a minimal competence may be sufficient to support.

Near the beginning of this book there is a story, 'City and Suburban', by New Zealand's most distinguished writer of fiction, Frank Sargeson; and at the end, one by Marilyn Duckworth, a young writer known chiefly for her novels. That Mr. Sargeson brings a high degree of consciousness to his story, while Mrs. Duckworth is still working largely by instinct, will be obvious enough. What interests me, however, is the qualities the two stories have in common. Neither seems to me perfect in form. Both present a recognizable New Zealand suburban scene, and introduce into it elements of fantasy and of horror. Both writers—but Mr. Sargeson especially—are possessed by an 'idea'. The ideas differ in detail, but they fit well enough together. They concern suburban life, affluence, conformity ('Pink? But that's *wrong*') and the rebellion of something that may as well be called 'the spirit' against these things. Simply *as* ideas, they are not ones to which I would find myself giving easy assent. What is it then, to which the 'ear' I have spoken of, has responded?

I hope it will be plain that I have not set myself this examination in order to pass with full marks, but only to push myself towards some kind of definition. There are stories it would be easier to analyse, if 'analysis' were called for; and others which are simply good and successful, in a way which leaves little to be said. But there are only a few, I think, in which, quite a part from the question of 'success', the qualities peculiar to *fiction* are so readily distinguished:

'Oh, I feel sick,' Mrs. Doubleday gulped, lying back on the tartan rug and placing a hand across her eyes. Her shopping bag

bosom divided over her ribs, while her soft chins multiplied......
... 'Find me the field glasses, Jeremy.'

(Marilyn Duckworth)

And as the handkerchief-draped horror went into the picnic bag,
out came the transparent packet of cholocolate biscuits....
... I recovered my speech only to say a thing which to Pam
would be irritating and silly, and which in the circumstances she
was quite right to ignore.
'For God's sake, Pam,' I said, 'why ever in the name of heaven
and earth did you insist they be called Happy and Glad?'

(Frank Sargeson)

Two picnics. In ten years time I may well have forgotten a good
deal of Mrs. Duckworth's story; but it is unlikely I will have forgotten the scene in which the suburban lady calls for her field
glasses. Nor does it seem possible that I will have forgotten any
detail of that perfect short story within what is perhaps an im-
perfect one, in which Mr. Sargeson's Happy and Glad bring to
their parents the severed finger they have found on the beach.

Why are such scenes memorable? Why is one compelled—
by that power which belongs uniquely to fiction—to store them
as if they were real? It is not to an 'idea' one has responded. There
is, I suppose it may be said, a 'perception'—about our society,
about ourselves—bodied forth in these scenes; but if so, it is a
perception more comprehensive, more satisfying, and more general
(its instance being more particular) than anything which may be
stated in intellectual terms.

There are, of course, stories which, for all their distinctness as
fiction, do resolve themselves in a statement. 'The trouble is ... '
O. E. Middleton's 'The Doss House and the Duchess' concludes,
'we forget the friends of our poverty.' It is the classic conclusion
to the classic pattern of the 'mateship' tale. The simple didacticism
has its charm, as it had in the early stories of Frank Sargeson. But
is it only for this we have come so far? What supports the statement,
surpasses it in claiming our attention, and lends to it in the end a
flavour almost of irony, is a quality everywhere present in the story,
but most clearly exemplified in that cool and terrifying moment
when 'a ripe melon falls from the sky and splits on the pavement'.

Can we call that quality the sense of style? If we can—and that
is how I believe it is best described—it must be distinguished from
'fine writing'. There are times, indeed, when writing which is
noticeably fine can seem evidence only of a fiction writer's effort,

and failure, to get through to his subject. The prose stands like a dead monument to his labour, and that is all we see. Maurice Duggan is perhaps better equipped to turn a sentence than any other New Zealand writer. Yet that is not the gift which makes 'Along Rideout Road that Summer' the remarkable story it is. It is not 'prose' that tangles the heel of the father, retreating from his discovery, in the 'bra' of the girl with whom his son has assumed the 'historic disposition of flesh'; nor is it 'prose' that sends him stumbling across the field his son has ploughed, 'scattering broadcast the white and shying gulls'.

If for my own purposes I have rejected in turn the quality of the 'ideas' and of the prose as measures of the quality of the fiction, it is not so that I may conclude with a general statement about the metaphysical, or metaphorical, 'unity' of the work of literature. Literature can look after itself, and has no need of our road-blocks and check-points along the variety of routes by which it may be approached. My concern has been, not to preserve it against in-filtrators, but simply to keep as close as possible to the experience of the common reader who will come to these stories as fiction. A professional critic might well study 'Along Rideout Road that Summer' simply as prose. A second might approach it sociologically, in terms of 'race relations'—and find in it a tone refreshingly casual and wholesome. A third, coming by a different route, might see it as a bringing together of two extremes—the literary and the actual—of the New Zealand consciousness. Each of these studies would have its point and its value. Each would contribute something to our awareness of the fact that Mr. Duggan has done something entirely new in this story. Yet none, strictly within its terms of reference, could quite deal, for example, with Fanny Hohepa's 'bra': that would be a detail, one of many left out of the account; and without such details, without the sense they cumulatively contrive for us of something *lived through*, none of those critical approaches—stylistic, sociological, historical—would be called for at all.

Can we go a short step further and allow that 'bra', tangled round a shocked father's retreating foot, to stand for what I have called the sense of style; and to see the sense of style in turn as the direct transmission of the writer's sense of life? It is this latter sense which generates his energy at the same time that it requires precision of him; and it is this, in the scenes I have used as touchstones, that has given to Frank Sargeson and to Marilyn Duckworth their gaiety, to O. E. Middleton and to Maurice Duggan their authority, in the midst of the horrors or the complexities or the absurdities they are conceiving.

Introduction

I could not, of course, insist that no other consideration than those I have indicated has at any point influenced my selection. A perfectly consistent editor would be rare, and perhaps no more satisfactory than any other. One or two stories may well have been included partly for the record—for reasons of history, or even of literary history. By far the majority, however, are here solely for the achievement of those possibilities which belong to fiction alone.

Readers will come to this anthology wanting to know, among other things, what developments are evident in the New Zealand short story since the publication of the previous World's Classics anthology. They will find their answers in the book as a whole, not in its introduction. There are, however, one or two extra-literary developments which may be briefly noted, since they may help to provide a context, and even perhaps an explanation, for the purely literary ones which the stories themselves will reveal. Chief among these is the rapid growth of a public for New Zealand fiction.

'New Zealanders', an American writer recently commented, 'are among the most literate people in the world, and they consume books about themselves more rapidly than the citizens of any other country.' It is something booksellers and publishers began to take note of in the 1950's. Now, of the books sold in any of the four main cities, about one-third are on New Zealand subjects and by New Zealand authors. At its simplest level, of course, this is an appetite for mirrors —and especially for those expensive mirrors (*New Zealand in Colour, New Zealand—Gift of the Sea*) which answer correctly to the question 'who is the fairest of them all?' As the appetite becomes more sophisticated it passes through popular to academic history, through journalism to sociology, through romance to fiction, and beyond all these, to poetry. We are, it seems and have been since about 1930, at that moment (a moment in history, but prolonged through several generations) when a new society defines its consciousness while that consciousness is forming; and we may hope only a little of what such a time can produce has yet been achieved.

It is largely this appetite at home that has produced the boom of the last decade in the publication of New Zealand novels and short stories abroad.* London firms publish our work partly because there is an English market for it; but principally because there is a market for it at home—one which will take more than half the

* of the twenty-one writers still living at the time of the publication of D. M. Davin's anthology, only four had published fiction in London. Of the same group, nine have now published there; and of the twenty-one contributors to the present volume, thirteen.

printing of any New Zealand work of fiction. We have not yet reached the time when—like some Australian works—any of our own are quite 'fashionable' in London: but we may expect that to come too, for better or for worse. And beyond the publishing industry there is another—the academic—which shows signs of turning in our direction: 'Commonwealth Literature', as a serious study, is already under way in both England and the United States.

One effect of these developments has been, I think, to increase the New Zealand writer's confidence and his sense of possibilities, and to broaden the scale on which he can work. Another, however, may be to promote the novel—that being the form publishers favour—at the expense of short stories.* One might expect, too, that something of the formulas of 'marketable' fiction would have begun to influence our writers. Such an influence may indeed be evident in recent novels; but I can see, as yet, only rare signs of it in short-story writing. There is still in New Zealand, as there was in the thirties and forties, evident devotion to the *craft* of the short story, not as a thing in itself, but as a means of getting at the exact flavour, the distinct feel, of our experience. It may be (one can only guess) that an overseas reader, or even a New Zealander accustomed solely to the conventions, social and literary, which shape so much of the fiction published in English, will find himself saying of many of these stories that this is not, after all, what he *expects* of a work of fiction. If so, he would do well to question his expectations first, and only second the credentials of the writers, all of whom have been through a school in which every statement is measured, not by the roundness of its vowels or the ease of its syntax, but by its power to reach out to, and grasp, a recognizable experience. It would be foolish to claim that all equally have passed through that school with flying colours; but none is unaware of its lessons.

C. K. STEAD

August 1965

---

* The contributors to this book have produced altogether about thirty novels, most of them in the last dozen years.

The Undertaker's Story

FRANK SARGESON
(*b.* 1903)

A stocky powerful man somewhat gone to seed, he was thrown out of a seaside pub one fine Saturday afternoon when I was sitting on the verandah.

The bar had been too crowded and noisy, too intolerably hot and sticky, and I had taken my beer outside, where the sun would be some time yet before it hit the bench against the front wall. A breeze off the harbour kept the high tide slapping at the sand, which sloped up until it met the concrete verandah flooring, but the glare and glitter was too trying on my eyes and I turned sideways on. The noise from within was a babble and roar, but the moment my ears began to pick out the sounds of a quarrel, it was strange to see how the backs that curved from the wide-open windows began to straighten. As the moment of climax approached they all disappeared.

Spluttering and blowing, his face red unshaved and swollen, he braked with his feet and grabbed at the jamb of the doorway, but so many were pulling and shoving he hadn't a chance. He went limp as they heaved him down the slope, and he lay like something washed up by the tide. It was as though he knew himself to have been defeated beyond all question.

They all turned and went inside again, dusting and straightening their clothes. There was no fuss, no sign of either malice or sympathy. A quarrelsome drunk had been dealt with. The faces at the windows looked the other way, and the backs curved out again.

There were two of us outside now, and while I was trying to work out the problem the incident had presented me with, there appeared in the doorway an elderly undersized man, very tidy in a panama hat, a maroon blazer and flat rubber-soled shoes. With his white tooth-brush moustache as well, he looked as though he had by some mistake dropped in instead of going to bowls. He had with him an old felt hat, which he dusted with his handkerchief as he went down the beach, and for quite some time he kept turning it in his hands as he sat beside the heap of discarded humanity. When he began to speak I could not hear what he said, but the heap immediately came to life. That hat was accepted, and soon they were sitting side by side with their backs to the pub as they talked. Or rather, while the older man went on talking.

I was moved, but perhaps my strongest feeling was one of gratitude that my problem hadn't had to be solved.

When they at last stood up and parted, it seemed that the drunk was perhaps not so drunk. Quite steady on his feet, he returned from along the beach for the ceremony of trust and friendship. Hands were gripped and held, placed on shoulders and left there. It was a sort of tableau, or they might have been figures on a frieze. Beyond them the sea's dark blue suggested melancholy, and the unceasing movement seemed not to hold out any promise of permanency for their bond, but at least they stood on sand that was solid and clean after the high tide, and there was the sunlight for an impartial golden blessing.

The elderly man gave me a nod when he re-entered the pub, and I was not surprised when he brought out his own beer.

Ay, he said, quite without any preliminaries as he sat down alongisde, ay. It is a sad thing when a man cannot forgive himself for his own failure.

This was direct and intelligent, somewhat unusual. Also, he spoke with a slight Scottish burr, which is often supposed to go with reticence.

I said I thought I understood.

Duncan, he said. I knew him when he was a Highland lad, a sturdy young bull of a lad that lived his days on the hills with the sheep. I remember well I saw few lads of his like when I went on my rounds to those Highland places.

Ay, he said — and it seemed not unlikely that the hills he looked at across the harbour, were re-shaping themselves into something rather different.

You're not a Highland man yourself? I asked.

No. I was a Paisley boy. My people settled from Lancashire, Manchester. I grew up a Lowland Scot, but except for a manner of speaking there's not all that difference. The Lowland Scot is Anglo-Saxon as you may remember from your schoolbooks, and much the same by nature according to the way I figure it out. But there is much to separate him from the Highlander.

You visited the Highlands? I prompted him.

I was a young man travelling with a line of knick-knacks. For the most part it was jewellery, cheapjack stuff. There was money to be had by my boss in Glasgow, but nothing much for a young fellow working on commission. The Highlanders were hard folk to persuade, and if it had not been for the lassies, with their liking to deck themselves out with a bit of finery—well, the order sheets I sent back to my boss would never have added up to much of a turnover.

But this Duncan? I prompted again.

Duncan, he said. I remember well I said to his mother, a Mrs. McGowan—I said the land's poor and the season is bad, and I don't forget there is always the landlord, but remember Mrs. McGowan I said, it's the townsman in the big city that's first to go without his supper when times are bad. I said it was good-bye to Scotland, for I was off to New Zealand, where by God's help and good luck I would make my fortune.

It must have been a long time ago, I said. How is it you remember so exactly?

Duncan, he said. It was Duncan. The boy was there in the yard, feeding a handful of grain to his mother's hens while I talked at the doorstep. He heard me say the name of this country.

How could I know, he continued, how could I know that name would never shift from the boy's memory?

So he followed you out here? I questioned, thinking I might cut down some of the story's trimmings.

It would be wrong to say that. He never remembered my face, and I did not recognize him until I heard his name called out and took stock of him. You see, I had not made my fortune after near on twenty years, and I had trouble enough to put thoughts of Scotland far from my mind. It was bad luck I took up with my old line of commercial travelling, although it did not look like bad luck at the time. I was employed by a grocery warehouse, and glad of my opportunity to see the country, but there is temptation for a young man when it is rare for him to sleep in any bed except what he can get at the country pubs. I don't mean to say I went to the bad with the drink, because your Scot is canny as a rule, and he has a great respect for book-learning. Many a night when there was drinking it would be no attraction for me, because I was lying on my bed with a book, and to this day I am a great reader of good books. But there is the temptation of woman, and that our Maker has decreed for the population of the world. No man may refrain, as you a young man will understand. But no great amount of looseness was ever in my nature, and I took my wife from a pub where I was in the habit of staying, a grand girl with a good hand for cooking, and a full bosom where any man might wish to pillow his head for his contentment.

Yes yes, I said, but what about Duncan?

Duncan, he said. If you are not in a hurry there is time to tell you about Duncan—and he was silent a moment while he appeared to gather up his threads.

My wife left me, and she took away the wee boy. I had never settled in this country, do you see?—even though it was ten or twelve years since I landed. I was still on the road, and it was no life for my wife. A woman should not be exposed to temptation when she has a husband to tend her. I tried, but I could not mend my situation, so I swore by God's help I would mend my ways in case I had another opportunity for settling. I thought hard and deep, and I decided to give up the road. I sat and looked at my soft hands, and I remembered about my grandfather. He was a master spinner, and he settled in the North because he hoped to better himself at the fine Paisley work. There was none of that sort of thing in New Zealand, but I remembered my bachelor uncle gave me a card-board box of carpenter's tools for my birthday when I was ten. It was because I had said I was going to be a carpenter. The tools were toys, which I was proud to bring out to show the visitors, but although there was a book of directions, and my uncle brought me pieces of wood, I was never known to try to use those tools. It all came back to me in my distress, and I decided (when I was near to turning forty, mind you), I decided I would make myself into the carpenter I said I was going to be.

And? I had to prompt.

Did you not see the big sign as you came through the town?

I thought a moment, and replied that apart from the hoardings, the only sign I could remember was the undertaker's.

That's it, he said. Robert Wilson is my name.

But, I was about to say, when he continued.

You see, I was a very determined man and I had made my decision. I learned the carpentry, and I did more by learning the joinery and cabinet-making. I discovered I had nimble hands when a delicate job was called for. I came over to the coast here, and I set myself up in the furniture line of business, but it would be untruthful to say I prospered. I made none of your cheapjack stuff, which the public preferred because of my prices. I remember well a customer said when I showed him a kitchen cupboard—he said I had put in enough work to make it watertight. He said I should have been a boatbuilder. Ah, but it was about that same time my opportunity came to me. There was just one other furniture-maker in the township as it was then, and he was the undertaker. He died, he was undertaken himself as you might say, and I made my arrangements to take over his business. Now wasn't that a strange thing?—it was honest work for living folk I had done, but the public wouldn't have it on account of the prices. I did not prosper until I worked for the dead man that could have no argument about the price, and no say about what I provided.

He paused, but he held up his hand when I opened my mouth to speak.

Duncan, he said. It was about that same time when I began the undertaking. It was unbeknown to me that Duncan was living behind the hills you see eastwards yonder as you come up the coast. He had taken up a bit of land in a ballot. It was O.R.P. if you understand, occupation with right of purchase, what is reckoned third class land. But alongside of him being hampered for lack of ready money, the floods washed out his fences, and the wind blew a gale that carried away his cowshed, and the lean-to where he lived until he could prosper. I learned the story of his misfortunes one day when I had business at the Court-house, and heard his name called out before the Justices for sheep-stealing. Duncan, I said, when they allowed me to talk with him, before he was taken away to be tried at the Supreme Court—Duncan, I said, do your time as you must if the judgment of the law goes against you, but don't lose heart man. Stand up on your own two feet and look folks in the face, for it is in the nature of man to fall according to the law of God. But all may hope to raise themselves by the help of God and man, and if the Almighty does his share so will I too.

You see, I am none of your strict Calvinists in my belief, he broke off to say.

I told Duncan I had not made my fortune, but I stood in a fair way to prosper, and if he would return to the district I would do everything on his behalf that lay in my ability.

And he did return, I said.

Yes. But not before I had lost sight of him for close on ten years. He was not much changed in his appearance, but I never knew a man so reluctant to speak. He scarce spoke a word to me as a boy, and I forced the answers from him that sad day he was brought to the Court, but now he spoke up only one answer when ten might be required. And not to hear his wife answer at all was very aggravating.

You see, he said after a pause, he had taken a wife, and the pair were like foreign immigrants to America that have not learned to speak the English language. But what was the more strange, it was rare you heard them say a word to each other—no, not even upon an occasion of importance as you will hear.

Now do you see? he went on, I had my doubts about them being married. They were matched like to like if you understand, and in the marriage state it is best for the dark to be set against the fair, and the light and merry against what is more sober. But I did an injustice. Duncan had his bit of money saved up, and wished me to help him on to the land according to the word I had promised. I had prospered and I was willing to honour my bond, and indeed it suited me well, because I had bought up sixteen acres of good dairy country going cheap beyond the town boundary. If Duncan would settle, he and his wife could milk for the town supply, and by delivering to the householder as well the profit would be increased. So we made an arrangement, but first I told Duncan there was just one matter. He was a man with a conviction, but that would never be held against him with me supporting him—and I explained how I now had the honour of sitting as a J.P. But there must be nothing irregular in addition that might cause people to talk, and if he would pardon me for mentioning it I would be favoured if he would show his marriage certificate.

Good Lord! I couldn't help exclaiming. And did he crack you?

I was aware of the risk, he went on. But do you see?—I knew if the marriage lines were shown swiftly, I could fairly reckon it was because they were in the possession of Mrs. McGowan, and instead of free choice, I could infer the probability of what the young people nowadays speak of as a shotgun marriage. And in the event, it turned out that Duncan's wife visited me immediately with the document I wished to see.

But there was no child, I said.

Ah, I'm coming to that. I supposed the child had miscarried, and there I had the explanation of two people, man and woman, bound up together as man and wife for no reason but the child. There was no child, but they were still bound. Duncan, a fine strong handsome man, was bound to a poor creature that carried scarce a hint of feminine flesh anywhere on her bones.

His pause was so long I had to say, And?

And I was deceived. They settled nicely, putting heart and soul and all the strength of their two bodies into the work on the land. But I confess I was very surprised to hear there was to be seen a wee boy running about the place, and sometimes riding on the float when Duncan came to town for the early delivery. I inquired, and I found he had been left with his grandmother, Duncan's mother-in-law, until they were settled. Not that I counted the circumstance against them, but it irked me to be deceived when I was right in my reckoning. And I still could not understand why they did not speak to each other, whatever the wrong that had been done, when they had the boy to compensate them for being bound. He was a merry lad, too young for his schooling, but fine strong and healthy. And he was equally fond of Duncan and his mother. He would run from one to the other, and although his frolics never persuaded either to speak except perhaps a syllable, I marked it one day when Duncan placed his hand on the child's head—because Duncan smiled, and that was a thing I had never known him to do.

Ah, but then it all happened, and it was sudden like the plague visited on the Egyptians by the God of Israel. I have no evidence that Duncan was in the habit of taking liquor privately, but occasionally of an afternoon, perhaps one day a fortnight, he would ride into town and drink until closing time. It was never reported to me he drank to excess and indeed it was complained by the barmen that he was the slowest drinker on record. But it did not matter how much he drank, he would never seek company in the bar. For my own satisfaction I ascertained that his wife did not sit wringing her hands waiting on his return, on the contrary she would have the milking done and everything washed up ready for the morning, so I did not consider I had any grounds for complaint. But so far as I can piece together the happenings, one late winter evening Duncan rode home and heard the cows bellowing on account of not being milked. His wife's excuse was Jock, the laddie—he had been taken ill with a bad stomach pain in the afternoon. He was tossing and delirious with fever, and the wife dared not leave him to walk some considerable distance where she could ring up the doctor. She asked Duncan to go and ring, but he was obstinate and said the boy would be well by the morning. He went to milk the cows, first forbidding his wife to leave the house, and swearing he would have no doctor calling, with authority to poison the boy with his medicines. The poor creature was distracted, but she obeyed her husband, and Duncan delayed returning to the house until the evening was well spent. She thought from the delay he had been for the doctor after all, but it was not so, and immediately he returned she risked disobedience, because although the boy had turned quiet he lay cold in a sweat—and when the doctor came at last, husband and wife were sitting each side of the bed, not speaking, but each clasping upon the boy's hands. And the boy was dead.

He was silent a moment, and the noise from inside the bar seemed suddenly very loud. I did not know what to say and said, I see.

But, he went on, there was more happened that winter night. The doctor got me out of bed to notify me on the phone. I could not sleep after such news, accustomed though I was to notifications of the kind so I dressed myself and drove out to the farm. I shut

off the engine to coast down the hill to the gate, and I considered
returning to town because there was no glimmer of light to indicate
they were not in their bed. But a light commenced to shine beneath
the macrocarpas that separated the garden from the paddocks,
so I walked up the track and rounded the house but I went no
further. There was toi-toi I could stand behind, and I could see
well that Duncan's wife was holding a storm lantern while Duncan
dug and chopped at the roots of the biggest tree. I heard him grunt
at his work but he never spoke, and he worked hard and fast
until there was a big hole tucked well in under the tree. Then I
had to hold in my breath as they passed near returning into the
house, but immediately they came again, Mrs. McGowan still
carrying the lantern but Duncan bearing a rough timber box.
He placed it well in the hole, and when he had finished throwing
back the earth and was stamping it with his feet, then his wife
placed the lantern on the ground and returned into the house.
Neither had spoke a word, but as for Duncan, when he had finished
stamping he picked up the lantern and stood before he returned
into the house. And I heard him say, Jock! my Jock.

For quite some time we were both silent, but the spell was
broken when he had to respond to greetings from a group which
came round the side of the pub to enter by the front door. It was
in any case high time for me to be out on the road, to wait for the
bus that would take me further up the coast.

I shouldered my rucksack.

Are they still living together? I asked.

Never. She left him after the inquiry.

And is Duncan still on the farm?

Never, never. He earns his bit of money here and there. He is
tipped for marking the scores in the billiard saloon.

Tell me, I said, did you ever marry again?

Ay, he replied, I married my housekeeper. It was in keeping
with my position when I was appointed a Justice of the Peace. My
wife is a fine figure of a woman.

There was an indefinable something about his eyes—what is
called a twinkle, I suppose.

And she has an excellent hand for cooking.

Yes, I said as I raised my hand for a goodbye. I'd expect that.

FRANK SARGESON　　　**City and Suburban**
(*b*. 1903)

To me, it more or less fixes the time I belong to if I say there was
always a war in progress when I was a schoolboy. To be more
exact, though—the Armageddon I refer to was the second one this
century. I remember particularly a teacher who plugged a line
about my lucky generation. Last time there had been some mistake
about the war to end war. But now, let there be no mistake about
it! There was a good time coming for all young people—golden
opportunities, glittering prizes later on; more to the point, generous
bursaries for all students with ambition. But in those days my
ambition was an opportunity denied me by the school leaving age.
My elder brother, a little too young for any of the services, was
establishing himself in a milk-round which could have been pro-
fitably extended if I had joined in as a junior partner. I was told
that in the meantime I must remain a schoolboy. It was suggested
that for compensation I might usefully dig for victory in the vegetable
garden.

Whenever there is any kind of petty crisis in my life that milk-
round will return into my mind as something I regret having missed
out on. Let's face it, I'm average. I have my university qualifications,
I am by profession an accountant, that's to say a partner in a
public accountancy business. I am the end product of what may
happen if you raise the school leaving age. Instead of neglecting
the opportunities provided (drawing my bursary for beer money),
I worked hard and I still do. I'm a married man with two youngsters
a home of my own and of course the car. Nothing alters the fact
that you have only to strip away the higher education to find me
average. If you like, the *new* average—the latter-day common
man, the runner among the ruck in the urban rat race. In secret I
yearn for something less complicated, let's say a milk-round and
an unworried living in a small country town. For committing myself
to paper I have the good excuse that I am at present enduring another
of my crises.

But first I must say that it was only gradually during my years of
exposure to the higher education that I discovered its two-sided
character. It takes you on a stroll through civilization's flower

garden (and I'm not being ironical—I am ready at any time to applaud the man who decides there's nothing in life to compare with reading, say, history).; and on the other hand it leads you to believe you are being singled out, made to feel important, assisted to get on and make a career—earn good money. So the question eventually comes up whether you can have it both ways; whether, having been shown around the garden you don't visit there any more, or whether (I am aware that I am changing the metaphor), you endeavour to arrange an uneasy marriage between what is of perennial appeal, and what has its day to day uses in keeping the wolf a long way from the door—in my own personal case one party to the marriage a business career, and the other, well, history. (That study does in fact happen to be my special cup of tea; but with my enthusiasm only moderately abated I could mention others, and will even go so far as to specify theology. Granted free choice of a career I might well have preferred to all others that of a learned clergyman—and the advantage of an efficient curate to attend to parish duties would have clinched the matter beyond all question.)

Now I have aimed at establishing myself as a man who can appreciate that some very attractive flowers grow on what used to be a kind of dung heap sometimes called by fanciful names (such as Leviathan); but which is nowadays more aptly described as a combined junk and gadget heap, praised-and-damned as the welfare state—or sometimes just praised as the affluent society. What are the advantages I derive from that appreciation? Has the higher education sold me an outsize pup or not? Answers to these questions wouldn't be just for me—as an accountant I would say that to reckon accurately the number involved could be a pretty sizeable job of computing, one requiring to be served by the latest model electronic machine if the population explosion and all such kindred phenomena are to be taken into account.

I expect my use of the marriage metaphor is significant. After all, everything we endure in this world is rooted in the married state —I mean it's the reason we are here unless we happen to be literal bastards. And I will say at once that I have no petty complaints about my wife. Since I began with women I have never been able to do without having one around. Pam is nicely put together, and I am confident about wearing qualities which should ensure that she remains for many years easy on the eyes. Also, being one hundred per cent woman, I can never see her landed in my own sort of jam —I mean to say I sometimes foresee the day when my life will be largely composed of an attempt to deal with long hours of boredom occupying the empty space between the morning and afternoon newspapers. That sort of horror will never be Pam's cup of tea, and even if it was she would never recognize it as such. There's a phrase (if I remember it was plugged by Spinoza), *sub specie aeternitatis*. To my certain knowledge Pam will never be plagued by the itch to relate her experience to any principle—I mean anything that might tend to upset her certainty about what is important in life and what isn't.

But it's time I came to the point—after all, I have mentioned a crisis.

It *would* be on a day like this (by far the best of our summer holiday), that our youngsters should come up the beach at low tide, and bring with them the finger they had found in one of their favourite rock pools.

'Mummy, look!' That was our boy, Happy. The pair of them had been disagreeing over who was to carry their find, which was cupped by Glad in her two hands. To me, it was as though I had never seen a finger so astonishingly large despite the wrinkles. The nail was intact and all had been washed white and clean. As an object composed of alabaster or translucent wax it could have been attractive—but there was no mistaking what it was.

As usual Pam was quicker than I was, and her technique within its own limitations coulnd't be faulted. While she whipped out a handkerchief she agreed with the young 'uns that they had found something very precious (Why! of all things! a new kind of shell— a *finger*-shell! Well!), and at the same time quite desperately fragile. Mummy would keep it for them, And now please would they go and find Mummy another of those pretty red and green stones— but wait a minute. ... And as the handkerchief-draped horror went into the picnic bag, out came the transparent packet of chocolate biscuits.

In the meantime I had been trying very hard to rid myself of the impression that what our children had found was somebody's severed phallus; and I recovered my speech only to say a thing which to Pam would be irritating and silly, and which in the circumstances she was quite right to ignore.

'For God's sake, Pam,' I said, 'why ever in the name of heaven and earth did you insist they be called Happy and Glad?'

The children had obligingly trotted off as suggested, and now Pam remarked that we must stroll casually about the rock pool area, just to be satisfied about any more human remains. And after that I must take the car to the nearest phone box and ring the police. We must hand over our gruesome relic and free ourselves of all responsibility. But there you are—my wife had used two words which belong to the stock in trade of one branch of the higher education. And in any case, once our children were beyond hearing I had groaned aloud.

'Pam,' I said, 'so long as we are at large in human society responsibility is our fate. No,' I added, 'our *doom*!'

My wife's sharp look at me was familiar—also her decision.

'All right,' she said, 'I'll go. Jellyfish.' She said too that I might try to make my conversation a shade more coherent—that sort of thing *could* be the sign of a mental breakdown.

I haven't mentioned that I met Pam during the time of our joint exposure to the higher education. She had begun with the fine arts, but changed to social studies—hence perhaps her flair (very evident during the time of our first encounters), for reconciling general theory and particular instance. Born myself to fumble any practical job in hand when it is unfamiliar, I was quick to admire and be grateful.

'While I'm gone,' she went on, 'I will trust you to be responsible for our children.'

I was not in the mood for arguing. When the children showed signs of disquiet over the sound of the car I shouted that Daddy would be with them soon, and to dispose of the jellyfish allegation I joined them by way of a circuitous route past the rock pool. There were no human remains so far as I could observe—as I told myself of course there wouldn't be. Despite what *actually* turns up, it's always the bits and pieces I *expect* to come in my direction.

When we were through with the police sergeant and his offsider, who turned up after the youngsters were in bed (being Pam, Pam had arranged for our children to be 'spared'), we had a row—the kind of rumpus which I foresee will be an annual event guaranteed to coincide with our annual holiday. And although there was no mistaking what grim finger had reached for the push button on this occasion, that is not to say *any* couple wanting a thorough-going occasion will ever lack a watertight excuse. Nevertheless, common stuff—I mean when the pair of us could be in no doubt what we were up to, yet found ourselves compulsively impelled to demonstrate how damnably ordinary we are. Pam is my own age exactly— which means she has come on right to the top of her form according to Kinsey. As for me, well, according to the same authority senility of that kind begins in males after sixteen. Not that I'm not the man to meet his marriage account as often as the wife likes to send in her bill—it's just that I am not always bright enough to conceal my surprise that pay-time has come round again so soon.

(I owe to my historical reading the discovery that according to Roman law a husband might discharge or withhold payment of the debt according to inclination. An Athenian husband on the contrary was by Solon's law required to make three payments a month. It was the Jewish people however, who had rules for special cases: a daily settlement of the debt was required from an idle but vigorous young husband, but twice a week from an ordinary citizen sufficed; once a week from a peasant, once in thirty days from a camel-driver, and once in six months from a seaman. But a student or doctor might resist all demands; and *no* wife who was in receipt of a weekly sustenance could sue for a divorce. I believe too that among the Jewish people polygamy would divide, without multiplying, the duties of the husband—and polygamy regulated in that way is something of which I could thoroughly approve. After all, it is not unreasonable for any man to wish for a number of wives sufficient to ensure there remains always one on duty.)

From my general reading I have gathered that back at the beginning of the century a wife would sometimes rebel against a husband to whom she was, according to her own view, 'just a plaything'. But from my experience I would think that modern times have tended to reverse that situation. Also, I will admit to irritating my wife by my failure to adopt what she considers the right attitude to our annual holiday—for her an extension of the child's experience of a beach holiday; that is to say golden days of sun sand and sea, in more exact words a daily round of fun and games but with the lid taken off. And no regrets, and no guilty conscience. And of course she's right in the pattern—you have only to check up on the statistics for spring births ('plum duff babies' is I believe the description bestowed by the nursing-home sisterhood).

But perhaps I can put the matter on a somewhat more refined level, if I say that for Pam our annual holiday is what the whole of life could be if we never aged (I mean beyond our maturity), and could always reckon on a large credit account at the Bank with never a moment's worry about its maintenance. There is something very pro-American about my wife, but money and consumer-goods are not what I mean. What you buy with money is the happiness which you never for a moment doubt is what you deserve, and may expect without any argument to the contrary. If you are disappointed in your expectations, then some two-legged scapegoat must be sought for immediately and made to take the blame. Tonight, before my wife slammed the bedroom door (leaving me to write this kind of last will and testament), I bitched back at her with the declaration that a more accurate view of our situation on this planet was held by the Greeks, for whom life was damned awful apart from a few happy moments for which they were no doubt profoundly grateful. And apart from her retort ('Ancient Greeks I'd give the whole damn lot for one decent American any day'), she remarked that she hoped I had considered the status of women and practices such as the exposure of infants—and that wasn't to mention slavery and what went on at stag parties. What did *I* think I knew about the ancient Greeks anyhow? Ha ha!

Now I expect I might have tried to patch matters up by making some kind of jest—perhaps by referring her to Kinsey, and Nature's cruel jest in throwing us into each other's arms at identical ages, when it would have been more satisfactory if her thirty years had been complemented by a mere sixteen years on my part (and ha ha to you). And no matter how vehement my wife's verbal reactions might have been, she would nonetheless have understood. But for me, to say any such thing would be merely to conceal the truth. To catch the interest of the parlour psychiatrist in her, encouraged by her social studies, I might perhaps have said that I could not rid myself of my first impression that it was some poor devil's severed member our youngsters had come up the beach to present us with. But what in the name of all that's *sub specie aeternitatis* would she have made of me if I had confessed the simple shocking truth —that even from her and my closest friends I conceal the melancholy which is induced in me by the afternoon slope of the summer sun? And that sex, Kinsey, and what have you are all the easiest kind of stuff to take compared to that horror?

Well, that's it. If these pages ever have a reader I would expect them either to ring a bell, or not to. It occurs to me that what our kids found on the beach might well represent somebody's drastic attempt at a solution (and it would make me very very angry to be reminded that what was found was a finger). Each man to his taste and his solution—and Pam by the sound of things behind the bedroom door has reached the limits of her patience. For that matter, so have I.

RODERICK FINLAYSON   **The Bulls**
(*b*. 1904)

The young new bull arrived at the farm that morning. He was a
handsome two year old Jersey, sleek and quiet eyed. Steve, the
drover from Matapoi, brought him along and turned him into the
yard. The old man and the boy came out and looked him over.
The boy could tell the old man was pleased with the bull by the
way he shuffled slowly around the yard with his hands behind his
back looking at the animal while he whistled a little through his
rangy moustache. The boy thought the bull looked good too.
    'Well, you can take the old fella, Steve,' the old man said.
    The drover didn't bother to reply. He was a thickset florid man
with a red-veined nose, hard unfriendly blue eyes, and close-cropped
sandy hair. His dog was a lean yellow cur, unfriendly too, slinking
and showing his teeth when the boy spoke to him. The drover rode
a gaunt chestnut mare so long-legged the man looked too tall in
the saddle. He sat staring hard down on the boy.
    'Wouldn't want to tag along with that man—not at any price,'
the boy thought, edging away from the unfriendly gaze.
    'Come along in, Steve, the missus has dinner on the table,' the
old man said. He looked at the boy. 'Come on, boy, don't keep us
waiting, looking like you're dumb.'
    The drover dismounted and led his horse to the water trough.
'Gotta be getting on the road,' he grumbled as if ungrateful for
the offer of a meal. 'You never know when it comes to getting an
old bull away from his home paddocks.'
    Nevertheless, once he was in the farm kitchen, he ate a real good
fill, gobbling great mouthfuls of beef and potato without any sign
of enjoyment and without speaking a word. But when he had had
enough and was handed his second cup of tea, he sat back and
smirked at the old man's wife. 'Meal like this here, missus, reminds
me of when I rode champion steeple-chasers and was feasted and
feted by the girls all up and down the country.' Having made this
statement he drank the tea in long sucking gulps and became as
morose as before.
    When the men left the house the drover went straight to his
horse and mounted. 'Come on, Thomson, where's the old devil?'

he shouted.

The old man with the boy went on foot to the back paddock, opened the gate and called to the big red bull. 'Hey-aah, bully! Hey-aah!' The red bull lumbered out with a slow toss of his horns. They followed him up the drive past the cowpaddock gate where he eyed the grazing herd.

'Run ahead and open the road gate, boy,' the old man said.

The old bull, sensing what they meant to do, balked at the gate. But the drover spurred his horse forward and cracked his whip angrily. The yellow cur snapped at the bull's heels and swung on his tail. And with the horseman lashing at his hindquarters, the old bull was rushed through the gate and out onto the open road. It was a back country road of sandy yellow clay now dry and dusty, and it twisted aimlessly among clumps of manuka scrub and native heather. Gorse grew thick along the barbwire boundary fences.

'Keep him at the bloody gallop,' yelled the drover. 'He won't get no chance to be no bloody trouble.'

But the old bull braked with his four legs bunched and turned quick as a cat turning to double back toward the gate that led to home and the herd. The drover swore freely and let out half-choked yells. His horse seemed to the boy to be far too long-legged for this kind of a job, and the man was too heavy and too high in the saddle.

The yellow dog yelped beside the bull. The old man and the boy tried to head the animal but he charged past and jumped the fence. He was in his home paddock again. Slowly he stalked toward the cows indignantly shaking his head.

'Do you think I have time to waste?' the drover shouted. 'Get him out of there, Thomson.'

Again the boy opened the road gate. Steve cantered in with his whip cracking and the yellow dog made straight for the bull, but neither man nor dog could get the bull near the gate.

'I'll turn some of the herd out with him,' the old man said. 'Run them up the road aways and then let them drop behind when we've got the old fella on the move.'

The drover cantered round the herd, and they got half a dozen cows and the old bull on the run. They stampeded them up the road, the cows moo-ing and blaa-ing at such unusual treatment, the bull tossing his head in agitation as he ran with the foremost cows. But Steve impatiently galloped among the mob and tried to rush the bull out ahead and up the road. The old fellow was too knowing. He swerved sharply into the gorse and leapt the neighbour's fence. There he stood in the strange paddock pawing the ground until the sods flew. Then he drove his horns into the broken ground and tossed the dirt high over his head.

The neighbour, a man named Jackson, had been watching from up by his shed. His herd in the next paddock was becoming restive and his bull was trotting excitedly up the dividing fence, so he put his two dogs on the intruder at the same time that the drover, who had swung open the road gate, now charged across the paddock with his dog. Steve slashed the bull's flanks with his stock-whip and the three dogs snapped and slavered at his heels forcing him over to the fence, forcing him to a short standing jump that brought him down on the wires with the barbs ripping his legs.

The old man called to the boy, 'Boy, we gotta get him on his way ourselves. That damn man's no good. He's only maddening the beast. Now be ready to head him away from home. You're young and nimble on your feet. I've got to keep at his heels.'

The big red bull was free of the twanging wires and was crashing through the manuka scrub. I'd like to stay handy to duck under that fence, the boy thought, but look out or you'll get pinned against that barbwire. Better keep to the open.

He was on his toes, tensed in the middle of the dusty yellow road. Suddenly he saw the bull coming, head low, neck arched. The little eyes were blood-shot and threads of saliva were trailing from the bull's lolling tongue. His flanks were streaked with blood and sweat and dust, and the places where the barbs had ripped were growing redder. The old fella's taking it hard, the boy thought, But he's dangerous like that, he reminded himself. He spread his arms wide and jumped up and down on his toes till the bull was almost up to him. Then he spun around and jumped aside into the manuka as the bull, made to change his course slightly, lumbered past, his great neck muscles bulging.

Boy, the boy said to himself, when it comes to leaving, you are as bad as that old bull.

The old man had the dog on to him turning him before the drover could catch up. They got the bull on the run up the road again, but again he skidded in the dust, swung around and charged back.

'Shake your coat at him, boy,' the old man shouted. 'Boss the bull, boss him'

The boy peeled off his jacket and shook it at the bull, jumped up and down shaking it in front of the bull. The bull changed course somewhat. The dog harried him, giving the boy a chance to jump clear of his path into the manuka. The bull crashed through the scrub, flattening the bushes in his way.

I must watch my step, thought the boy. Better not slip on a stone or trip in the scrub.

Again the old man and the dog turned the bull, again the boy
danced and pirouetted in front of him and kept his eyes away from
home. These actions of the boy with his flapping coat, the old man
with his prodding stick, his whoops and cries, where not without
a plan. If they did not drive the bull up the road at least they kept
him from home. It was a game of chase, a game between dancing
toes and pounding hoofs around the scattered manuka clumps by
the dusty yellow road. No one, neither the bull nor the men would
admit defeat.

'We cannot drive him, boy,' the old man gasped when he found
a chance to be near the boy. 'We must wear him down. It isn't
hard to wear him down when you are young and nimble on your
feet. Keep in front of him.'

The old bull was no longer so nimble on *his* feet. Gradually
they were wearying him. He panted, and his tongue lolled. The
unconcerned drover left him to the man and the boy on foot.
Sour faced, he sat on his tall horse at the roadside, while he rolled
a cigarette.

The old man and the boy were tiring too. With his cigarette
unlit the drover quickly uncoiled his stock-whip and gave a mighty
crack. 'Leave him to me,' he yelled. Spurring his horse forward,
whistling his eager yellow dog, he made a final charge that carried
the stumbling bull before him up the road, with no chance of turning
back.

'That's goodbye to him,' the old man said. 'That's goodbye.'

A cloud covered the sun, and the boy, standing still on the road
watching the distant lumbering bull, felt the chill of the evening
breeze. He shrugged into his old brown coat.

Next day after breakfast, the old man said, 'Well, now we must
ring the young one.' He and the boy went out to the stockyard where
the young bull was. He looked at them with great wondering eyes.
His coat was sleek and the muscles rippled when he moved.

The old man walked as he often walked, with his hands loosely
clasped behind his back, but now in his right hand he carried a
length of rope. He walked with a shambling sideways gait, and he
did not look at the bull. But the bull kept his eyes on the man. Not
looking at the bull but slowly shambling as though to go past him,
all the time drawing nearer the animal, the old man slowly and
casually backed the bull into the corner where the bail post was.

The bull constantly shifted ground to keep his eyes on the old
man. Then the old man flipped a noose of the rope over the bull's
horns, over his head, and threw his weight on the rope as the bull

backed, and took a turn around the strong post. As the bull kept backing round and round the shortening rope pulled his head down to the post.

'Now we have him where we want him,' the old man said. 'Have you got the things?'

The boy had the necessary things—the bright new copper ring and the steel spike and the old tin can and 'dopper' black with cattle tar. He put these down on the dry hard ground near the post. The bull was rolling his eyes till the whites showed, his curling tongue licked at his nostrils and he panted a little.

'Hold the rope, boy.' As the boy kept the rope taut, the old man took hold of the bull by the horns as though to wrestle with him and slowly he forced the bull to his knees and then right off his feet so that he rolled over and lay on his side in the dust.

'Now hold him by his horns,' said the old man.

The boy grasped the strong young horns.

'Now sit on his back—up there by his neck. That's right. Hold him down while I do the job.'

'How can I hold him down if he goes to get up?' asked the boy.

'Don't you worry boy. It's just sitting there that does the trick,' the old man said.

So the boy sat on the bull's back. He could feel the muscles quivering, the nerves twitching, beneath the sleek hide. On his bare legs where jeans had slipped up, he could feel the animal warmth and the silky smoothness. He looked at the nervous rolling eye, the clean sharp young hoofs. He slipped his hand from one curved polished horn and fondled the thick curls below it. Some of the bull's great strength seemed to fill the boy's slender body. Soon he would be leaving the farm. He, and the old bull, would be gone—and this young bull and the old man left.

Yesterday and today I've bossed two bulls, the old one and the young, he thought, and I feel fine. Going out into the world, leaving this farm, don't worry me any more.

The young bull trembled all over and gave a low moaning 'blah'. With the steel spike the old man was piercing the flesh between the nostrils. It was tough going. Sweat dripped from the old man's brow and his hands were trembling before the steel came through. Then he pulled the spike out and reached for the cattle tar and put a daub of that on the wound. The bull sniffed the stinging fumes and bowed his head, his whole body relaxing.

'Now hand me the ring—and the screw and the screwdriver,' the old man said. But now he was shaky and nervous and the old blunt fingers fumbled with the little screw after he had forced the open ring through the bull's nose. 'Here boy, you do it,' he cried at last. 'Your fingers are still young and nimble.'

So the boy slid from the bull's back and fixed the ring in the bull's nose and the job was done. The old man undid the rope and the young one, after lying inert for a few moments, felt that he was free and slowly got to his feet. He gave another low 'blah' and shook his head and ambled off. Then he broke into a trot and then into a gallop, cavorting a little as he went, so very young and nimble on his feet.

The old man watched him go. Slowly he gathered up his things and shambled towards the house. The boy followed him with just a bit of a swagger in his walk.

No Man is an Island

JAMES COURAGE
(1905–1964)

There was a girl in that nursing-home who had tried to throw herself from a New York skyscraper. Her name was Suzanne and she was twenty-four years old. I was about twice her age—a fact she tried to make little of by addressing me as 'honey' in an accent not native to her. The nursing-home was in England and, like Suzanne, I was a patient in it.

'Why did this thing happen to you in America?' I asked, when she first told me the trouble.

'Why? That's quite a story, honey. Anyway, I was promptly popped into a place called Bellevue, where the nurses were brutes and not a bit gentle to me.'

'Bellevue's supposed to be the best mental hospital in New York,' I told her.

Suzanne stared at the floor of the lounge. 'I only like people who are gentle, not the violent ones. I hardly know you, stranger, but I can tell you wouldn't do me an injury.'

I was taken aback. 'Why should I?'

But the effort of finding an answer was too much for her. She muttered a word or two then walked away, trailed at a short distance

by the private nurse who kept an eye on her. I had already reached
the conclusion that Suzanne was a bit of a lost soul—and looked it.
  Her dress, for instance. Or rather her pecular collection of garments. A pair of indigo-blue jeans, ending six inches above the
ankles; a crumpled red shirt; a grey, dirty duffel-coat without
a hood (I think this had been shorn off with scissors); a pair of
beach-sandals with string soles. Her brown hair was cut in shortish
tufts which fell forward to her eyebrows. Her face was narrow and
would have been handsome in a fallen-angel fashion but for a
slight flattening of one side of the nose, where the skin was whiter
than the rest. I noticed also that she carried about with her a stick
or a staff; sometimes an ordinary garden-stake, pointed at one
end. She explained these weapons by saying that she had rheumatism
in the legs. I had reason, from the first, for not being quite so sure
of this explanation.
  'Do you want me to hit you?' she asked me casually not long
after we'd met.
  'Some other time. Not today, thanks.'
  'Or perhaps you'd prefer being split with an axe?'
  'Is that a habit you picked up in New York?'
  Her lips went hard and straight. Then her mind or her attention
wandered. 'No man is an island,' she said vaguely, 'no woman either.
Old Donne knew. So did old Titus Andronicus by that boy called
Shakespeare. ... But Shakespeare wouldn't ever have been in
New York, would he?'
  'No,' I said, 'it isn't probable.'
  'I'm English, you know. Born and brought up in London. Only
my mother's an American.'
  I was curious enough to ask how, after the skyscraper incident,
she had managed to get back to this country.
  'My father got me flown over in a plane.' Her voice was once
more logical, even cordial. 'It was a special plane, with a nurse
and an attendant. We flew all one night over moonlit clouds. It
was just like being in heaven, only I was doped in case I tried to
throw myself overboard. I wanted to, too, just to lie on all those
clouds.'
  'You've had a tough time of it.'
  She shut her eyes. 'Yes honey. Il pleure dans mon coeur comme
il pleut sur la ville. The French are bastards but they understand
suffering.'
  'And the Americans?'
  'Bastards and sweeties, all mixed up.'
  I asked her where she had lived in New York.

'Near Greenwich Village. I was painting pictures for an exhibition.' She laid down her stick and sat beside me on the sofa. 'Why are you in this place?' she demanded.

I was in no rush to talk about myself. 'Nervous trouble,' I said briefly. This fortnight is supposed to be a rest-cure.'

Suzanne puffed cigarette smoke towards the ceiling. 'Hell would be a rest-cure just as good,' she said presently. 'Do you feel any better since you arrived?'

'Not much, or only when they give me a pill—one of these tranquillizers.'

'I take them too. But only after lunch. I feel fine in the mornings, before the day starts to crack me up. How long were you in bed here before they let you downstairs?'

'Four days... no, five, I think.' The drugs and the curtained room had made the time indefinite, endlessly nocturnal. Only bits of it were in focus—the charnel odour and cold-scorching taste of paraldehyde in a medicine glass; the whiff of my own sleep-sweat rising from my pyjamas when I woke; the blue uniform of the night-sister and her Garbo-like face. Time had not mattered, until one afternoon the resident psychiatrist had said I could get dressed and find my way downstairs for tea ('Talk to the other patients. You'll find they all have their problems. And the nurses'll help you if your legs feel uncertain'). So I had shaved, dressed myself and gone groggily down into the greenish garden-light of the main lounge. There were only seven up-patients that day, and one of them had been this girl, Suzanne, staring at the white egg of my face and at the pin-stripes of my blue suit and wanting somebody new to draw her out of the mortuary of herself. We had talked and I had heard about the skyscraper.

'Tell me something, honey,' she said now. 'What month is it?'

I thought of looking into my pocket diary then decided against the effort. 'The beginning of May,' I said at a guess.

'I hate the spring. It's like getting drunk, and then it's over.' Suzanne laughed aggressively before peering more closely into my face. 'You look as though you'd know a lot about life, if I could ask the right questions.'

'I know a little. Not enough.'

'One never gets the right answers until it's too late.' She shook her head. 'I'm talking too much. Do I bore you, stranger? Only birds ought to chatter.'

Her nurse appeared beside us with a little tray and a glass of water. 'Suzanne, I've got a pill here for you.'

'All right, all right. Let the nightingale be silent and take her pill, if she must.'

One afternoon she had a visitor, a slim man, natty, with a shine of black hair on his skull. I saw the pair of them talking together on the croquet-lawn before they came indoors, arm in arm, for tea. An hour later, after pointing her stick in my direction, she led the visitor across to my chair.

'This is my father', she told me. 'He's come from London in the train.'

Seen close to, her father's face had a glazed, indoor look. The eyes were shrewd, also very determined to be sociable in front of his difficult daughter. He pumped my hand pleasantly.

'You're both of you wearing the same kind of suit,' Suzanne observed, 'except that my father's got a double-breasted waistcoat.' With her stick she pointed out the very Savile-Row waistcoat to me. Sweet, isn't it. I always like men's clothes better than women's.'

'You're improving, Suzanne,' the father said benignly. 'You're looking better too.' He was already putting on his overcoat. 'I must get back to town,' he excused himself to me. 'This place is very remote for transport.' He shook my hand again. 'I'm glad Suzanne's found somebody to talk to here. It's lonely for her.' He was gone.

'Did you like my father?' Suzanne demanded of me that evening. 'Did you really think he was kind?'

'I saw no reason not to.'

'He loves me,' she brooded. 'Not a great deal, but some. More so now than he ever has before. But he works too hard, he drives himself all the time, making money, filling up his life. He's a barrister.'

I asked her if she were an only child.

'No, I've got brothers. I always wanted to be like them. They got all the attention and I was only an appendix—' she corrected herself '—an appendage or whatever it is.' She offered me a cigarette from a packet still shiny with cellophane. 'My father brought me these. I love him very much. I wish I knew if he loved me.'

'If he didn't he wouldn't have come so far to see you.'

'He's too thin but I liked his waistcoat.' She laid her open hand, suddenly and lightly, on my wrist. 'Did you know I'm a witch? I can make people love me by giving them the magic touch.'

'Teach me how it's done', I suggested.

She snatched her hand back, closing it into a fist. 'No, I'm tired now. Where's that damn nurse of mine?' She called out the nurse's name in a shrill voice: 'Bridget!'

The Irish nurse disentangled herself from a game of cards across the room. 'I'm here, my dear,' she said calmly.

'Get me one of my pills.' Suzanne had already started up the stairs, thumping the banisters with her staff. 'I'm in the mood to hit somebody unless I lie down.'

The nurse ran after her patient. 'There's nothing to hurt you here, Suzanne, nothing at all. Your father's gone.'

If Suzanne had quite a story I had yet to piece it together.

Each day, as the duration of my drug-sleeps lessened, I was allowed to spend a longer time downstairs, away from my room. The patients I met were not the same ones every afternoon: some stayed in bed under treatment, some went out with friends, some went to the cinema in the town, a few were released to return home. But Suzanne was always there, sometimes wandering about the lounge and garden, sometimes sitting mutely with her staff across the thighs of her jeans, sometimes simply examining the other patients with a malign stare. She was not to be escaped, even if I had found her boring. But she did not bore me. I wanted to know more about her.

One particular afternoon she discovered me trying to play the piano in the lounge. It had been a good piano once but had been thumped-on and a few of the notes were apt to stick. I was attempting to remember one of the shorter pieces from Schumann's *Carnaval* when Suzanne's voice rasped at my elbow.

'You play well, honey. Don't stop.'

'I've let my fingers get stiff.'

'One of the patients here sings. You must have seen her; she's that Indian woman.'

Yes, I had certainly seen the Indian woman, a creature of much animal grace. I had admired her polished hair, the sari-like dresses that clung to her body, the diamonds and pearls she wore against her golden skin.

'I call her The Lotus,' Suzanne said. 'Wait, I'll fetch her— she's downstairs for a few hours—and you can play her accompaniments.'

Before I could object that my sight-reading was indifferent she had found The Lotus and brought her to the piano. The Indians' actual name was complicated, so I shall call her The Lotus. That afternoon she had only one song she wished to sing, the music of which she unearthed from a pile of tattered sheets already on top of the piano. The song or aria was *Mi chiamano Mimi* from *Boheme*. Luckily it had a simple piano accompaniment.

'I can't sing well any longer,' The Lotus warned me in a fluting accent, 'but let us try.'

'I shall listen,' said Suzanne. 'I shall sit in the stalls and listen.'

She squatted on the floor behind us and puffed at a cigarette in an amber holder.

'Cosi gentil il profumo d'un fior,' sang The Lotus.

She had an astonishing voice, a heady soprano like a white wine. She took her high notes with power, while I struggled with the piano and my own anixety. We went through the song twice before I asked The Lotus where she had had her voice trained.

'At Milan. One of the best sopranos at the Scala taught me.' Her black eyes brimmed with tears. 'But now I do not practise. I no longer even sing to my husband or my little child.'

'But your voice is still lovely,' Suzanne interrupted from the floor. 'As lovely as you are.' And, scrambling to her feet, she flung an arm round the Indian woman's shoulder. 'We mustn't cry, sweet lady; any of us. You must think of Buddha.'

The other shrank away. 'I am not a Buddhist and Buddha does not comfort me.'

'I'll comfort you instead,' Suzanne soothed her. 'Were you born beside a lake?'

'Yes,' said The Lotus, surprised.

'I knew it.' Suzanne's eyes glittered. 'I'm clairvoyant, you see, when I want to be. You're a Lotus beside a lake.'

'Lotuses grow only in the south and I was born in Kashmir,' the Indian woman protested.

To me you are a Lotus and my love is like a red red rose gazing at you.

'You say peculiar things. Suzanne, I do not understand all you mean.' The Lotus wiped her tears, bowed to me and left us, gliding away with dignity.

'Of course,' Suzanne shrugged, 'she is crazy. Anyone as clairvoyant as I am can see that at once. She's got everything bottled up inside her. The doctor's going to give her an injection tomorrow evening to make her talk.'

'What happens if she talks in Kashmiri?'

'I wouldn't know. Perhaps it doesn't matter in psychiatry; it's the release that counts. Play to me again.' She tapped the piano-keys with her stick. 'If music be the food of love, and all that.'

But after two minutes of Beethoven she drifted away, murmuring that Beethoven was a violent man. I did not see her again until the following afternoon, when her greeting was aggressive:

'I'm fed up with everyone in this place. They're a lot of neurotics. Come out and walk with me, honey. But wait first while I get my hat.'

The May sunlight was bright enough to make even a child look wrinkled round the eyes. At any rate, Suzanne's hat was enormous, a Mexican or Palm Beach sun-hat of plaited straw, about eight feet round the brim, with a high nipple of a crown on top. Worn with her frieze-coat, sandals and staff, the hat turned her into a pastoral figure like a pilgrim in an old picture.

'I have to wear this thing,' she explained the hat, 'or the sun hits me on the roof of my brain.'

The lawn round us was very green, with orange and white azalea petals blown along the edge of the grass. The rhododendrons were in flower. Suzanne and I strolled past the croquet-hoops and turned to look back at the high brick flank of the nursing-home. The tops of the trees reached to the third storey, below the Kentish sky. The building had once been a Victorian private house.

'Not as tall as a skyscraper,' I observed aloud.

Suzanne shivered. 'I didn't jump,' she said presently. 'I stood on the sill of the window where I could see all the cars in the street below, like fleas on a hedgehog. I watched them. I was thinking: "When I'm found among the cars nobody'll know whose my body is. I'll be nothing again, as though I hadn't been born." Then I had a black-out and woke up yelling in a Bellevue ward, with a bucknigger of a nurse telling me to shut my mouth. ... Does it sound simple, honey? A simple act of will I failed in?'

'You haven't told me what led to it,' I reminded her.

Angrily she shook her head under the hat. 'New York'll see me again,' she said. 'I'll go back and conquer the damn place as 'Id meant to.'

I asked her about the pictures she'd painted.

'They were good. I was putting that city where it belonged, among the shapes of hell. I'm no fool as an artist.' She prodded the lawn with her staff then wanted to know about my own work. Was I a writer?

'Of a kind.' Writers were unsatisfactory people and I did not want to say too much. 'I got stuck in a book I was doing.' I explained. 'I couldn't sleep and the strain cracked me up.'

'So serious?'

'Serious enough to bring me here. It linked up with too much else inside me.' I was anxious not to sound pontifical.

'Do you live alone?' Suzanne asked.

'Mostly. My wife died.'

'Solitude breeds fiends. They come out of the walls.' Suzanne looked at the sunlight falling safely on her hands. 'They can't get at us here but I know their faces, the fiends from the dark.'

Lightly I suggested that the dark might be, for each of us, our

childhood rather than any malevolent unconscious. The fiends
came out to claim a compensation later, in our desire to reshape
a reality we'd been scared of. It sounded plausible, but Suzanne
frowned.

'Why do you paint your pictures?' I asked.

'When I don't get enough love I paint, honey. It's like that, and
it works. Or it worked until last year.'

Our stroll in the sun had brought us close to four of the other
patients who were beginning a game of croquet on the uneven
grass. Suzanne halted and fixedly stared at one of the players,
a young man with curly fair hair and a tweed jacket. He stood within
six feet of us.

'I don't like that man,' she said to me loudly. 'He's dangerous.
His eyes are full of axes.'

The young man glanced round. He had been about to strike
one of the croquet-balls, and the mallet remained slightly raised
in his hands. As a joke he swung the mallet in Suzanne's direction.
Glaring at him she pushed her hat back, her sandals feeling for
a stance on the grass, her breath hissing. At the same time I was
aware that her nurse, who had been walking unobtrusively behind
us, had run forward and was beside her.

'Now Suzanne, there's no harm at all,' the firm Irish voice insisted.
'Mister Dick's a nice boy. You've played cards with him....'

Suzanne relaxed. 'I don't like young men,' she said. 'Go away,
Bridget.'

'You'd like to have a little pill, wouldn't you.'

'I don't want any bloody little pills.' Suzanne turned her back on
the nurse and the croquet-player and calmly came back to her
conversation with me: 'Let's talk of art and love again, honey.'

Art and love, however, had had a check. The most we could
manage was a word or two about music.

'The Lotus must sing for us again,' Suzanne said at a tangent.

'I'm going to her room tonight to talk to her after the injection.'

'I doubt if you'll be allowed to see her.'

'When I want a thing,' Suzanne said, 'I get it. You'll find that
out, you writer who gets stuck.'

At nine in the evening, however, while Suzanne was still in the
lounge and before I had gone up to bed myself, The Lotus appeared
in the doorway, her black eyes distended.

'Not for twelve years have I felt so happy,' she cried, swaying
towards us .'One little needle in the arm and I am drunken, I am
marvellous.'

She had had her abreaction-treatment, had been helped to her room, but had escaped the night-sister and come downstairs. Now Suzanne guided her into a chair by the fire and forced a cigarette between her shaking fingers. 'Tell us, honey,' she besought The Lotus, 'what did you confess?'

'What did I say to the doctor? I can't remember. . . . Everything, nothing, my life.' The pearls on her neck gleamed as she let her head fall back. 'I feel so light, so floating,' she sighed in rapture.

Suzanne knelt before her, laying her cheek against the Indian's flower-printed dress. 'Did you tell the secret of the lotus in the lake?'

'I think you are mad, Suzanne, to say such things.'

'I am not mad, and you are a lotus.'

'I'm anything you please,' the Indian woman laughed. 'Tonight I feel the unity of life.'

The skirts of Suzanne's dirty coat spread round her on the carpet. 'Sing to me, Lotus,' she begged in a pure, tender tone, most strange to hear. 'I want to be a child.'

The Lotus began to sing in a muzzy, chuckling manner. She sang part of a Mozart aria, quailing at the higher notes. It might have been the performance of a sleep-walker, except that she paused once or twice to draw on her cigarette. Suzanne did not stir or speak until the end of the song.

'I want to confess too,' she murmured then. 'I want to tell somebody what's in my heart. Not a damn soul will listen.'

She did not look at me, and her abrupt scornful laugh might have been meant for the fire in the grate.

'I'm not a child. . . . Let me see him.'

Suzanne's voice reached me indistinctly from the passage outside my room. It was about eight o'clock in the morning. One of the nurses had just collected my breakfast tray, and it was to her Suzanne had spoken. I heard the nurse say that something was not allowed. The two voices faded away. I was drowsy and sank back into sleep. This was to be my last morning of sedation. Meanwhile such dreams as I had were not of Suzanne.

It was not until mid-afternoon, when I was downstairs, that she caught up with me. 'I tried to break into your room,' she announced. 'I wanted to talk.'

'How's The Lotus, after last night?'.

'In bed, feeling bad, the poor sweetie. It's that sodium stuff she was given... Let's go for a walk.'

With Suzanne trailing her huge hat against her knees we went out on to the gravelled drive below the steps of the house. Again the sun shone. The lawns, freshly-mown, appeared to be divided into ribbons that took the light like satin. The air was hot on our heads.

'We can walk in the shade,' Suzanne said. Ignoring her nurse, who had followed us and was pinning on her white cap, she prodded at the moss of the path with her staff, then laid a hand with one of her 'magic' gestures on my elbow. 'The Lotus opened her soul to the doctor but I can talk to you instead.'

'About New York?'

She nodded. 'How I came to get there, in the first place.' Her mother, she told me, had introduced her to an American woman on a visit to London, a woman of character and elegance who ran a fashion house on one of the streets near Central Park. Her name was Myra Gibbons. She had proposed spontaneously that Suzanne should return with her to America. Myra's husband could later arrange an exhibition of her pictures at one of the smart galleries.

'I asked my father's advice,' Suzanne said. 'He told me I wasn't to bother him, but he gave me the money to go. So I flew over with Myra. I'd been moping in London, going to the Slade, and this New York trip was a break, like some sort of dream I was in.'

She had been speaking with perfect lucidity. Now, as she slashed with her staff at branches and leaves beside the path, she began to hesitate. I had to bring her back to the point in her story where she had found a room for herself in New York. At first she'd known nobody in the city but Myra, and Myra was busy all day with her fashion house.

'Besides,' Suzanne continued, 'her life was different than I'd imagined. She'd jumped on a roundabout...'

'A roundabout,' I filled the pause.

'That husband she had was her third. Myra was forty—older than that, I guess—but Bob was just a cute good-looking boy of twenty-five; more like a son than a husband. Mostly he lived on her money, playing round with little jobs in television or arranging shows in art galleries.' Suzanne paused. 'Can you guess what's coming, honey? That boy had too much charm to be safe. I don't know what he wanted—it wasn't bed—but I was lonely and he took me to places and cracked up my painting to me. Myra may have told him to do it—at least to begin with—but I lost my way. I'd never thought I could love anyone of my own age before, and it hurt. Things began to go wrong with me.'

Suzanne took off her hat, to rumple her hair and gaze up at the sun. Presently she came back to her story. She had taunted Myra with Bob's youth and a row had started. Bob himself stopped being so attentive. Suzanne's notes to him went unanswered or led to explosive late-at-night conversations on the telephone. A winter passed. Suzanne found that the plan for her exhibition had been cancelled behind her back.

'Why didn't you come home to England?' I asked.

'My father didn't want me, any more than Bob did, or Myra. I was lost, My God, I was lost.'

The lost feeling had led to prolonged depressions. The climax had arrived one Sunday morning when she had somehow forced her way into Myra's apartment: she had been met by Bob—'that rattlesnake in a dressing-gown'—who had not chosen his greeting politely. In fact unless she stopped intruding between husband and wife he would split her head open with any convenient axe he could find. Murder would be a pleasure, possibly a duty.

I put the obvious question: 'What did you do?'

'You know what I did. I found the highest window I could. That's what I did.'

We sat down on an iron seat against the rhododendrons at the side of the path. Suzanne showed me a profile of pain, the eye savagely concerned with recollection. Her story hadn't perhaps been as important in itself as the release of telling it: moreover, I suspected that her trouble must have gone further back than New York. At any rate I was far from ready for the exact words she now flung at my head:

'Why don't you come back to New York with me?'

An answer wasn't easy. 'What would we do there?' I said after a moment.

'You could finish your book and I'd go on with my painting.'

I imagined our profoundly irregular existences. 'Listen, Suzanne—'

'What's so difficult about it?' She stared at me fiercely and aggressively. 'You're no older than my father—you've seen him— and you could ask me to marry you.'

I had to say something, and I said it as gently as possible: 'I don't want to offend you—'

'You wouldn't offend me.'

'I don't want to offend you,' I repeated and got to my feet. 'Shall we walk? The sun won't harm you if you put on your hat.' I moved to retrieve her hat from where it stood propped against her staff at the end of the seat further from me. Perhaps the movement was too near, too alarming, for her self-control.

She was very quick. She had grabbed the staff and raised it at me, above my head, before I could draw back. I had to use all my strength to wrestle with her, holding the staff away from me, forcing it aside, disarming her.

'Now that's no way to behave, no way at all.' Suzanne's nurse had given a loud yelp from under the trees and had rushed forward to help me. Together we tried to calm Suzanne.

It was not easy. Her shaking mouth and the intake of her sobs as her anger dissolved were difficult to watch. No man is an island, I thought; no woman either; and I was involved in compassion for her. It was some time before I was able to leave her with the nurse.

Another twenty-four hours in the nursing-home, another night of the sleep I had needed, and I was due to go back to London.

'Shall I say goodbye to Suzanne?' I asked her nurse, Bridget. 'Will it upset her?'

'Have you forgiven her for yesterday?' the nurse said judiciously.

'These odd things happen. I wasn't harmed.'

'Then give her a goodbye.' Bridget peered from the window beside us. 'She's only a step away, out there in the sun. I'm keeping an eye on her.'

I found Suzanne sitting on the wheelbarrow. Beside her, seated on a garden-roller, was the curly-haired young man of the episode on the croquet-lawn a week before. Their faces were friendly.

I told Suzanne I was leaving.

'Dick and I were talking about Shakespeare's wife,' she said. 'She was one of the witches in Macbeth.'

'I'm leaving, Suzanne,' I repeated. 'Is there anything I could do for you?'

'Nothing.' Her voice had only a slight tremor. 'I've decided against America—unless Dick will come with me.'

My taxi was already waiting. I went to collect my suitcase from the hall.

OLAF RUHEN
(*b.* 1911)   # My First Whale

My first whale was a great blue cow, placidly taking a little brief sunshine in Porpoise Bay, a stretch of exposed water immediately adjacent to the most southerly portion of the South Island of New Zealand. She was an enormous beast, lying quiescent in an area of dancing blue water with one fin upraised; and I knew she was a cow, because she was suckling her calf.

I call her 'my first whale' because of the personal nature of the relationship we established, though I had, of course, encountered other whales before her.

Whales, indeed, have always impressed me, even when, as in my earliest years, they were represented only by a flurry on the distant horizon, where some cruising cetacean fought or frolicked with its attendant killers, shovelling the ocean up towards the sky with its great flukes and generally behaving like a small boy let loose. And, like most other people, I have seen them lifting their hundred-odd tons clear of the water in joyful leaping, or cruising sociably alongside an ocean liner.

I came to a closer acquaintance of whales under my first skipper, a great-hearted trawler-man named George Tulloch, who I am certain is, as of this moment, a not unobtrusive occupant of the Valhalla section of Heaven. While he was alive I was forever expecting him to hoist the Jolly Roger on his wallowing, rolling monstrosity of an undersized steam-trawler. He was certainly closer, spiritually, to an eighteenth-century pirate than to a pre-Christian Viking; but he is bound to be out of his period.

It was small wonder that those placid but stubborn individualists, the whales, sought George's company. For a period of four months, whenever we sailed from Port Chalmers and cleared Cape Saunders to head south, we were met by a large, snub-nosed whale of indeterminate variety but bearing an individualistic, irregular, sulphur-coloured patch high on its port beam. This friendly fellow used to travel with us all the way down the coast to the fishing-grounds, flick a demonstrative tail as we shot the trawl and disappear. He was never seen in the company of any other boat, and we appreciated the compliment.

On another occasion we passed a school of black-fish—little blunt-headed whales perhaps twenty feet long, travelling in threes like an army, in a column half a mile long. The leader, out in front, spotted George (for George was indissolubly identified with his craft) and, presumably with ecstatic cries of joy, whipped round and rubbed his back under the keel. For a quarter of an hour the little ship protested as the following files dived down to exploit the backscratching qualities of the trawler, bumping and rubbing with ardour and appreciation, and then went on their way.

Once, too, we passed a school of cowfish—smaller cetaceans allied to the porpoises, but fifteen feet long, salty in colour and having a falcate dorsal fin in place of the more usual rounded one. They were cow-cowfish, each accompanied by a baby perhaps a couple of feet long. And each cow was teaching her calf those delightful acrobatics with which cowfish, porpoises and the black animals mistakenly called grampuses herald a change in the wind.

One mother leapt high, performed a somersault-and-a-half and landed solidly on her side; and immediately her baby followed suit. Another simply sunfished—perhaps she had given birth to an awkward child. Another was doing simple back-flips, and still another performed an evolution which I have since identified as a 'roll off the top.'

There were eight cows in all, and eight calves, and each pair was performing an entirely different evolution, over and over again, and all in unison. It was noticeable that the babies were fully as graceful as their mothers, and also that they were not breathing so hard. Even more noticeable that there was no sign of father.

But perhaps the closest I came to making the acquaintance of a whale—this, of course, before my first whale—was on an occasion when I had been fishing for some months with Sucky Smith. Sucky was not his real name, but people called him Sucky to distinguish him from his brothers, who were called Dummy and, with a change of simile perhaps, 'Couta.

Sucky was a solid little warrior, and reasonably imperturbable. He wore, habitually at sea, a triple oilskin shirt which pulled over his head with no buttons to catch in nets and lines, a sou'-wester and another garment more like a school-girl's gym tunic than anything else. It was also of oilskin, and stretched from just below his shoulders past his knees; where it yielded place to Sucky's thigh-boots. It was a very useful garment, but Sucky always wriggled out of it before he came in sight of the fish-wharf at nights, and hid it under a pile of gear where people would not see it.

It was early in the morning, perhaps five-thirty, and we were thirty miles out at sea with our first twenty lines fishing. I was inside the engine-room attending to chores there, and the figure of Sucky, sitting in his ridiculous outfit at the tiller, completely filled my view of the great outdoors.

Suddenly I saw Sucky leap to his feet with a stricken expression, so old-fashioned as to approach the childlike, on his weather-beaten face. He was so startled that he forgot about the tiller absolutely.

He dropped the sandwich he had been eating for lunch (we

always lunched before the sun rose) and didn't even bother to try to rescue it from the seawater which washed about his feet in the cockpit.

By all that I knew something absolutely unforeseen had happened, so I put down the oil-can and came out.

I was too late. The disturbance had been a whale, and it was still in veiw, but by now it was perhaps fifty yards from the boat. It looked enormous. I twitted Sucky with being frightened of a whale, and he said very indignantly that the beast had not frightened him. It had sneaked up on him and breathed out, and the noise of the escaping gases, rather like the vented steam from a railway-engine (but kept from me, of course, by the clatter of the engine) had stood a good chance, he thought, of ruining his hearing.

While we talked, the whale passed the buoy of one of our dan-lines. It was a five-gallon paint-drum, which was connected by seventy fathoms of line to a fourteen-pound-grappling on the bottom, sixty-five fathoms down; and we hoped to pull about three hundred pounds of fish on it. It was stayed tight back by a three-knot tide acting on all that depth of line; but as the whale passed close along-side cutting out a steady ten knots, the bouy came to life, and spun round in a slow circle perhaps a chain in diameter, completing the circuit twice before coming to rest again. The tremendous surge of the whale's wake thus visually evidenced sobered me, and from that moment my respect for the whale was born.

A month or two later a fisherman I'll call Spider was leaving the harbour at one o'clock in the morning when his forty-foot craft ran high and dry in an area supposed to be occupied by deep water. At the time Spider was at the tiller and his mate was in the engine-room in approximately the same position I had occupied in relation to Sucky, and in a similar boat.

The mate, believing they were half a mile off coures, yelled some pleasantry to Spider about wrecking the something-or-other launch and received no answer, rather to his surprise, for Spider had an extensive vocabulary and was quick to take offence. The boat was so far out of the water that it had rolled on its side, and the screw was racing in dry air.

However, before things could be righted, quite suddenly the boat was launched again, spinning along at seven knots as though nothing had happened. The answer was that they had run hard aground on the back of a sleeping whale. Spider was speechless for several minutes. He had a long session in the pub that afternoon, and for several nights thereafter his sleep was interrupted by the returning vision of a set of great flukes, blotting out half the stars in the sky.

These incidents have been brought back to me by a series of recent readings about whaling, all purporting to present modern whalers as perhaps the last of the muscle-bound adventurers of the masculine world; men who can shoot two thousand tons of meat before dinner. This is to me a wrong and impossibly romantic view of mechanised mariners who cruise up to unoffending whales in sixteen-knot vessels, shoot them with explosive harpoons and radio the position of the corpse to a tug. Svend Foyn, who invented the proto-type method, can be venerated as a businessman but as an adventurer, never.

However, one of these writers came up with an illustration which lends some colour to these recollections of mine. A whale's tongue, he says, is the weight and roughly the size of a whole elephant!

It is even more impressive to think of the blue-whale as the possessor of a two-ton tongue than, simply, as the greatest creature that has ever inhabited the earth.

And it makes you think of the cold courage displayed by those men who, not so long ago, used to pull out to sea in small boat, hook themselves to a whale with a harpoon and a length of Manila and ride out the struggle for a day or two, now and again pulling in under the menace of that enormous tail to tickle up the beast with a stabbing-lance.

Those were the days, as George Tulloch and others used to tell me, of wooden ships and iron men; displaced forever by the iron ships and blockheads of the late nineteenth century.

In George's store, amongst a conglomeration of varied rubbish, Japanese glass-floats and mechanical coilers, anchors and shackles, and ancient wicker-baskets, was the head of a harpoon, looped to take a light Manila line. The flange of the three-inch barb was hinged and held close to the lance by a wooden match, which was intended to break after the point had penetrated the whale's thin black hide. The haft was open, so that the wooden shaft might fall away immediately out of any chance of interference with the line.

With only this weapon, bare-handed men fought the greatest creature on earth, and sometimes, as in the case of the killer or the cachalot or others of the toothed whales, it was a creature capable of great savagery. An amateur blacksmith could have made one of these weapons in an hour.

But to get back to the animal I call my first whale. I was not surprised to find it there in Porpoise Bay, because, for some reason, although it was open to almost every wind that blew, Porpoise Bay was a noted haunt of every warm-blooded animal that swims the Southern Oceans.

In those days, just under twenty years ago, it was no uncommon thing to be invited to a game of tig by a bunch of young and trusting seals gambolling on the beach where once three-hundred diggers sifted the sands for gold; and porpoises, grampus and whales all waited there awhile on their migrations. The bay was shaped rather like a boat-builder's G-clamp; with a ragged fringe of rocks, sharp and ugly, in place of the screw.

At that end of the bay there was no beach but a petrified forest, to be found in the guide-books under the name 'Curio Bay'; with stumps, fallen logs and other curiosities faithfully reproduced in hard, yellow stone.

Much of it has since been carried away by tourists, and decorates dusty mantelpieces in Invercargill and other towns of the South land. At the upper end of the G, at just about the position of the serif on the letter, the Waikawa River flowed into the sea. Its estuary formed a harbour, once used by commerce but now dilapidated and delinquent. In the settlement of Waikawa, a mile or two up the river, I was trying to establish myself as a fisherman.

I had a little thirty-two foot schooner, a good sea-worthy craft which I worked single-handed by means of a number of jury-rigged appliances which brought the engine-controls to the tiller. In this craft, which some forgotten owner had christened *Alice*, I used to go drifting for blue-cod, crayfishing in season, setting dan-lines for groper all about the southern ports and even trawling from time to time. In fact my best successes were with trawling, although, particularly in those days of low prices (seven-and-six a hundred pounds for lemon-soles), they were nothing to write home about.

I came out in the bay on this morning, and inside the line of reef, where the water continually boiled, I saw the blue whale. There was something strange about her, and I went closer to investigate. As I came up I saw that she was lying on her beam-ends, as it were, with her starboard fin deep in the water and her port fin in the air, gesticulating from time to time. When I was closer still I saw she was feeding her calf.

I had never seen anything to make me afraid of whales, except for a rather shaken Spider in the pub on that earlier occasion, and I cruised up under power to observe what I considered a rather rare phenomenon of natural history.

I suppose I got within thirty yards. It seemed much closer at the time, and I estimated with some coolness and clarity that the whale was at least three times the length of the schooner and possessed a greater beam. The calf was nuzzling under the port flipper, and I was approaching at slow speed from the port quarter. At thirty yards, as I say, the whale moved. Without disturbing the calf in the least she turned and faced me, very quietly and deliberately. That was all.

I swung *Alice* round very neatly, I thought, and applied full throttle. *Alice* was capable of eight knots, but it seemed to me she was not delivering it. I looked back at the whale, and though she had not moved there seemed a speculative look in her eye, and there was no way of telling what stage the baby had reached in its feeding. I went inside the engine-room and found the spark was not fully advanced. I adjusted it and went outside. I had been right, I found, and *Alice* was getting along at least half a knot faster.

My first whale was well astern.

HELEN SHAW   **The Bull**
(*b.* 1913)

Miss Valentine, staggering under the weight of a great hamper basket, burst out of the hall of the house onto the verandah, defiantly attempting to look less than her years in flamboyant scarlet, but in blissful ignorance of the black petticoat that was dipping down below her gaudy hemline.

'There you are, father dear,' she warbled, brushing Mr. Valentine's ear with her grey curls as she kissed him.

'I've told you before to be careful of my ear, Lulu, *careful!*' the old man snapped back. Cantankerous as usual, he sat in the sun in his pyjamas and plum coloured velvet coat near the red and blue glass that closed in one end of the verandah. And where was his daughter going with 'her cabin trunk,' he inquired sarcastically, then, when she said it held currants she had picked for a neighbour, he scoffed and groped through his pockets for the brush to groom his venerable dog. 'Why don't your friends cultivate their own garden, my girl?' he asked as he explored his dog's black and tan coat for fleas. 'Sit up, Skipper, and listen to the human race following-my-leader calling baa, baa, baa, just listen to us, sir.' Mr. Valentine mimicked, menacingly smacking up clouds of dust from the tartan rug tucked round his knees. 'I'll remind you, Lulu, you're standing *in my sun*, girl, in my *s-u-n*,' he bellowed suddenly.

'Now, father, I'll only be gone a minute, father, really father,' Miss Valentine said gaily, and hovered over him, kissed the white plume on his bald head, then hurtled across the tennis court in youth's gaudy colours that so accentuated her age.

The Valentine's dog stretched itself, rose, and walked round in a circle, an unforgettable smell wafting up from its body, then it yawned 'and lay down, servile nose on its master's boot. Through his binoculars Joseph Valentine watched his daughter retreating into the shrubbery. 'There goes a supporter of lost causes, sir,' he said, talking down to the dog and thinking of the dining room walls that were plastered with Lulu's paintings of waterfalls and pungas. 'Pungas! Scatter my ashes over the honest to God tussocks, Skipper, and preserve me from the sly, dripping green bush,' he shivered, 'though I suppose she enjoys herslef, sir,' the old man continued, his voice becoming more charitable as the sun warmed his hands.

He sat very still staring at bees crawling in and out of the geraniums that lapped the edge of the verandah. He could see them cleaning their thin, active legs. Legs! He hadn't the strength for sky-larking left in *his* legs. 'And the whole place to ourselves, sir,' Mr. Valentine grunted, but the dog, bothered by flies, scratched its rump half-heartedly and snored off to sleep again, and soon the old man followed suit, falling rapidly into a light nap of troublesome dreams.

Back again in the Supreme Court he found himself defending his great-grandfather, Ebenezer Valentine, for an unknown and mysterious crime, with magnificent eloquence until old Judge Y. intimated it was futile proving a dead man's innocence, but would Joseph rid the Court of the bees that were swarming in a corner of the gallery, whereupon Joseph gallantly removed his wig and pitched it overhand into the heart of the swarm which caused one bee to sail down straight into Joseph's eye and sting him so that he couldn't move, speak or breathe. Softly, softly he crumpled up and fell down at Judge Y.'s feet, paralysed.

'What the devil's the meaning of it, sir?' Mr. Valentine snapped, as he woke with pins and needles to find the dog up on his knees. 'Down, sir,' he commanded, and it was then old Joseph saw the bull—an enormous, cinnamon brown, dirty cream, hulking brute, all ugly head and shoulders, glaring at him out of the geraniums with mean, unpredictably mean eyes—and less than a couple of yards between himself and the danger.

'Almighty God,' the old man swore, as he laid his stiff, mittened fingers on the dog's snout. 'It's going to be a case of mind over matter, over matter, do you see, Skipper, over matter,' he babbled, still keeping his eyes on the bull and feeling excitedly around for his binoculars, at the same time trying to steady his feet in preparation for the move he had got into his head was essential. Slowly the old barrister rose up out of his bursting leather chair that for years had been disgorging horsehair. 'Forgive us our sins and trespasses, and trespasses,' he repeated until he had his spindly legs under control, then up he swung the binoculars and hurled them backwards through the coloured glass behind his head. The window broke and the bull bellowed. Its head went down, but then it lumbered round into a wanton retreat crashing over precious shrubs and tearing its way like a tornado through hedges.

Never in all his life had the old man felt so cold. His head seemed empty, his fingers were like ice; he slapped his dog's sides and pulled its ears for warmth and friendship, then set off along the verandah in his queer, high-stepping way to see the men who swarmed in from the street with ropes and pitch-forks settle their account with the recalcitrant bull, and presently was rewarded with a view of the captured beast being led away meek as a lamb.

Now was the Valentines' garden emptied of danger and filled with the aftermath of alarm as Lulu rushed towards old Joseph screaming, 'Dear father, coming father, speak to me father,' and stumbled up onto the verandah throwing freckled, sunburned arms round his scraggy neck. 'Father, speak to me,' she panted. 'Father!'

He snapped his violet lips shut in her flaming face and proceeded inside, very shaky, but leaning on her until they reached the high-ceilinged, bottle-green bedroom where he undressed and climbed up into the double bed and stretched out under linen sheets and a crackling white counterpane.

'What are you looking at? Don't stare at me,' he roared. 'Brandy! And a hot bottle! And don't dream, girl,' he bellowed, as with a glaring blue, glittering eye he observed her scuttle from the room dropping numerous hairpins as she ran.

He slid his teeth into the mug of water on the cabinet and wound up his watch, then, beginning immediately to fume, he reached for his stick at the head of the bed and thumped hard on the floor with it for Lulu's services, but the moment she appeared he closed his eyes and foxed until she had supplied him with his brandy and hot bottle.

'And eighty-nine next June,' he boasted, when she had been and gone for the last time, and he sat up in bed and looked at himself in the mirror and stroked his moustache and swallowed his brandy, recalling how he had battled with the bull, when suddenly he heard the verandah window breaking again and the noise of glass splintering inside his head. 'The devil, what's that?' he cried, and poked into his ear, but in spite of his strong will and his patriarchal pride and arrogance, again the window broke; and broke and broke and broke inside his head, as if once was not enough to impress Joseph Valentine with the wonder of his aged body that still had breath left in it. Finally, like a warning voice that is carried out to sea by the roaring of waves, the tinkling of the glass grew fainter and fainter, became but a small echo wandering through colossal caves and then was lost, so that at last the old man was able to rest.

With the sheet drawn up to his chin, Joseph lay staring at a fly that buzzed inanely round and round in slow circles round and round above his snowy plumed head until at last the noise of his triumphant sleep filled the whole house with a mighty crescendo of thanksgiving.

A. E. BATISTICH
(*b.* 1915)

The Gusla

The girls were clucking about the house like hens, getting ready for the visitors from Auckland. Wherever he went, the old man found himself in the way. He went out to sit on the step. Maybe a man could have a smoke in peace there. But no. Not there, either.

'Dad!' It was Lina calling from the upstairs bedroom. 'Haven't you changed into your other clothes yet?'

No, he hadn't. And he wasn't going to, either. If these smart Inglezi from the city didn't like the look of him in his old pants they needn't like him at all. Collars and ties! They were all right for weddings and funerals, but this dressing up for dinner in your own house to please your daughters! He was still muttering to himself when Katie came out and took up Lina's cry.

'Dad! Not changed yet!' And there was their mother wringing her hands in the doorway. 'Simun! You should not make your daughters ashamed. Wearing those old clothes and all these fine people coming. A lawyer and a doctor, and the school teachers.'

Well, when she put it like that. A lawyer and a doctor. Now there were people you took your cap off to in the old country and bowed to and called '*Gospodin*'* reverently as if you were speaking to God. Here they come to your house, marry with your daughters perhaps. And why not? Lina and Katie were fine girls, and there was a nice sum of money in the bank for both of them, and when he and Mara had finished with the farm, whose would it be but theirs?

And when he looked out across the valley there was all the farm before him. His farm that he'd made from a gum-field. The best farm in the district. He could see the fruit trees stretching down the slope, the vines yellowing in the autumn sun. The cellars where the vintage was stored in fat barrels that had painted on them 'Yelena', his mother's name. All this he'd got for himself, and by heaven, he was proud of it all.

'Simun!' It was Mara pleading again.

'All right, all right,' he said placatingly, 'I'll just finish this pipe, then I will come.'

'Dad!' said Lina in exasperation.

'Dad!' echoed Katie, like a parrot. Of course he was a darling, but Lord! let him remember which forks you picked up for dessert, and which for the main course like she'd told him.

At last everything was ready. The house waited only for the arrival of the guests. And here they were. A long, low American car swung into the driveway. The cherry trees seemed to bow low in greeting.

'Hi, there!' the girls waved from the terrace, and the car pulled up and its load of smartly dressed young people spilled out on to the path. Three young men and two girls, all looking like people from the picture page of a magazine, but Lina and Katie looked as good as any of them and he was a proud man to see it.

All through the dinner Simun felt like a man who had strayed into the wrong life. He felt the girls' eyes on him all the time. The neatly placed knives and forks and spoons mocked him with their confusion. Which was for what? 'Ach!' he said aloud, 'three forks to have a dinner. Where I come from one was always enough.' He looked up to see Lina and Katie looking at him with fixed unhappy expressions,

*Sir

so he tried to talk of something else, but it was just as bad. His English became tangled with the old country language, as it always did when he was excited, and the guests were smiling, but the girls weren't. So he retired behind his moustaches and the unhappy contemplation of the maze of knives and forks before him, to ponder on the things that happen to a man, just because he has the bad luck to get rich.

The girls, now. They should be courting in the district. This going away to school in the city had given them ideas. Look at Marko's two sons, now. Fine boys. But would Katie and Lina look at them? It was the likes of those boys he'd like to see the farm passed on to. And when he thought of those two lads he felt a moment's envy. Marko and he had come out to New Zealand together, forty and more years ago. In the long years since, he had made out best. Marko just managed. But it was Marko who had the sons. Marko who lived the way he liked. It was in Marko's big kitchen that he really felt at home himself, now.

Soon after the meal was finished, he excused himself quickly. The young folk were going to dance to the radiogram. He couldn't help himself. 'This shuffling! Call that dancing! Now when I was a young fellow we *enjoyed* our dancing. Then it was who could go the fastest, and the accordion playing like it didn't know how to stop. Remember the accordion, Mama!' He turned to Mara but she had gone. 'Dancing!' he snorted angrily at the radiogram. Even if it had cost a hundred pounds, it was an invention of the devil—a *machine* to make music with!

As he left the room he heard one of the visitors saying, 'Isn't your father a character—right out of a book!' He was snorting so loudly to himself that he didn't hear what Lina and Katie had to say in reply.

Mara was already in the kitchen when he got there. Lucy, the girl who had come in to help, was busy at the sink. He saw, when he spoke to Mara, that there were tears in her eyes. 'Simun!' she reproached him. 'You should not talk like that. You shame the girls. You shame me, too!'

When he saw Mara looking at him like that, he felt ashamed of himself too. He looked up perplexed and lost. Nothing was right. There was Mara with an apron tied around her best dress and sleeves rolled up to elbows, looking anything but happy, and in a confused way he saw that it was all wrong for them. 'I should have stopped when the farm was paid for,' he thought. 'Too much money is mixing us all up. Marko and his family, they stay the same. I go there and it is their old friend they welcome. It is like we have never left Dalmatia.'

And there was Dalmatia, getting farther and farther away from him, leaving him out on a limb to belong nowhere. Sometimes when he looked at his daughters he wondered what his mother would have made of these hard, bright girls, smoking cigarettes like men, wearing trousers like men. Flesh and bone of that strong old woman. The same eyes. The same features. But how different! And he wondered too what they would make of her.

'I am going down to Marko's,' he said suddenly. 'I am no good here.'

At Marko's they were glad to see him and hear all about the girls and Mara. They sat around the big table and talked, Marko and he remembering their first years in New Zealand together, Rosa listening and smiling. She made coffee the old-country way, and they drank that and then they opened a bottle of Marko's best wine and there was more talk, and somehow the conversation got around to Simun's grandfather, and the *gusla* playing, and the singing of the songs of *Kralyevich Marko* and *Kossovo* and the Turkish *Begs*.

Long after he left them the conversation stayed in Simun's mind. The gusla, now. He remembered how when he was a boy, his grandfather had taught him to play it. The four notes up and four notes down, on its twisted horsehair string. Played to the singsong of the storyteller's chant. And the idea was born to get a gusla from the old country to be a kind of charm to keep him from too much loneliness in his age.

But it was more than that. When the letter came from Auckland stating that the gusla had arrived, and would he please call at Her Majesty's Customs and collect it, it was like a long exile that was over. He hid the letter, telling no one why he was going to Auckland. At the Custom's Office they had looked at the strange instrument and made a guess at the duty to be paid on it. For Simun, he had a gusla and that was enough.

And there it was beside him in the car. He kept looking at it, putting out his hand to touch the wood, to feel the smoothness of the goatskin belly. All the way home he wanted to sing. And he did. Out loud to the New Zealand countryside of *Marko Kralyevich* and his horse, *Sharats*. Of the wars with the Turks, and the girl who came down to do her washing in the sea. And that blue, blue *Yadran*, the name the Dalmatians have for the Adriatic sea they sing to, as to a woman. '*Oy Yadrane, Oy Yadrane!*' he sang, and the gusla sang with him, snug in its tasselled case.

He showed it to no one. Not even to Mara, but hid it in the old

house that no one went to now. It was inhabited only by the scuttling
spiders and the wind, and every night when the girls sat over their
dinner, or played the radiogram and entertained their friends, he
went down to the house and played his gusla and sang to himself.
They could have all their fine parties. He had something of his own.

When he was practised enough he went with the gusla to Marko's,
to surprise them with it. 'A gusla!' Rosa cried, and hugged it and
kissed it and cried over it as if it was a living thing. And for the
three of them it was as if they were standing in their own place, the
village at home where the gusla had come from.

Simun sat down on one of Rosa's kitchen chairs, placed the
gusla in position between his knees and drew the bow across its
one string. He began to sing in a low, chanting voice. 'In the morning
went the maiden, the dear Maid of *Kossovo*... and all day sought
her brothers on the field of woe.'

Then Marko took it and it was his turn now to play and sing,
and his song was of the gusla itself, the wood it was made from,
the young kid from whose belly its skin was taken, the bow of
fine horsehair that played on the gusla, wooing from her the songs
she would sing.

Rosa was a woman. The gusla was not for her. But she was allowed
to hold it, to feel the wood, to marvel at its silken tassels.

When Simun came back to his own house he saw that the girls
still had their visitors. The blinds were up and he could see the
young people dancing. The noisy music of the radiogram screamed
out into the night.

A sudden rage possessed him. He waved the gusla at the unseen
monster. 'We'll show you—this and I!' he shouted. 'Music is for
a man to make, not a machine. Like this!' And drawing the bow
across the gusla he began to sing loudly and defiantly of the *Kossovo*
maiden and the nine brothers she found dead for Serbia, the nine
Yugovichs dead on bloody *Vidov Dan*.*

* St. Vido's Day.

E. S. GRENFELL   # Old Tolly
(*b*. 1916)

Sunday afternoon, and in the cold bathroom the old man was shaving. Although it was fully an hour before sunset, he had pulled on the electric light, but finding it insufficient had stood a lighted candle on the shelf above the hand-basin.

He shaved laboriously, with trembling deliberation, the razor crackling slowly over his lean jaws. After every third stroke of the razor he wiped it carefully on a strip of newspaper. He was a tall, big-boned man; the mirror being too low he had to bend his knees slightly. Crouched in the wavering lemon light, his elbows upraised, he looked like some gaunt and dusty bird of prey. The jerky rhythm of his right arm was like the slow and painful flexing of a decrepit wing. But his left hand was still, spread fingers drawing the flaccid skin of his face tight against the crackling blade. From time to time he put his razor down to wipe the blurred mirror with a towel, or to twist doggedly but ineffectually at a bath tap which dripped, dripped, taunting his innate sense of orderliness.

Mumbling to himself about the tap he shaved on with finicking concentration until he had scraped the last fleck of lather from his face. When he had cleaned and dried his gear, he washed noisily in a full basin of cold water, vigorously, with great drowning gasps. Wet and freshly shaved, his skin had momentarily the gloss and tautness of health, in the weak candlelight. But with the drying of his face, and the snuffing of the candle, the illusion ended.

It was a grey cadaverous face with high sunken temples, the top lip long and pointed, cheek-bones flat and simian; a penny could have rested in the gaunt hollow beneath each foggy eye. A face redeemed from mere comic ugliness by the repose, the dignity of a contented old age.

Coughing drily, the old man padded out to the kitchen where he poked up the range fire and drew the kettle over. And the time? Nearly four-fifteen, he saw, and in the glass of the pendulum clock caught a reflected glimpse of the sky beyond the window already smoky and reddening with frost.

He pulled on his boots and an old blue and black striped blazer and went out to the little shed at the end of the garden. In one corner stood two sacks of potatoes and his garden tools; opposite, a pile of forcing frames. Suspended under the ceiling on a strip of wire-netting hung last season's onion crop, and on the walls, besides a grass-catcher and empty paint tins and worn bicycle tyres, were two hopeful attempts at decoration—a large lithograph of Admirals Jellicoe and Beatty, and a weather-stained almanac depicting three kittens and two balls of wool in a wicker-work basket.

Along the wall nearest the doorway was a row of crude drawers with pieces of strap leather for handles. One by one, the old man pulled each drawer clear of the frame and carried it to the daylight, raking through each rusty, dusty collection of bolts, screws, split-pins with a long, patiently probing forefinger. A reddish dust began to fill the little shed. Near the end of the row he paused in his search to blow his nose vigorously, a loud, querulous toot into a blue spot handkerchief. Then he went on with his search. The last two drawers contained larger articles—short lengths of bicycle chain, old dented door-knobs, round tobacco tins of parsnip and sunflower seeds.

Baffled, he stood on the asphalt outside the shed door, tugging at the lobe of his right ear. For some time he stood there patiently struggling with his failing memory. Then suddenly he turned, bustled back into the shed.

On a ledge above Admirals Jellicoe and Beatty was a pile of floor polish tins. In the second one he found a tangle of tiny expansion springs and three tap washers. The old man selected the shapeliest of the washers and going back to the house, to the bathroom, stuck it upright in the cake of soap in the hand-basin. Now, he told himself, I'm bound to see *that* in the morning.

At four-thiry he went outside to cover his chrysanthemums. The frost had flared even higher into the sky. One wall of the house, the east, was windowless, and snug under it grew the row of chrysanthemums, the drab limp leafage propped by manuka poles strong enough to support a sapling. The old man was thorough. Thoroughly now, he began to spread scrim over the protective framework, shuffling back and forth along the row to tuck under a protruding branch, or to ease the scrim away from a taller plant. Now and again he glanced up anxiously at the low pinkish sky as if he saw the frost suspended there like a raincloud, ready to fall at any moment. My own fault if they cop it, he thought. Messing about, wasting time.

His movements had a jerky urgency as he took a bucket from the wash-house and hurried out into the street, driven by the thought that somehow, somewhere that afternoon he had wasted valuable time.

The street wound along the ragged fringe of a small city, houses on only one side of it, and flanked on the south by a branch railway line—three trains a week and specials on Show Days. On the far side of the line were low swampy paddocks dotted with tussock; then a straggle of weather-board houses almost encircled by macrocarpas; beyond again, the sour, gently rising countryside.

The small corrugated iron shed on the far side of the line to which the old man made his way was used by surfacemen for the storage of tools, and occasionally a trolley. Behind the shed leaned a tumbledown wooden urinal, and a tap at which he began to fill the bucket. At the first clang of metal on metal, the horse cropping fifty yards away down the narrow railway paddock raised its head, stiffened its body expectantly, watching for the old man, gave a whinny of recognition when he emerged from behind the green rotting wall of the urinal.

For two months now the old man had been watering the horse. Its owner, a bottle-dealer, had temporarily retired from business. Plenty of easy money to be made just now, he said, without jogging round the streets in the cold. In the summer he'd probably get stuck into it again. She was a good little business.

A shiftless, mean-faced fellow, he snatched eagerly at the old man's offer to water the horse.

At first the horse had been none too sure of its new benefactor, had watched askance as he carried bucket after bucket over to the half-barrel, intimidated by the scarecrow figure, by the man's jerky flapping movements over the awkward fence and over the soft, uneven ground. A week later the horse was twenty yards nearer to the barrel, his rump towards the man, swinging his head in a wide arc as he cropped, all unconcern, all quivering alertness.

But now, two months later, the horse reached the barrel ahead of the old man who took some time to clamber through the sagging railway fence. Now, as the first bucketful of water curved down, he nudged gently, approvingly at the barrel with his nose—a habit which never failed to amuse and flatter the old man. He had worked in towns all his life and had handled nothing larger than a domestic cat. Seeing the horse accept him he was proud, as if he had tamed a fierce, intractable animal.

It took longer than usual to water the horse. The ground was frozen underneath, but the surface had thawed throughout the day and had not yet hardened again. A patch of sticky, slippery ground by the fence which skidded away underfoot like grease on concrete forced the old man—much against his will—to go carefully, to take time. Still, he managed to spare a minute to stand companionably beside the horse, listening to the greedy, crunching sound of it drinking. Then, like some huge regurgitating bird, he hawked twice and started off back to the house to change his clothes for his next job.

This was a dusty, dirty job, not warranting cleaner clothes, but it was a paid one and when he went to it he put on his second-best suit along with a sterner sense of responsibility. From April to September he tended the heating system of the neighbouring Presbyterian church, twice a Sunday, before each service. For this, the Deacons' Court paid him twenty-five pounds per season, to the satisfaction of both parties.

The house had chilled in his absence. Pulling down the kitchen blind his hand touched the window: it was like a sheet of ice. He put a heaped shovel of coal on the fire, and went into all the rooms in turn, shutting the windows against the creeping frost, peering around suspiciously for disorder before he left.

The rooms were scrupulously clean and tidy, the linoleums rich glossy reds and pale shining greens, plain, the patterns having long been polished away. Here and there the old man had spread sheets of newspaper. On his daily rounds of dusting, polishing, titivating, he stepped carefully on the islands of newsprint. Sometimes he went in stockinged feet. In the bedrooms the covers had the stiff perfection of a showroom display. Made of cheap sateens they shone like polished sheets of coloured metal. And on the walls hung relics of the past life of his family—photos, hair-ribbons, a certificate which stated that Margaret A. Tollis had passed the Leauge of Nations Examination for 1929, and in his own room, two of his late wife's hat-pins stuck behind the architrave of the wardrobe door.

The smallest and barest in the house his own room had an iron bedstead, a tall, lowering chest-of-drawers, a small cane bedside table and on it a black-faced alarum clock, a spectacle case, a bottle of cough mixture and his two books—*Ben Hur* and *For the Term of his Natural Life*.

He changed hurriedly in the cold bedroom. His thin hairy thighs were wide apart; beneath the pink flannel undershirt they had the absurd, wide-spaced spindliness of a child's drawing. Wheezing and shivering he struggled into the brown tweed suit. Like all his suits it fitted him in three places—the shoulder-blades, the elbows and the knees.

In the scullery, he knotted a scarf around his throat and spread the ends over his chest, buttoned his coat over them. A flat brown cap like a wilting mushroom, and he was ready.

On the way down the street he saw no one. It was the deadest
hour, between tea and church. Silent on their withered lawns the
houses were white-faced mausoleums. All seemed deserted, their
occupants having perished from cold and boredom and loneliness.
They had the merest, the most evanescent signs of life—a pale
flag of smoke on a chimney, the glimmer of a fire in a front room
window like the flicker of interest in a dull apathetic eye. Darkness
approaching, the frosty air had become tangible, congealed into
a white, stinging haze. There were a few high, dim stars.

Only two blocks from his house, the church stood at a bleak cross-
roads. Small and well-designed, its brick facade had been recently
oiled and the coping white-washed. Bright in the gathering white
haze it looked like a large freshly iced cake. Inside, it smelled faithfully and anciently of religion; the incense of varnished pews and
dusty coco matting.

Groping in the fusty darkness of the back vestibule for the cellar
key, the old man noticed a ribbon of light beneath the vestry door.
Someone coughed, a chair scraped—his friend the parson pottering
about. He thought: Well, it's his big day, he *ought* to be here on the
job.

Still thinking of the parson and his soft, one-day-a-week job, he
went round to the lee side of the building and opened the cellar
door, switched on the light. The cellar was deep and very narrow,
like a concrete slit-trench there underneath the church, but its atmosphere was warmish. Moisture glistened on the walls; at the far end
the boiler squatted in a dark cavity. The old man had to go
down on hands and knees to peer into the firebox, prostrate, it
seemed, before a stern pot-bellied idol.

After he had raked the ashes away a small heap of live coals still
remained from the morning's stoking, and on these he built a fierce
bright fire with dry fruit-case timber; then adding coal eventually,
shaping a little amphitheatre of fuel in the firebox with the careless
assurance of an expert. His movements were clumsy but calculated;
in the confined space the shovel struck repeatedly on concrete and
metal, sending up a clangour of activity into the crisp air above.

Approaching, the young minister grinned. Could be a smithy,
he thought, descending. Or someone repairing a railway engine.

The old man was peering critically into the open firebox, studying
his handiwork ,the slowly expanding circle of low flame.

'Hello there!' said the parson, and when the old man jumped as
always, continued as always with his weak ecclesiastical joke.

'One thing I know, Tolly,' he said, 'old Nick will get a first-class
stoker when you pass on.' He was a humorous-minded, broad-

minded young parson, very handsome, very self-confident.

The old man spoke his first words for that day. 'Should've been lit earlier,' he said, not turning. 'You'll want plenty of heat tonight.'

'I've got some red-hot stuff for them myself, Tolly,' the young parson laughed. 'They'll sweat all right.'

Straightening slowly, the old man turned a flushed, prim-lipped face to the parson. He liked the young man as a person; he deplored him as a parson. He thought the lad showed a lack of taste in his frivolous attitude to his job. Of course he himself held with the churches—they kept the nation from going off the rails. Look what happened to the Russians when they tried to do without churches— turned into a mob of worthless red-feds. All this although he didn't attend himself, not having the time. 'Look, the coal's got far too low,' he said. 'You'll have to get on to them. And keep at them or they'll put you off.'

'I'll make a note of that,' grinned the parson.

'You'd better ring tomorrow, first thing.'

'Yes sir,' said the young parson. 'I'll do that.' He backed meekly up the steps, nodding, his eyebrows assenting, his face boyishly and comically servile.

'And keep at them,' said Tolly sharply, to the disappearing legs.

After tea, Tollis had a letter to write, Remembering it at odd moments throughout the day he had felt quite important. A letter to write. Some business to attend to. He sat for a while after tea at the bare table, thinking out the letter and listening to the children's song service. Important and studious, he sat staring at a spot above the lintel of the scullery door, tapping fingers fumbling for the lively rhythm of the chorus, his mind fumbling for the words of the letter.

Then the service ending, the tinkling cymbals of the children's voices giving way to the sounding brass of the preacher, he switched off the radio and spread before him on the table a writing-pad, a bottle of ink, pen, an extra blotter. Both the pad and the pen were new, specially bought for the occasion.

He knew exactly what he wanted to say to Margaret, wanted to thank her and yet to say firmly and definitely, 'no', Because she was asking him to do the impossible. The more he thought of it, the more impossible he saw it to be. He saw the horse standing beside an empty barrel, the people sitting in a cold church, the chrysanthemums cut and blackened by the frost, the house going to rack and ruin. It was clearly impossible.

The pen was like a straw in his thick fingers. He puffed and writhed with the agony of transferring that crystal clear vision of impossibility from his mind to the devilishly thin paper with a devilishly sharp and wayward pen.

But crouched doggedly over the pad, his long nose tracing each spluttering stroke of the pen, after many blots and muttered damns he accomplished the letter.

Dear Margaret, he wrote, I now sit down to write these few lines in reply to your letter which got here Friday last. I am in quite good nick so dont worry. We have had a lot of frosts this winter three on end so far this week. Your new place must look very nice but you shouldn't have gone to the trouble of doing up a room for me as I have too much on my hands just now to come up there. As for me just playing bowls and billiards day in and day out all I ask is, can you see me? I dont know about getting a big price for the old place it wants a lot of doing up but as I was saying to Eric the other day, itll see me out. Your mums old school-mate Janey Andrews called in to see me the other week she was down on holiday just the same old six and eight but very deaf and failed a lot. Glad to hear that Arthur is doing so well and that you have got shifted into the new place but I wont be coming up in the meantime.

Love, he added, and meant it. He was fond of his children, but he mistrusted them. They were forever making some impossible proposal, 'all for his own good'. He had to be always on the alert.

Tollis folded the letter carefully into a stamped envelope and addressed it to his daughter in a town several hundreds of miles away. Seen in writing, a sprawling unfamiliar word, the town seemed even more remote to him. He could have been writing to the moon.

Anyway, she's got plenty to do without looking after me, he thought, going out with the letter, picturing her as a young bride absorbed in her own affairs and not as a middle-aged woman with time on her hands and affection to spare.

Outside, it was bright, icy moonlight and freezing hard. At the first sting of the bitter air he tucked his chin deeper into the thick knot of scarf. Frost glittered across the rooftops, and the smoke from neighbouring chimneys rose in white frozen columns. A crop of scarf, the drooping beak of his cap, the sharply out-thrust sleeves of his over-coat—he looked more than ever like some huge ungainly bird as he waded through the haze of frost across the crisp and crackling grass to his front gate.

Going down the street he whistled softly into the scarf; his echoing footsteps stalked him from behind the whitening hedges. Soon he had the snug feeling of lonely independence which these winter walks always gave him—the primitive joy of pitting his body against the cold and the wild weather, and emerging from the encounter invigorated and unscathed. In winter, too, there was little likelihood of meeting people with nothing better to do than to chatter.

The letter-box stood on the corner opposite the church. As he posted the letter he looked across to the church, noticed that the moonlight cast his shadow almost to the steps, and laughed gently remembering how the young parson had recently said, 'You ought to be ashamed of yourself, Tolly, never darkening a church door. But I'll have you a Deacon yet.' And 'Can you see me?' he had asked.

Then he stood transfixed by closer memories. His thoughts ran together like beads on a wire... the church, the young parson, the letter, that impossible proposal. 'Bowls,' he breathed softly over the wall of scarf, the word freezing into a little white feather of contempt.

He tugged the peak of his cap firmly down over his eyes and set off northwards with a brisk, stiff gait, an old contented man with no time to waste, heading for nowhere in particular.

MAURICE DUGGAN
(1922–1975)

In Youth is Pleasure

Hopkins had learned the translation by heart: with a pretence of difficulty intended to give his listeners the impression that he was translating at sight, he read slowly, filling the long pondering gaps of silence with a rush of words, and pausing again. He stood, huge and uncomfortable, at the edge of his desk and the book lay awkwardly in his hands. His eyes as he recited were fixed not on the lines of print but on the indifferent drawing which, as an aid to vocabulary and a key to the story below, headed the page. His voice, frequently mispronouncing, jerked sporadically forward like a fly trapped in a cobweb, faded a moment into silence and rose again with its suggestion of frenzy and tedium: it was not enough to hide his pretence.

—Stop, called Brother Mark. I say stop.

And as the recounting drone, telling its rote tale of sentry geese, choked like some stalled motor into silence the small, furtive, inattentive noises of the class died also. One by one the heads came up and one by one they swung about. Brother Mark and Hopkins were at it again: the play was on. As if above that other arena of spectacle and savagery the whole class leaned forward into the familiar drama which, because they were young, jaded them less in its familiarity, in its pattern too often rehearsed than, tiered in the hot imperial amphitheatre, it must have jaded those others.

Brother Mark stepped down into this almost tangible sense of expectation, rested a moment daintily poised on his dancer feet and began to sidle, to mince forward, threatening down the aisle. Hopkins, now with his mouth fixed as if in silent enunciation of his last word, raised his eyes slowly above the top of the breast-high book: like dancer or boxer, insolent and assured, smiling a very small smile that did not reveal his carious teeth, Brother Mark came on.

—We did not remember, he lightly mocked, so much of the scholar in you. He made a sly and bitterly amused appeal to the watching boys. I confess, he primly announced, I'd be put to it myself to do as nicely.

Hopkins blushed; the blood climbed over his face into his galleried ears. Brother Mark's eyes, winking and dancing in malicious delight, took him in from head to foot. Hopkins, under that stare, began to squirm: his socks with their striped turn-down of green and white had fallen over the tops of his heavy boots; his serge shorts, ending tightly above his grotesque knees, seemed about to split over his things—the tight cloth shone and bulged. Through the open neck of his shirt the hair could be seen, growing high up to the base of his neck, where it had been trimmed in an even line. His ears, dark with embarrassment, stood hugely out.

—Proceed, said Brother Mark. He rose on the balls of his feet and bending at the knee rocked forward. Proceed, he said.

Hopkins bent again, searching the meaningless page, searching his dumbed memory, pleading with his great slow tender eyes for the print to yield up, in some secret communication, its little mystery. His breathing in the quietened room came slow and heavy. Thirty heads and the eyes of Brother Mark watched and waited, and alone in the arena of that attention Hopkins felt ungainly and afraid. The palms of his hands began to sweat: the lines of print blurred under his eyes.

—Proceed, said Brother Mark. We are waiting.

The boys, feeling themselves enticed, conspirators and partners to this baiting game, shuffled and giggled: the sound rose abruptly and stilled. Brother Mark, frowning archly, placed himself at Hopkins' shoulder and peered down in enlightened contempt at the elementary page. His forefinger, precisely manicured, with a pale

moon gleaming in the pale nail, poked forward and prodded with
disdain at the point on the page where the reading had been interrupted: his eyes peered up, quizzical and sure, into the face of the
boy who was a full head taller than himself.

—The soldier, Hopkins bellowed.

—*Of* the soldier, surely, Brother Mark cut softly in. *Of* the soldier,
wouldn't you agree? The soldier, do you see, possesses something.
And Brother Mark's eyes examined a Hopkins bereft of all possession.

—Of the soldier, Hopkins parroted, staring down to where the
finger rested elegantly on the page. Of the soldier, he muttered, and
was silent.

—What? said Brother Mark. What of the soldier?

—I forget, Hopkins got out.

—Forget? Brother Mark exquisitely questioned. How forget? Isn't
it all down there? The finger reared and fell. It isn't something to
remember: come.

The page on which the finger lightly rapped trembled in the huge
hands. The thirty heads watching from all sides offered neither
assistance nor sympathy. Brother Mark raised his eyes and gazed
about with an air of simulated wonder. His eyes looked out from
under jet brows: he leaned forward. Hopkins, struck by that stale
breath, drew back: the movement was slight but Brother Mark
caught it.

—War, rapped Brother Mark. You see it?

—War, cried Hopkins, suddenly safe; and his doubled thumbs
erectile and huge rose like twin horns on either side of the cupped
book. War, he cried, and caught the thread and bolted on, bellowing
through his flawless and cribbed translation, shouting in a meaningless rote while he watched the menacing finger retreat diagonally
across the page.

—Enough, cried Brother Mark. Enough.

Once again the drone fell away: Hopkins' face, red and miserable,
swung round.

—We think, said Brother Mark, you are not playing fair. We
think, he menaced, that you are cheating.

—No, Brother, Hopkins said.

—No? said Brother Mark. Now it would seem that you are lying.
Cheating and lying both. You would do well to think of your soul.

—Turn back, Brother Mark said. But without waiting he snatched
the book, turned back half-a-dozen pages and thrust it back into the
hands that were cupped still, the thumbs dejected, as though they
had held it without interruption. Try that, Brother Mark said.

The class stirred again and settled: the summer sun shone into the room and the motes of dust, in inappropriate gaiety, danced before the green board chalked with sums. Through the silence a shout of laughter from a distant class-room mocked and died: Hopkins looked down.

—Regina, Hopkins read.

—Oh, in English, please, said Brother Mark.

—The queen, Hopkins said.

The silence tautened and drew out.

—Last week's lesson, said Brother Mark.

—The queen, Hopkins began again.

—The queen; the queen; shrilled Brother Mark. Get on. Get on. What queen: where? In irate and delightful fancy his eyes, as for that regal one, searched the room and his voice, whinnying in frenzy, rang out: Get on.

But he had shatttered the conspiracy; the power relaxed. Faced with something that was not foreseeable or safe the boys' condoning interest flooded back so that once again there remained only that spectacle which, objective and judicious, they continued to watch.

Hopkins, challenged, could not meet it, could not keep up the inconsiderable pretence: the book sank slowly and the mournful face, no longer searching for that assistance once denied, swung slowly across those other glances which, meeting his, fell away or stared back imperious, curious and removed. Brother Mark stepped forward and a floorboard creaked and from a crack between the boards a small volcano of dust erupted among the bright motes, filtering still. The manicured hand reached forward, miming a gesture of plucking at something odious, and nipped, thumb and forefinger, into Hopkins' ear. Under its bite Hopkins shuffled forward with his eyes watering in pain; near the blackboard he was swung about until, clownish and wretchedly benign, he faced the facing class whose eyes like magnetised needles swung to that north, trembled, and stayed. The sun struck full on his great thighs; he was released. The book fell from his hand and at the noise the class shifted again, as if so small a detail brought to the tension some relief, let them off from whatever feelings—censure, sympathy, pleasure, condonation, pain, delight—isolate or complex, rose to their sense.

It was left to some other boy to read the passage: Brother Mark commanded the smallest. He came forward to the chosen place, so close to the body of Hopkins that he almost touched him and could smell the peculiar smell of sunwarmed cloth. Hopkins over-topped him: the smaller boy was set like something precious and human and compact within the mere animal mass of that greater bulk.

—Go on, Simpson, Brother Mark said.

Slowly and accurately, in a piping voice that as much as his size seemed to mock the ungainly Hopkins, Simpson read on. The very force of the authority which commanded him released him from blame, released him from any duty to contest it—as though being commanded by a force of grand compulsion should alter the relation between wrong and the doing of wrong. Simpson did not mock: he had been chosen to mock, and there lay all the difference; or so he consoled himself. There was no way out, no way other than to transfer that petty and womanish venom to his own head: he did not care for Hopkins enough for that—no one, it seemed, did care—and he was not brave enough, or foolhardy enough, to venture such a thing on its own account. Even among schoolboys, his actions seemed sturdily to proclaim, there is that sense of aptness; a natural prudence which suits itself to the occasion. This was not the first time Hopkins had been baited nor did anyone think it would be the last. They accepted all that happened as something which, determined beyond them, carried its own air of permanence and order.

The class grew restless under Simpson's unoffending voice: they stirred with the sound the watchers make when—as on the wall of the cave—the flickering pictures fail and the sense rises over them of how they are crammed, only human, into that sudden dark.

—Enough, called Brother Mark, consumed perhaps with a similar feeling. Go back to your place, Simpson.

Hopkins, doubled forward as though that paining hand nipped still at his ear, bent immobile in effigy of resignation and obscure despair, did not look beyond the heavy toes of his besmirched boots. He feared to find, in the eyes beyond, not the dispassion which he knew would be there, but sympathy which, even mistakenly, he knew he could not meet. He could not have sworn he was being truthful in so standing there; he knew for an instant that he had not done as much as he might have done, as much as, through all his fright, he could have done. Buried far down under his present despair was a bile of slow anger, a record of outrage. They were feelings, no more, but too much present for denial: they bore him along and yet kept him oafishly there, scapegoat to the class, because he had caught, like one glancing dance of light, the almost lost gleam of something there was not time—and never would be, perhaps—to examine. It underrode everything and was to him no more than suspected; and yet it was the reason he would have turned from sympathy: it had no presence and was not more than an ambience, a faint aura of something that, though obscure and lost, yet shone to his dozing mind with its suggestion of guilt and delight. He stayed bent forward and waited the next move: the little flame of anger burned up.

Brother Mark, gay again and smiling, regretting with light impatience that he had run the risk of losing face, of seeming even for an instant to have lost, stepped lightly up on to the teacher's dais.

—There is so little point, Hopkins he smiled, in denying it. You mustn't think we are all fools. You cheated, you know; you cribbed and you lied to cover it up. That isn't, and he smiled again, the way a grown man is expected to behave.

Hopkins, finding no relief but only a further threat in the light, reasonable voice, shuffled one foot over the dusty boards: under his tight shorts the muscles shifted.

—Admit it, Brother Mark lightly advised. Admit you were lying and cheating.

Hopkins' reply, hollow and averted, was lost.

—It is, and Brother Mark addressed the class, such a waste to put such a fellow to the classics. A convoy, do you see, must take its speed from the slowest ship: we all suffer through such a dunce.

Brother Mark's shepherding eye went out over his class and returned, light and contemptuous, to the dunce: his palms, turned theatrically upwards, rose as he shrugged and his eyebrows, arch and arched, comically indicated his despair. What could he do, he pleaded in eloquent silence, with such a dunce? How should he deal with such stupid deceit? His smooth voice prodded again at the slumbering bulk of Hopkins who protested no more than by moving his feet. A laugh skittered through the room.

—I am afraid, Hopkins, sympathised Brother Mark, that in our opinion you must be held unsuitable for any but the grosser tasks of this world. We are thirty-two in this room; and yours are the only boots with dung on them. Brother Mark, struck with this thought, paused, and then went on. Your parents would be ill advised to spend any more money on you. There must be country jobs you could do, surely? He sniffed fastidiously as if those blowing country smells were striking up from Hopkins' boots. There is nothing we can do, Brother Mark said, and his head struck forward and his eyes flared: nothing at all for such a massive dishonest lout.

A small drop of saliva fell from his lips to the back of his wrist: with a gesture of amusing exaggeration Brother Mark drew forth his handkerchief and wiped it away. Not until he finished and raised his eyes did he see that he had gone too far. He had but a moment to compliment himself that he was a match for any overgrown boy before he retreated an involuntary step and came up against the edge of the reading stand: the handkerchief like some lax signal of

premature surrender trailed from his hand. In silence and as one
the thirty boys craned forward.

—There is no other way, the Brother Superior said. We will have
to let him go.

—Without an explanation? Brother Ignatius asked.

—How, queried the Brother Superior, would you propose explaining? Or what?

—He had been baited, Brother Ignatius said. For a long time, by
all accounts. You'll admit there's an end to turning the other cheek.

The Brother Superior smiled, almost with sadness.

—Not, he said, a Christian end. But that I blame him, don't think
that.

—Has anything been said to Brother Mark?

—A reprimand, is that what you mean? the Brother Superior
said. I have spoken to him. It isn't possible to change a man's nature.

—The man in question, Brother Ignatius said, might be reminded
that it is, on the other hand, possible to lose his soul.

It drew no rebuke. They sat on either side of a table covered with
green baize: a shaded lamp burned between them but left them both
in shadow. Hopkins' school reports were spread before them.
Brother Ignatius, much older, leaned back into his chair and through
some trick of the light his cheek-bones seemed to have fallen in and
his eyes looked out from their ancient shadow.

—Brother Mark, the Brother Superior said, has, I think, learned
a lesson. A painful one, in its way, he added.

—He has so many lessons to learn, Brother Ignatius said. There
hardly seems time for them all. I hope it lasts, that's all.

—It's left its mark, the Brother Superior said, and frowned at the
unintended pun. But why didn't the boy come to me before?

They looked with a common impulse towards the door; it too was
covered in green baize: the Brother Superior had a fear of draughts.

—The sanctum sanctorum, Brother Ignatius mildly joked. He was
afraid, I suppose, It wouldn't be an easy thing to do, especially for
a boy like that: or for anyone. The place has an air.

—Yes. But it's curious, and the Brother Superior lightly touched
the papers. He doesn't get marks in anything but botany and divinity.

—But? Brother Ignatius said. The world, surely?

—You know what I mean, the stern tones rebuked.

—It won't be easy to explain, Brother Ignatius said. What he did
was both justified and wrong; right and wrong, so to say. It will
seem like splitting hairs, to him.

—Oh wrong for discipline, wrong for the college, yes. But do you see a way of keeping him on? I'll confess I don't.

—Brother Mark might go, Brother Ignatius said.

—That's flippant, the Brother Superior said. You know that isn't possible. You're not being much help.

—It's not something I like, Brother Ignatius said.

—He's not stupid: the boy, I mean. But I quite see that there is something in his slowness that could be immensely irritating. Not that I'm making excuses, you know that. The whole thing is unpleasant. I've put him in the infirmary.

—Him? said Brother Ignatius. We're all turned about, surely?

—It's the only separate place. But what worries me is how best to go about things. He had no explanation, the Brother Superior said. Except to say he was sorry. And yet if I write to his parents and say that he isn't to blame and then in the same breath I say that I've expelled him, what will they think? What would anyone think? I can't hand them a dilemma like that; to say nothing of how it might reflect on us.

—Let him go, Brother Ignatius said, stirring. There's nothing else for it. Perhaps God and nature will know what to make of his good marks; perhaps he'll be taken in hand. There's nothing we can do: we aren't organised for such decisions. Right and wrong: it's splitting hairs. And yet, if we look for the evil, where are we then? Right in the mire, I'd say; uncomfortably close to home.

With great dignity the Brother Superior stood up: his impersonal eye roved over the walls of the room: he brought his unrelenting glance back to Brother Ignatius.

—And do you think, the Brother Superior said, that you have that thought entirely for your own?

Hopkins sat on the edge of one of the beds in the small two-bed infirmary. The other bed was empty and, on both, the white covers shone with a bleached purity. The room held nothing more: it had a faint smell of damp kapok and disinfectant and common soap. The window was open and the sun was going down: the clear window pane shimmered with light. The afternoon breeze tugged at the austere curtains and blew into the room the shouts of boys out on the playing fields, the sound of a motor-mower tracking over the summer grass, the smells of dust and summer, of hot bitumen and cooking food. Hopkins' face, patched with freckles and surmounted with a shapeless brush of pale hair, wore an expression of tiredness and gloom: his great spaniel eyes were closed but he was not alseep.

He knew what was coming: could anything be surer? He would be sent home, that was plain enough. His parents would be disappointed and grave but they would not punish him. Their aged faces rose to his mind: he felt himself as bent already under their perplexed and injured eyes, under their dumb reproach. They had sacrificed for him and he had let them down. From the world, those imagined eyes proclaimed, we would expect such things, but not from you. And in the over-furnished room hallowed to such occasions his mother would wait, with a tenderness that was more remorseless than blows, for the moment which would prise from him those assurances, those lies if need be, which would reaffirm her in her belief that he was, in spite of it all, a good boy yet at heart.

—I'm sorry Hoppy, Simpson said: and Hopkins, who had not heard him come, opened on him eyes framed still in a clown's sorrow and despair. I'm sorry, Simpson said, but what could I do?

The huge head shook and the hair trembled: Hopkins did not speak.

—I've scrounged a biscuit, Simpson said, and as to something hardly human offered the wholemeal square he had bartered for with a day-boy.

Hopkins took it: he broke it in half and put both halves in his mouth where they stuck a moment before he chewed and swallowed. Both boys were aware of a tension between them.

—Thank you, Hopkins said formally. He picked a crumb off the hairs on his chest and put it into his mouth.

—He's a bastard, Simpson said, loudly and with daring. Everyone knows that.

—It doesn't matter, Hopkins said.

—What will they do? Simpson said.

—Send me home, I suppose.

—Expel you, you mean? Simpson said; and put so bluntly it overcame them both. There was, after all, between them some bond and they looked at one another with an expression near to awe. They had touched on something; they had acknowledged between them that unspoken and even unconsicious conspiracy that proclaimed, in the face of everything, their belief in a functioning standard: they were related in a conspiracy which, allowing for the absence of anything as definite as friendship, yet proclaimed, crudely and impermanently perhaps, their belief in some sort of justice. It was unadult, and perhaps between now and maturity they would forget it; but it was impelling and real.

—Will you go? Simpson asked. But he was not interested in the answer: he knew Hopkins would go; how could he do otherwise? No: what held him there was the feeling that something more was to be done. The precise moment for leaving had not come; and so, between them, Hopkins and he acted it out.

—I'll have to, Hopkins said.

—Won't your family make a stink?

—No, Hopkins said; they won't.

—Won't you even get a hiding? Simpson curiously asked.

—Not a real one, Hopkins said.

—I'll write you, if you like, Simpson said.

—If you want to. It doesn't matter.

—Are you mad at me? Simpson asked.

That was the point: they recognised it at once. Simpson hung, waiting for an answer. He wouldn't write; they both knew that. Simpson did not want Hopkins' friendship, and they would not be friends, but that Hopkins should know, should say, that under that force there was nothing else he could have done—that, to Simpson, was important.

Hopkins sat on: under the shouts that blew in, fainter now, through the open window, he stirred; he looked at the white beds; a bird chuckled in a tree. He wanted only to be on his own again and to have it all over, all done with. It had nothing to do with him for, even as they spoke, his sentence, he did not doubt, was being lightly decided behind the green baize door. What did they say? He squeezed his eyes shut as if in this way he might hear, but when he opened them again there was only Simpson waiting still, still to be satisfied. It was, Hopkins realised, out of his hands; it had always been so. Soon enough it would be his mother making a demand that in no way differed from this. He looked at Simpson gravely, lugubriously.

—Are you mad? Simpson said.

—I don't blame you, if that's what you mean, Hopkins said. Why should I? It hadn't anything to do with you. He stood up. Who has it to do with? he wondered to himself.

Simpson came round the edge of the bed. Across the white cover, and with all the solemn jesting of those who have found treaty, they touched hands.

—Anyway, Simpson said, it isn't much of a place. And he was gone.

Hopkins crossed the room, lumbering, and with his huge hands erased the impression of Simpson and himself from the white beds. He went to the window. The bird in the tree choked on a note and gave up, disgruntled. Two floors down the quadrangle lay, empty except for the Brother Superior walking towards the infirmary. Hopkins waited: the last of the sun shone like pale spears on the stones: the poplars shivered and stood up into the evening air: in puckish thanksgiving the bird found its song.

MAURICE DUGGAN
(1922–1975)

Along Rideout Road that Summer

I'd walked the length of Rideout Road the night before, following
the noise of the river in the darkness, tumbling over ruts and stones,
my progress, if you'd call it that, challenged by farmers' dogs and
observed by the faintly luminous eyes of wandering stock, steers,
cows, stud-bulls or milk-white unicorns or, better, a full quartet of
apocalyptic horses browsing the marge. In time and darkness I
found Puti Hohepa's farmhouse and lugged my fibre suitcase up to
the verandah, after nearly breaking my leg in a cattlestop. A journey
fruitful of one decision—to flog a torch from somewhere. And of
course I didn't. And now my feet hurt; but it was daylight and, from
memory, I'd say I was almost happy. Almost. Fortunately I am
endowed both by nature and later conditioning with a highly develop-
ed sense of the absurd; knowing that you can imagine the pleasure
I took in this abrupt translation from shop-counter to tractor seat,
from town pavements to back-country farm, with all those miles of
river-bottom darkness to mark the transition. In fact, and unfortunately there have to be some facts, even fictional ones, I'd removed
myself a mere dozen miles from the parental home. In darkness, as
I've said, and with a certain stealth. I didn't consult dad about it,
and, needless to say, I didn't tell mum. The moment wasn't propi-
tious; dad was asleep with the *Financial Gazette* threatening to
suffocate him and mum was off somewhere moving, as she so often
did, that this meeting make public its whole-hearted support for the
introduction of flogging and public castration for all sex offenders
and hanging, drawing and quartering, for almost everyone else, and
as for delinquents (my boy!).... Well, put yourself in my shoes,
there's no need to go on. Yes, almost happy, though my feet were so
tender I winced every time I tripped the clutch.

Almost happy, shouting Kubla Khan, a bookish lad, from the seat
of the clattering old Ferguson tractor, doing a steady five miles an
hour in a cloud of seagulls, getting to the bit about the damsel
with the dulcimer and looking up to see the reputedly wild Hohepa
girl perched on the gate, feet hooked in the bars, ribbons fluttering
from her ukulele. A perfect moment of recognition, daring rider, in
spite of the belch of carbon monoxide from the tin-can exhaust up

front on the bonnet. Don't, however, misunderstand me: I'd not have you think we are here embarked on the trashy clamour of boy meeting girl. No, the problem, you are to understand, was one of connexion. How connect the dulcimer with the ukulele, if you follow. For a boy of my bents this problem of how to cope with the shock of the recognition of a certain discrepancy between the real and the written was rather like watching mum with a shoehorn wedging nines into sevens and suffering merry hell. I'm not blaming old STC for everything, of course. After all, some other imports went wild too; and I've spent too long at the handle of a mattock, a critical function, not to know that. The stench of the exhaust, that's to say, held no redolence of that old hophead's pipe. Let us then be clear and don't for a moment, gentlemen, imagine that I venture the gross unfairness, the patent absurdity, the rank injustice (your turn) of blaming him for spoiling the pasture or fouling the native air. It's just that there was this problem in my mind, this profound, cultural problem affecting dramatically the very nature of my inheritance, nines into sevens in this lovely smiling land. His was the genius as his was the expression which the vast education-al brouhaha invited me to praise and emulate, tranquillisers ingest-ed in maturity, the voice of the ring-dove, look up though your feet be in the clay. And read on.

Of course I understood immediately that these were not matters I was destined to debate with Fanny Hohepa. Frankly, I could see that she didn't give a damn; it was part of her attraction. She thought I was singing. She smiled and waved, I waved and smiled, turned, ploughed back through gull-white and coffee loam and fell into a train of thought not entirely free of Fanny and her instrument, pausing to wonder, now and then, what might be the symptoms, the early symptoms, of carbon monoxide poisoning. Drowsiness? Check. Dilation of the pupils? Can't check. Extra cutaneous sensation? My feet. Trembling hands? Vibrato. Down and back, down and back, turning again, Dick and his Ferguson, Fanny from her perch seeming to gather about her the background of green paternal acres, fold on fold. I bore down upon her in all the eager erubescence of youth, with my hair slicked back. She trembled, wavered, fragmented and re-formed in the pun-gent vapour through which I viewed her. (Oh for an open-air job, eh mate?) She plucked, very picture in jeans and summer shirt of youth and suspicion, and seemed to sing. I couldn't of course hear a note. Behind me the dog-leg furrows and the bright plough-shares. Certainly she looked at her ease and, even through the gassed-up atmosphere between us, too deliciously substantial to be creature down on a visit from Mount Abora. I was glad I'd combed my hair. Back, down and back. Considering the size of the paddock this could have gone on for a week. I promptly admitted to myself that her present position, disposition or posture, involving as it did some provocative tautness of cloth, suited me right down to the ground. I mean to hell with the idea of having her stand knee-deep in the thistle thwanging her dulcimer and plaintively chirruping about a pipe-dream mountain. In fact she was natively engaged in expressing the most profound distillations of her local experience, the gleanings of a life lived in rich contact with a richly understood and native environment: A Slow Boat To China, if memory serves. While I, racked and shaken, composed words for the plaque which would one day stand here to commemorate our deep rapport: *Here played the black lady her dulcimer. Here wept she full miseries. Here rode the knight Fergus' son to her deliverance. Here put he about her ebon and naked shoulders his courtly garment of leather, black, full curiously emblazoned—Hell's Angel.*

When she looked as though my looking were about to make her leave I stopped the machine and pulled out the old tobacco and rolled a smoke, holding the steering wheel in my teeth, though on a good day I could roll with one hand, twist and lick, draw, shoot the head off a pin at a mile and half, spin, blow down the barrel before you could say:

Gooday. How are yuh?

All right.

I'm Buster O'Leary.

I'm Fanny Hohepa.

Yair, I know.

It's hot.

It's hot right enough.

You can have a swim when you're through.

Mightn't be a bad idea at that.

Over there by the trees.

Yair, I seen it. Like, why don't you join me, eh?

I might.

Go on, you'd love it.

I might.

Goodoh then, see yuh.

A genuine crumpy conversation if ever I heard one, darkly reflective of the Socratic method, rich with echoes of the Kantian imperative, its universal mate, summoning sharply to the minds of each the history of the first trystings of all immortal lovers, the tragic and tangled tale, indeed, of all star-crossed moonings, mum and dad, mister and missus unotoo and all. Enough? I should bloody well hope so.

Of course nothing came of it. Romantic love was surely the invention of a wedded onanist with seven kids. And I don't mean dad. Nothing? Really and truly nothing? Well, I treasure the understatement; though why should I take such pleasure in maligning the ploughing summer white on loam river flats, the frivolous ribbons and all the strumming, why I don't know. Xanadu and the jazzy furrows, the wall-eyed bitch packing the cows through the yardgate, the smell of river water... Why go on? So few variations to an old, old story. No. But on the jolting tractor I received that extra jolt I mentioned and am actually now making rather too much of gentlemen: relate Fanny Hohepa and her uke to that mountain thrush singing her black mountain blues.

But of course now, in our decent years, we know such clay questions long broken open or we wouldn't be here, old and somewhat sour, wading up to our battered thighs (forgive me, madam) at the confluence of the great waters, paddling in perfect confidence in the double debouchment of universal river and regional stream, the shallow fast fan of water spreading over the delta, Abyssinia come to Egypt in the rain... ah, my country! I speak of cultural problems, in riddles and literary puddles, perform this act of divination with my own entrails: Fanny's dark delta; the nubile and Nubian sheila with her portable piano anticipating the transistor-set; all gathered into single, demesne, O'Leary's orchard. Even this wooden bowl, plucked from the flood, lost from the hand of some anonymous herdsman as he stopped to cup a drink at the river's source. Ah, Buster, Ah, Buster. Buster. Ah, darling. Darling! Love. You recognise it? Could you strum to that? Suppose you gag a little at the sugar coating, it's the same old fundamental toffee, underneath.

No mere cheap cyn...sm intended. She took me down to her darkling avid as any college girl for the fruits and sweets of my flowering talents, taking me as I wasn't but might hope one day to be, honest, simple and broke to the wide. The half-baked verbosity and the conceit she must have ignored, or how else could she have borne me? It pains me, gentlemen, to confess that she was too good for me by far. Far. Anything so spontaneous and natural could be guaranteed to be beyond me: granted, I mean, my impeccable upbringing under the white-hot lash of respectability, take that, security take that, hypocrisy, take that, cant, take that where, does it seem curious? mum did all the beating flushed pink in ecstasy and righteousness, and that and that and THAT. Darling! How then could I deem Fanny's conduct proper when I carried such weals and scars,

top-marks in the lesson on the wickedness of following the heart.
Fortunately such a question would not have occurred to Fanny:
she was remarkably free from queries of any kind. She would walk
past the Home Furnishing Emporium without a glance.

She is too good for you.

It was said clearly enough, offered without threat and as just
comment, while I was bent double stripping old Daisy or Pride of
the Plains or Rose of Sharon after the cups came off. I stopped what
I was doing, looked sideways until I could see the tops of his gum-
boots, gazed on *Marathon*, and then turned back, dried off all four
tits and let the cow out into the race where, taking the legrope with
her she squittered off wild in the eyes.

She is too good for you.

So I looked at him and he looked back, I lost that game of stare-
you-down, too. He walked off. Not a warning, not even a reproach
just something it was as well I should know if I was to have the
responsibility of acting in full knowledge—and who the hell wants
that? And two stalls down Fanny spanked a cow out through the
flaps and looked at me, and giggled. The summer thickened and
blazed.

The first response on the part of my parents was silence; which
can only be thought of as response in a very general sense. I could
say, indeed I will say, stony silence; after all they were my parents.
But I knew the silence wouldn't last long. I was an only child (darling,
you never guessed?) and that load of woodchopping, lawnmowing,
hedgeclipping, dish-washing, carwashing, errandrunning, garden-
choring and the rest of it was going to hit them like a folding mort-
gage pretty soon. I'd like to have been there, to have seen the lank
grass grown beyond window height and the uncut hedges shutting
out the sun: perpetual night and perpetual mould on Rose Street
West. After a few weeks the notes and letters began. The whole
gamut, gentlemen, from sweet and sickly to downright abusive.
Mostly in mum's masculine hand. A unique set of documents reek-
ing of blood and tripes. I treasured every word, reading between
the lines the record of an undying, all-sacrificing love, weeping
tears for the idyllic childhood they could not in grief venture to
touch upon, the care lavished, the love squandered upon me. The
darlings. Of course I didn't reply. I didn't even wave when they drove
past Fanny and me as we were breasting out of the scrub back on
the main road, dishevelled and, yes, almost happy in the daze of
summer and Sunday afternoon. I didn't wave. I grinned as brazenly

as I could manage with a jaw full of hard boiled egg and took Fanny's arm, brazen, her shirt only casually resumed, while they went by like burnished doom.

Fanny's reaction to all this? An expression of indifference, a down-curving of that bright and wilful mouth, a flirt of her head. So much fuss over so many fossilised ideas, if I may so translate her expression which was, in fact, gentlemen, somewhat more direct and not in any sense exhibiting what mum would have called a due respect for elders and betters. Pouf! Not contempt, no; not disagreement; simply an impatience with what she, Fanny, deemed the irrelevance of so many many words for so light and tumbling a matter. And, for the season at least, I shared the mood, her demon lover in glossy brilliantine.

But as the days ran down the showdown came nearer and finally the stage was set. Low-keyed and sombre notes in the sunlight, the four of us variously disposed on the unpainted Hohepa verandah, Hohepa and O'Leary, the male seniors, and Hohepa and O'Leary, junior representatives, male seventeen, female ready to swear, you understand, that she was sixteen, turning.

Upon the statement that Fanny was too good for me my pappy didn't comment. No one asked him to: no one faced him with the opinion. Wise reticence, mere oversight or a sense of the shrieking irrelevance of such a statement, I don't know. Maori girls, Maori farms, Maori housing: you'd only to hear my father put tongue to any or all of that to know where he stood, solid for intolerance, mac, but solid. Of course, gentlemen, it was phrased differently on his lips, gradual absorption, hmm, perhaps, after, say, a phase of disinfecting. A pillar of our decent, law-abiding community, masonic in his methodism, brother, total abstainer, rotarian and non-smoker, addicted to long volleys of handball, I mean pocket billiards cue and all. Mere nervousness, of course, a subconscious habit. Mum would cough and glance down and dad would spring to attention hands behind his back. Such moments of tender rapport are sweet to return to, memories any child might treasure. Then he'd forget again, Straight, mate, there were days especially Sundays, when mum would be hacking away like an advanced case of t.b. Well, you can picture it, there on the verandah. With the finely turned Fanny under his morose eye, you know how it is, hemline hiked and this and that visible from odd angles, he made a straight break of two hundred without one miscue, Daddy! I came in for a couple of remand home stares myself, bread and water and solitary and take that writ on his eyeballs in backhand black while his mouth served out its lying old hohums and there's no reason why matters shouldn't be resolved amicably, etc, black hanging-cap snug over his tonsure and tongue moistening his droopy lip, ready, set, drop. And Puti Hohepa leaving him to it. A dignified dark prince on his ruined acres, old man Hohepa, gravely attending to dad's mumbled slush, winning hands down just by being there and saying nothing, nothing, while Fanny with her fatal incapacity for standing upright unsupported for more than fifteen seconds, we all had a disease of the spine that year, pouted at me as though it were all my fault over the back of the chair (sic). All my fault being just the pater's monologue, the remarkably imprecise grip of his subject with the consequent proliferation of the bromides so typical of all his ilk of elk, all the diversely identical representatives of decency, caution and the colour bar. Of course daddy didn't there and then refer to race, colour creed or uno who. Indeed he firmly believed he believed, if I may recapitulate, gentlemen, that this blessed land was free from such taint, a unique social experiment, two races living happily side by side, respecting each others etc. and etc. As a banker he knew the value of discretion, though what was home if not a place to hang up your reticence along with your hat and get stuck into all the hate that was inside you, in the name of justice? Daddy Hohepa said nothing, expressed nothing, may even have been unconscious of the great destinies being played out on his sunlit verandah, or of what fundamental principles of democracy and the freedom of the individual were being here so brilliantly exercised; may have been, in fact, indifferent to daddy's free granting tautologies now, of the need for circumspection in all matters of national moment, all such questions as what shall be done for our dark brothers and sisters, outside the jails? I hope so. After a few minutes Hohepa rangatira trod the boards thoughtfully and with the slowness of a winter bather lowered himself into a pool of sunlight on the wide steps, there to lift his face broad and grave in full dominion of his inheritance and even, perhaps, so little did his expression reveal of his inward reflection, full consciousness of his dispossessions.

What, you may ask, was my daddy saying? Somewhere among the circumlocutions, these habits are catching, among the words and sentiments designed to express his grave ponderings on the state of the nation and so elicit from his auditors (not me, I wasn't listening) admission, tacit though it may be, of his tutored opinion, there was centred the suggestion that old man Hohepa and daughter were holding me against my will, ensnaring me with flesh and farm. He had difficulty in getting it out in plain words; some lingering cowardice, perhaps. Which was why daddy Hohepa missed it, perhaps. Or did the view command all his attention?

Rideout Mountain far and purple in the afternoon sun; the jersey cows beginning to move, intermittent and indirect, towards the shed; the dog jangling its chain as it scratched; Fanny falling in slow movement across the end of the old cane lounge chair to lie, an interesting composition of curves and angles, with the air of a junior and rural odalisque. Me? I stood straight, of course, rigid, thumbs along the seams of my jeans, hair at the regulation distance two inches above the right eye, heels together and bare feet at ten to two, or ten past ten, belly flat and chest inflated, chin in, heart out. I mean, can you see me, mac? Dad's gravesuit so richly absorbed the sun that he was forced to retreat into the shadows where his crafty jailer's look was decently camouflaged, blending white with purple blotched with silver wall. Not a bad heart, surely?

As his audience we each displayed differing emotions, Fanny, boredom that visibly bordered on sleep: Puti Hohepa, an inattention expressed in his long examination of the natural scene: Buster O'Leary, a sense of complete bewilderment over what it was the old man thought he could achieve by his harangue and, further, a failure to grasp the relevance of it all for the Hohepas. My reaction, let me say, was mixed with irritation at certain of father's habits. (Described.) With his pockets filled with small change he sounded like the original gypsy orchestra, cymbals and all. I actually tried mum's old trick of the glance and the cough. No luck. And he went on talking, at me now, going so wide of the mark, for example, as to mention some inconceivable, undocumented and undemonstrated condition, some truly monstrous condition, called your-mother's-love. Plain evidence of his distress, I took it to be, this obscenity uttered in mixed company. I turned my head the better to hear, when it came, the squelchy explosion of his heart. And I rolled a smoke and threw Fanny the packet. It landed neatly on her stomach. She sat up and made herslef a smoke and then crossed to her old man and, perching beside him in the brilliant pool of light, fire of skin and gleam of hair bronze and blue-black, neatly extracted from his pocket his battered flint lighter. She snorted smoke and passed the leaf to her old man.

Some things, gentlemen, still amaze. To my dying day I have treasured that scene and all its rich implications. In a situation so pregnant of difficulties, in the midst of a debate so fraught with undertones, an exchange (quiet there, at the back) so bitterly fulsome on the one hand and so reserved on the other, I ask you to take special note of this observance of the ritual of the makings, remembering, for the fullest savouring of the nuance, my father's abstention.

As those brown fingers moved on the white cylinder, or cone, I was moved almost, to tears, almost, by this companionable and wordless recognition of our common human frailty, father and dark child in silent communion and I too, in some manner not to be explained because inexplicable, sharing their hearts. I mean the insanity, pal. Puti Hohepa and his lass in sunlight on the steps, smoking together, untroubled, natural and patient; and me and daddy glaring at each other in the shades like a couple of evangelists at cross pitch. Love, thy silver coatings and castings. And thy neighbours! So I went and sat by Fanny and put an arm through hers.

The sun gathered me up, warmed and consoled; the bitter view assumed deeper purples and darker rose; a long way off a shield flashed, the sun striking silver from a water trough. At that moment I didn't care what mad armies marched in my father's voice nor what the clarion was he was trying so strenuously to sound. I didn't care that the fire in his heart was fed by such rank fuel, skeezing envy, malice, revenge, hate and parental power. I sat and smoked and was warm, and the girl's calm flank was against me; her arm through mine. Nothing was so natural as to turn through the little distnace between us and kiss her smoky mouth. Ah yes, I could feel, I confess, through my shoulder blades as it were and the back of my head, the crazed rapacity and outrage of my daddy's Irish stare, the blackness and the cold glitter of knives. (Father!) While Puti Hohepa sat on as though turned to glowing stone by the golden light, faced outward to the violet mystery of the natural hour, monumentally content and still.

You will have seen it, known it, guessed that there was between this wild, loamy daughter and me, sunburnt scion of an ignorant, insensitive, puritan and therefore prurient Irishman (I can't stop) no more than a summer's dalliance, a season's thoughtless sweetness, a boy and a girl and the makings.

In your wisdom, gentlemen, you will doubtless have sensed that something is lacking in this lullaby, some element missing for the articulation of this ranting tale. Right. The key to daddy's impassioned outburst, no less. Not lost in this verbose review, but so far unstated. Point is he'd come to seek his little son (someone must have been dying because he'd never have come for the opposite reason) and, not being one to baulk at closed doors and drawn shades, wait for it, he'd walked straight in on what he'd always somewhat feverishly imagined and hoped he feared. Fanny took it calmly: I was, naturally, more agitated. Both of us ballocky in the umber light, of course. Still, even though he stayed only long enough to let his eyes adjust and his straining mind take in this historic disposition of flesh, those mantis angles in which for all our horror we must posit our conceivings, it wasn't the greeting he'd expected. It wasn't quite the same, either, between Fanny and me, after he'd backed out, somewhat huffily, on to the verandah. Ah, filthy beasts! He must have been roaring some such expression as that inside his head because his eyeballs were rattling, the very picture of a broken doll, and his face was liver-coloured. I felt sorry for him, for a second, easing backward from the love-starred couch and the moving lovers with his heel hooked through the loop of Fanny's bra, kicking it free like a football hero punting for touch, his dream of reconciliation in ruins.

It wasn't the same. Some rhythms are slow to reform. And once the old man actually made the sanctuary of the verandah he just had to bawl his loudest for old man Hohepa, Mr. Ho-he-pa, Mr. Ho-he-pa. It got us into our clothes anyway, Fanny giggling and getting a sneezing fit at the same time, bending forward into the hoof-marked brassiere and blasting off every ten seconds like a burst air hose until I quite lost count on the one-for-sorrow two-for-joy scale and crammed myself sulkily into my jocks.

Meantime dad's labouring to explain certain natural facts and occurrences to Puti Hohepa, just as though he'd made an original discovery; as perhaps he had considering what he probably thought of as natural. Puti Hohepa listened, I thought that ominous, then silently deprecated, in a single slow movement of his hand, the wholly inappropriate expression of shock and rage, all the sizzle of my daddy's oratory.

Thus the tableau. We did the only possible thing, ignored him and let him run down, get it off his chest, come to his five battered senses, if he had so many, and get his breath. Brother, how he spilled darkness and sin upon that floor, wilting collar and boiling eyes, the sweat running from his face and, Fanny, shameless, languorous and drowsy, provoking him to further flights. She was young, gentlemen: I have not concealed it. She was too young to have had time to accumulate the history he ascribed to her. She was too tender to endure for long the muscular lash of his tongue and the rake of his eyes. She went over to her dad, as heretofore described, and when my sweet sire, orator general to the dying afternoon, had made his pitch about matters observed and inferences drawn, I went to join her. I sat with my back to him. All our backs were to him, including his own. He emptied himself of wrath and for a moment, a wild and wonderful moment, I thought he was going to join us, bathers in the pool of sun. But no.

Silence. Light lovely and fannygold over the pasture; shreds of
mist by the river deepening to rose. My father's hard leather soles
rattled harshly on the bare boards like rim-shots. The mad figure of
him went black as bug out over the lawn, out over the loamy furrows
where the tongue of ploughed field invaded the home paddock, all
my doing, spurning in his violence anything less than this direct
and abrupt charge towards the waiting car. Fanny's hand touched
my arm again and for a moment I was caught in a passion of sympathy for him something as solid as grief and love, an impossible
pairing of devotion and despair. The landscape flooded with sadness
as I watched the scuttling, black, ignominious figure hurdling the
fresh earth, the waving arms seemingly scattering broadcast the
white and shying gulls, his head bobbing on his shoulders as he
narrowed into distance.

I wished, gentlemen, with a fervour foreign to my young life, that
it had been in company other than that of Puti Hohepa and his brat
that we had made our necessary parting. I wished we had been alone.
I did not want to see him diminished, made ridiculous and pathetic
among strangers, while I so brashly joined the mockers. (Were they
mocking?) Impossible notions; for what was there to offer and how
could he receive? Nothing. I stroked Fanny's arm. Old man Hohepa
got up and unchained the dog and went off to get the cows in. He
didn't speak; maybe the chocolate old bastard was dumb, eh? In a
minute I would have to go down and start the engine and put the
separator together. I stayed to stare at Fanny, thinking of undone
things in a naughty world. She giggled, thinking, for all I know, of
the same, or of nothing. Love, thy sunny trystings and nocturnal
daggers. For the first time I admitted my irritation at that girlish,
hic-coughing, tenor giggle. But we touched, held, got up and with
our arms linked went down the long paddock through the infestation
of buttercup, our feet bruising stalk and flower. Suddenly all I wanted and at whatever price was to be able, sometime, somewhere, to
make it up to my primitive, violent, ignorant and crazy old man.
And I knew I never would. Ah, what a bloody fool. And then the
next thing I wanted, a thing far more feasible, was to be back in that
room with its shade and smell of haydust and warm flesh, taking up
the classic story just where we'd been so rudely forced to discon-
tinue it. Old man Hohepa was bellowing at the dog; the cows rocked
up through the paddock gate and into the yard: the air smelled of
night. I stopped; and holding Fanny's arm suggested we might run
back. Her eyes went wide: she giggled and broke away and I stood
there and watched her flying down the paddock, bare feet and a
flouncing skirt, her hair shaken loose.

Next afternoon I finished ploughing the river paddock, the nature of Puti Hohepa's husbandry as much a mystery as ever, and ran the old Ferguson into the lean-to shelter behind the cow shed. It was far too late for ploughing: the upper paddocks were hard and dry. But Puti hoped to get a crop of late lettuce off the river flat; just in time, no doubt, for a glutted market, brown rot, wily and total failure of the heart. He'd have to harrow it first, too; and on his own. Anyway, none of my worry. I walked into the shed. Fanny and her daddy were deep in conversation. She was leaning against the flank of a cow, a picture of rustic grace, a rural study of charmed solemnity. Christ knows what they were saying to each other. For one thing they were speaking in their own language: for another I couldn't hear anything, even that, above the blather and splatter of the bloody cows and the racket of the single cylinder diesel, brand-name Onan out of Edinburgh so help me. They looked up. I grabbed a stool and got on with it, head down to the bore of it all. I'd have preferred to be up on the tractor, poisoning myself straight out, bellowing this and that and the other looney thing to the cynical gulls. Ah, my mountain princess of the golden chords, something was changing. I stripped on, sullenly: I hoped it was me.

We were silent through dinner: we were always silent, through all meals. It made a change from home where all hell lay between soup and sweet, everyone taking advantage of the twenty minutes of enforced attendance to shoot the bile, bicker and accuse, rant and wrangle through the grey disgusting mutton and the two veg. Fanny never chattered much and less than ever in the presence of her pappy: giggled maybe but never said much. Then out of the blue father Hohepa opened up. Buster, you should make peace with your father. I considered it. I tried to touch Fanny's foot under the table and I considered it. A boy shouldn't hate his father: a boy should respect his father. I thought about that too. Then I asked should fathers hate their sons; but I knew the answer. Puti Hohepa didn't say anything, just sat blowing into his tea, looking at his reputedly wild daughter who might have been a beauty for all I could tell, content to be delivered of the truth and so fulfilled. You should do this: a boy shouldn't do that—tune into that, mac. And me thinking proscription and prescription differently ordered in this farm world of crummy acres. I mean I thought I'd left all that crap behind the night I stumbled along Rideout Road following, maybe, the river Alph. I thought old man Hohepa, having been silent for so long, would know better than to pull, of a sudden, all those generalisations with which for seventeen years I'd been beaten dizzy—

but not so dizzy as not to be able to look back of the billboards
and see the stack of rotting bibles. Gentlemen, I was, even noticeably, subdued. Puti Hohepa clearly didn't intend to add anything
more just then. I was too tired to make him an answer. I think I
was too tired even for hate; and what better indication of the extent
of my exhaustion than that? It had been a long summer; how long
I was only beginning to discover. It was cold in the kitchen. Puti
Hohepa got up. From the doorway, huge and merging into the night
he spoke again: You must make up your own mind. He went away,
leaving behind him the vibration of a gentle sagacity, tolerance, a
sense of duty (mine, as usual) pondered over and pronounced upon.
The bastard. You must make up your own mind. And for the first
time you did that mum had hysterics and dad popped his gut. About
what? Made up my mind about what? My black daddy? Fanny?
Myself? Life? A country career and agricultural hell? Death? Money?
Fornication? (I'd always liked that.) What the hell was he trying to
say? What doing but abdicating the soiled throne at the first chal-
lenge? Did he think fathers shouldn't hate their sons, or could help
it, or would if they could? Am I clear? No matter. He didn't have
one of the four he'd sired at home so what the hell sort of story
was he trying to peddle? Father with the soft centre. You should,
you shouldn't, make up your own mind. Mac, my head was going
round. But it was brilliant, I conceded, when I'd given it a bit of
thought. My livid daddy himself would have applauded the perfect
ambiguity. What a bunch: they keep a dog on a chain for years and
years and then let it free on some purely personal impulse and when
it goes wild and chases its tail round and round, pissing here
and sniffing there in an ecstasy of liberty, a freedom for which it has
been denied all training, they shoot it down because it won't come
running when they hold up the leash and whistle. (I didn't think
you'd go that way, son.) Well, my own green liberty didn't look
like so much at that moment; for the first time I got an inkling that
life was going to be simply a matter of out of one jail and into another. Oh, they had a lot in common, her dad and mine. I sat there,
mildly stupefied, drinking my tea. Then I looked up at Fanny; or,
rather, down on Fanny. I've never known such a collapsible sheila in
my life. She was stretched on the kitchen couch, every vertebra
having turned to juice in the last minute and a half. I thought maybe
she'd have the answer, some comment to offer on the state of dis-
union. Hell. I was the very last person to let my brew go cold while
I pondered the nuance of the incomprehensible, picked at the du-
bious unsubtlety of thought of a man thirty years my senior who
had never, until then, said more than ten words to me. She is too

good for you: only six words after all and soon forgotten. Better, yes, if he'd stayed mum, leaving me to deduce from his silence whatever I could, Abora Mountain and the milk of paradise, consent in things natural and a willingness to let simple matters take their simple course.

I was wrong: Fanny offered no interpretation of her father's thought. Exegesis to his cryptic utterance was the one thing she couldn't supply. She lay with her feet up on the end of the couch. brown thighs charmingly bared, mouth open and eyes closed in balmy sleep, displaying in this posture various things but mainly her large unconcern not only for his tragedy of filial responsibility and the parental role but, too, for the diurnal problem of the numerous kitchen articles, pots, pans, plates, the lot. I gazed on her, frowning on her bloom of sleep, the slow inhalation and exhalation accompanied by a gentle flare of nostril, and considered the strength and weakness of our attachment. Helpmeet she was not, thus to leave her lover to his dark ponderings and the chores.

Puti Hohepa sat on the verandah in the dark, hacking over his bowl of shag. One by one, over my second cup of tea, I assessed my feelings, balanced all my futures in the palm of my hand. I crossed to Fanny, crouched beside her, kissed her. I felt embarrassed and, gentlemen, foolish. Her eyes opened wide; then they shut and she turned over.

The dishes engaged my attention not at all, except to remind me, here we go, of my father in apron and rubber gloves at the sink, pearl-diving while mum was off somewhere at a lynching. Poor bastard. Mum had the natural squeeze for the world; they should have changed places. (It's for your own good! Ah, the joyous peal of that as the razor strop came whistling down like tartar's blade.) I joined daddy Hohepa on the verandah. For a moment we shared the crescent moon and the smell of earth damp under dew, Rideout Mountain massed to the west.

I've finished the river paddock.

Yes.

The tractor's going to need a de-coke before long.

Yes.

I guess that about cuts it out.

Yes.

I may as well shoot through.

Buster, is Fanny pregnant?

I don't know. She hasn't said anything to me so I suppose she can't be.

You are going home?

No, Not home. There's work down south. I'd like to have a look down there.

There's work going here if you want it. But you have made up your mind?

I suppose I may as well shoot through.

Yes.

After milking tomorrow if that's okay with you.

Yes.

He hacked on over his pipe. Yes, yes, yes, yes, yes is Fanny pregnant? What if I'd said yes? I didn't know one way or the other. I only hoped, and left the rest to her. Maybe he'd ask her; and what if she said yes? What then, eh Buster? Maybe I should have said why don't you ask her. A demonstrative, volatile, loquacious old person: a tangible symbol of impartiality, reason unclouded by emotion, his eyes frank in the murk of night and his pipe going bright dim, bright as he calmly considered the lovely flank of the moon. I was hoping she wasn't, after all. Hoping; it gets to be a habit, a bad habit that does you no good, stunts your growth, sends you insane and makes you, demonstrably, blind. Hope, for Fanny Hohepa.

Later, along the riverbank, Fanny and I groped, gentlemen, for the lost rapport and the parking sign. We were separated by just a little more than an arm's reach. I made note then of the natural scene. Dark water, certainly; dark lush grass underfoot; dark girl; the drifting smell of loam in the night: grant me again as much. Then, by one of those fortuitous accidents not infrequent in our national prosings, our hands met, held, fell away. Darkness. My feet stumbling by the river and my heart going like a tango. Blood pulsed upon blood, undenied and unyoked, as we busied ourselves tenderly at our ancient greetings and farewells. And in the end, beginning my sentence with a happy conjunction, I held her indistinct, dark head. We stayed so for a minute, together and parting as always, with me tumbling down upon her the mute dilemma my mind then pretended to resolve and she offering no restraint, no argument better than the dark oblivion of her face.

Unrecorded the words between us: there can't have been more than six, anyway, it was our fated number. None referred to my departure or to the future or to maculate conceptions. Yet her last touch spoke volumes. (Unsubsidised, gentlemen, without dedication or preamble.) River-damp softened her hair: her skin smelled of soap: Pan pricking forward to drink at the stream, crushing fennel, exquisitely stooping, bending...

And, later again, silent, groping, we ascended in sequence to the

paternal porch.
  Buster?
  Yair?
  Goodnight, Buster.
  'Night, Fanny. Be seein' yuh.
  . . .
Fourteen minute specks of radioactive phosphorus brightened by weak starlight pricked out the hour: one.

In the end I left old STC in the tractor tool box along with the spanner that wouldn't fit any nut I'd ever tried it on and the grease gun without grease and the last letter from mum, hot as radium. I didn't wait for milking. I was packed and gone at the first trembling of light. It was cold along the river-bottom, cold and still. Eels rose to feed: the water was like pewter; old pewter. I felt sick, abandoned, full of self-pity. Everything washed through me, the light, the cold, a sense of what lay behind me and might not lie before, a feeling of exhaustion when I thought of home, a feeling of despair when I thought of Fanny still curled in sleep. Dark. She hadn't giggled: so what? I changed my fibre suitcase to the other hand and trudged along Rideout Road. The light increased; quail with tufted crests crossed the road; I began to feel better. I sat on the suitcase and rolled a smoke. Then the sun caught a high scarp of Rideout Mountain and began to finger down slow and gold. I was so full of relief, suddenly, that I grabbed my bag and ran. Impetuous. I was lucky not to break my ankle. White gulls, loam flesh, dark water, damsel and dome; where would it take you? Where was there to go, anyway? It just didn't matter; that was the point. I stopped worrying that minute and sat by the cream stand out on the main road. After a while a truck stopped to my thumb and I got in. If I'd waited for the cream truck I'd have had to face old brownstone Hohepa and I wasn't very eager for that. I'd had a fill of piety, of various brands. And I was paid up to date.
  I looked back. Rideout Mountain and the peak of ochre red roof, Maori red. That's all it was. I wondered what Fanny and her pappy might be saying at this moment, across the clothes-hanger rumps of cows. The rush of relief went through me again. I looked at the gloomy bastard driving: he had a cigarette stuck to his lip like a growth. I felt almost happy. Almost. I might have hugged him as he drove his hearse through the tail-end·of summer.

BILL PEARSON
(*b.* 1922)

At the Leicesters'

I often went to Mrs. Leicester's on a Sunday afternoon, plodding
a dusty couple of miles from the arid glare of the camp to the irrigated greenery of the settlement. And it was worth it, if only for
the air-cooling system installed in her sitting-room or the jug of
iced tea standing on the cooler. Once when Miss Leicester offered
me a second glass I jumped up to pour it myself, but she beat me
to it and knocked the jug over, broke it and spilt the tea into the
works of the cooler. 'It's just as well I broke it, and not you,' she
said, grimly ironic as she rang for the servant and clicked her tongue
over the price of a new jug.

Mrs. Leicester was French by birth and the widow of an English
judge. She hadn't seen London since the last century, or Paris in 20
years; and she was an authority in her way on the mosques of
Cairo. On a Saturday afternoon she'd be sitting on a folding camp-
stool outside Bab-el-Luk station, troops would gather, Miss Leicester would collect a small donation from everyone, Mahmud the
policeman would summon gharries, and then a procession of half-a-
dozen gharries would take us off to a mosque. Once, through Mrs.
Leicester's good favour with the Moslems, we even got into Imam
Shafe'i, usually too sacred for infidels.

But Mrs. Leicester was getting on for eighty. She couldn't ne-
gotiate stairs any more; and the gharry drivers wouldn't trust their
nags to long journeys or uphill climbs, so it was only a small
regular cycle of mosques we visited.

Once I sat beside Mrs. Leicester in the front gharry with three
other servicemen. Cramped as we were, I felt honoured. It was Bairam; we called it their Christmas. The Egyptian kids were unusaully
clean and spruced up, they were laughing and they were more than
usually on the bludge. One of them leapt up on on to the mudguard
and called Mrs. Leicester by her name —or as near to it as his arabic
could make it—and she held out her gloved hand for him to kiss.
'Would you mind giving him a small something?' Mrs. Leicester said.
'I would have to take my gloves off.' A RAF bloke beat us all to it
and gave the kid a two-acker piece.

Mahmud the policeman was a bulky genial fellow; he was her

official protection in journeys through the slummy approaches to the mosques. He always made sure no one but he assisted Mrs. Leicester's failing limbs from gharry to the mihrab of a mosque. Every Bairam Mrs. Leicester would take up a collection and buy him a present; this time the RAF bloke had been collecting: he performed the duty with the fervour and persistence of a lackey. He asked me twice had I 'contributed to the cause,' and didn't appear to believe me when I told him I'd given something to Mrs. Leicester the Sunday before. What they gave Mahmud I don't know, but no doubt he was as pleased as he was when I let him have some smokes in the portal of Ibn Kalaun and didn't ask more than the Naafi price, and then as he fished for the money, relented and said they were a gift—it was Bairam. To show his appreciation he shouted me a gharry ride back to the New Zealand Club—it was a distinction to be seen riding with an Egyptian policemen in white, and soldiers stared at me wondering if I'd been mug enough to let a wog police-man arrest me. Whether he paid or claimed a free ride out of tribute to his profession I didn't find out. Mahmud said once, 'With the Egyptian it's always baksheesh; baksheesh all the time. No good.' It was no wonder that we liked him.

You met a variety of people at Mrs. Leicester's. She would sit, the nucleus of a doting group of Tommies, Yanks and French civi-lians, much as the Frenchwomen who ran the 18th century salons must have sat. She would be genial and expansive, and for four hours she dispensed knowledge and wisdom to adulant troops. 'There are consolations in being old,' she said. 'One grows accus-tomed to so much more attention.'

* * *

There was the Swiss woman who'd been rereading Dostoevsky and spoke with a passionate intensity. She was in a dilemma over her servant. who kept helping himself to her clothes, her money, anything he wanted or could sell. She had tried talking to him, offering to help him out with a loan, at which he'd protested his innocence, then admitted everything and in a wave of high resolu-tion promised to take nothing again; only to start on another bout of theft a few days later. She had tried ignoring her losses, but they continued. 'What—what am I to do?'

Miss Leicester, I think, suggested the police.

'Yes, yes, the police!' the Swiss woman said. 'But what good does that do? He would go to gaol, he would be ill-treated, he would come from gaol with a square cut from his hair, and he would be a con-

firmed criminal. I feel I cannot condemn him to a life of crime. It
is so perplexing!'

There was the RAF bloke with a moustache and a sort of bank-
clerk's smugness, the one who had collected for Mahmud's present.
He spoke of the Immobilia Building with a sneer, as if it were the
crowning damnation of modern streamlined synthetic civilsation;
once when someone mentioned an 18th century Turkish *sebil*, he
said with kindly disdain, 'But it's a little modern for me.' He always
saw to it that newcomers were given the Family Bible, two volumes
of detailed photos of Cairo mosques, from Amr to El Rifa'i. This
day a Kiwi came in—I thought he looked like a Southland farmhand
—and the Tommy unloaded the Bible on him. But the Kiwi was just
back from Italy. 'I've seen that before,' he said and looked to Mrs.
Leicester busy with a Yank and a Wren. Failing Mrs. Leicester,
the Kiwi turned to me, dipping into 'Plights and Pull-throughs in
the Middle East.' He said, 'Oh, that's M. I knew M. When we
were in Egypt we went everywhere together. All Cairo—the pyramids
—Alex.—Sakkara—everywhere. Then I went to Italy. He did the
Middle East. I did Italy. Every town you can think of. I've spent
thousands of lire on photos. I've sent thousands of photos home—
thousands!' It seemed as if these war years were the crowning
episode of his life, the justification of all those years in Tuatap mud;
he was seeing the world, hoarding up impressions, experiences, mar-
vels and customs, enough to impress the neighbours for a lifetime.
I envied him.

Then another RAF bloke came, a photographer. 'Our *great*
photographer,' Mrs. Leicester always called him. He brought a
box of his photos every time because he knew he was expected to.
She had asked him once could she use some of them to illustrate
her next book on mosques; he'd hinted it wasn't done to ask un-
commercial favours of a professional. 'Most people are glad to
have their photographs included in *my* books,' she'd said.

And then the little Jewess blew in, all hustle and vivacity. Mrs.
Leicester had mentioned before that a Waac would be coming to
play for her; 'if she is not first rate as a player, certainly she is well
within the third grade'; coming from Mrs. Leicester this was praise
indeed. The Sunday before there had only been four of us, myself,
another Kiwi, the Swiss woman and the Jewess; and she had told us
of her first days in Palestine. 'I went to Tel Aviv,' she said. 'And it
was oh, so—terrible for the beginning. I did not have any money
and if you have no money in Tel Aviv it is so hard for you. I had to
work for a family who had come from Poland and wash their clothes
and polish their floors—but oh, more than everything, I missed the

piano. I would have given *anything* to be able to play. And you
know, they have concerts there in Tel Aviv—beautiful concerts
with wonderful players, and I had never enough money to pay to
go to any. So do you know what I did? I would climb up the back
stairs, behind the concert hall—you know?—and stand there to
listen to all the concert. It was so good. But then I answered an ad-
vertisement and began to teach a little boy to play the piano; and
his father said I could work there, and if he paid me less, I could
play the piano in my spare time. He did not pay me so much, but
it was something to have the piano. They gave me only my breakfast
and I could not afford to buy any other meals. Do you know what
I would do? I would be so hungry. Well, you know those little
shops that have in their windows sausages and meats and things
like that? Well, I would stand in front of one at night-time, and in
my imagination, I would eat up every one of them until I was absolutely full.'

'You wouldn't get very fat on that,' the Kiwi said.

'No, but so I could pretend to myself—you know?—that I was
not hungry. It was so hard. But then I had the piano.'

'And your mother, all this time?' Mrs. Leicester asked.

'Well, when I had saved enough money, I wrote to my mother
and asked her to come out to me. But she wrote: "I am too old to
leave Germany now. This is my home, this is my country. It would
be like to uproot an old tree. I could not face it." So then the war
came, and I do not know if she is alive or where is she. But I think
she must have died. If she is dead she will have missed so much
suffering anyway.'

She started to play then, and she was good. And on this later
Sunday after we'd sat primly round the tea-table those of us who
were 'musicially inclined' went to the drawing-room, the others
went back to the library to browse. We listened and we clapped.
'But please don't ask me to play again,' the Jewess said. 'Every time
you ask me and I play again and then I think I play too long. Every
time when I go I *reproach* myself.'

'Well, there's no need for you to reproach yourself,' Miss Leicester said, gently ironic.

When it came time to go and we were each taking our turn at
shaking Mrs. Leicester's hand, the Kiwi obtruded a stock of war
experience. As he came to Mrs. Leicester he said, 'What surprised
me about Italy was the way the churches are still standing. In the
middle of a bombed-out village you can always count on the church
standing.'

'That is because the allied airmen aim carefully so as to not to damage sacred buildings,' said Mrs. Leicester.

'Oh no! Don't run away with that idea. Oh, no!' The Tommies
behind the Kiwi were embarrassed at this intrusion of intense
opinion; in the middle of a formal ceremony, the Kiwi had thrown
a spanner into the works. 'Because sometimes they do hit the churches, but when they do, you can always be sure, the altar's still standing, and if the altar isn't, then the crucifix is. Oh, it's uncanny! Uncanny!'

*   *   *

It was the RAF photographer who first made me look for it. We
went back to Cairo one Sunday and went to the Club for a cup of
tea, and there was another Tommy with us. 'The Leicesters have
quite a reputation here for being beggars,' the photographer said.
'They make it a practice to go to the Baron's for dinner every Saturday after their excursion. I don't think the Baron is inhospitable,
but the point is that he's tied down to entertain then regularly every
Saturday.' Well, the photographer knew the best society in Cairo,
a certain professor, the Baron, members of the Anglo-Egyptian
Union. It wasn't that, like the professor, who had started with Mrs.
Leicesters' tours for soldiers in the previous war, he was a pupil
who'd outgrown his teacher; he'd met the Leicesters in the course
of his work, but he'd always done his own hunting out of old Mos-
lem buildings, climbing on to littered roofs of private houses, barg-
ing through slum tenements to get a better view of them.

A memory came to me of Mrs. Leicester lamenting a recent down-
pour and the flood it had caused; muddy water rose in the house,
ruined a carpet and spoilt the bottom row on her bookshelf. She'd
filed a claim for compensation from the government, but she didn't
expect much. She spoke of it repeatedly as a tragedy, worse one
would gather, than that of the fellahin who lost their mud huts.

'Wouldn't it be a case like that of some people I know in England?'
the other Tommy said. 'People who are old and not earning anything.
They really have lots of money but they are frightened it won't last
them till they die. And they become very niggardly, unnecessarily so.'

Well, I thought, what did it matter? She was a likeable woman
and it's comforting to say, 'We all have our faults'. I'd seen this
Baron once; a retired Swedish diplomat. He'd come to Mrs. Leicester's for a book and he bowed to us and said, 'Good evening,
gentlemen': his charm and grace made you feel formal and at ease
at the same time, Mrs. Leicester asked him would he take the young
Jewess into Cairo with him, she was in a hurry to return. The Baron

went into a huddle with himself. 'Well, she would be obliged to sit with the chauffeur. I'm afraid the back seat is full. I have some friends waiting, you see. But then, she would be only sitting *next* to the chauffeur. That doesn't involve her being attached to him, does it? She would still be travelling with our party.' The problem solved, the Jewess went with him.

But Mrs. Leicester was secure in her good terms with Egypt. Mahmud would shepherd her till she gave up her tours. Boys would climb on to her gharry to kiss her hand and ask a small something. It was Miss Leicester who wasn't so sure.

*   *   *

Miss Leicester ran a school for Egyptian girls in the Saida Zeinab district, a huddlement of dry dingy dusty earthen houses. She had a flat in Cairo itself, where she held down an office job at a petrol agency: she could say she was independent, she wasn't living on her mother.

One day we were talking about Britain and the Middle East and Miss Leicester said, 'England is tired of it all. She wonders is it worth it. She'd like to wash her hands of it all.' And the England in Miss Leicester's proud expatriate spinster's face was getting tired too. It was the pride of one who refuses to see the gesture of contempt, pretends not to hear the insult, would ignore the spittle on her shoes.

She ran the school off her own bat and in her spare time. (Most business places close down for the afternoon in summer in Cairo.) You felt it was her gesture of idealism, perhaps a salve to the uneasy conscience of a guest who felt she'd overstayed her welcome. She was doing her little bit. But anyway it was a change to see little Egyptian girls clean and happy, to see them sewing and singing instead of sitting dully on heaps of dirt, with flies asleep on their faces, dodging the sun. The emphasis was on propriety, on the nice way of doing things, good manners and a cheerful disposition, the Golden Rule: all Miss Leicester's stubborn and modest idealism went into the place. She boasted that once she'd told them of children in Upper Egypt who'd lost their homes in a Nile flood; whereat the girls had offered to forego the milk she bought them if she'd put that money to helping the destitute children. It wouldn't be much, but it was the gesture.

She showed me a tray full of dolls, tea-cosies and coverlets they made. They were for sale. 'All the proceeds go to the Red Crescent,' she said. 'Of course, there's no obligation to buy.' Well, the cheapest thing was twenty ackers, I had only ten till pay-day. 'I'd rather make a small donation,' I said, trying to sound noble. I signed in the visitors' book, amongst the doctors and lawyers and army officers who'd been along; and I gave her my widow's mite.

She let me loose in a cupboard full of little garments the girls had sewn, and in their scramble to bring out things to impress a visitor, the girls pulled out a little china vase that held pins, It broke, and when Miss Leicester came along and saw it, her face showed that that was one planned improvement postponed, perhaps another pupil who wouldn't be enrolled. She clicked her tongue, and said, 'What a pity. They're so hard to replace.' She had to contend with a lot of things; the rising cost of living was big amongst them. Well, I'd have liked a lot to pay for it, but I'd given her the last of my money.

So it was with rather a guilty conscience I smiled back to their charming goodbye, and thanked Miss Leicester when I got out of her battered little car. 'One does what one can'; praise bounced off her like drops of water from a duck's back; one tried to be realistic.

*   *   *

Miss Leicester's flat was just off Soliman Pasha. It wasn't a classy district, no green irrigated shrubberies, no yard at all. One of many huddled flats, with cramped balconies and shutters pinned back by the windows from which in the early morning would droop, like lolling tongues, bedding put out to air. There would be French and Italian and Turkish families in this street, and may be an Egyptian public servant with a son at university.

I had to wait a few minutes before she opened the door. I didn't know which floor she was on, and a servant I asked didn't seem to understand me. I didn't belong there and he wasn't going to encourage a soldier to be near the place. And then, by chance, Miss Leicester opened her door. I explained, and 'Oh,' she said self-righteously. 'My card is here, isn't it? Yes!' and she pointed to a grimy unobtrusive pair of names by her doorbell. It was as if she wouldn't have forgiven herself if her card hadn't been there; almost a social misdemeanour.

'I'm so pleased you've come,' she said.'Won't you care to join me at tea? I've been dreading so much this meal. Sister Annette went this morning. You know when one has been living with a person for two years, one becomes quite attached...This will be my first meal alone. Everything reminds one...

She looked out the window and listened: the air was full of the noise of Cairo reawaking to the cool of evening—hawkers' cries, taxi-horns, gharry hoofs: music to her native ears, but music that had fear for her expatriate soul. But one had to be brave; she turned and served me some salad.

'She went for an indefinite period,' she said. 'She will be away all the summer in any case. But her permit expires in three months; if she stays longer she will find it difficult indeed to enter the country again. And then the European winter will be so cold with the shortage of fuel, and after six years of Egypt she will notice the cold. I think she'd be most unwise to stay. I do hope she comes back.'

There wasn't much I could say to comfort her; I wasn't wedded to the country like her and I could only egg her on in her effort to be cheerful. We finished our cold meat and salad. There was still some in the bowl. 'Will you have some more?' I said no; I'd already eaten at the barracks; I'd only joined her to be sociable. She helped herself to some more. 'The servant would only eat it,' She explained. 'You know at one time one kept one's servants in food, and they always ate what was left from the meals. But later it was more convenient, especially when one's servants didn't live on the place, to pay them the equivalent in wages. But they still expect the food, and one knows they will eat any leavings. So that... she paused, holding the salad spoon in mid-air and confided ... when it's a case more of greed than of hunger, one feels one can eat more with an easy conscience.' The words trailed tentatively. She looked at me for confirmation, and though I tried, I'm afraid I didn't help her out. I tried to look agreeable, but I was thinking, out of pity more than anger, what she'd come to. A proud unbeaten Englishwoman, daughter of the judges, administrators and cotton-growers, running a school from charity, but beaten at the money game, outwitting her servant, and feeling she was cheating.

I didn't stay long; her rooms were an oasis of English taste and respectability in a desert of dirt and graft, but it was a dull and depressing oasis, its waters were brackish, its palms bedraggled. I had come for a food-parcel she was posting a friend in England: military mails were so much more certain than Egyptian mails these days.

'What will the postage be, can you tell me?' she said.

'I'll be able to wangle it for nothing,' I said, and I knew she was relieved.

PHILLIP WILSON
(*b.* 1922)

It was Easter

I went into the place and took a quick look round in case there was anyone I knew. But there was no one. I couldn't see very well after being in the sun for so long, and the sounds of the voices and the shadowy figures seemed strange. It made me feel worse than ever. I had to tell somebody. It was simply terrible.

Christ, it's simply awful!

I must have been saying it to myself all the time, running along the white sand road by the beach looking for someone else. I thought I would surely find a cobber in the pub. But I couldn't see a soul as I stood there trying to get my breath, with the sweat trickling under the edge of my hat and down beside my ear. Then it started to come out on my forehead and ran into my eyebrows. My hand was shaking when I wiped it from my face. I hadn't noticed that before. And, my heart was going like an outboard motor. I must have lost my nerve badly. I wanted a drink, and went over to order a double whiskly. but there wasn't any whisky on. Not until five o'clock. So I had to have a beer. O boy, it was good! I was waiting for the second when I realized there was one of them I knew after all. Now I could see better I recognized her at once.

She was near the other end of the bar working the pump and filling handles four at a time for a bunch of Maori boys. It was the usual Saturday crowd and they were laughing and giggling and having the time of their lives blowing what was left of the week's pay. Some had a two-up school going in the corner. I saw the pennies flash high in the air, heard the excited calls: 'Come in, spinner! Come in, spinner!' Heard them clink on the floor, heard the shouts and groans, saw the fives change hands. They looked so happy that I wanted to go and tell them.

'There's a dead man down the road. Hanged himself from the rafters in the barn and now he's dead. I know because I just seen him.'

I really felt like walking up and saying that, but then the awful thought of it came over me and I started to shiver and I felt cold and my guts seemed to clog and sink inside me. My legs wouldn't hold me up properly, so I leaned against the bar. It was like I was going to faint and I was running wet all over, in an absolute lather I could feel it pouring under my armpits and I couldn't stop myself from trembling. I suppose it was partly the beer that made me perspire so much, but I was afraid, too. I was just sick with fear.

'Mary,' I called.

She looked round and saw me and came to where I was leaning against it.

'Feeling thirsty?' she said.

'Yes, beer,' I said, without thinking.

She smiled at me.

'One long and cool.'

'O Mary', I said. 'I've just seen a dead man. He was swinging there and his face was black and his tongue sticking out and it was swollen and black too. His eye was wide open and he was looking at me when I came in, only he swung round then and I could see the back of his head. He was dead all right, must have been since yesterday. I swear he was staring at me. He wanted to say something, only he couldn't because his tongue was filling up his mouth.'

She looked at me.

'O Mary,' I said, 'It was terrible. It was awful! He was swinging there dead as a rabbit. What am I going to do?'

The perspiration was streaming down my face now I was telling her about it and going through it again.

'Pretty hot today, ain't it, Freddie,' she said.

'Give me another beer, Mary,' I said.

'There's one waiting.'

I hadn't noticed, but there was a full handle on the bar. It must have been there all the time I was talking. I drank it off at once without stopping and put the empty on the bar. I wiped my mouth with the back of my hand. Then I wiped the sweat off my chin. I didn't feel so bad now I'd told her.

'A dead man,' I said.

She just kept on looking at me.

'Where was he?'

'Down in the barn.'

'Which barn?'

'Out the other side of town, by that old farmhouse where nobody lives.'

'What were you doing there?'

'Mary,' I said. 'What's that got to do with it?' There's a dead man in the barn. Hanged.'

'Have you told the police?'

'No,' I said. 'I was scared stiff. I came here as fast as I could. I had to tell someone, it was so terrible. I never thought of going to the police.'

'Well, you better tell them now.'

'I can't, Mary,' I said. 'I'm shaking all over.'

She looked at me.

'You tell them, Mary,' I said.

She just kept on sort of looking at me.

'Riding them up,' I said. 'The old red barn out by the edge of town. Tell them I told you. I can't. I think I'd be sick if I had to tell it over again.'

'Freddie,' she said. 'You're not making this up, are you?'

'No!' I said. 'Honest to God I'm not, Mary. I saw him, I tell you. Swinging there and his face all black with it.'

Suddenly I knew she didn't believe a word I was saying. She thought I was just after a free beer. She thought I was crazy with the heat and the sun.

'It's true, Mary,' I said. 'Come down yourself and I'll show you.'

'Down there with you?' she said. 'Now? Not me, Freddie.'

Everyone in the bar was looking at us but I didn't care. He was dead and she wouldn't understand. I listened to the big South Pacific rollers thudding on the beach. And yesterday I'd heard the toll of church bells. It was supposed to be Easter!

'I think you're talking a lot of bull,' she said.

I just couldn't credit it, that she didn't believe me.

'A dead man,' I said.

She shook her head and walked away to the other end.

'Three straights and a dash?' she said to the Maoris, and gathered the empty handles in her fingers.

I turned round to go out of the place. I wiped sweat off my eyebrows and from my lips. It stung like salt. Surely I didn't look as bad as that? I wasn't crazy, was I? I went to the right in the blinding heat and headed for the police station. I kept muttering to myself all the way along the footpath by the sea. Surely *they* would realize. But Mary! To think I would kid her. About a thing like that! I balled my fists up tight and started to run again.

Well, it was simply incredible, that's what it was.

PHILLIP WILSON
(*b*. 1922)

End of the River

With the motor-bike banging away beneath us it was like watching a movie flashback to be riding on the pillion behind Anthony to the lower reaches of the river. We had heard the big fish were lurking there, and it took me back ten years to the days when we had gone fishing together on the Waikato, camping out in the open for weeks before the beginning of the new term. He had both our rods balanced across his knee, and I had the rest of the gear slung in a bag over my back. This was the outing we had been promising ourselves for some time, ever since he had told me he had been picked to go to Rome, to study for a Doctorate. In a way it was his own private farewell to arms.

It had been quite a triumph for him, everybody said, to have won his achievement so young, and there was quite a bit of envy among those of us who knew him well. It wasn't just becasue he was the only Catholic among us. What aroused us more than anything, I suppose, was the fact that it was because of his religious beliefs, the very thing that used to make us feel superior to him, that he was getting the kind of opportunity which was denied to others whom we thought more worthy. And I, who had been his closest friend, the only one with whom he had persisted in corresponding during the war when we were so completely cut off from one another, I who should have had the least cause for envy, was wrenched with despair that life should have treated him so well and me, with my jaunty, self-assured nihilism, so shabbily.

It was typical that he was not a bit triumphant about his success, but had only smiled benignly when I accused him of it, admitting his good fortune with a quiet grin on those blubbery lips that seemed designed more for sensual enjoyment than for the ascetic life he had laid out for himself. Yet it must have been there before the war, that determination to make a name for himself in his chosen filed, even in those student years when we were both involved to within an inch of our physical capacities in Latin texts and the literature of the seventeenth century, but with such, as I saw now, disparate aims. How much more must the exaltations and groanings of Crashaw and Donne, or the blind severities of Milton, have affected

him than they did me, who thought I had penetrated to the very
sap of their divine wisdom? And how he must have laughed at old
Herbert, whom I had worshipped second to the greatest of them for
his calm Protestant faith amid all that torment. In my blindness I
had not seen that it would inevitably lead to something like this, and
I was paying for it now, remembering that he had not only made no
excuse for his beliefs but had even hinted once or twice at his theo-
logical aims. Looking back, I had to admit that there had been a
certain steadfastness about him that we didn't have, and a humility
too, something that we in our arrogance could not understand.

Now, in the moment of his impending departure, I could see the
thinness of the thread which had held us together for so many years.
There had been nothing emotional in our friendship at first. It was
based on the fact that he had always had an answer to my arguments
and I the perfect rebuttal, as I thought, to his. We had been thrown
together through a spirit of competition, because we were both
near the top of our class, fighting for the scholarships that were in-
variably awarded to someone else. And liking the texture of each
other's minds we had stuck together, arguing with the prodigious
gravity of young men, sharpening our minds and realizing our
dependence on each other only when we were apart. It may have been
because I was younger than he was, and less sure of myself, but often
when my intellectual conviction deserted me and I saw the darkness of
unbelief stretching out like a sea, suggesting everything but yielding
nothing as true and faithful as his own spiritual refuge, I had wondered who would be proved right in the end. It was always my buoyant
Marxism against the solidity of his ancient hierarchy, and I could
not conceive of any battle being won by the spirit of conservatism
among men who were free and without fear. Yet the pattern of our
own lives was proving me wrong, and while the last and most important scholarship had been won by him after all, I was left with
no other outlet for my energies than a school-teacher's classroom.
He would come back, if he did, one of the most important men in
New Zealand in some ways, while my own liberalism would expire
among acrid chalk-dust and the crude guffaws of boys.

Was I wrong after all? I only knew that when he went he would
take with him my assurance, for it had been supported largely by the
wall of his argument. Unknowingly I had leant on him, and without
him I would be lost. At any rate, on that day at the end of 1941 when
we were all unceremoniously conscripted into the army after our
students' year of grace, myself to end up in the sweat of an air force
squadron in the Pacific and he in the equally debilitating humidity
of a naval patrol off the coast of West Africa, there was no tear in

the shabby garment of our friendship. So that now, in the autumn
of 1950, we were trying to experience it all again in one last glorious
burst before he departed for his long-sought Armageddon and left
me to vegetate on these barbaric shores.

The road was deep in yellow dust, and as we bumped blindly
round a corner we came upon an odd sight. It was the first curious
happening of that strange day. We saw an old truck come whirling
towards us, wrapped in its own individual dust cloud, from the
centre of which came the unmistakable sound of bagpipes. I turned
my head as it passed and saw a woman reclining against the back
of the cab in a bathing costume, blowing furiously on a set of pipes.
I couldn't make out the tune she was playing in the instant before
they had passed, but it sounded to me like the keening of a tormented
soul.

'Did you see it?' I yelled in Anthony's ear, and he shouted something rude against the wind, grinning widely, while his fair curly
hair tossed above the handlebars. It seemed a dirge for our cooling
friendship, and I hated its voluptuous reminder of the past.

We rode on, locked in a contentment which even that sad omen
could not spoil, watching the river stream out beside the road like
a silver flame in the sun, It flowed like a parched tongue between
brown fields spattered with rushes and cabbage trees, poor land that
grazed a few sheep and an occasional dry cow belonging to a syn-
dicate in town, as decadent-looking with its limp wire fences and
gorse-covered hillsides as the deserted farmhouse we could now see
standing along by the shore. It was only on the higher range of the
Orongorongos, where the bush still stood secure, that we sensed
the full grandeur of what the valley must have been a hundred years
before.

Just after we came to the old homestead a second peculiar incident
occurred when a man dressed in city clothes, his coat and tie in his
hand and with dusty black shoes on his feet, came running down the
hill across the river where a side road had once wound up to the
ruined lighthouse on the cliff. He hopped across by the swing-bridge
and proceeded to stride along the road in the direction we had come
from, without so much as a glance at us as he walked on, lonely and
eyeless behind his glittering spectacles. We wondered where he had
come from and where he hoped to get to that day, since there was
no dwelling of any kind for miles around, and he had no car or even
bicycle as far as we could see. But was it Anthony or myself I saw
there? Again I was afraid.

We decided that I should fish the lower part of the river from the
bridge up, and that Anthony should go back along the road for

about a mile and fish upstream from there, leaving the motor-bike against a fence post so that I could ride on and catch him when I got that car. The water was deep and a light green colour, lovely to look at and promising even greater treausres to a careful angler, and a light southerly blowing up from the mouth put a ripple on the water at times, which was just what we had bargained for on this particular day. I started off with a small dry fly, working upstream and casting in all the likely places. I saw several medium-sized trout, but couldn't get any to rise, and I soon began to wonder whether I shouldn't try a different tackle. It was strange water to me, but it seemed a very promising river indeed, except that I wasn't sure how to get the fish out of it.

Anthony had gone back up the road. I could see where he had left the bike shimmering in the sunlight, and with this promise of company before me I was beginning to get a little frustrated and lonely, when I came around a gorse bush and saw one of the biggest trout I think I have ever seen. He was swimming lazily up against the current, wiggling his fins idly as if he had no aim at all in life, until he darted suddenly forward, causing a great commotion in the water, and I realized that this monster was chasing the shoals of tiny mullet that came up into the mouth of the river from the sea. I quickly put on a matuku, the largest wet fly in the box, and began to go after him as if my existence depended on his being landed.

Although I didn't disturb him or even attract his attention at first, I followed him stealthily up the river until I got out on a gravel spit that extended into the middle of the stream just below some old sheep yards. Here he was chasing a bunch of small fry in the shallows, and I saw him turn half out of the water with a devilish roll as he went after them. Then as I wound the line over my left hand I realized that he had lost the mullet and was following my lure. As he struck at it I lifted the tip of the rod high in the air before he shot away downstream. I shouted with excitment as the rod strained and bent like a whip beneath his power, and I fought him for fully fifteen minutes, standing there up to my ankles in the shallow water and feeling a deep pleasure such as I hadn't known since the days we had flown our planes out over Rabaul during the war. The tension that built up in me from a fear that the light tackle I was using wouldn't hold him found its relief when he did break it at last, snapping the cast off just above the hook in a final desperate attempt to get away. Somehow I was glad I had lost him, for he seemed too magnificent a fish to end his life in such a way.

I was trembling all over as a I ran up the bank with my rod to find Anthony, but when I saw him coming and heard him say he hadn't seen a thing except eels, I felt flat and disappointed in a moment and was even more glad that my own hands were empty. He was ready to pack up and go home then, and didn't believe me at first when I told him of the enormous fish I had hooked and fought with. We sat down on the warm grass in the shelter of a bank and ate the sandwiches we had brought, while the sun struck down at us from the lip of the hills. I was a little sorry for him, as I hadn't been since hearing the news, and he put his arm around me and we lay there in perfect tranquillity while I told him about it again, feeling the pleasure of his comradeship like wine as he murmured how lucky I had been. Gradually he leant over as if he wanted to kiss me, so strong was the leaping of our blood to each other, and the steady softness of his stare transfixed me as he leant his body against mine and gripped my arm with his hand. A question shone in his eyes and with the golden sun behind his curls he seemed to take on the aura of a saint as that full inflexible lip dropped over me. I began languidly to yield to the force that was in him, and felt the shadow of something beyond my understanding cross my face for a moment, as the sun went down below the ridge and left us there with the first darkness of evening covering the grass and the river.

What had happened to us? I asked myself. I thought of Anthony's nonchalant reminder that we would have to move smartly to get home before night made the climb out of the valley too hazardous. What did they really mean? I wondered, thinking over the events of the day: the woman with the bagpipes, the solitary man far from home, the big fish I had caught and lost in the river. What passions were contained in that moment when Anthony had leant over me with the smile of a lover on his face? In my mind I caught an echo of the renunciation that shone upon his brow, yet what use was a crown of thorns when life was taking from us the one consolation we had known?

The valley was like a desert and we seemed back in the wilderness as we travelled beneath the winnowing moon-light, empty, mindless, no longer linked as one upon that warm machine. What was this country to him now, with its spirits of old tangata haunting the tree-tops and its grey tombs of men who had already lost their heritage in a life more lonely than death, where sheep and land and home were valued more for the money and days of horse racing they could provide than for anything affecting a man's soul? I was caught in a flux of emotion in which nothing had any significance any more but the fact that I was losing my closest friend. Why could we not roll up in our blankets by the roadside and sleep there before returning to the city that held his future so inexorably in its grasp?

Why could we not talk all night about past triumphs and the glory
of a youth that would soon be lost to us forever? The engine roared
on as we mounted the hill to the summit and saw the Hutt lights
beneath us like a bed of glowing rain. I had lost him at last. My
shallow integrity had failed me, while the nub of his conviction
carried him far from my grasp to a land from which he might never
return; into the ecstatic presence of a God he had made part of
him. And on this ominous shore it seemed the mists of Hades slowly
descended, enveloping me but leaving him to ride majestically on
into a radiance that was denied my sight and a warmth that would
never touch my aching heart.

DAVID BALLANTYNE   **Other Gardens**
(*b.* 1924)

I

My husband was expecting a visitor, so I left him reading the Sunday
papers—he thought it broadening to buy them all; the *News of the
World*, he asid, was as instructive in its own way as the *Observer*—
and escaped to the common. My ground-floor tormentors were, as
I had hoped, too involved in rest-day rituals to notice my flight, and
although there was a moment in the hall when I seemed to hear Mrs.
Fenner calling to one of her daughters to see who was making for
the door, I later reasoned that she had more likely been demanding
from her bed that the kitchen radio be turned up.

I had come to value the common not so much for its own sake—
there was days, particularly in the unexpected heat of the first summer, when I hated it—but simply as *somewhere to go*. We had gone
there together, Bernard and I, in the slate-grey weeks that followed
our arrival in London, and I remember how awed we were as we
walked on a snowy day along the path that encircled the pond
in one corner of the common. The skinny trees were black where
they were not white, and all over the common there was only grey
or brown where there was not black or white. 'It's like a photograph,'
Bernard said. I said the earth was so hushed. 'Like a photograph,'

he said, and said again many times in the several weeks left of winter. Afterwards, when I began going alone to the common, I was seldom touched by its seasonal aspects, could not tell you when I noted signs of the miraculous spring I had been warned to watch for, nor which day it was when the sun I thought I had lost shone from a sky as high and as blue as any I could remember, nor even when I heard for the very first time (so it seemed) the sound of leaves falling. I became aware of these things accidentally; they were small interruptions. If it were sunny, I risked resting in the wild grass; if it were cold, I stamped my feet and swung my arms as though exercise were my only reason for being there. Whatever my preoccuptaion, I was always aware of the others who used the common. We shared that place.

Anyway, on this particular Sunday afternoon, I was elated about dodging Mrs. Fenner and her spies, and not too sorry either to be away from the room where Bernard would now feel free to enjoy the scandals that for my benefit he pretended to disdain. (How gravely he had looked up from his *Observer* to wish me a pleasant stroll!)

I was half-way across the wider part of the common—it narrowed at the pond end with the inroads of war-time allotments—before I realised that something special was in the air. I stopped. It was still too early for the people of this suburb to be out taking what they could of the pallid winter sun; they seemed to need the approach of dusk to bring them out. But surely there were more bicycles than usual? And such strangely naked-looking bicycles. They were bumping across the common from all directions. Riding them were the sharp pale youths who had looked so boyish when I first saw them in the High Street, but so disturbing when I was closer that I had wondered if they had ever been innocent.

Well, they were innocent today. And they held me for an hour while they raced their bicycles around a miniature dirt-track close to the railway line on the far side of the common. They were skid-kids, two teams of them—Greyhounds and Panthers, according to a blackboard near the starting-point. They raced four at a time two from each team, and they jabbed their iron-tipped leather speedway boots furiously on the pedals, they bucked and skidded their machines on three furious circuits of the track. But the fury was quiet, so quiet. Tyres scraped in the dust, metal occasionally clinked against metal; yet from neither the riders nor the watchers who had somehow appeared at the low stick fence enclosing the track was there a sound.

I stared at the yellow-shirted Greyhounds and the green-shirted Panthers, and presently I realised that, irrespective of team colours, they formed two classes—the skilled and assured ones who went immediately to the front and remained there, and the straining followers who opened and shut their mouths in wordless desperation as they lunged for illusory openings.

Among the skilled ones was youth wearing a black-and-white check cap. His face was expressionless, his lips did not part, and although his busy legs won him every other race—every one he competed in—he let no smile temper superiority that to me seemed contemptuous. I watched him closely. I admired him, then I was troubled by him. I tried to be interested in other riders, like the crew-cropped Panther whose silken green scarf lifted briefly in its owner's most strenuous efforts before falling as *his* hopes were doomed to fall. Always, though, I returned to that cap, that blank face.

For some time after I left them I could see those skid-kids going round and round and round. I could feel the intensity of the silence in which they laboured.

II

I had smoked my last cigarette. Even for me, this was fast smoking; I had set out with nearly a full packet.

I smiled at the thought of myself standing entranced by the stick fence, popping cigarette after cigarette into my mouth. No wonder my lips were tender, my throat parched.

Now I must visit my friends at the café, I *must* have cigarettes.

I longed for a cigarette. I wished I had saved one, only one.

The café was twenty minutes away. How could I last that long? Perhaps there was a packet in my other coat? But my other coat was back at the flat, and I did not want to return to the flat yet.

No, there was no alternative. You *will* do these silly things. Oh, you pest!

Perhaps I said this aloud. More likely, Patty Fenner needed no such excuse to stare. I wondered if she had been watching the skid-kids and had seen me; it would be something else for her to pass on to her mother, just as she was now passing on other gossip about me to a youth in drainpipe trousers. Patty was a kittenish-looking girl with a small cheeky body and a tiny white face; she had big brown eyes. I suppose she was pretty. To be honest, there was a time soon after we moved into the flat when I was able to compliment Mrs. Fenner on the good looks of her children—and no reservations. I was friendly enough with her then to be told about her jolly times during the war. During the war she had apparently moved in higher social circles than she did now; she was especially tickled by the memory of a party where a fellow-guest had been an actor named (she said) Dean Jaguar. I used to study her old face, her greying blonde hair and her sagging figure, and I used to wonder why she did not talk of the blitz, why she talked only of parties. Her interest in pleasure was so obvious that I believe I felt warm towards her.

But that was ages ago. Before the trouble.

I made the mistake now of watching Patty and her boy friend. I should not have watched them, I should have taken the other path, the one past the pond end of the common. I could have reached the street that way.

Still, my mistake scarcely excused the abuse Patty threw at me.

'Big-head!' she shouted. 'Mind your milk-bottles!'

She shared the joke with her boy friend and off they went, shoulder to shoulder in delight.

Well, at least I knew where I stood with this Patty, this girl in the black duffle coat. She came out into the open. She shouted. She could be recognised.

The others, my other enemies, were so furtive, so teasing. If I were to tell, for instance, how I found myself beside one of them at the local cinema, people would want to know *How*? *What did he say*? *Did he touch you*? and so on. They would not think it important that he wore a curious spotted ring; they would not appreciate how subtle these others were.

Patty, at any rate, was not subtle. Childishly she called me Big-head, added a reminder of the occasion her mother's night visitors kicked and smashed the bottles I had placed on the front steps; she wanted to set me thinking about the nastiness that followed my suggestion to Mrs. Fenner that her visitors might at least have picked up the pieces. I had something to grasp when it was Patty's kind of insult.

So I was not too disturbed as I made my way along the path. Patty had taken my mind off the skid-kids, if not off my need for a cigarette.

III

I knew them as Henry and Tess. Why were they my friends? Because I ate often in their little café when Bernard's job took him out of London. Because they were at once affectionate and matter-of-fact in my presence. Because they reminded me in some ways of the people of my childhood. Also, though this affected me hardly at all, Henry had had war-time associations with New Zealanders and would sometimes ask me to repeat my assurances about the happy life awaiting the immigrant in New Zealand. I knew very well he had no deep interest in New Zealand, nor in me. But he was friendly and so was Tess and they committed me to nothing.

'Cigarettes, dear?' said Tess before I had reached the counter.

'I've been watching the Greyhounds and Panthers,' I told her.

'Yes, dear?' she said interestedly.

'One of the Greyhounds was particularly fast, Tess,' I said. 'He wore a check cap. Goodness, he was purposeful.'

'It keeps them out of mischief,' Tess said.

'They were *all* so purposeful,' I said, taking a cigarette from the packet she passed me. 'But the one in the check cap was successful too. That seemed to make a difference, Tess.'

'Well, it keeps them out of mischief,' Tess said.

'The others would never be as fast as *he* was,' I said. 'But they wouldn't give up. And he knew they wouldn't give up. He knew they would always be there behind him. You know, Tess. *Striving*.'

'Yes, it keeps them out of mischief,' Tess said.

I wondered whether to have a cup of tea. I was the only customer in that shabby café and accordingly felt composed. 'Oh I *will* have one,' I said. 'One of your lovely cups of tea, Tess.'

I watched her put three cubes of sugar on the saucer.

Then Henry, who was carrying a vase of red and purple anemones, came from the kitchen and nodded to me. 'Nice enough day for you?'

'I've been on the common,' I told him.

'She's been watching the skid-kids,' Tess said.

'A nice day for the skid-kids,' Henry said. He put the flowers on a glass case of sandwiches and cakes.

'I thought they were so...so purposeful,' I told Henry. I drank some tea.

'It keeps them out of mischief,' Tess said.

'Perhaps so,' said Henry, his gaze on my cigarette fingers. He had once suggested that a holder would keep my fingers from staining. I lowered my hand.

A young couple entered the café; I must hurry.

I waited until I fancied Henry and Tess would not notice, then I stepped out into the High Street. Dusk was near enough now and there were more strollers. Noisy youths, men in tweed caps and belted gabardines, gaunt women and self-contented women, grubby barefoot kids and rosier kids with socks to their knees, dark-stock-inged girls with amazed eyes and high hair.

I was well aware that if I could be pursued once I could be pur-

sued any number of times. I had been pursued one day by two men
in black coats, so I had to be always watchful, even on a Sunday
afternoon in the High Street.

My trouble began...I suppose it began when I refused to lend
Mrs. Fenner the sugar she had sent Patty up for. I refused because
I was tired of lending her sugar, feeling that if she could entertain
as she did most nights she could afford to buy sugar. I was, I thought,
reasonable about it; I am always reasonable. I gently warned Patty
and her sisters that they must stop pestering me. I was working at the
time, and it seemed I was no sooner home of a night than the begging
knock sounded on the door. It was this, in fact, that helped to send
me to the café when Bernard was out of town.

I am not saying, though, that it was the only cause of the trouble.
An involved situation arose, for instance, because another tenant,
a Miss Lily, used to come down from the attic to chat with me over
a cup of tea. Mrs. Fenner did not like Miss Lily and warned me in
the early days of the spinster's vicious tongue, as she put it. Anyway,
it was from Miss Lily I learned of Mrs. Fenner's adventures. I don't
believe I ever got them all in sequence, but they had much to do
with a soldier-husband returning from the wars, booting out the
fellow who had moved in while he was away, then moving out himself. Later there were other men. Oh, it was so sordid and my interest was strictly polite. Indeed, I doubt if Miss Lily would have kept
it up if Bernard, who sometimes joined our little tea parties, had
not encouraged her. I don't know how often he murmured 'Freudian'
as he drew on his pipe and nodded for her to continue. And although
'Freudian' is his favourite irrelevancy whenever people's relation-
ships are being discussed, his use of it has never depressed me as
much as it did during Miss Lily's visits. Naively, I was pleased when
she found herself a room in East Finchley; there would be no more
tea parties, no more dirty looks from Mrs. Fenner, I would have
peace.

I was not to know that Mrs. Fenner, the star tenant, had some
sort of influence over the landlord, a dentist who came across from
Hampstead once a month to collect the rent and the meter coins.
How otherwise could she have persuaded him to let the attic to the
Liverpool newly-weds? At first they were sociable, so sociable that
the girl once told me there was something about her husband, who
was short and wore rimless glasses and smirked, that frightened
her. She did not elaborate, and when the bumping began on the
floor above I supposed it was connected with whatever was frightening the wife. This bumping, which was like furniture being moved
or a broom continually whacking bare boards, went on for hours

at a time. I said nothing, I did not complain. Yet soon the girl
would not look at me if she saw me on the stairs or near the bathroom we shared. So that I became certain Mrs. Fenner had been
speaking to her about me. The old girl was after me, sure enough.

Well, that was how the trouble began. But this Sunday afternoon,
surprisingly, I was not pursued. I say surprisingly because only
the other night I had given Mrs. Fenner a new grievance. I had
overheard a front-steps conversation between Patty and a girl named
Elsie, a frequent visitor to the Fenners. It was late and I was sitting
smoking a cigarette at the streetside window of our flat; the voices,
these voices, meant nothings to me, only that Elsie had evidently
been to the local and was quarrelsome. My window was open.
I could not *help* hearing what was said. Elsie said something about
Patty's mother 'knocking off' some silverware, a remark which instantly had Patty whispering urgently about the need to talk quietly
—an extraordinary need for any Fenner to seem aware of, I must say.
'Knocking off' I took to mean thieving, but I did not gasp at the
revelation or, I thought, react in any other way. It may be that I
moved in my chair; at any rate, Patty was suddenly looking up at
the window and yelling 'Old cow! Mind your own business!' I
imagine she lost no time in telling her mother about Elsie's in-
discretion and my nosiness. For my part, I left the bedroom and
went into the living-room, and I looked at Bernard who was absorbed, as he had been for nearly a fortnight, in a book about the
French Foreign Legion. But I did not interrupt him. Why should I?
'Your imagination in form, eh?' he would have said.

IV

My husband's visitor this Sunday was a young man in well-cut
grey trousers, navy blazer, white shirt, black-and-yellow tie and
brown suéde shoes. I gave him a happy smile. It was a happy
smile because I had been undetected by the Fenners on my way up
the stairs.

'Ah, the wanderer returns!' said Bernard.

He was happy, too. He was happy because he had a visitor,
somebody with whom he could discuss his career as a window-
frame salesman—happy, to be fair, because he liked the company of
enterprising people.

The young man's name was Don. The usual things were said—
yes, I loved London; yes, it was stimulating to be in a city where
there was so much to do, so much to see.

'She's a dinkum Kiwi, our Joan,' smiled Bernard, waving his

pipe. 'Don't let her fool you, boy. She'd go back like a shot on the first boat if she could.'

Don looked astonished. 'You *would*?'

How did it go? Like this: 'When I remember the years I wasted back there, when I think how bored I'd be at this moment...' I shook my head.

Don was relieved. 'I see what you mean,' he said.

'Besides, I have Bernard to think of,' I said. 'Bernard has so many chances over here.'

Bernard, of course, put in: 'The perfect wife, Don.'

And that, I reckoned, was as good a cue as I was likely to get. 'Mind if I leave you two alone for a few minutes?' I asked. 'I *must* take off my shoes.'

'Go right ahead, honey,' said Bernard. 'Don and I can cope. Eh, Don?'

I went to the bedroom and I looked from the window. Dusk darkened the sycamore in the garden across the street.

I lit a cigarette and walked from the brown-green-orange rug near the window to the dark-green rug near the door, then back again, and I continued walking from one rug to the other. I knew that while Bernard had his own entertainment primarily in mind when he invited people around, he also hoped they would help to divert me. I should meet nice people, he said. And his visitors were certainly nice. Nice in the way you expect New Zealanders to be in London. Unfortunately, I was fed up with ambitious young men and excited travellers. I recalled the couple, back from a car tour, who were full of an adventure that had occurred in Berlin: the husband had joined a group of tourists staring at a Russian colonel and presently had shouted, 'Up you, Old Horse!' He had spoken these cheeky words to a Russian and, my God, he had escaped! I recalled the man who had driven to one of the Duke of Edinburgh's polo meetings and had later, during a fuss about parked cars, found himself next to the car in which the Duke sat, and, my God, if the Duke hadn't winked at him! All of which pleased Bernard very much. Wasn't it exhilarating to think of New Zealanders touring Europe, New Zealanders being winked at by Royalty! As for what the visitors made of Bernard: I expect they were satisfied, he generally listened attentively (with clever interjections) before starting his own contribution. Only once had he been disconcerted. Why he should bring a Canadian psychologist to the flat puzzled me then and does now, it really does. Why he should flounder into Couéism when his none-too-searching questions had already disclosed that the psychologist, besides disapproving of generalisations about

complexes, was sophisticated enough to take an irreverent view of
Freud and, I'm bound to say, of Jung and Adler as well—why
Bernard should mention Coue did not puzzle me then and does
not now. I felt sorry for him and when the edgy psychologist had
gone I soothed him and flattered him until he was back to feeling
that every day in every way he was getting better and better...

I lit another cigarette and told myself I should be out there preparing a meal; even now Bernard would be pelting his guest with
cheerful references to the inner man, light relief after his grave
account of how he intended entering politics when he eventually
returned to New Zealand. Oh, perhaps another quarter-hour, I
decided.

I stopped by the window. There was nobody beneath the sycamore. Nor could I hear the Fenners. But of course they always
saved their best efforts until they knew I was alone; they did not
bother Bernard at all—or, if they did, not so much so that he was
tempted to examine his belief that this was an excellent flat; so cheap,
so handy to the buses, so handy to the High Street, so handy to
the common...far enough out to give one a feeling of earth rather
than stone close by.

I drew the curtains, crossed to the light switch, waited a moment
after switching on the light, then forced myself to go to the dress-
ing-table mirror.

V

'The important thing.' Bernard told us over the remains of the
meal, 'is to *make* them accept you. What's a compromise here and
there? If they like to think I'm an Australian, let them—if it will
help me make a sale. If they're happy about spotting my accent they're
more likely to save me a lot of time-wasting wheedling.' He raised
his eyebrows.

'Not a dinkum Kiwi attitude,' Don joked.

'How's that?' Bernard asked seriously. 'Look at it this way,
Don—'

'I was kidding,' Don said.

'Don't you agree it's the tendency for the New Zealander to be
sat upon?' asked Bernard. 'You get a lot of New Zealanders bringing over easy-going New Zealand ideas. And they don't suit the
place. Correct?'

'Is it a bad thing to be easy-going?' asked Don.

'Now that's the question!' cried Bernard. 'You see, Don, my
theory is that people over here reckon New Zealanders are only

colonials after all—they can be pushed about. The Aussie, on the other hand, has always made it bloody clear he *won't* be pushed about. That's the Aussie way. The Kiwi way is to say "She's jake" and take what comes. The Kiwi doesn't hit back. The Aussie hits back. Why else do the English, with *their* dreadful accents, think the Aussie accent is so dreadful? It's because the Aussies get under their skins. The Aussies are tough. You *must* be tough over here.'

'I see what you mean,' Don said. 'You mean that's why you don't mind being mistaken for an Australian?'

'It's a compliment,' Bernard laughed. 'But, boy, do they hate me behind my back!' He gazed at Don. 'I didn't get this far by worrying about *that* sort of thing, though. Never did care what people said about me. I was a depression kid, you know. My people didn't have much money, so I left school before I wanted to. But that didn't stop me from getting an education, Don. What if I did have to pick it all up myself? It's the kind of education that sticks, in my opinion.' He pointed his pipe at me. 'Take Joan,' he said. 'She came from a humble country environment—small-town, like myself—but her people had just that little extra in the way of cash, they could afford to send her to High School and University. Now I don't want to boast, Don, but I think if you were to ask Joan whether she thought my course in self education had been a success—I reckon she'd back me up on that. Eh, Joan?'

It was difficult to be still. I wanted to be away from them. 'Bernard is an enthusiastic reader,' I told Don.

Don noted this pensively.

'I read and I *think* about what I'm reading,' Bernard said. 'A lot of readers skim, you know, Don. I'm not a skimmer. Once I take on an Upton Sinclair, for instance, there's no holding me until I've got that book whacked. Same with anything else I tackle. Even music. Nearest we had to music in *my* childhood home was *Hallelujah I'm a Bum*. These days I can listen to Chopin, say, or Puccini for hours—*and* enjoy them. I'm a great man for opera—'

I happened to be sitting at this moment on the ugly old sofa under the living-room's high windows. Stripped cottage-weave curtains fell behind the sofa and one of them was not quite in place and I found myself looking through the crack and, since it was now night and I could see nothing, thinking of the view as it had been on a certain evening in late summer. It was one of the evenings when Bernard was away peddling window-frames; otherwise there should have been nothing special about it. But I remembered, as though it were only yesterday, how I sat in the long dusk and watched from this window. Past the overgrown arbour in the garden of our place—the garden we were not permitted to use because it went with the ground-floor flats, including Mrs. Fenner's—was the tall spidery tree that stayed bare longer than any other tree in the neighbourhood. Smoke drifted among the trees in the gardens that stretched away from me towards the higher ground where the red buses went by. There were apples and pears in these gardens, there were lawns and flower-beds, there were television aerials on many of the chimney-pots silhouetted above the red and grey-brick homes. Indications of cosiness. Had it been envy I felt that night? I could not remember. I remembered wishing I had written to my sisters back home, even to my acquaintances back there. But I had nothing to tell my sisters, they who had frowned about Bernard ('Is he *really* your type, Sis?') and about England ('Isn't it *terribly* distant, Sis?') Nor did I wish my one-time acquaintances to talk of me; let those who knew us be content with Bernard's breezy bulletins. So it was only a passing weakness that night; the letters remained unwritten. How long, I now asked myself, must exile last? One of Bernard's visitors, a journalist named Plimpton, had said it was two years before he 'got the feel of the place' and another two years before he decided that London was 'the expatriate's only possible home'. But how long for me? Three years? Four? Five?

'I reckon about five years, Don,' said Bernard airily. 'Time enough for a fast worker, eh? Mind you, if I'm an executive at the end of five years, I'm not likely to turn it in. I'm working on another angle too—but keep this under your hat. I might be able to work it so they send me to New Zealand. They're thinking of branching out with factories in the colonies—the Commonwealth. And if they want somebody for New Zealand...eh?'

'I see you have it all planned,' smiled Don.

'I'm right on top of things, Don,' said Bernard. 'That's the only way to be, take it from me. Joan will tell you. Joan, you'd agree with that, wouldn't you? I've always been on top of things—especially since we came to England.'

I looked at Don. I said: 'Before then, too.'

'Especially since we came to England,' said Bernard. 'But that's enough of that, Don my lad. A man needs a drink after that lot. I'll take you down to my local. Always introduce the boys to my local.'

Always? Apart from a certain Canadian psychologist, I thought. Don looked at me.

'That's all right, mate,' said Bernard. 'Joan doesn't want us cluttering up the place. Prefers to be on her own. She doesn't like the noise. Isn't that right, honey? I tell you, Don, she left her job—

good job as a typist at the Temple—she left there because it was too noisy. The Temple!' He laughed.

I could see that Don was not convinced. So I said with a smile: 'I wanted a holiday.' That sounded lame, so I added: 'It was so foggy.' Then, briskly: 'I must look for another job.'

'Don't worry, honey,' said Bernard. 'You have a good rest. We'll never be short of cash while I'm in gear. Ready, Don? Want you to sample an ale I regard rather highly. I won't be long, Joan.' He pecked my cheek, said: 'Not too long, anyway.'

'Have a good time,' I told them. 'Mind the traffic.'

'She's kidding,' I heard Bernard telling Don as they went out, 'No traffic in this neck of the wood.'

VI

Perhaps he was right, I thought as I did the dishes. Perhaps I *had* left the Temple job because of the noise. Voices, after all, were noise. Ordinary voices. Somebody speaks to somebody else; the voice is meant to be heard by a third person—by me, for instance. An employer speaks of what *he* believes to be a fact, and in his voice is much more than the wish to correct; there is smugness, contempt, irritation, anger. Seldom compassion. Oh, and don't forget the voices from faces that twist in pity when *you* speak.

I clattered the dishes. 'Dear Bernard,' I said, 'there is noise—and noise.'

Mrs. Fenner obviously believed the same. For her radio suddenly surged into a blast of 'Stars Shine in Your Eyes', and I wondered why the radio did not fall apart, I wondered how it was possible for a radio to be so loud and not fall apart.

I put the dishes on the gas-stove rack and drew the curtain around the corner that served as a kitchenette. Bernard would expect a white shirt for the morning; shiny collar, of course. His face would drop if the shirt were not pressed and gleaming when he returned from the local. But what could I do against that blasting below? It would persist too; Bernard's departure had been noted.

I turned on our own radio and selected one of those B.B.C. 'portraits' in which a succession of players, pretending to be contemporaries of the victim (in this case, Dr. Johnson), recite breathlessly in voices that are now stern, now chatty, now coy, and so on. I found it frightening and, thankful Bernard was missing it ('The Great Cham once said...'), turned off the radio and went to the bedroom.

Without switching on the bedroom light, I lit a cigarette and walked from rug to rug until the cigarette burned down. Then I lit another cigarette and sat on the edge of the bed.

I heard whistling. What sound, if any, did a black-bird make at night? Was this mimicry?

I did not go to the window.

Presently the whistling stopped, and I was left wondering: *Why have Henry and Tess changed?*

I recalled the curiosity with which Henry in particular had eyed me in the café today. His manner, the way he carried the anemones. Like a man who had been told things and was not yet certain how to handle me. Essentially good-natured, he had been reluctant to offend —or to rouse? And Tess, Tess could have been talking of an imbecile when she told Henry how I had been watching the skid-kids. Repeating her comment about keeping the skid-kids out of mischief! There was more to *that* than I had realised at the times. How obvious! She might as well have added 'Get the point?'

Still, I tried not to be bitter. I must be reasonable. Really they were a good and simple pair; it was embarrassing for them to have me in their cafe. Very well, I would spare them embarrassment; I would stop going to the cafe.

By the time I returned to the living-room to iron Bernard's shirt it was as though losing one's friends were something that happened every day.

VII

Bernard was, as usual after his pub visits, very solicitous. His solicitude was intended, I knew, to cover up ale-prompted elation.

He thanked me for ironing the shirt.

I asked him if he had enjoyed himself.

'Got trapped into darts,' he said. 'That Don fellow, he's an ass with darts. In other ways too, eh?'

'He seems earnest,' I said.

'I think he's finding the going a bit tough over here,' Bernard said, shaking his head. 'Catching on that London can be heartbreaking.' He thought this over, then remembered the next questions. 'What sort of day did you have, honey? Where did you go this afternoon? How was the walk?'

I shrugged. 'Same old walk. Same people. Same dogs.' He was staring. 'Yes,?' I asked.

'Your lipstick,' he said. 'Your lipstick's lopsided, honey. Doesn't cover your lips properly.'

'Have you only just noticed?' I asked. 'Your friend Don noticed.'

I laughed. 'It fascinated him.'

Bernard frowned. 'You put it like that on purpose?'

'I *intended* adjusting it,' I said. 'I forgot.'

'Looks odd,' he said. Then he was suspicious. 'Have they been bothering you again?'

'Who?' I asked, wide-eyed.

'Down below,' he said.

'Mother Fenner tortured her radio as soon as you went,' I said.

'And Patty was hostile earlier on—when I was watching the skid-kids.' I spoke calmly.

'Skid-kids?' he asked.

'Greyhounds and Panthers,' I said. 'On the common.'

'You mean you watched those skid-kids all afternoon?'

'I couldn't stop looking,' I told him.

'What about the noise?' he asked.

'There was no noise,' I said.

'Honey, I heard the noise from here,' Bernard said. 'I could hear the crowd. I mentioned it to Don. I said to him there must be something doing on the common.'

'It was the silence that surprised me,' I said. 'Those boys were so quiet—' I stopped.

'What's the matter?'

'Something *is*,' he said.

'No, nothing,' I said.

I was thinking of myself in a black-and-white check cap, pedalling round and round and round—and of Bernard trying very hard to catch me.

I wished I could weep.

DAVID BALLANTYNE
(*b.* 1924)

A Leopard Yarn

I believe in one God the Father Almighty Maker of heaven and earth and of all things visible and invisible light of light begotten not made and was flesh Crucifixus etiam pro nobis . . .

I sat staring at my grandfather. My grandfather was big and stout and rosy-skinned, and he had a white, sharp-pointed moustache. He had worked on ships, travelled round the world, worked in snooty hotels and timber camps and, it seemed to me, just about everywhere. My mother used to tell how he brought back from the islands in the Pacific great clusters of bananas and heaps of pineapples and oranges. That was in his younger days. Every night now he ate spud and sausages, smacking his lips, going chup-chup-chup, winking at me. Every night, too, he told yarns.

This night I was sitting across the table from him, my eyes open wide. The radio on the sideboard was playing brass-band music, I remember.

From the sink, my grandmother called: 'For goodness' sake hurry up with that meal! If you got home at the right time, if you didn't go gallivanting round the pubs, you wouldn't keep us so late.'

And, as Grandad's fork went up with the last mouthful, his plate was whisked from the table.

He winked at me. 'Doesn't give a man a chance, does she, Roy?'

I looked at him and I thought how he always reckoned I was the best in the family because I stood guard for him outside the pub on Saturday afternoons, watching for Grandma, and when we were home I wouldn't tell where Grandad had been all afternoon. Sometimes, though, I would not get the warning through in time and Grandma would burst into the pub at full steam, grab Grandad and push him out into the alley, and we'd all hurry home.

'What was school like today, Roy?' Grandma shouted above the noise of the radio.

'Not bad, thanks,' I told her.

'Did you know your prayers?'

'Every one.'

'Truly, Roy?'

'Every one,' I said.

'Well, what's the first you say?'

'Oh, you know,' I said.

'Roy, what's the first prayer you say?'

'I believe in one God the Father Almighty Maker of heaven and earth and of all things visible and invisible—'.

'The Creed!' shouted Grandma, delighted.

'You're a clever boy,' Grandad told me.

'He's got more brains than you, anyway,' Grandma said.

'You're right there,' Grandad said.

'I *haven't* got more brains than Grandad,' I told Grandma. 'He's got more—'

'Roy, don't contradict,' she said.

It was about half past seven the radio announced that a leopard had escaped from the zoo and everybody had better keep a pretty close lookout if they didn't want to run into danger.

I sat tight on my chair. Thinking of a leopard loose in the world scared me a bit, and I tried to forget about it because I didn't want anybody to guess how scared I was.

'You know, Roy, I'd hate to meet a leopard,' Grandad said. 'Unexpectedly, like.'

'You'd run a mile,' Grandma said.

'I wouldn't say that,' Grandad said. 'I don't believe I'd run.'

'You'd run, all right,' Grandma said.

'What *would* you do, Grandad?' I asked.

'I'd kill the beast, son.'

Grandma was placing the tea dishes in the sideboard. 'Just listen to him,' she said.

'I wouldn't be frightened,' Grandad said. He gazed at me. Then he said: 'Look, Roy, I'll go out after the beast. I'll go right this moment. Lend me your airgun and I'll shoot that leopard.'

Maybe he really would shoot the leopard, I thought. I had got the airgun for a birthday present, but my mother would not let me use it because she said such things were dangerous. I was sure she would let Grandad use it, though. I ran into the front bedroom where she was writing a letter to my father, who was away working in the country, and I got the airgun from the wardrobe and told her Grandad wanted it so that he could shoot a leopard. She followed me back to the kitchen.

I gave Grandad the airgun.

'Dad, your'e not going out at this time of night, are you?' my mother said.

'Too right I am,' Grandad said. He was on his way to the door.

'You can't be!'

'I'm going out to shoot that damned leopard that's escaped from the zoo,' he said. 'It was on the radio.'

'Dad, come back!' my mother said as he reached the door.

Grandma was arranging ornaments on the mantelpiece .'Let him go if he wants to,' she said.

Grandad went out, the airgun pointing downwards.

I sat in a chair by the stove. I stared through the grating at the ashes starred by red embers. I wished my mother had not been there so that I could have gone with Grandad. Everything was very quiet.

All things visible and invisible lights of light begotten not made . . .

How many leopards had he killed by now?

But maybe the leopard would kill him. Maybe poor Grandad
would never again eat spud and sausages, and there would be no
more Saturday afternoons outside the pub, no more big oranges
and Lucky Packets as rewards.

I could imagine man-eating leopards tearing my grandfather to
bits.

'Hope nothing's happened to him . . . eh, Grandma?'

'You go to bed, Roy,' Grandma said.

'It's only eight o'clock,' I said.

'Well, stop talking about your grandfather,' she said. 'You're
disturbing my sewing.'

'Can I go outside?'

'What on earth for?'

'Nothing.'

'What?'

'A little look. That's all, Grandma.'

'Well don't be too long.'

Outside in the still summer night there were slithering insect
sounds, and crickets sang in the paddocks. Then a slight breeze
rustled the passionfruit vines. Corners held scents and shadows,
over everything was a purple sky. But there was no sign anywhere
of my grandfather.

I went back inside.

'Well?' asked my mother.

'Nothing,' I said.

'He'll be all right,' Grandma said.

She and my mother went outside at half past eight, and I followed
them.

There was still no sign of Grandad. He was lost.

'I'll look up the road,' I said.

'Only to the corner then,' my mother said.

'Yes,' I said.

I ran very quickly for nearly a mile. When I reached the Royal,
I felt my way down the dark alley and knocked on a door at the
end. About five minutes after I knocked, the door opened and I
blinked into light; I could see nothing for a smudgy blue cloud and
I stared hard, trying to see through it.

'Have you seen my grandfather?' I asked the woman in the blue
kimono.

'Have I seen your *what*?'

A Leopard Yard   111

'My grandfather.'
Her face was very white, her lips very red. 'What does your grandfather look like, sonny?'

I believe in one God O Grandad a big man a stout man rosy skin snowy-
white moustache sharp-pointed light of light begotten not made Cru-
cifixus . . .

'And does he own a white-handled pocket-knife, sonny? Does he?'
She was kidding. I laughed.
She laughed, too.
'And what might your grandfather's name be?' Her scent, or
something, made me gasp.
'His name is Foley,' I said.
'An Irish name,' she said. 'I like Irish names. And what's *your*
name?'
'Roy,' I said. 'Roy McKay. My father's a carpenter. My father's
built some of the biggest freezing-works in New Zealand.'
'I'm very impressed, Roy,' she said.
'Do you know where my grandfather is?' I asked.
'I won't be a minute, Roy,' she said. 'I think I can help. Hooray
for the Irish! And the Scots, of cousre.'
I had felt the change inside me from the first moment the cloud
floated round me. Now the kimono lifted as she went down the
passage, and I shuffled my feet while I waited. Then Grandad was
there, smelling of booze, and I supported him down the alley to the
street, and I remembered the leopard and asked Grandad what had
happened to the airgun, and I couldn't understand his mumbling,
and when I eased my grip he flopped to the gutter, just about asleep,
just about.
'Hell, Roy, I'm tired, tired.'
'Where's the airgun, Grandad? What have you done with the airgun?'
'You get it, Roy. I'm very tired.'
So I went back along the alley, and once more she opened the
door for me.
'Have you seen my airgun?' I asked, deep in scent.
'What would I be doing with your airgun, love?'
'Grandad was going to shoot a leopard, he borrowed my airgun,
now he hasn't got it.'
'What did you say he was going to shoot, Roy?'
'A leopard.'
'Oh,' she said. 'Well, please come in, Roy.'

I followed her along the passage, and at the door to the room I took in everything: single bed against the left wall, a dresser, a small gasburner, table at the right side, window with pink curtains at the end, blue and yellow rug on the floor, two empty beer bottles on the table, some glasses, the bed mussed-up, the bed very small, the bed. No gun, though. She had hidden the gun.

'Come in, love,' she said. 'How old are you, love?'

'Ten,' I said.

'Double figures,' she smiled.

'Yes,' I said. I couldn't see the gun.

'You're a big boy for your age,' she said.

I thought of my skinny long legs and blushed.

'I bet you're smart at school,' she said.

'I'm not bad,' I said. In the fields near Saint Benedict's Convent I used to lie morning after morning, the bell ringing away the periods, the bell-tower sharp against the sky.

'Say something you've learned,' she said.

'A prayer?'

'Anything. A prayer would do.'

She lay on the bed. The kimono was open at the top, her skin was clear and pinky-white.

'This prayer is what we say every day,' I said.

'I'm listening, love,' she said.

Credo in unum deum Patrem omnipotentem factorem caeli et terrae visibilium et invisibilium. And in one Lord Jesus Christ the only be-gotten Son of God light of light true God of true God . . .

'We say it every morning,' I said.

'Good for you,' she said. 'Tell me about your grandfather, Roy.'

It was simple talking to her then. I told her how Grandad had worked on ships, how he used to bring fruit home from the islands in his younger days, how he loved eating spud and sausages, chup-chup-chup, and how he liked telling stories.

She lay curled up on the bed, like the women in pictures, red lips, white face, sometimes in the middle of a cloud.

Suddenly I had to go. 'I have to go now,' I told her.

She stood up hurriedly. She stood right in front of me, put her cupped hands over my cheeks, looked into my eyes. I did not want to see her breasts as she seemed to press them against me, but I could not look up once I had looked down. She had to push my head back, and I saw that she was smiling. I felt the softness of her skin through the kimono, and there was the warm and scenty smell of her body, and there were her hands stroking my face.

She embraced me.

I did not know what to do.

She let me go.

'Would you like some lemonade?' she asked.

'No thanks,' I said.

'Try some,' she said.

'No,' I said.

'I bet you're thirsty,' she said.

'No, I'm not.'

'I bet you are.'

She crossed to the dresser and when she had poured the lemonade into a glass, the drink fizzling, I did feel like it and I drank it all. Then she got me some cookies and I ate these, too. I liked her and I did not want to leave this room. She was nice.

Remembering the airgun, though, I began squinting round the room.

'What's up, love?' she asked.

'I want my gun,' I told her.

'Persistent young devil, aren't you?' she said.

She looked under the bed, drawing up her kimono and staying bent over for several seconds. When she stood up she had the gun in her hand. She gave it to me.

'I thought Grandad lost it,' I said.

'Well, you've got it now.'

'Thank you very much.' I did not move.

You'd better go now,' she said. 'Your mother would be angry if she knew you were here.'

'I like being here,' I said.

'Go home, Roy,' she said.

I went to the door, wanting to leave, yet not wanting to.

'Goodbye,' she said.

I said goodbye back and I never saw her agian. Not in that room, her breasts against me, her warm woman smell, her hands upon my cheeks.

I found Grandad in the gutter.

'I've got the gun, Grandad. What about the leopard? You going to shoot the leopard?'

The street lamp shone shades of yellow and green on my grandfather. He must get to his feet, down the main road to home and bed. First support from the lamp-post, then on feet, walking, staggering.

He said suddenly: 'Dont' tell them.'

'You know I won't tell,' I said.

Crucifixus etiam pro nobis Grandad . . .

I knew there were no pellets in the gun, and I was glad it was
unloaded because I had the idea it would be heavier if it were loaded.
Grandad, leaning on me, was enough of a weight.
A dog tore past us, barking at another dog. Both dogs crashed
through a hedge into the paddock by the road. Then silence.
My grandfather stopped. He stood as though waiting for some-
thing to happen.
'What's the matter, Grandad?'
'I heard it, Roy.'
'Dogs, Grandad.'
'It's the leopard, Roy.'
'No, Grandad—'
'Give me that gun! I want to shoot the leopard.'
I handed over the gun and let him go. He crawled through the
hole in the hedge, disappeared.
I looked up and down the street. Then I got on my hands and
knees and followed my grandfather.
While I crawled, I remembered everything that had happened in
the past hour. I tried to put that room from my mind. I tried to
concentrate on the lemonade and the cookies. But it was no use;
I kept remembering the kimono, the voice, the hands upon my
cheeks.
I crawled on, and I knew where I was. I was near Saint Benedict's
Convent, I had hidden in this grass.
Grandad sprang into the air. To his left was the outline of the
convent bell-tower.
'Grandad!' I called.
He had the gun to his shoulder. He took aim, pulled the trigger.
The click was loud.
'I got it!' he shouted. 'I got the leopard! I got it, I got it!'
I knew he wasn't really drunk. He was just trying to make me
forget the room.

JANET FRAME   **The Reservoir**
(*b.* 1924)

It was said to be four or five miles along the gully, past orchards
and farms, paddocks filled with cattle, sheep, wheat, gorse, and the
squatters of the land who were the rabbits eating like modern sculpture into the hills, though how could we know anything of modern
sculpture, we knew nothing but the Warrior in the main street with
his wreaths of poppies on Anzac Day, the gnomes weeping in the
Gardens because the seagulls perched on their green caps and showed no respect, and how important it was for birds, animals and
people, especially children, to show respect!

And that is why for so long we obeyed the command of the
grownups and never walked as far as the forbidden Reservoir, but
were content to return 'tired but happy' (as we wrote in our school
compositions), answering the question. Where did you walk today?
with a suspicion of blackmail, 'Oh, nearly, nearly to the Reservoir!'

The Reservoir was the end of the world; beyond it, you fell;
beyond it were paddocks of thorns, strange cattle, strange farms,
legendary people whom we would never know or recognize even
if they walked among us on a Friday night downtown when we
went to follow the boys and listen to the Salvation Army Band
and buy a milk shake in the milk bar and then return home to find
that everything was all right and safe, that our mother had not
run away and caught the night train to the North Island, that our
father had not shot himself with worrying over the bills, but had
in fact been downtown himself and had bought the usual Friday
night treat, a bag of licorice allsorts and a bag of chocolate roughs,
from Woolworth's.

The Reservoir haunted our lives. We never knew one until we
came to this town; we had used pump water. But here, in our new
house, the water ran from the taps as soon as we turned them on,
and if we were careless and left them on, our father would shout, as
if the affair were his personal concern, 'Do you want the Reservoir
to run dry?'

That frightened us. What should we do if the Reservoir ran dry?
Would we die of thirst like Burke and Wills in the desert?

'The Reservoir,' our mother said, 'gives pure water, water safe to drink without boiling it.'

The water was in a different class, then, from the creek which flowed through the gully; yet the creek had its source in the Reservoir. Why had it not received the pampering attention of officialdom which strained weed and earth, cockabullies and trout and eels, from our tap water? Surely the Reservoir was not entirely pure?

'Oh no,' they said, when we inquired. We learned that the water from the Reservoir had been 'treated'. We supposed this to mean that during the night men in light-blue uniforms with sacks over their shoulders crept beyond the circle of pine trees which enclosed the Reservoir, and emptied the contents of the sacks into the water, to dissolve dead bodies and prevent the decay of teeth.

Then, at times, there would be news in the paper discussed by my mother with the neighbours over the back fence. Children had been drowned in the Reservoir.

'No child,' the neighbour would say, 'ought to be allowed near the Reservoir.'

'I tell mine to keep strictly away,' my mother would reply.

And for so long we obeyed our mother's command, on our favourite walks along the gully simply following the untreated cast-off creek which we loved and which flowed day and night in our heads in all its detail—the wild sweet peas, boiled-lolly pink, and the mint growing along the banks; the exact spot in the water where the latest dead sheep could be found, and the stink of its bloated flesh and floating wool, an allowable earthy stink which we accepted with pleasant revulsion and which did not prompt the 'inky-pinky I smell Stinkie' rhyme which referred to offensive human beings only. We knew where the water was shallow and could be paddled in, where forts could be made from the rocks; we knew the frightening deep places where the eels lurked and the weeds were tangled in gruesome shapes; we knew the jumping places, the mossy stones with their dangers, limitations, and advantages; the sparkling places where the sun trickled beside the water, upon the stones; the bogs made by roaming cattle, trapping some of them to death; their gaunt telltale bones; the little valleys with their new growth of lush grass where the creek had 'changed its course', and no longer flowed.

'The creek has changed its course,' our mother would say, in a tone which implied terror and a sense of strangeness, as if a tragedy had been enacted.

We knew the moods of the creek, its levels of low-flow, half-high-flow, high-flow which all seemed to relate to interference at its source—the Reservoir. If one morning the water turned the colour

of clay and crowds of bubbles were passengers on every suddenly
swift wave hurrying by, we would look at one another and remark
with the fatality and reverence which attends a visitation or pro-
phecy,

'The creek's going on high-flow. They must be doing something
at the Reservoir.'

By afternoon the creek would be on high-flow, turbulent, muddy,
unable to be jumped across or paddled in or fished in, concealing
beneath a swelling fluid darkness whatever evil which 'they,' the
authorities, had decided to purge so swiftly and secretly from the
Reservoir.

For so long, then, we obeyed our parents, and never walked as
far as the Reservoir. Other things concerned us, other curiosities,
fears, challenges. The school year ended. I got a prize, a large yellow
book the colour of cat's mess. Inside it were editions of newspapers,
The Worms' Weekly, supposedly written by worms, snails, spiders.
For the first part of the holidays we spent the time sitting in the
grass of our front lawn nibbling the stalks of shamrock and reading
insect newspapers and relating their items to the lives of those living
on our front lawn down among the summer-dry roots of the couch.
tinkertailor, daisy, dandelion, shamrock, clover, and ordinary
'grass'. High summer came. The blowsy old red roses shed their
petals to the regretful refrain uttered by our mother year after
year at the same time, 'I should have made potpourri, I have a
wonderful recipe for potpourri in Dr. Chase's Book.'

Our mother never made the potpourri. She merely quarrelled with
our father over how to pronounce it.

The days became unbearably long and hot. Our Christmas pre-
sents were broken or too boring to care about. Celluloid dolls had
loose arms and legs and rifts in their bright pink bodies; the invisible
ink had poured itself out in secret messages; diaries frustrating in
their smallness (two lines to a day) had been filled in for the whole
of the coming year... Days at the beach were tedious, with no
room in the bathing sheds so that we were forced to undress in the
common room downstairs with its floor patched with wet and
trailed with footmarks and sand and its tiny barred window (which
made me believe that I was living in the French Revolution).

Rumours circled the burning world. The sea was drying up,
soon you could paddle or walk to Australia. Sharks had been seen
swimming inside the breakwater; one shark attacked a little boy
and bit off his you-know-what.

We swam. We wore bathing togs all day. We gave up cowboys
and ranches; and baseball and sledding; and 'those games' where

we mimicked grown-up life, loving and divorcing each other, kissing and slapping, taking secret paramours when our husband was working out of town. Everything exhausted us. Cracks appeared in the earth; the grass was bled yellow; the ground was littered with beetle shells and snail shells; flies came in from the unofficial rubbish-dump at the back of the house; the twisting flypapers hung from the ceiling; a frantic buzzing filled the room as the flypapers became crowded. Even the cat put out her tiny tongue, panting in the heat.

We realized, and were glad, that school would soon reopen. What was school like? It seemed so long ago, it seemed as if we had never been to school, surely we had forgotten everything we had learned, how frightening, thrilling and strange it would all seem! Where would we go on the first day, who would teach us, what were the names of the new books?

Who would sit beside us, who would be our best friend?

The earth crackled in early-autumn haze and still the February sun dried the world; even at night the rusty sheet of roofing-iron outside by the cellar stayed warm, but with rows of sweat-marks on it; the days were still long, with night face to face with morning and almost nothing in-between but a snatch of turning sleep with the blankets on the floor and the windows wide open to moths with their bulging lamplit eyes moving through the dark and their grandfather bodies knocking, knocking upon the walls.

Day after day the sun still waited to pounce. We were tired, our skin itched, our sunburn had peeled and peeled again, the skin on our feet was hard, there was dust in our hair, our bodies clung with the salt of sea-bathing and sweat, the towels were harsh with salt.

School soon, we said again, and were glad; for lessons gave shade to rooms and corridors; cloak-rooms were cold and sunless. Then, swiftly, suddenly, disease came to the town. Infantile Paralysis. Black headlines in the paper, listing the number of cases, the number of deaths. Children everywhere, out in the country, up north, down south, two streets away.

The schools did not reopen. Our lessons came by post, in smudged print on rough white paper; they seemed makeshift and false, they inspired distrust, they could not compete with the lure of the sun still shining, swelling, the world would go up in cinders, the days were too long, there was nothing to do, there was nothing to do; the lessons were dull; in the front room with the navy-blue blind half down the window and the tiny splits of light showing through, and the lesson papers sometimes covered with unexplained blots of ink as if the machine which had printed them had broken down or rebelled, the lessons were even more dull.

Ancient Egypt and the flooding of the Nile!

The Nile, when we possessed a creek of our own with individual flooding!

'Well let's go along the gully, along by the creek', we would say, tired with all these.

Then one day when our restlessness was at its height, when the flies buzzed like bees in the flypapers, and the warped wood of the house cracked its knuckles, out of boredom, the need for something to do in the heat, we found once again the only solution to our unrest.

Someone said, 'What's the creek on?'

'Half-high flow.'

'Good.'

So we set out, in our bathing suits, and carrying switches of willow.

'Keep your sun hats on!' our mother called.

All right. We knew. Sunstroke when the sun clipped you over the back of the head, striking you flat on the ground. Sunstroke. Lightning. Even tidal waves were threatening us on this southern coast. The world was full of alarm.

'And don't go as far as the Reservoir!'

We dismissed the warning. There was enough to occupy us along the gully without our visiting the Reservoir. First, the couples. We liked to find a courting couple and follow them and when, as we knew they must do because they were tired or for other reasons, they found a place in the grass and lay down together, we liked to make jokes about them, amongst ourselves. 'Just wait for him to kiss her,' we would say. 'Watch. There. A beaut. Smack.'

Often we giggled and lingered even after the couple had observed us. We were waiting for them to do it. Every man and woman did it, we knew that for a fact. We speculated about technical details. Would he wear a frenchie? If he didn't wear a frenchie then she would start having a baby and be forced to get rid of it by drinking gin. Frenchies, by the way, were for sale in Woolworth's. Some said they were fingerstalls, but we knew they were frenchies and sometimes we would go downtown and into Woolworth's just to look at the frenchies for sale. We hung around the counter, sniggering. Sometimes we nearly died laughing, it was so funny.

After we tired of spying on the couples we should shout after them as we went our way.

> Pound, shillings and pence,
> a man fell over the fence,
> he fell on a lady,

and squashed out a baby,
pound, shillings and pence!

Sometimes a slight fear struck us—what if a man fell on us like
that and squashed out a chain of babies?

Our other pastime along the gully was robbing the orchards,
but this summer day the apples were small green hard and hidden
by leaves. There were no couples either. We had the gully to ourselves. We followed the creek, whacking our sticks, gossiping and
singing, but we stopped, immediately silent, when someone—
sister or brother—said, 'Let's go to the Reservoir!'

A feeling of dread seized us. We knew, as surely as we knew our
names and our address Thirty-three Stour Street Ohau Otago
South Island New Zealand Southern Hemisphere The World,
that we would some day visit the Reservoir, but the time seemed
almost as far away as leaving school, getting a job, marrying.

And then there was the agony of deciding the right time—how
did one decide these things?

'We've been told not to, you know,' one of us said timidly.

That was me. Eating bread and syrup for tea had made my hair
red, my skin too, so that I blushed easily, and the grownups guessed
if I told a lie.

'It's a long way,' said my little sister.

'Coward!'

But it *was* a long way, and perhaps it would take all day and night,
perhaps we would have to sleep there among the pine trees with the
owls hooting and the old needle-filled warrens which now reached
to the centre of the earth where pools of molten lead bubbled, waiting to seize us if we tripped, and then there was the crying sound
made by the trees, a sound of speech at its loneliest level where the
meaning is felt but never explained, and it goes on and on in a
kind of despair, trying to reach a point of understanding.

We knew that pine trees spoke in this way. We were lonely listening to them because we knew we could never help them to say it,
whatever they were trying to say, for if the wind who was so close
to them could not help them, how could we?

Oh no, we could not spend the night at the Reservoir among the
pine trees.

'Billy Whittaker and his gang have been to the Reservoir, Billy
Whittaker and the Green Feather gang, one afternoon.'

'Did he say what it was like?'

'No, he never said.'

'He's been in an iron lung.'

That was true, Only a day or two ago our mother had been re-
minding us in an ominous voice of the fact which roused our envy
just as much as our dread, 'Billy Whittaker was in an iron lung two
years ago. Infantile paralysis.'

Some people were lucky. None of us dread to hope that we would
ever be surrounded by the glamour of an iron lung; we would have
to be content all our lives with paltry flesh lungs.

'Well are we going to the Reservoir or not?'

That was someone trying to sound bossy like our father,—'Well
am I to have salmon sandwiches or not, am I or have lunch at all
today or not?'

We struck our sticks in the air. They made a whistling sound.
They were supple and young. We had tried to make musical instru-
ments out of them, time after time we hacked at the willow and the
elder to make pipes to blow our music, but no sound came but
our own voices. And why did two sticks rubbed together not make
fire? Why couldn't we ever *make* anything out of the bits of the
world lying about us?

An aeroplane passed in the sky. We craned our necks to read the
writing on the underwing, for we collected aeroplane numbers.

The plane was gone, in a glint of sun.

'Are we?' someone said.

'If there's an eclipse you can't see at all. The birds stop singing
and go to bed.'

'Well are we?'

Certainly we were. We had not quelled all our misgiving, but
we set out to follow the creek to the Reservoir.

What is it? I wondered. They said it was a lake. I thought it was
a bundle of darkness and great wheels which peeled and sliced you
like an apple and drew you towards them with demonic force, in
the same way that you were drawn beneath the wheels of a train
if you stood too near the edge of the platform. That was the terrible
danger when the Limited came rushing in and you had to approach
to kiss arriving aunts.

We walked on and on, past wild sweet peas, clumps of cutty
grass, horse mushrooms, ragwort, gorse, cabbage trees; and then,
at the end of the gully, we came to strange territory, fences we did
not know, with the barbed wire tearing at our skin and at our skirts
put on over our bathing suits because we felt cold though the sun
stayed in the sky.

We passed huge trees that lived with their heads in the sky, with
their great arms and joints creaking with age and the burden of
being trees, and their mazed and linked roots rubbed bare of earth,

like bones with the flesh cleaned from them. There were strange
gates to be opened or climbed over, new directions to be argued
and plotted, notices which said TRESPASSERS WILL BE PROSECUTED
BY ORDER. And there was the remote immovable sun shedding without gentleness its influence of burning upon us and upon the town,
looking down from its heavens and considering our infantile-
paralysis epidemic, and the children tired of holidays and wanting
to go back to school with the new stiff books with their crackling
pages, the scrubbed ruler with the sun rising on one side amidst the
twelfths, tenths, millimeters, the new pencils to be sharpened with
the pencil shavings flying in long pickets and light-brown curls scal-
loped with red or blue; the brown school, the bare floor, the clump
clump in the corridors on wet days!

We came to a strange paddock, a bull-paddock with its occupant
planted deep in the long grass, near the gate, a jersey bull polished
like a wardrobe, burnished like copper, heavy beams creaking in
the wave and flow of the grass.

'Has it got a ring through its nose? Is it a real bull or a steer?'

Its nose was ringed which meant that its savagery was tamed,
or so we thought; it could be tethered and led; even so, it had once
been savage and it kept its pride, unlike the steers who pranced and
huddled together and ran like water through the paddocks, made
no impression, quarried no massive shape against the sky.

The bull stood alone.

Had not Mr. Bennet been gored by a bull, his own tame bull,
had been rushed to Glenham Hospital for thirty-three stiches?
Remembering Mr. Bennet we crept cautiously close to the paddock
fence, ready to escape.

Someone said, 'Look, it's pawing the ground!'

A bull which pawed the ground was preparing for a charge. We
escaped quickly through the fence. Then, plucking courage, we
skirted the bushes on the far side of the paddock, climbed through
the fence, and continued our walk to the Reservoir.

We had lost the creek between deep banks. We saw it now before
us, and hailed it with more relief than we felt, for in its hidden course
through the bull-paddock it had undergone change, it had adopted
the shape, depth, mood of foreign water, foaming in a way we did
not recognize as belonging to our special creek, giving no hint of
its depth. It seemed to flow close to its concealed bed, not wishing
any more to communicate with us. We realized with dismay that
we had suddenly lost possession of our creek. Who had taken it?
Why did it not belong to us any more? We hit our sticks in the air
and forgot our dismay. We grew cheerful.

Till someone said that it was getting late, and we reminded one another that during the day the sun doen't seem to move, it just remains pinned with a drawing pin against the sky, and then, while you are not looking, it suddenly slides down quick as the chopped-off head of a golden eel, into the sea, making everything in the world go dark.

'That's only in the tropics!'

We were not in the tropics. The divisions of the world in the atlas, the different coloured cubicles of latitude and longitude fascinated us.

'The sand freezes in the desert at night. Ladies wear bits of sand...'

'grains...'

'grains or bits of sand as necklaces, and the camels...'

'with necks like snails...'

'with horns, do they have horns?'

'Minnie Stocks goes with boys...;'

'I know who your boy is, I know who your boy is...'

> Waiting by the garden gate,
> Waiting by the garden gate...

'We'll never get to the Reservoir!'

'Whose idea was it?'

'I've strained my ankle!'

Someone began to cry. We stopped walking.

'I've strained my ankle.!'

There was an argument.

'It's not strained, it's sprained.'

'strained.'

'sprained.'

'All right sprained then. I'll have to wear a bandage, I'll have to walk on crutches...'

'I had crutches once. Look. I've got a scar where I fell off my stilts. It's a white scar, like a centipede. It's on my shins.'

'shins, funnybone...'

'It's humerus...'

'knuckles...'

'a strained ankle...'

'a strained ankle...'

'a whitlow, an ingrown toenail the roots of my hair warts spinal meningitis infantile paralysis...'

'Infantile paralysis, Infantile paralysis you have to be wheeled in a chair and wear irons on your legs and your knees knock together

...'

'Once you're in an iron lung you can't get out, they lock it, like
a cage...'

'You go in the amberlance...'

'*ambulance*...'

'amberlance...'

'ambulance to the hostible...'

'the *hospital,* an *amberlance to the hospital*...'

'Infantile Paralysis...'

'Friar's Balsam! Friar's Balsam!'

'Baxter's Lung Preserver, Baxter's Lung Preserver!'

'Syrup of Figs, California Syrup of Figs!'

'The creek's going on high-flow!'

Yes, there were bubbles on the surface, and the water was turning muddy. Our doubts were dispelled. It was the same old creek,
and there, suddenly, just ahead, was a plantation of pine trees, and
already the sighing sound of it reached our ears and troubled us.
We approached it, staying close to the banks of our newly claimed
creek, until once again the creek deserted us, flowing its own private course where we could not follow, and we found ourselves
among the pine trees, a narrow strip of them, and beyond lay a vast
surface of sparkling water, dazzling our eyes, its centre chopped
by tiny grey waves. Not a lake, nor a river, nor a sea.

'The Reservoir!'

The damp smell of the pine needles caught in our breath. There
were no birds, only the constant sighing of the trees. We could
see the water clearly now; it lay, except for the waves beyond the
shore, in an almost perfect calm which we knew to be deceptive—
else why were people so afraid of the Reservoir? The fringe of young
pines on the edge, like toy trees, subjected to the wind, sighed and
told us their sad secrets. In the Reservoir there was an appearance
of neatness which concealed a disarray too frightening to be acknowledged except, without any defence, in moments of deep sleep
and dreaming. The little sparkling innocent waves shone now green,
now grey, petticoats, lettuce leaves; the trees signed, and told us to
be quiet, hush-sh, as if something were sleeping and should not be
disturbed—perhaps that was what the trees were always telling us,
to hush-sh in case we disturbed something which must never ever
be awakened?

What was it? Was it sleeping in the Reservoir? Was that why
people were afraid of the Reservoir?

Well we were not afraid of it, oh no, it was only the Reservoir,
it was nothing to be afraid of, it was just a flat Reservoir with a

fence around it, and trees, and on the far side a little house (with wheels inside?), and nothing to be afraid of.

'The Reservoir, The Reservoir!'

A noticeboard said DANGER, RESERVOIR.

Overcome with sudden glee we climbed through the fence and swung on the lower branches of the trees, shouting at intervals, gazing possessively and delightedly at the sheet of water with its wonderful calm and menace,

'The Reservoir! The Reservoir! The Reservoir!'

We quarrelled again about how to pronounce and spell the word.

Then it seemed to be getting dark—or was it that the trees were stealing the sunlight and keeping it above their heads? One of us began to run. We all ran, suddenly, wildly, not caring about our strained or sprained ankles, through the trees out into the sun where the creek, but it was our creek no longer, waited for us. We wished it were our creek, how we wished it were our creek! We had lost all account of time. Was it nearly night? Would darkness overtake us, would we have to sleep on the banks of the creek that did not belong to us any more, among the wild sweet peas and the tussocks and the dead sheep? And would the eels come up out of the creek, as people said they did, and on their travels through the paddocks would they change into people who would threaten us and bar our way. TRESPASSERS WILL BE PROSECUTED, standing arm in arm in their black glossy coats, swaying, their mouths open, ready to swallow us? Would they ever let us go home, past the orchards along the gully? Perhaps they would give us Infantile Paralysis, perhaps we would never be able to walk home, and no one would know where we were, to bring us an iron lung with its own special key!

We arrived home, panting and scratched. How strange! The sun was still in the same place in the sky!

The question troubled us, 'Should we tell?'

The answer was decided for us. Our mother greeted us as we went in the door with, 'You haven't been long away, kiddies. Where have you been? I hope you didn't go anywhere near the Reservoir.'

Our father looked up from reading his newspapers.

'Don't let me catch you going near the Reservoir!'

We said nothing. How out-of-date they were! They were actually afraid!

O. E. MIDDLETON   **Saving the Breed**
(*b*. 1925)

Never saw such a great pack in all the King Country, as old Charlie's.
See him coming in from the back country at mustering-time with
a mob of two thousand or so and his dogs handling each woolly
as though its fleece was worth its weight in gold, which it wasn't
in those days.

Up in front would be Slick, the leader, stepping along in a queenie
way with his tail hypnotising the front of the mob and the usual
goofy look on his face. He was more like an overgrown shorn lamb
than a dog, even to the colour of his crinkly coat. A real dreamy,
dopey sort of dog you'd say at first look, yet the sheep would follow
him anywhere.

Out on the flanks might be Jessie and Dave, two young beardies
whose main job was heading, and shepherding the stragglers would
be Charlie's strong-eyes, Beau and Belle.

You wouldn't notice Dan, the yellow backing dog until the mob
got boxed at a gateway or crossing a bridge. Then Charlie would
give him the word and he'd be up over their backs barking and
grinning and barking here and there, and in to heel with the mob
running freely again before you knew what was up.

He was a great man with dogs, was Charlie, and he seemed to
love all his dogs the same, and they him. Couple of times someone
offered him big money for two good huntaways and he turned them
down and each time the dog got sick and died or was killed. He
was dead scared of getting any more offers in case he was tempted
to accept, for the dog's sake.

But nobody would have been silly enough to try and buy his eye
dogs. A stranger on the road maybe. But then Charlie would have
rolled himself one and looked up at the hills and pretended he
didn't hear.

You just couldn't translate two dogs like Beau and Belle into
cold cash. It wasn't that they were Charlie's bread and butter or
the reason why he was reckoned to be the best shepherd in the
district. Given the right stuff to work on he could have turned out
any number of useful dogs in a year or two. But Beau and his sister
were the kind you own only once in a lifetime.

Charlie had got them as pups from some breeder up North and wanted some more by the same sire some day. The old dog had been imported but they hadn't had much luck with bitches until one had thrown Beau and Belle.

Beau was a tall dog. High in the shoulder and broad across the chest, with bulging, wide-apart eyes. He carried his ears pricked all the time, could steady a big wild wether with one look and do anything Charlie asked him, even to circus tricks.

Belle was like a smaller copy, more nuggetty, but still powerful. She was short-haired like her brother but had less white on the throat. Charlie prized her for the pups she was going to give him through her father, the old dog up North...

Charlie was a slow, quiet man with a lanky build. To look at his face you'd think he had been a fisherman, it was so leathery and wrinkled by years of being out on the hills in all weathers. Come to think of it, he *was* a bit like a fisherman the way he worked his team. See him drag a gully full of tomos and patches of scrub and guarantee if you went over it all on foot afterwards you wouldn't find one straggler. Just as though someone had been over it with a piper net.

Lot of people took Charlie for a fool with his slow ways and the way he had of sitting slumped in the saddle when he was on a long drive. Like the lorry-driver who saw him trailing a herd of steers one day and thought he could get through by blowing his horn and not reducing speed.

Charlie woke up in time to see one of his young dogs yelping off the road with a crushed foot and the truck half-way through the herd.

He moved so fast then that he had his horse blocking the way by the time the truck came out the other end and the things he said to that driver and the fiver he got, on the dot, toward veterinary expenses, are now local history.

Shearing-time was always a worry for Charlie and his team, but not because of the extra work. They would be up about two every morning for weeks without complaining and have a full shed every day, ready for an early start as long as the weather held. Out in the paddocks they worked together like a good line of backs, but as soon as they got near the homestead Charlie would start to worry.

What with the dogs the roussies and penners-up and daggers brought to give them a hand in the shed and yards and the others the shearers brought, so they could go after pigs when it was too wet to shear, the station wasn't safe for a self-respecting pack.

Belle would be locked up securely until the last stranger and his dog had left the bunkhouse, and people at the Store even said that Charlie's suspicions didn't stop at dogs. He just wouldn't take any chances with Belle and when you realised that she was the last hope of her line, you couldn't blame him.

Then there would always be the odd ewe with a few teeth-marks showing up once the wool was off and someone would always trot out the old theory about eye dogs being biters. And Charlie would have words with the boss and threaten to leave, until a shearer caught the culprit in the act. And, sure enough, it would be some saw-toothed pup of a penner-up, and not Beau at all. Charlie himself would chain the rascal for the duration and thank heaven it *hadn't* been Beau, because that was one thing you *couldn't* be certain about with a strong-eye.

But aside from shearing and crutching times, life was good at the station and with Belle hitting four, Charlie started thinking seriously about the litter he wanted and how he would have to be dropping a line to the breeder up North. .

Day he got that reply from up North, Charlie walked right out of the store without even ordering his groceries. Weeks after, people said, he would pass you on the road without so much as a good-day, and looking as though all his team was down with distemper.

If ever a man was sorry he had waited too long with a bitch. it was Charlie. After all his careful handling and hoping and looking forward to training young dogs of the same breed when Beau started to show signs of wear! Now he would have to go outside the strain and get the best cross he could. The old dog up North was dead.

What made Charlie sour was that he had only lost a leg. Proper care and a good vet and he'd still have been a great dog to breed from. But no, they had destroyed him, and he the last of the imported stock. It was enough to make a saint swear. And Belle due on again any time, too...

But he wasn't a man to get a snitch on his neighbours because of a bit of bad luck and it wasn't long before he was his old self again.

A few weeks after, people began to notice that the pack was one shy. There was Slick, the beardies, Dan and Beau—but no Belle. With dogs as well-known as Charlie's you couldn't help noticing, but if you said anything about it to Charlie, all you got back was a quiet grin and some slow remark about the weather.

Real man of mystery he was those days. Puttering round the whare at all hours, having packets of special dog-food sent down from the city and picking them up from the store without a word of explanation.

Not even the boss knew exactly what was going on. Every time he went down to the whare to have a word about the stock, there would be Charlie, fussing around a new pen he'd built near the door. But try and get any news out of him and he shut up tight as a fresh-water mussel.

Still, he couldn't keep a story like that corked-up for ever and it wasn't long before the whole district knew Charlie's star bitch was due to pup.

Even then he wouldn't let on whose dog it had been, but that didn't stop every cocky for miles trying to book a pup.

It was shearing-time again before anyone got a look at the little fellers, but no one needed a second go to see that Belle had thrown the real thing. There wasn't an odd one among them and every one had the black and white, and full eyes of the old strain.

Only thing was they were a bit small-boned, but Charlie said that was one of the risks in that kind of cross.

But the pick of the litter was better even than he had hoped. He was broad-chested and well-marked, with big wide-apart eyes.

Charlie called him Beau Bells.

O. E. MIDDLETON
(*b.* 1925)

The Doss-house and the Duchess

How beautifully named are the streets of our poverty! Piety, Pleasure, Parliament and Humanity Street. All over the world, the poorest places with the richest names, until, one day, there is Paradise Street....

On the grey stone curbing opposite the Mission, a knot of seamen. Stiff-legged and slow, Magee is coming down the street. Lewin's sharp elbow works at our ribs.

'He's had another jab. See how pale he is!'

Magee declines to sit on hard stone. He leans against the corner railings and takes his time about unwrapping a brand-new packet of Woodbines.

'Have you heard the news, me boys?'

'What news is that?'

'About Her Royal Highness?'

Lewin has heard. It is written all over his avid face, across his cringing shoulders. Nothing pleases him more than to dole out hot dollops of gossip. He is our rumour-monger, our harbinger, our spy. But he shuts up and waits for the cigarettes to be dealt out.

'You mean about *her* coming down to Paradise Street to look over the Mission?'

Magee lights up carefully and hands over the match. We hold the flame right at the ends of our Woodbines so that only the tips catch fire. Oh the fine flavour, the perfume of the pale blue smoke when you have been without...!

'Sure that's it. All the beachies at Northend are talking about it. It's in the paper she's opening the new hostel, then going on a tour of the docks.'

Blackie pulls out the *Mail* which he carries folded small in his hip pocket and smoothes it out. We lean over it, breathing in each other's smells as we devour that fat print. *Duchess to open new club for Seamen*, it says. We are famished for more, but there is nothing about us. Not a miserable crumb about her coming down to the Mission.

'May I be struck dead if it's not the truth!'

'Ah don't speak so, Kevin boy!'

'...You'll see soon enough that it's right. Eleven o'clock to-morrow morning.'

'Who was it told you then, Kevin?'

'I keep my ears open....'

'It wouldn't have been that tall fruit up at the clinic?'

'No, it would not!'

'And how is the arm today, anyroad?'

'A little better, thank you.' Stiffly he straightens, shoves himself off the railings and coasts across to the Mission.

'He's got a bad one this time, it seems....' Our eyes linger on the open doorway full of fellow-feeling.

Blackie says it is time for the tea-shop, but Lewin says he will stay at his post on the corner where he sometimes waylays affluent strangers.

Blackie is proud of his new find. Luckily for us, the dockers are very particular about their sandwiches. All the crusts are cut off and piled in wooden trays. If you are nice and civil, the girls who work in the teashop will let you help yourself to them.

The crusts are good and crisp. They fill our guts and our pockets to overflowing.

We pile the rest into a shoe-box for later.

Inside the café, the dockers munch their barbered bread, stamp their feet, swig huge mugs of tea and coffee. Oh the joyful noise of men with jobs! The din of their cheerful voices chivying the girls, chaffing each other; the clumping of their well-booted feet, the scrape of benches, drift through the kitchen. Like sweet scraps of sound, they fall among us in the alley as we stow away the last crusts.

Blackie catches the eye of a bustling girl: 'Say thanks, Mary! see you tomorrow if it's O.K....?'

She flashes us the dazzling, unseeing look of an angel—or a goddess. Even Blackie is subdued. Only Dougherty saves our wretched manhood.

'Sure we'd all come up here on our knees just for one sight of your darling face!'

The tinkle of laughter warms our backs as we pick our way among the dustbins.

'Oh the bliss of a full belly! And what wouldn't I give now for another of Magee's smokes. ...!'

'If he's not gone through them yet, there'll still be one more apiece when we get back.'

Once again we drag over the dreary miles of dock cobbles, climbing cleated gangways, searching shifty eyes for a glimmer of hope. The usual round and the same stale answers on every ship: 'All hands are hired through the Pool. Are you established members of the Pool?'

Why do they think we are tramping fifteen miles of dockside, when the other way, you have only to show your papers at the Pool office, and wait for a ship?

'Oh did you see that loaf?' Dougherty is making a mental meal as we come down the last gangway. '... Sitting up there on top of the locker, and that Peggy too miserable even to offer us so much as a drop of tea!'

'The Limey bastard!' Blackie's spit on the cobbles speaks for Dougherty and me. Between our sweaty feet and the uneven stones there is a mockery of leather. Out of reach in every way, the dock train glides back on smooth rails. Clattering drays and rumbling lorries go by laden with bales and crates. One dray grinds slowly past piled with boxes and cartons stamped with a black fern leaf.

'Say how would it be to try to speak to the Duchess?'

'About getting us a ship, you mean?'

'Why not? The interest of the Commonwealth, and all that......'

'You're crazy. You wouldn't get near her.'

'You'd have more show trying to put the bite on the Pope.'

Half-way home, we pass the ruin of the warehouse cellar, bared by bombs.

'See there!...And there!' It is Dougherty's ritual. He is like someone catching lice on himself, or inspecting old wounds as he picks out the iron rings where slaves were tethered.

It is growing dusk as we strike the bottom of Paradise Street. The empty spaces left by the war are noisy with children and from his pitch near the tobacconist's the old man growls the names of the evening dailies. Lewin is waiting for us, hands in pockets, his triumph showing in a raggy whistle that puckers his face.

'What do you know, a geezer threw me a dollar! Coffee will be served in the lounge. ...!'

In the last of the day, the bare brick and cold stone of the street soften to warm browns. As we converge on the Mission, Lewin getting his share of crusts and talk, a ripe melon falls from the sky and splits on the pavement. Fingers knead the flagstones among the scatter of seed and pulp as we draw near and the trunk and legs of this guy flutter in a way that is almost human.

'Hey! You below! Tell the office to phone the police!'

The square, white, undeniably human face of the detective looks down sternly from an open third-storey window.

Dougherty's eyes shoot sparks upwards: 'It's a priest and an ambulance, and not the police he's wanting, I'm thinking.' Mechanically he crosses himself, looking down.

Why are the voices of the children suddenly still?

Through the door of the Mission, and from hiding places up and down the street, men hasten to view this insect squashed on the footpath.

'What was he doing?'

'How did it happen?'

'Caught in the act ...?'

'He won't do that again!'

Breathless, we escape from the press of eager bodies and stand, uneasy yet strangely renewed, on its fringe.

'I think *I'll* just ...' Lewin, his wealth forgotten, bends over the gutter vomiting bread. Only Dougherty, calm and pale, stays to help the ambulance men.

Amid the dying talk which follows the ambulance, Lewin wipes his mouth, Dougherty makes another cross in the air.

'He'll not be signing on for any more trips. ...'

'Did you know him then ...?'

Two uniformed men are talking to the plain-clothes man and the skipper of the Mission. All eyes, a thin child pushes her way among the legs and gazes at the smear of thick juice.

'Go on! Hop it girly!'

Why is it not until we smell the harsh disinfectant, hear the wet sound of the janitor swabbing the flag-stones, that Dougherty and I feel anything? Vanquished at last, we too bend over the gutter.

'Can't take it, uh, you guys?' jeers Blackie as we join the others in the Mission café. Even Lewin is perky again with coffee in his belly and a new fag in his face.

'Did you see his face?'

'His own mother wouldn't have recognized him!'

'Someone said he was from Dublin way, but what's it matter now? May he rest in peace, poor fellow.'

There is a glisten of sweat on Magee's brow, a sombre look in his eye:

'As like as not it was him took that fine razor of mine. But who can say what a man will do if he's pushed far enough?'

Slowly, we have drifted back into our haven. Some of us have on our best shore-going shirts, and those with a change of socks and underpants have put them on.

Before long, the Ladies' Welfare Committee will ask for volunteers to stack chairs and tables against the wall and the café will resound to the jolly laughter of decent, plain girls and to the twanging of the piano. But you never know your luck in a big ship, and where else can we go anyway?

'You staying for the social, Blackie?'

'Bet your life! Wouldn't miss the free tea-and-tabnabs. Besides, I kinda like homely girls. ...'

Of course we are all staying for the Mission social, to clasp clean girls and dance decently to the piano whose chords are already heavy with tomorrow's hymns.

The floor is clear, the pious, black-suited man with the stiff collar seats himself at the piano and already a couple of young officers have whisked away the only presentable girls. Magee is explaining to a motherly woman who bends over him that he is unable to dance since he strained his back and Blackie carefully stubs out and pockets his fag and takes the floor with a hefty, bespectacled lass. Lewin leaves us with a leer and sidles up to a kindly-looking committee-woman.

There is more than one kind-hearted tart in the town. The street outside is quiet now but an odour of carbolic still hangs around the entrance. Certain of the flagstones gleam in the light from the street lamp. The words of an old sea-shanty begin to go around in my head and stars are twinkling through the dirty cloud above the street.

'Coming-ready-or-not!' calls a clear young voice from one of the empty spaces between the buildings.

The old man has left his pitch outside the tobacconist's. In his place, a trim young tart shows her wares to anyone who will look.

How long can you survive on an alien shore, fed only by hope and the company of fellow-exiles?

'Don't talk to *me* about the Commonwealth!' Blackie snarls at us on our bad days. 'If the god-damned Commonwealth meant anything we'd all be drawing the dole like every other mother-loving beachcomber in this God-forsaken, Limey hole!'

Young Maggie May mistakes my lingering look and follows me with sweet words.

At the bar, Clara is too busy to do more than buy us a drink between customers and I am suddenly too tired or too fussy to wait till she's finished work.

Even the young fellow in the sea shanty had to go back to Paradise Street. Sooner or later, we all have to drift back there to our home, the Mission: beds 1/– in the dormitories and if you have another shilling you can walk into the dining-room and sit down to a hot meal and take as much bread from the common plate as your belly and your pockets can hold.

The Mission is a place to doss for the night; somewhere to meet your mates, swap news or stories; have a shave or a wash, rinse out your sweaty socks. It was built for us in the days of sail by God-fearing merchant-philanthropists of the town whose wealth came in ships from all over the Empire. We are grateful for the disinterested goodness of heart which built the Mission and for the upright men who run it. The marks we leave on the smooth walls of the lavatories, the shapes we draw and the words we write, testify to our gratitude and manly joy.

Unbidden, we crowd into the upstairs lounge on Sunday mornings for the devotional service and offer prayers for our benefactors.

Sometimes, it is true, there is a misunderstanding, and a seaman who has skipped church finds someone else has been given his bed. The Mission is a popular place, especially in cold weather, and it is often hard for the skipper to decide which of us are the most deserving.

But to be one of the volunteers who bullock the piano up the stairs on Sunday morning, or at least to be seated with your red-backed hymn book in plenty of time, and so catch the skipper's eye as he counts heads, takes a great weight off the poor man's mind.

'Guess I'd better drift back, Clara.'

'Do you have to go right away?'

'There's a posh visitor coming down our way in the morning.'

'Go on ...!'

'A duchess of something or other.'

'She can wait!'

A big West Indian drifts across to our table. His name is Daniel Defroe and he has just acquired some money and the itch to spend it.

'How are things, Johnny Kiwi?'

'Lousy as ever, Dan. How are the rats of Parliament Street?'

When he laughs it is like a ferocious black cat licking its chops and there is a sound from deep in his chest like the rustle of bamboo leaves.

'We're managing to keep them at bay, boy.'

Dan and some friends spent two years on the beach in London, living in cold, crowded basements in Cable Street. One terrible Winter, two of them managed to find work as builder's labourers, but Dan ended with pneumonia.

'How's the chest now?'

'Sound as a bell now, man. I'm eating like an old horse these days.'

He is working in the kitchen of a hotel and manages to stoke up his big boiler when the chefs have their backs turned. Why should I stand in his way if he wants to let off some perfectly good West Indian steam?

They are putting back the chairs and tables in the café. Blackie and his filly have vanished. Lewin still has the ear of the committee-woman and Dougherty has turned in. But Magee has saved me two slices of cold plum duff from supper. As we go up the stairs, he shares out another Woodbine.

'With luck there'll be another few bob from me Mum in the post Monday.' He has to pause on every landing, flexing his hams like an old horse with stringholt.

In the pale light of bare bulbs, the rows of black iron cots seem like racks. ('Seamen's carcasses stowed, 1/– per night. Please keep your streets tidy!')

At least, this way, we are snug and warm for a few hours, we who have come through the trials of the sea only to succumb to the ordeals of the shore. ...

'I wonder if they'll bring her ladyship up here?'

We have taken off our shoes and tied them to the bedrail by the laces. Magee has slipped his purse inside his underpants and our clothes are rolled under our heads or stuffed under the mattresses.

'Are you serious?'

A warm, familiar smell fills our nostrils. It is the odour of ill-fed, ill-washed bodies mingled with the sour smell of disappointment.

'The day I ship out of here,' Magee whispers in the dark, 'I'll get a sub from the old man and stand you boys a pint of Guinness each. . . .'

'The day you ship out, Blackie and I will be well away. . . .'

'No, the day I ship out of here. . . .' Obstinately his voice drones on softly, full of hope, full of dreams.

When the bell goes at seven, daylight slanting through the narrow casements recalls us to our world and Blackie's immaculate cot.

'Come on now, all you lads! I want everyone up and spruce for our royal visitor.'

The skipper himself strides among us in his best dark suit laving his hands. Two window-cleaners who have followed him in begin washing the grime from the panes which filter light to us from the dark side of the street.

'Can you beat that! They're even washing the windows!'

Magee twists in his cot, making a face, and up and down the room, the racked sleepers squeak their cots, hawk, fart, cough and ease themselves awake.

Lewin leers at us from the other side as he pokes his legs into his pants.

'Come on me loyal lads! Shake a leg!'

There are women on their knees scrubbing floors, polishing brasswork; men in shirt-sleeves dashing about, getting in each other's way.

Dougherty and I are the guests of Lewin and Magee at breakfast and there is a great stowing away of bread in case Blackie comes back empty.

'Well, mates, Mrs. Lewin's little boy Hector did a bit of all right for himself last night, anyway.'

It seems the committee-woman lent him ten shillings and promised to help him get a job as a waiter.

'Was that heifer of Blackie's the same one he had a fortnight ago?'

'No, a different one. That other one didn't come back.'

The desk clerk, the skipper, the old janitor and the extra helpers are still scuttling about. Magee makes a funny remark about them and bids us goodbye.

On the grey stone curbing opposite the Mission, the usual knot of loungers spreads itself in the thin sun. A red-haired donkeyman is having his say about the royal family. We have heard it all before, but it warms us, draws a few snickers of approval. Sunday in Paradise Street, and on top of it all, a royal visitor. . . .

Somewhere off the coast, a small tanker ploughs for port with spirit from Aruba. The consul told us she is three men short, so we have looked her up in *Lloyd's Shipping News*...

A little dark steward from Manchester tells of an experience with royalty in one of the Cunard ships. It is an obscene story and the hard faces of the buildings opposite throw back our gusty laughter. Between my cracked shoes lies a granite pebble. It is rounded and hard and with a polish like smooth varnish. Without thinking, I pick it up and fret it against my trousers.

The stone begins to weigh heavy in my hand. It is as hard and un-yielding as this shore. Although my ears follow the comical, jerky talk of the man from Manchester, my hand would like to hurl this stone against the dour face of this Northern city.

At the top of the street, a skinny figure swings into sight. Even this far off we can see the swagger in his rolling walk. Lewin has seen him and nudges Dougherty. Several pairs of envious eyes pilot him in as he catches sight of us and crosses over.

The talk has strayed from its starting-point and has settled around our favourite subject.

'Oh Boy!' Blackie lets out as he parks his lean nates on the kerb. A flourish as his hand goes into his shirt pocket, a flash of colour and bright cellophane and he is offering us real American cigarettes.

The stone falls back into the gutter, Lewin's trap drops open, Dougherty lets out a soft 'Mother of God!'

But for the moment, Blackie says not a word. With a half-smile he slits his eyes against the smoke, glances towards the far end of the street and cocks an ear to talk.

It is almost time for the service. The skipper trots out of the Mission, polishing his knuckles in his palms. He looks up the street and down, takes off and polishes his glasses, puts them on again and bolts back into the Mission.

Reluctantly, we drift across to the dark side and through the door. Upstairs, a mournful-looking cadet is handing out the tattered books. Shamefacedly, we shuffle into the dark-panelled room, take our places on the benches. Pale as ever, Magee slips in and drops into the place we have saved for him.

Some of the hymns make us laugh. '...Some poor wretched, struggling seaman, You may rescue, you may save,' is one. The way the skipper stands up and sings it with his blue chin moving solemnly up and down has Blackie and me in fits. From what dizzy heights they look down on us, these self-righteous Victorian hymn-writers!

As usual, we end by singing 'For those in peril on the sea,' and the skipper says 'Let us pray' and bows his head. When he has scanned us carefully over the tops of his spectacles, he begins intoning the prayers.

'...And lead us not into temptation, but deliver us from evil...'

'Amen!' we say fervently. It is the only part of the programme which has any real meaning for us.

As soon as the service is over, the skipper says we may remain seated until the arrival of our royal visitor. He looks at his watch scurries downstairs and we let out gusty sighs and forced coughs as we shrug off the gloom and hand back our hymn-books.

From their dark frames on the dark walls, the stern fathers of the Mission look down on us. Their likenesses endure like the iron and coal of their era, the dark solid furniture they bequeathed us.

But what have they done with that poor sinner who tried to deliver himself from the third floor window?

'Here she is! Here she is!' A chorus of awed whispering as charwomen and cleaners fly for their peep-holes. Sounds of slamming car doors, of more hushed talk, then silence.

'They're coming up ...!' Lewin's slantwise face listens for us, registering every sound from below. The pianist holds himself stiffly on his stool, squaring his narrow shoulders. Blackie has stopped breathing.

An old fellow we have not seen before, but who looks like the Mission's patron saint, bursts in and babbles: 'Her Royal Highness, The Duchess of——.'

In she comes like a barque in full sail. Tall, clean lines, fine clothes....What more can you say?

The red-haired, cockney donkeyman is the first to his feet; the small dark man from Manchester is only a split-second behind him.

A puff of wind to my left and right and Blackie and Dougherty are upright. Further along the bench, Magee gets slowly to his feet, a dark look on his face.

The donkeyman's back and red neck hide the duchess from me and me from her, but over the head of the little man from Manchester, the skipper sends me steely signals Blackie begins to tug my arm in a half-hearted way, but soon stops.

The skipper's face is going red and his eyes seem watery behind his spectacles. By the time the piano has galloped through the national anthem, he is staring at the wall above my head.

Those who have handed in their names are being presented to the tall elegant woman who smiles simply and unaffectedly and touches their hands with the tips of her gloved fingers. There are three cadets in the queue and a young officer from one of the Canadian Pacific ships.

Blackie is full of sorrow. 'Oh boy, you're for the block for sure! They'll lock you up in the tower.'

Lewin is agog, though silent, but Magee leans across, his hand to his mouth:

''Tis what we all should have done. The best of luck to you boy!!'

'He's right! I'm a son-of-a-bitch to have let you down. If only we'd gone into a huddle about it beforehand. . . .'

She is gone as suddenly as she came, so now we can enjoy another of Blackie's virginias. More slamming of car doors and purring of muted engines and they have left the street.

The skipper reappears in the doorway of the lounge and gives us one of his watery smiles. 'Could I see you in my office, Mr. Bell-ringer?'

Dark looks from Magee, Dougherty and Blackie. Lewin is neutral.

'You did what we all should have done. Don't let him bother you. He can only throw you out.'

How sweetly the flavour of certain moments lingers in a cigarette.

The skipper has recovered his self-possession and is gently laving his hands.

('Blessed are the meek, my friends!')

'Ah yes, ah, Mr. Bellringer. I have no intention of asking you for an explanation for what was obviously a premeditated act of dis-respect and disloyalty. It is my duty to see that beds go to the most deserving cases. As from now your bed is cancelled and you are no longer welcome here.'

He pushes over a slip of paper and a florin. The slip says 'Refund on bed No. 33. Sun., Mon., 2/–.'

The others are waiting outside. Blackie, his hands deep in his pockets, kicks at the kerb with his scuffed, pointed shoes.

'That Bible-banging, psalm-singing old scrawler. . . . !'

'There's one thing,' Dougherty remarks gently, 'you've no luggage to worry about.'

Blackie flourishes his packet. Solemnly we pluck out cigarettes, apply fire.

'We'll all go with you up to the new place. It's only a couple of miles. Their beds are dearer, but we can always have a whip-round.

'. . . If the old —— hasn't been on the blower to the skipper up there. . . .'

'The day I ship out of this place. . . .' Magee mouths darkly at the street.

Blackie signs across to Lewin and we head out of the lower end of the street towards the dock cafe.

There are not so many crusts today because there are not so many dockers at work. But Blackie and the others insist they are not hungry. They make a fine parcel of the crusts and the bread we saved at breakfast, in the *Lloyd's Shipping News* and Dougherty bears it before him as if it were the host.

'First thing in the morning, we'll go and see the consul. Is that a deal?'

Stiff-legged and slow, Magee drags at our side.

'Would you take a job now, Kevin, if it was offering?'

'Just as soon as I get over my strain, like. . . .'

'This is the route the Rolls Royces took.'

'I'd sooner do it in one of them than in these. . . .' Through a hole in his pointed shoe, Blackie's yellow sole accuses us like an eye.

'. . . And to think there's a fine top-coat in Kelly's pawnshop you could have had the use of these cold nights.'

We are in the main drag. Lewin buys a copy of the *News of the World* and reads out the choice bits to us. There is a photograph of a fossil man who lived a million years ago. Blackie points out that he looks like the skipper of the Mission. There is another picture of a Greek shipping magnate on the beach at Cannes with a long-limbed film star. Her husband is suing for divorce and citing the Greek.

A millionaire has jumped from a skyscraper in New York and there are tens of thousands homeless after a tidal wave in Japan. . . .

'Nothing about a geezer who did the swallow-dive out of the Mission!' Lewin raises his snout above the ink-smelling sheets.

'. . . May God have mercy on his soul,' one of us says mechanically.

'Happened too recent,' Blackie says flatly. 'Anyway, who wants to read about that? Why, it might have been one of us here now.'

But Lewin's face tells us he is not satisfied. He has been cheated of something he could have talked about, fondled, believed in. How can you be sure a thing happened until you read about it in the paper?

There is still an argument going on when I come out of the new swing doors.

'They only have cubicles here. They're 3/– each.'

'That old skunk at the Mission didn't reckon you could afford one of those or he'd have telephoned for sure.'

Cheerfully, Blackie counts out a florin, a sixpence and two hexagonal threepenny pieces. 'I've got a date with Priscilla in an hour. But Joe and I'll see you outside here at nine tomorrow.'

Dougherty passes me the bread. The package is still warm from his big Irish hand.

'See you in the morning then.' A surely nod and he swings away beside Blackie.

'Watch it, mate!' and Lewin has darted off too, his banner furled, his eyes not missing a face among the leisurely Sunday strollers.

Now there is only Magee.

'You might as well take these. . . .' He is slipping a new packet of Woodbines into my pocket.

'No Kevin. A couple's plenty. . . .'

'Hush man! There'll be word from me Mum tomorrow for sure.'

'Anyway, I'll be seeing you.'

'Sure. . .'

'Maybe we'll all ship out together if the three of us miss the tanker. . . .'

'Why not? Your boys need someone to keep an eye on you, especially Blackie. Someone with experience.' He pronounces the word with the second syllable drawn out to emphasise its weight and meaning.

'Look after yourself. . . . And thanks.'

There is nothing beautiful about the name of the street where they have built the new seamen's hostel. It is called Bond Street or Stock Street—something like that.

But the berths smell of linseed oil and new paint and their windows face the sun. When you pay your three shillings at the desk the clerk gives you a big clean towel and there is ample hot water in the shower and soap in the handbasins.

If it is only for one night, then all the more reason to make the most of it. Tomorrow, anything might happen—or nothing. Tomorrow they might give us the dole.

. . . 'Oh yes, Mr. Blackadder and Mr. Bellringer. Your forms have come through now at last, I'm happy to say. Sorry about the delay and the little misunderstanding. Hope you have not been too much inconvenienced. Since you are British Subjects and have paid taxes in your own countries, you are of course entitled to full unemployment benefits here.' The little clerk at the Labour Exchange who has always been so peevish and short with us because of our outlandish accents, beams at us full of respect and hands over two envelopes. Inside there are government cheques for £18 in back pay for each of us.

'If you will just sign here. . . and there, and call here every Thursday from now on with the regulars. . . .'

. . . Or tomorrow might be another of those grimy, drizzly days when the early workers pull down the brims of their caps, huddle into their mufflers and coat collars and hurry along with their eyes on the greasy pavement. One of these days when exiles warm themselves with remembered sunshine, feed on a forgotten plenty. How many more treacherous tomorrows lie in wait for us before we exhaust our store of charms or join the ranks of the immune?

Is it possible that out of this already tainted tomorrow will come a small steel ship with deliverance for three? That there will be something to Lewin's advantage, mail for Magee....?

We are sitting in the firemen's mess. Dougherty is on watch with a Swede.

'Boy those fish-balls were good....'

'If I eat another hunk of bread and smør it'll be all I can do to stand....'

The messboy's discreet ropesoles pad patiently to and fro.

'They saved our lives, eh Kiwi, these Square-heads?'

'Amen!'

The messboy flits from his cubbyhole and stands beside the table, smiling with his pale Northern eyes.

'You like our food....Yess?'

'Yes!'

'That's good, no?'

'Good ship, good people!'

'Yess, I think so.'

Already Blackie is losing his haggard, hungry look. We like to sit in the mess long after the meal, talking and smoking American cigarettes, savouring our good fortune.

'I wonder if poor old Kevin's still going to the clinic?'

'... And do you reckon Lewin was on with that committee-woman?'

'Not a doubt of it!'

'...Say, did I ever tell you about Priscilla? Now there was a dame for you!'

The trouble is that once we are at sea again, we forget the mean faces, the false hearts, the ugly lives. And sometimes too, we forget the friends of our poverty in the streets with the beautiful names, and those others who have become immune.

JACQUELINE STURM **For all the Saints**
(b. 1927)

I hadn't been working long at the hospital before I noticed Alice.
She was the kind of person who stands out right away in any crowd,
even in an institution where everyone has to wear a nondescript
uniform. At first I thought it was her Maori blood—she was at least
halfcaste—but there were several other Maoris on the staff and a
few Raratongan girls too, so that colour didn't really make much
difference unless someone started a fight, and then the important
thing was not the kind of person you were but what side you belonged
to. But to get back to Alice. If it wasn't colour, I decided, it certainly
wasn't glamour either that made her so notable, far from it, though
some might have thought her handsome in a dignified statuesque
kind of way. She was a tall heavily-built woman round about the
thirty mark, though it was hard to guess her age, with smooth black
hair drawn tightly back into a bun and a smooth pale olive skin that
never showed the slightest trace of make-up. Over the usual blue
smock we all had to wear, she wore a long shapeless gown, always
spotlessly white and just showing her lisle stockings and black
button-up shoes. From what I could make out, her work was like
her uniform scrupulously clean and neat and done quietly and
methodically without fuss or bother, in spite of the first cook who
would have hustled an elephant. She was the kind of woman boss
who is happiest cracking a stock-whip. But even after I had noted
these details about Alice and the deliberate way she moved about
the kitchen, seldom smiling and never joining in the backchat with
the porters, I still wasn't satisfied. I felt there was something else I
couldn't recognize or understand because I had never met it before,
some indefinable quality that made her quite different from the rest
of us.

I was a servery maid in the nurses' dining-room, and my chores
often took me across the corridor to the main kitchen where Alice
worked. I made overtures whenever I got the chance, offering to
help lift things I knew she could manage quite easily by herself,
smiling and nodding and generally getting in her way. Nice day,
I'd say, or going to be hot again, but never a word back did I get.
Sometimes she'd respond with a grunt or smile or scowl, but most

times she would just walk away, or worse still, wait silently for me to move on. This went on for several days, but Alice wouldn't be hurried—she had her own way of making introductions.

One morning I went as usual to collect several big enamel milk jugs from the freezer outside the kitchen door—this was my first job every day—and I was just reaching for a jug when *clump*, the heavy door slammed shut behind me. I put the jug down very carefully. *Keep still*, someone shouted inside me, as every muscle in my body threatened to batter me against the four inches of door, *don't move, keep still*! I waited till the shouting had stopped, and then I very gingerly approached the barrier and tapped on it timidly like a guilty child outside the headmaster's office. Are you there? squeaked a voice I didn't recognise, as though it were using a telephone for the first time. It's me here, can you hear me? I waited several lifetimes for the answer that didn't come, then turned away slowly like the lion on the films. Jugs, I thought dully, looking at a wall of them, nice useful harmless things jugs. But at that the whole shelf began to slant and sway drunkenly. I'm at a party, dozens of people around me, talking and laughing and singing and stomping to hot boogie-woogie. I strained my ears to catch the sound. Drip went a drop of icy water on the concrete in front of me. Now we're all sitting on the floor round a blazing orange fire, eating steaming savs and drinking hot hot coffee and playing a quiet sort of guessing game. I concentrated on a large wooden box against the far wall. How many pounds of boxes to a butter, no no, how many pounds of—the door swung open slowly behind me, and I crawled back to light and warmth and sanity. Alice was propped up against the kitchen door, tears rolling down her face, and shaking so much with laughter I thought her head would fall off.

'Good joke, eh?' she gasped, while I tried to force my knees to keep me upright, 'funny, eh?' And she gave my shoulder a thump that sent me sprawling into the kitchen like a new-born lamb. From now on, I told myself afterwards, rubbing salt into my wounds, you're going to mind your own darn business. But the next morning when I came on duty, the milk jugs were waiting in the servery. Alice had been to the freezer before me.

After this, Alice and I got on like a house on fire, and it wasn't long before the rest of the staff saw what was happening and started giving me advice. It might have been because they didn't like Alice, or because I was a new chum and as green as they come and they thought I needed protecting, but whatever the reason, several of them took me aside, and told me Alice was a woman with bad blood, a treacherous character with the worst temper on God's earth, and the kind of friend who would turn nasty over nothing at all. Soon after, I found out what they really meant and why Alice was the terror of the kitchen.

It had been a particularly trying day, with the thermometer climbing to ninety degrees by mid-morning and staying there, and everybody got so irritable they didn't dare look each other in the eye. I was the last to finish in the servery and thought I'd pop into the kitchen and say goodbye to Alice before I went home. The huge cavern of a place was nearly empty and uncannily quiet. The cooking coppers round the walls had boiled all their strength away, the big steamers that stood higher than a man had hissed their life into the air around them and the last tide of heat was ebbing slowly from the islands of ovens in the middle of the floor. Alice was alone with her back towards me, mopping the red tiles with long swinging movements, never going over the same place twice, and never missing an inch. As I watched her from the doorway, the little man who worked in the pot-room slipped through a side door and cat-stepped it daintily with exaggeration over the part Alice had just washed. She leaned on the mop and looked at his dirty footmarks with an expressions face. A minute later he was back again, singing in a weak nasal voice through the top of his head.

'Ah'm a leedool on the lornlee, a leedl on the lornlee sahd.' He brushed against Alice and blundered into her bucket so that the soapy water slopped over the sides. 'So sorree,' he backed away, but he was too late. Alice had him firmly by the coat-collar, lifted him off his clever feet, and shook him up and down as I would shake a duster. As she threw him half the length of the kitchen through the door into the yard, I crept down the corridor, remembering the freezer and feeling that thump on the shoulder again.

But the next day I found out something much more important about Alice than the quality of her temper. She came and asked me if I would write a letter for her. I was a bit surprised and wanted to know why she didn't do it herself. She couldn't. She had never learned to read or write. At first I was incredulous, then as the full significance of the fact sank in, I was horrified. Words like progress civilisation higher standards and free secular compulsory, sprang to their feet in protest.

'Why, Alice, why?'

'My mother was not well when I was a little baby so she gave me to my Auntie who took me way way out in the country and the two of us lived there on Auntie's farm. My Auntie was a very good woman, very kind to me, but she could not read or write and school was too far away so I never learned. I just stayed at home with

Auntie and fixed the farm, But one day when I grew big Auntie said to me, we've got no more money Alice, so you must go away and work and get some money and bring it back to fix the farm. So I did, And now I am writing to Auntie to say I am getting the money fast and will come back very soon.' I tried to guess Alice's age once more, decided on thirty again, and reckoned that Auntie might have been about twenty when Alice was 'given' to her. That made her at least fifty now—getting a bit old for fixing farms.

'You read and write, Jacko?' That was the name she liked to call me.

'Oh yes, I read and write.'

'You pretty clever, eh Jacko?' she asked wistfully. 'You better show me how.'

And so, every afternoon for the next two or three weeks, I tried. The two of us were working the same broken shift from 6.30 a.m. to 6.30 p.m. with an hour for lunch and three hours off in the afternoon. We started with writing, but I had to give up, I just couldn't take it. It was far worse than working in the pot-room. Alice would grip the pencil as though it were a prison bar and strain and sweat and grunt and poke out her tongue, and I'd sit beside Alice and strain and sweat and grunt and poke out my tongue. I rummaged round the bookshops down town and eventually found an easy learn-to-read little book, strictly unorthodox, and not crammed with highly coloured pictures of English villages and stiles and shepherds in smocks and meadows with ponds and oak trees and sheep with the wrong kinds of faces and bluebells at the edge of the wood. Our book was illustrated in red, white and black, and the few words on each page were put in little boxes, and you jiggled them round so that each box had a slightly different meaning though the words were nearly the same. I would say—first box: look! here is a dog; the dog's name is Rover. And Alice would repeat it after me slowly, pointing at the right box and looking intently at the words and the picture, and then she would roar with laughter and slap the book and very often me too. It was fun for both of us at the beginning and Alice went ahead like nobody's business, but towards the middle of the book the boxes got bigger and the pictures fewer and the game became hard work. One morning I noticed Alice was looking pale and very glum. Her work in the kitchen was as good as usual but she dragged her feet listlessly and kept her eyes down even when I spoke to her. In the end I asked her what was the matter. At first I thought she wasn't going to answer, and then she burst out—

'That damn dog, Rover! All night I try to remember what he did when he jumped over the gate, but it was no good, I couldn't think. All night I try to remember and I got no sleep and now I'm tired Jacko, tired tired.' And to my dismay the immobility of her face broke for the first time, wrinkled up like a child's, and a tear slipped down her cheek.

'Look, Alice,' I said, feeling smaller and more helpless than I'd ever felt before, 'you don't want to worry about a silly old dog or a book or reading or anything', and I steered her into the corridor where the sharp kitchen clowns couldn't see her crying. 'Look, it's a lovely day. Let's have a holiday this afternoon. Let's pretend it's someone's birthday and have a good time. Oh damn, we can't, it's Sunday. What can we do, Alice?'' I waited while she struggled with her voice.

'You do something for me, Jacko? You take me to church to-night, eh?'

She was waiting for me after work. I took one look at her, closed my eyes, and opened them again carefully. She was looking happier and more excited than I had ever seen her, the despair and tiredness of the morning had quite gone, but so had the neat uniform. She was wearing a long pale sink garment that looked suspiciously like a nightgown, and round her neck she had tied a skinny mangy length of fur that even a manx cat wouldn't have looked at twice. But it was the hat that took my breath away. I had only seen such a hat in old photos or magazines about Edwardian England. It was a cream leghorn with a wide flopping brim, dark red roses round the crown, and a huge swaying moulting plume that almost hid her face. I didn't have a hat with me, but I reckoned Alice's would do for the two of us.

'I think I'll go home and see Auntie for a little while. I've got some money for her, and when I've fixed the farm I'll come back again.' She showed me her suitcase. 'I'll catch the 10.30 rail-car to-night.'

We were a little late for church, and as we crept in, all eyes swung in our direction, and stopped. That's right, I thought, take a good look, you'll never see another like it again. The summer evening sun streamed through the clear glass window and showed up mercilessly like strong electric light on an ageing face, all the drabness of the grey unadorned walls, the scratches on the varnished pews, the worn patches in the faded red carpets, the dust on the pulpit hang-ings, and the underlying greenness of the minister's old black suit.

'For all the saints, who from their labours rest', squeaked the small huddle of people like someone locked up in a freezer. I shifted my weight from one foot to the other and leaned against the pew in front of me. Ahmmmah, droned Alice happily above everyone else, except the big-bosomed purple-gowned over-pearled organist, who pulled all her stops out and clung to the top notes like a determined lover. Alice was holding her hymn book upside down.

After the service I took Alice home for supper. She seemed a little lost and rather subdued in our sitting-room, and sat stiffly on the edge of a chair with her knees together and her hands gripping each other in her lap. I made several unsuccessful attempts to put her at ease. and then I noticed she kept glancing sideways at the piano that stood in the corner.

'Would you like to play the piano, Alice?' I suggested. She jumped up immediately with a delighted grin and walked over to the music stool.

'Dadadaeedeeda', she sang on one note, and thumped up and down the keyboard. Fifteen minutes later, she turned to me. 'Pretty good, eh? I know plenty more. You like some more?' And she settled herself down for the rest of the evening before I could reply. My mother got up hastily and went out to the kitchen to make the supper. When the time came to go, Alice looked very solemn and I feared a repetition of the morning crisis. But I was wrong.

'I got something I want to show you, Jacko', she said. 'I've never shown anyone before.' And she handed me a folded piece of old newspaper. 'That's a picture of my uncle, He went away before my Auntie got me. My Auntie says he's the best man she ever knew and one day he'll come back and look after me and Auntie and get money to pay for the house and fix the farm. He's got a good kind face, eh Jacko?' I peered at the blurred photo. A group of men were standing behind a central figure sitting in the foreground, and underneath, the caption read—'This is the last photo to be taken of the late Lord Tweedsmuir, Governor-General of Canada, well known throughout the English-reading world as the novelist, John Buchan.' My mother looked over my shoulder.

'But surely you've made—' I stopped her with a sharp dig in the ribs.

'Yes, Alice', I said, 'he has got a good kind face, and I'm sure he'll come back.'

It was bright moonlight at the station. Small groups of people stood around waiting to see others off in a rail-car that looked much too small and toy-like for the long journey round the foot of the hills that lay to the north-west of the town. Alice gripped my arm till my eyes watered, and then she mistook that for something else and gripped harder still.

'Goodbye, goodbye,' she waved out of the window, the plume shedding feathers over everything near her. 'See you soon, Jacko, goodbye.'

But I never saw Alice again. I stayed on at the hospital for the rest of the summer and then went south to another job, and Alice hadn't returned before I left. Auntie must be sick, I thought, or maybe it's taking her longer to fix the farm than she expected. Several months later I received a letter from my mother. 'I've got some news for you,' she wrote. 'Alice came back not long ago, but her place in the kitchen was taken, so they found her a job in the laundry. She got on all right at first, but soon there was more of the old trouble, and when she nearly strangled one of the other women, things came to a head and they had her put away quietly. There was quite a bit about it in the paper, but of course she wouldn't know that. Poor Alice. Do you remember how she played the piano that night and showed us a photo of her "uncle"? And oh, my dear, till your dying day, will you ever forget that hat?'

RENATO AMATO   # Perspective
(1928—1964)

It had been raining for three days or four, and it was nearly Summer. At times I forgot and thought it was still Winter.

There were those pools of shining water, that night, at one o'clock, throwing up the reflections of the lights from the lamp-posts, and not a soul in the streets.

There was a beggar who, I said to myself, was a friend of mine. He didn't know it. I had seen him sleep for two nights on end, curled up on the step of a tobacconist's shop, under the rain, and now I had gone out again looking for him. Instead he was not there: he had gone and vanished who knows where. So, I stood in the rain and felt a secret desire to catch pneumonia or a rheumatic fever.

Pat pat on my shoulder.

I wanted to find that beggar and talk to him and give him a bed and take him home: he shouldn't have disappeared.

I crossed two or three shining streets: the water glowed against the lamp-posts; when I turned my face up to look at it, it fell on my

glasses and made me blind. Then I took my glasses off, and it seemed
to me that all those threads of water were just streamers of tiny candle lights in a church at Christmas. Without my glasses, I always
thought I was like a mole burrowing its way through the bowels of
a mountain.

Pat pat on my shoulder. You poor man, you.

First my friend, the beggar; then my blindness, when I didn't
want to be in a church or underground; and then, those other
reasons.

I mean those other reasons that nobody knows and that everybody, maybe, only talks about with himself, when there is no
one, not even a beggar, around. And even then, who knows....

I went on for a little while looking at everything through the tears
of my lenses. My shoes were full of water and my trousers shapeless
from the knees down.

'Oh' I said 'for a taxi.' I wanted one, as people want a home, or a
woman, or—what is everything in one thing—money.

First the beggar; then the rain; then the taxi. I bet I didn't know
myself what I wanted.

There were no taxis around. The houses were dark: I must have
started to think of all the people behind those wet walls and those
shuttered windows, and then my thoughts must have got lost among
a thousand undefined faces, here and there, going off in a thousand
different directions.

'Well,' I said 'where now?'

It started again. It was useless: I didn't really have any choice. I
had to go, clippety-clop, like an old horse who knows his way home
by instinct; I had to go to her, because—funny thing—she was my
home to me.

I knew I would find her busy, but I shut that out of my mind. She
would be moving from one to the other of those five bedrooms of
that place and I would be in one of them waiting for her. I only
hoped they still had a room vacant.

When I reached the small square that was criss-crossed by five
or six tramlines, I was nearly happy.

The building was huge; the great oaken door on the street was
locked and I opened the small postern with a pass-key. I bent and
went in and, while going in, I thought of myself with a shrug of
self-pity. What was the matter? Didn't I know she was a ....? But
when it came to that I couldn't say it. I couldn't even think it.

In the large carriage-way the only light came from a small electric
bulb burning in front of a statue of the Virgin Mary. She was standing on a small shelf in the wall, and, as usual, from pitying myself,

I went on to pity the people who have the Faith. Shrug shrug. We all need a walking stick: the girl up there needs this; I need her; and it struck me that nobody needed me. Not even the beggar, the one I said was a friend of mine.

You poor man, you, again.

I went up those damp steps; the girl was there, in a flat on the third floor.

I was cold.

It came out of my lips, unbelieving and slow: 'Who knows why she doesn't want to love me.'

And it was the same way I had asked myself why the beggar was not there and the taxi. But this time the question lingered in my mind with a sort of hopeful smile and a pain in my body. It was always like that. My friend who didn't matter; the taxi that wasn't there: they didn't matter, but this girl, oh, she did. And her love had to come.

I kept thinking that hers were only a woman's ways; and it didn't matter to me that one could sleep with her just by taking a room in her place and paying.

I went up slowly, all wet and dripping, feeling my way up those steps I knew by heart. I thought that I might be too late; that there would not be any rooms left. And, if that had been the case, I wouldn't have known what to do. I wouldn't have wanted to knock at another door of another of those flats in the building and find another girl who wasn't her. Because, in a way, if it was her as a woman that I wanted, it was also something else of her that I wanted and that only she had. I was ashamed of it: not so much of wanting to make love to her on one of those iron beds in one of those cold rooms, but rather of wanting that something else from her which I could not define very well in my mind and which I called 'love', because it was easy and seemed to make things clearer.

I used my knuckles to knock, instead of pushing the electric button, and waited. It was the same sort of waiting I had had on my first date with a girl and I thought that it was either because I was growing old or because I had lost my senses.

Then there was a shuffling of feet along the corridor, the inner door was opened, a man mumbled from behind the door.

'It's me. Can I have a room?'

'What a rotten time to bother people and wake them up,' he said.

'I couldn't make it earlier. Have you still got a room?'

'The last one,' he said.

He went behind the desk, turned the register towards me and got my money.

'Where is she?'

'I don't know. But I'll tell her you are here.'

'Yes. Hurry.'

And I felt at home, the old horse in the stable, as soon as I got into the room and started taking my clothes off. It didn't matter which of those five rooms it was, it was home to me, more than the place I had myself.

I got undressed and waited. I took my glasses off. I heard the man go to another room and say something. I knew that he was telling her about me and I knew she had been lying with another man, a salesman or a sailor, or a peasant from the country. I knew it; I knew it and, still, when I imagined her talk from behind a door just barely open, I didn't think of the other man in her bed or of what they had been doing. Every time I thought of her. I always saw her as if she were really mine and nobody else's, as if—in the world—there were only the two of us.

Then the bathroom door was opened; she ran the water, beyond the partition wall of my room, and I followed her movements and imagined her dry herself and spread talcum powder on her body, until the skin on her stomach became whiter and smoother and perfumed.

Then the bathroom door opened again and she came into my room, without knocking, wearing a light, cotton dressing-gown with a discoloured floral pattern.

'I am sorry I am late. It rained. Did I wake you up?'

'No.'

'Come here,' I said and took her by the hand and started leading her towards the bed and searched her body with my other hand, lifting open her gown and looking and grasping her and feeling at peace.

I could see her black hair fall down in short waves towards her shoulders and frame her quiet, unmoved profile as we went slowly together.

I never called her by name, I never spoke to her of the things one is supposed to speak about to one's sweetheart: I only wanted her to love me, because of a strange quality she had of looking like.... That was something I had never consciously stopped to analyse.

If my life depended on it, I would not be able to describe her. Perhaps I never cared about what she looked like or what her name was; perhaps that is why I always took my glasses off when I was with her. I could vaguely see her hair, sense the way she breathed and walked. But, more than actually knowing her, I had her there only to spark off my own imagination, so that her reality could be made to fit my idea of her.

I can't say why it was her that I needed more than anybody else. My love for her might have stemmed from the way she had of saying very little and seeming to know, at the same time, exactly what I expected her to do. I can't be sure, because I have never worked in a field and I have never followed a team of oxen dragging a plough and breaking the ground: but I have heard it said that they, the men who work the land, come to look upon oxen as indispensable partners, as precious, necessary helpers.

It must have been the same for me with this girl. And she was indispensable to me, for some odd reason, because, maybe, I am a man and this is what men are like.

We went towards the bed. It was cold: we walked over the parquet and I suddenly realized that we were going very slowly. I pushed her and I held her and she yielded to me and that was good, because, then, I forgot my misery, or my loneliness, or the long walk and the rain and the wait and the silly reasons for not wanting to come.

She lay down, relaxed, and turned her head to follow me as I went to the switch and put the light off. And when I went back, with my weight and the feel of my skin, and my hardness and my all-important urgency, I found her there, the way I remember I found the warmth of the earth, in the old Summers I spent in the country. I lay, then, with my face down, and stretched and felt the hay in the air, and—to me—the world was nothing but the piece of ground I stretched on, with my arms thrown open, as if on a Crucifix. And the'thing was the same; this girl was that piece of ground now, that made a graceful gesture to welcome me and shelter me and let me rest. She even sighed, the way the wind breathed over my head, through the branches of a tall mulberry tree.

She always sighed, to regret perhaps the fact of her own womanhood, and it was her sigh that maybe I did not want anybody else to hear. It seemed to open for me the doors to a world that, in my mind, had to be only mine. She was not, then, whatever she was, whatever we call girls anybody can have, but all the girls of this world, all the women I had ever wanted, a nameless, faceless symbol for all those others that I had met and lost or failed to notice or failed to hold.

When we parted, I kissed her face and I caressed her. She was there, as foreign and distant as a body from another planet, placid and untouched as if she had been a rock on a mountain slope.

Her body was cold. I imagined the colour of her skin, I felt the goose-pimples on her arm. 'Here. Cover yourself,' I said.

'I'm all right,' she said. 'I'll have to go soon.'

'Come on. Let's have a cigarette.'

'Just one.' I fumbled around and found my cigarettes on the bed-side table-top. The pack was damp. I lit one for her and one for myself, and saw her by the light of the match, still uncovered, still lying where I had pushed her. I didn't want to see her.

'Come on. Come under the blankets. You are cold.'

When she did not move or even seem to have heard me, I pulled her and forced her to move.

'Oh,' she said.

'Why don't you love me?' I said. But, more than the fact of her love, I wanted only her words: I only wanted her to say 'Yes, I love you. There is nobody else that matters.' Only those words, and I knew I would have never returned to see her; I knew I would have always had for her that desire of treating her as part of the darkness.

'Silly,' she said. 'Isn't this enough.'

'It doesn't touch you. You don't get involved.'

'Sure I do. I liked it, you know.'

'No; you didn't,' I said. And that was maddening. Because it was the knowledge I thought I had of what she thought, that I wanted her to prove to me. It was maddening to see that something could happen which I could not understand.

'If you did, why don't you say you love me?'

'You men are crazy,' she said. 'You come and want things and keep on wanting things and every time you get then you don't know what to do with them.'

I lay there and I was stunned by what she had said, because I couldn't see how she could know. What was me and my secret seemed to be as open to her as if I had told her myself.

'But there are things that matter,' I said.

'Like love?'

'Yes, yes,' I lied.

'You talk like a book,' she said. 'You're nice, though. You make me die every time.' She inhaled her smoke and the tip of the cigarette glowed and then she breathed noisily out.

'What about the man who runs the place?' I said suddenly. And I would have liked it to sound very angry, very manly, very jealous.

'What about him?'

'Do you love him?'

'God, no. What a funny idea. That would ruin the business.'

'But he does it, docsn't he?'

'Just a fancy, every now and then,' she said: 'but I don't treat him different from any other customer. He is good to me, you know.'

Now I wished she were silent again. She stirred and lifted herself up and stretched her body over mine to reach for the ash-tray on the bed-table and I felt that same thing again and I put my arms around her.

'I love you very much,' I said.

'Let me go now. I'd better go.'

'No.'

I let her go: that soft, warm body of hers that was really all that mattered.

'All right. I'll wait,' I said.

She went out and the room was again cold and I started to wait. She always played some trick on me; she always told me lies; she promised something and then she forgot about it and apologized with a silly sort of laugh.

I had never seen her when she lied, because her lies were told when I could not see her, and I never knew if lies—had I been able to see her—could have been read on her face.

I knew she would not be back as soon as she had said. There were other doors to be opened and other things to be done. But that was something I didn't want to remember.

The rain was going on outside. Falling with a dull sort of laving sound, running down the windowpanes and making no noise.

I remembered the beggar, whom I had missed, and I thought that I had never really wanted to meet him: one is charitable out of a sense of frustration, only when one can't do the things one wants to.

For the things one wants to do, like this thing here, with this girl, one might even at times give up the things one loves most: like the girl I wanted to marry, who'd said she was too nice to be a woman to me.

Which would be a childish thing to do.

Although, what was the difference been this girl and that. When I took my glasses off, I only saw a woman's hair. And whether it was this woman's or that other one's, it didn't really matter.

What had never changed was 'Why don't you love me?'

An unmanly, plaintive way of being a man.

If one thinks of it.

I heard the shuffling of feet in the corridor and I thought 'this time she told the truth. Here she comes;' instead, it was the bathroom door that opened again.

Was she taclum-powdering herself? She always carried that baby-smell with her. Stronger than any man's smell I'd ever smelled on trams and buses and trains and in the country, among people who never wash, not even when they die.

And then I was floating like that, from one thing to another, thinking, suddenly, why things like this—people say—aren't any good, since they take the madness out of you and make you fit ideas in some sort of perspective that wasn't there before.

What else is there?

God? Money?

Give me this any day. God can wait; I can't.

And I don't know if it was God that heard me, but the person in the bathroom thundered away and, really, it was just as if the voice of God had shaken me up. Then the rasp in a man's throat before the spitting.

I must have been dozing.

The water flushed down the drain, and I shivered.

I would have run away now, if it had not been for her promise that she would be back soon.

And, in a sense, I did run away, because I fell asleep and didn't wake up until she came into the room again and slid into my bed and nudged me.

There was a hint of grey in the room, by then, filtering through the slats of the shutters, and I could hear the clanging of the early trams coming up from the streets.

I was on her again, with the same hunger as before and a sort of revengeful spirit that only a man can feel and made me want to break things up and pry and destroy. As if I were trying to say something to her, that I could not say in any other way.

Only when I heard her sob, I said 'Why don't you marry me?'

She was silent for a while and I said it agian.

Then, slowly, the quality of her sobbing changed. There still was a heaving in her body, but it had quickened now.

'What is it?' I said.

'I am laughing,' she said.

'What for?'

'Because I know you.'

'Sure you do.'

'How long have you been asking me to marry you?'

'I don't know. I've been coming here for quite a while now....'

'I know that. How long would you say?'

'A year, maybe.'

'Maybe,' she said. 'Every fortnight, for a year, you've been coming here at one o'clock in the morning and paid your money and had your fun....'

'No, no,' I said. 'Not fun....'

'Call it what you like. But you know something?'

'What?'

'I am a new girl. I've only been here two months.'

And she laughed aloud this time and I had to think to understand what that meant, because she didn't seem to be talking sense to me. What did she mean?

Why didn't she stop laughing?

'Shut up,' I said, and I shook her and, if she hadn't stopped, I would have strangled her.

'Well?' she said.

'You're lying. You think you're being funny.'

'No. Look,' she said, 'what's my name. Do you know that?'

'Betty,' I said.

'No.'

'Of course it is.' But by then I had lost whatever conviction I might have had. I only wanted to try and find a reason, for my own peace of mind, why she should be acting like that.

Because it was an act.

'You know?' she said. 'The chap who runs the place told me about you. He's had three other girls in here, before me, and you never noticed. I didn't believe it; I even made a bet with him.'

'You're joking.'

'No. I wouldn't have told you, if I didn't think it is for your own good.'

I couldn't see why her telling me should be for my own advantage, and I didn't care. But what I resented was the tone of her voice, the implications that I could draw from her words. I couldn't bear the thought that she would think herself in a position to help me, when, all the time, I had wanted her to give me her love so that I could protect her. No: it wasn't like that. It would have taken more scavenging, more fingering and probing than I was prepared to do, more self-baring than I thought advisable, to find out, or, better, to express clearly what was behind my love for her love.

'What do you know?' I said. 'What do you think you know about me? And what does the boss know? And what do you think you are?'

'Take it easy,' she said. 'You think you're just yourself: the only one, nobody else like you. I know better. If nothing else, I ought to know men, oughtn't I?'

That was what I didn't want: I didn't want her to know me, the way I didn't want to know her. It was my privacy, and she was robbing me of it. And I was there, naked inside and out, looking like something that was me, in the hands of this girl; something I could vaguely recognize, something vaguely familiar and, at the same time, something I'd never come face to face with before.

And it was, also, as if she had taken the crutches away from under my arms and I were hesitating on the verge of a step I knew I couldn't make.

'All the sailors who come here,' she said, 'want to marry the girl they've done over.'

'I am not a sailor.'

'All the drunks.'

'I am not.'

'They've got their dreams. They think they are big; they think they're generous.'

'I am me. And you don't know me.'

'Still want to marry me? Still want me to love you?' she said.

'Go away,' I said. 'Go away. Don't bother me.'

'Next time you see me, you'll know who I am, won't you?' She slid out and walked quietly towards the door and it was then, in the light of the day that had come into the room, that I thought of the quality in her—in them—that appealed to me. She was, to my glassless eyes, the usual indistinct shape she had always been: her back broad and solid; her head slightly bent forward as if she were pulling who knows what heavy load; her flanks moving alternately at each step she took. And there was not a ripple anywhere. But, there it was: the thing I wanted a woman to have. It was the unstirring submission of an animal sent to pasture in the fields, to munch its cud unknowing and unruffled, warm and heavy, useful, a whole genus away.

'I'll never see you again,' I cried after her. 'You're only a....' but, when she turned towards me, I couldn't say it. 'I'll never see you again.'

'See if I care,' she said.

When she slammed the door behind her, I found myself frozen in a sitting position, suddenly aware of all the waking noises in the place and suddenly trying to remember which were the words that I had said and which were those that I had only thought, wondering desperately whether anybody had overheard me.

I crept down under my covers and pulled the blankets over my head and waited for the time when everybody had gone.

Down there, in there, I was again safe.

'Never again,' I said to myself. 'Never again.' I always said that: every morning I woke up in one of those rooms in the place, I always make that resolution and I always forgot it ten days or two weeks later. But, now, there would be no longer any reason to break it. What was the girl's name? How could I have thought I loved her, when all the time it wasn't her?

I dressed slowly, trying not to make any noise, and walked out on the corridor, with my eyes on the floor —so that nobody could see me—and down the stairs, to go and look for my....

NOEL HILLIARD
(*b.* 1929)

A Piece of Land

I

The station bell rang. 'All seats please!' the guard shouted. Two Maoris gulped their tea and, leaving the cups on the window-ledge, swung on to the platform of a second-class carriage. The engine hissed steam.

They sat in opposite seats beside an open window. Both wore tight suits badly in need of a pressing, and their ties sat uncomfortably under fixed collars; plainly they were used to wearing nothing but a singlet, dungarees and hobnailed boots six days a week.

'They don't stop long enough you can cross the street for a beer, eh?' said Mutu Samuel, the larger and older of the two.

'Hah!' Joe Tuki grinned. 'I suppose they frightened their railway cafeteria what-you-call it might miss out on the takings.'

The train gathered speed. They rested their elbows on the sill, sharing a packet of tobacco, listening to the urgent ping-ping-ping of crossing bells.

'I could do with a good feed,' Mutu said.

'Me too. Boy! they had some *kai* up there at that *tangi*. Stretch my stomach!' Joe patted his belly. 'Take it a month to get back to normal, I suppose.'

'It's a long time since I had a *hangi* chicken.'

'Long time since I had anything at all out of a *hangi*. You see that pig before they cut it up? It must've been two-fifty pounds easy.'

'Good to have a bit of taro again, too.'

'We should've brought a root with us, try to grow it at the mill.'

'No good up there. Soil too dry, I think. All that pumice.'

The clash of couplings and the hammer of wheels roared through the carriage as the guard opened the door in a flurry of wind, clicking his clippers. 'All tickets for Turama, please. All tickets for Turama Junction.'

'That's us,' Joe said. 'You got the tickets?'

Mutu took a chafed old wallet from his inside pocket and flicked among papers. 'Yeah, got them.'

'Thank you. . . .' The guard clipped, biting his tongue. 'I'll hang on to these now, if you don't mind.'

'Okay, chief.'

The guard swayed down the aisle: 'All tickets for Turama. . . .'

'That was the last station before home, eh?'

'Yes, the last.' Mutu put his wallet away. 'I won't be sorry to get home, either.'

'Me too. Get some hot *kai* into me. Sandwiches and soft drink, they only bloat you. Like a cow in clover.'

Mutu leaned on the sill. 'Funny thing, you know, when we get home we're glad to be there. That's home. And yet people ask you, Where you been these last few days? you'll tell them, Oh, I've been up home. . . up home for the *tangi*.'

'Yes, you don't know where to call your home. Up there, down here. Both home, I suppose.'

The train crossed a viaduct; underneath were willows and a muddy creek.

'It looks different up there now, Joe,'

'Hardly know it for the same place.'

'All the trees I remember, they're chopped down. I had a garden there, one time, back of the old cow-shed, when I was a kid. Only a few thistles there now. You never tell there was ever a garden there.'

Joe nodded. 'You remember that creek use to be near the big ngaio in the pig-paddock? I caught an eel there once, fat as a car tyre. Now it's only a little spring, that creek. Hardly even any water cress. They going to dump a load of rocks on it, cover it right up. Too much bog in the winter, Wiki says.'

'I suppose you go away from a place, you expect to find everything the same when you go back, even after ten. . . fifteen years.'

Smuts from the engine whipped through the window. They sat in silence, each with his own picture of the vanished idyll.

Suddenly Joe leaned forward. 'You hear what old Paikea Te Pano said about us having land left to us up there?'

Mutu did not respond to his urgency. 'Yes, I heard him. I always knew I was going to get some land, but I never knew how much or where abouts.'

'I never knew about me, being only a half-brother, you know. Be good to go back up there on to your own land, eh, Mutu?'

'Be good, all right.' He tossed his open hand. 'But we don't know where it is, anything about it. Old Paikea didn't know.'

'I heard him say there was timber on it. You hear him say that? You remember when we was all in the whare at the back after we come home from the church? He said it then. He said there was timber on it.'

'I never heard him say that.' Mutu chuckled. 'But I noticed he was full as a bull in no time.'

'He'd know, though, just the same, full or not. He knows all about the land up there, all the families, who's got what.'

'What did he say?'

'He said you and me both got land left to us, and there's timber on it.'

'Timber!'

'Yes, timber.' Joe paused for a moment. 'That's something we know a bit about eh? I been in mills ...let me see ... I suppose about eighteen years now, you take all the different ones, not counting the war. I wouldn't be much good on the farming, now, I been away from it for too long. But timber, that's different.'

'Timber, eh! If there's enough of it we might be able to mill it and sell it. You and me, Joe. Mill it and sell it.'

'Easy, once you get the gear, some big company back you. Or the Maori Affairs, they might. These firms I work for, different years, they might back me.'

'Get the gear, and we mill our own timber! I think the Maori Affairs back us, all right.'

'Buy a truck, cart it out.' Joe made a sweep with his hand. 'You and me in the bush, Mutu. Working for ourselves, eh!'

'Be great, all right. I never worked for myself in my life before. And we get enough timber to make houses for ourselves, Joe.'

'You bet! My axe...it'll work better for me then! Build our own houses with our own wood. Don't need too much money to cover yourself, that way.'

Mutu creased his forehead, baffled by his own obtuseness. '*Pai kare*! when I heard old Paikea say that about the land, I never took much notice. Never thought!'

'Same with me! I said to myself, I suppose it's only a strip of someone's farm, can't do nothing with it. But when he said about the timber....'

Mutu was suspicious. 'You absolutely certain, now, he said there was timber on this land? You sure he wasn't talking about someone else's place? Did he say what kind?'

'No, nothing. He only just said what I told you.'

'Well...we have to write to the Land Court, find out.'

Joe held on, fiercely. 'Old Paikea wouldn't say that if it wasn't right! He was full when he said it, but I never heard of him saying anything that wasn't right, whether he's full or not.'

'We should've thought to ask them before we came away. Ask all the old people, see what they know about it. Did you ask any of them?'

'No, I never thought. It's only since we got talking about it now, I see what there might be in it for us. No, I never even thought. I was too busy meeting everyone, trying to remember the nâmes.'

'The same with me. It's no good, you go away from your people a long time, when you go back you got to *titaha* your brains, try to remember.'

'Yes, you feel a stranger with your own bones. You forget all the old ways. Me, now. . . there I go walking into the meeting-house with my shoes on. Someone have to tell me to take them off. A man feel silly when someone have to tell him a thing like that.'

'I forget, too,' Mutu said. 'There's the old *kaumatuas* talking away to me in Maori and I don't know half what they're saying. I got to bob my head, you know, make out I understand.'

Joe leaned forward, his face alight, and thumped Mutu's thigh. 'But if we go back up there, Mutu, go on to land of our own, we won't be strangers any more.'

'No. We'll be a family again.'

Something in the ring of the word *family* moved them deeply. They sat in silence looking through the window. Paddocks, rows of poplar, cabbage-trees beside a raupo swamp, a corn-crib needing new nails.

Mutu touched his chest with his fingertips. 'Look at me, Joe. All my life I been going from place to place, living in rented houses. I never had nothing. People say to me. Where you from? . . . I don't know what to tell them. Other Maoris, you ask them where they come from, they'll tell you straight away. Up North, or East Coast, or Down South, wherever it is. They ask me, I tell them where I was born, but I don't feel like that's my place, you know?'

'I know. The only time you ever go home is when someone dies. That's no good.'

'See, I been living away from there since I was a kid. I don't feel like Matiti's my home. You ask me, Where you from? I might tell you Auckland, or Kopuawhara, or Te Kuiti, any other place I've lived, wherever I've worked, where I got friends. I'm at home where my wife's people are, just as much. All those places I rented a house, they're all homes to me. They still my home, even if they don't belong to me.'

Joe nodded. 'Same with me and Hemaima's people. We lived there three, four years after we got married. There's her place, that's a home. There's Matiti, that's a home, you might as well say. There's the mill, Turama, that's a home now.'

Mutu shook his head. 'It's no good. I want my kids to know they belong somewhere. People say to my kids when they grow up, Where you from? they can say Matiti! and they know that's right, that's the dirt under their feet when they grew up. They know that's their place, the family is there, the old poeple, Polly and me. Wherever they go, they know they can always come back. Not like their old man, don't know where he's from, can't make up his mind what to tell people.'

The train slowed down past a surfacing gang. In the seat across the aisle a Maori woman slipped her breast into her baby's mouth. Heavy bush spread over the distant hills.

'Great, to get a bit of land up there, Mutu.'

'Great, all right. You got a bit of land, you know you're safe. You own something, they can't touch you.'

'When we get home, you write to the Land Court, find out about that land.'

Mutu rubbed the back of his head, frowning. 'I'm not much on this writing, Joe. Never was. My teacher call me blockhead at school.'

Joe considered. 'I know what. See old Waitangi Matthews, he's a J.P., something high up. Get him to write the letter for us.'

Mutu shook his head. 'That's no good. He's East Coast, he don't know the *hapus* up our way. He might want me to tell him all the ins and outs. Anyway, it's our land. I can try to do it myself. Work it all out, and then we get Hinemoa to write it.'

'All right. We both think about it, you and me, try to remember all we can, and I come up to your house one night, and we work out what we going to put. We both write the letter.'

The whistle shrilled three long blasts. Joe looked out of the window. 'Here's the junction now. Same old water tank!'

'We get a taxi at the station. Sling my overcoat, Joe.'

'I hope Hemaima got something hot on the stove.'

A cold, damp wind blew off the bush through the godforsaken little station. Torn posters flapped. Mutu pulled on his overcoat. 'Be great to get out of this dump,' he said.

II

Hemaima Tuki spread over a couch in the Samuel living-room.

Between her large knees a two-year-old boy clad in only a short
singlet sat playing with cotton-reels on a string. Polly Samuel was
squeezed in beside her, knitting. Through the open window from
the mill across the paddock came the ringing whine of saws tearing
through *totara*. The room smelt of boiled-over milk, meat on the
turn, burnt fat. Photographs, most without mounts or frames,
covered the mantelpiece: heads of old folk, smiling groups with
arms around each other's shoulders, one of Mutu holding a large
eel on a twist of wire. In the middle of the floor a sullen, pretty girl
of fifteen sat at the table fiddling with the shuttle of a treadle machine.

'Hinemoa, set the table,' Polly commanded.

The girl did not look up. 'Aw, Mum, I want to do my frock.'

'Do it after! Get all that stuff off the table. And give the fire a
stoke.'

'Aw!' The girl tossed her hair back and pouted. Very slowly she
rolled up the material and pushed the machine into the front bedroom.

'Girls....' Polly fussed. 'They get about fourteen, fifteen, into
high school, they start to get ideas about themselves.'

'Me, I sometimes wonder if they're better when they're small or
when they're big,' Hemaima said. 'When they're little you think
you can't wait till they grow up and get out from under your feet.
And when they grow up they get so cheeky, so full of themselves,
you wish they were little again.'

'I think they're best round about four. When they're two, three,
you can't seem to do nothing with them.'

'That's just my Jackie,' Hemaima ruffled the hair of the boy
between her knees. 'You tell him not to do something, the minute
your back is turned he go and do it. And Joe's no help to me these
days. Since he got back from that *tangi* he's been talking nothing
except this land they supposed to have at Matiti. He sits there at
night just staring into space.'

'The same with Mutu. I say something to him, he says Eh? I say
it again, he says Eh? What's that? He never even went to the football
on Saturday.'

Hemaima nodded towards the mantelpiece. 'He be pleased when
he see that letter.'

Polly smiled. 'Joe too. I suppose they'll go straight off to the pub.'

'Don't blame them, too. I be glad to get out of this dump!'

'Yeah, eh! I been living in mill houses ... let me see...oh, I
don't know. Since the war, anyway.'

'I hope your land and our land is close together. Then we just
be able to pop in like we do now.'

'What sort of house you going to get Joe to build for you fellows?'

'Well, I want three bedrooms, and if there's any more kids we can build on. I'm going to have a great big sitting-room with an open fire for me to cook my bread. A big room where all the people can fit in when they come to see us.'

'These mill houses, there's no room for you all to get together.'

'Be good to have a big room with a wide fireplace. Build the house around the fireplace. These fellows here, they think you only have a fire for cooking. They don't know, eh?'

'They don't know! These houses, they're all the same.'

Hemaima spread her arms. 'I want a big wide fire to do my cooking. Bake the bread like my grandmother use to. Joe can make one, with dirt.'

'I wonder how much land we'll have for a garden?'

'If yours is close to ours, we can join it all together. Get the plough in to turn it over. Save all that digging.'

'Have fruit trees too. No more shop fruit, all bruises.'

'We get a horse, the kids can go for rides on the sand like *we* use to.'

'And the way it flicks when you pat it, eh!'

They thought of when they were young and bare-footed and eager, in places far away.

Hemaima said, 'Joe's going to buy a truck to cart this timber they're going to cut. And at the weekend we can put the kids on the back and go for a ride to the beach. Take our lunch. Bring home driftwood for the fire.'

'I saw some nice blue check stuff in the Farmers catalogue. I think I'll buy that for my curtains.'

Jackie eased clear of his mother's knees and began to pick at the frayed end of the mat. Hemaima reached over and cuffed him.

'I'm going to have inlaid lino,' she said. 'No more mats and sacks! We can cure some sheepskins, dye them, like my mother use to. Nice on the floor if you got a baby just crawling.'

'If we live close together we can share the same carshed.'

'Send an order to the shop every week. Live out of the garden. Plenty of corn! *Kumaras!*'

'We keep a couple of cows. And some fowls.'

'Joe says there's a creek there. We can keep ducks in the creek. I like duck eggs in a cake.'

'You never see duck eggs here, eh? And plenty water cress, *puha, tawharas*. There might be some flax!'

'A long way to the pub. I suppose Joe start making home brew again.'

'Eeeeh! I suppose him and Mutu make a brew together.'

'Be good!' Hemaima beamed. 'Get everyone in on Saturday night! Big room, everybody got somewhere to sit down. Big fire going!'

'If they make plenty money out of this timber, after a while we might get a fridge. Make ice blocks for the kids.'

'No more rent to pay!'

'Get a great big radio. Plenty of records.'

'Nobody to moan...complain if you make some noise.'

The thrill of having something good to look forward to was new and strange.

Polly said, 'I been telling everyone we going away since Mutu said about this land.'

'I bet they all jealous!'

'Course! I don't think there's anyone living here that isn't dying to get out of it.'

'Great, to get away from the bush, out into the country again. See the sun come up in the morning. Get your washing dry! There's not a thing in our house that hasn't been damp since the day we got here.'

'It's the same with all our things. When we go to Matiti I'll get Mutu to make me one of these clotheslines turns around in the wind.'

'The kids can go to a Maori school. This school here, I don't know what they doing half the time. Young Sonny don't seem to know nothing.'

'I know! Same with Willie. If Mutu does all right out of this timber, we can send Hinemoa to one of these big girls' schools in Auckland—Queen Victoria, some place like that.'

'Beauty boy!' cried Hinemoa in the next room.

'What you doing in there?' Polly called.

'What you think? My frock for tonight. You kicked me off the table so I'm in here on the bed.'

Polly lowered her voice. 'Do her the world of good to get away from here,' she confided. 'What's there for a girl in a place like this? Nothing! They sit around playing cards, talking boys half their time. What a collection of boys they got here! Do her the world of good to get out of it.'

'Ae,' Hemaima nodded. 'Did you hear what happened about Bella's girl....'

Mutu sauntered across the paddock and eased through the wire of the back fence. 'Willie!' he shouted. 'Get these shoes off the step!'

'Hullo, here comes the old man,' Polly said. 'In a bad mood too.'

Willie, greasing the chain of his' upturned bike, made no move. 'They only my sandshoes.'

'You leave them here for people to tread on, you get a hiding next time!'

'They only my *sand*shoes. . . .'

'Nemmine! You shift them!'

He left his boots at the door and came in. '*Tena koe*, Hemaima. Good to see you! Where's Joe?'

'Down the pub, I suppose.'

'That's where I should be, too. *Pai kare*! I'm hungry!'

'There's a bit of brisket there in the pot,' Polly said.

Mutu peered at her. 'Eh? Where's those mussels?'

'We ate them.'

'What?'

'Well, what you think we going to do with them? Sit here all day look at them?'

'By . . . my stomach been talking to me all day about those mussels. You leave some for me?'

'Try in the safe.'

Mutu opened the safe and lifted out a chipped enamel dish. 'Eh! Just as well!'

He took a knife from the drawer and sat at the table, screwing the mussels open and sucking up the juice before eating.

'What you worried about that for, man?' Polly teased. 'You get this place of ours at Matiti, you can go to the beach every day if you want to. Get plenty mussels...*paua*....'

'...*kina*...*pipi*...flounder....' said Hemaima.

'Beauty! Toheroa, too, if we're lucky. Use to be lot there one time. You had plenty these mussels, Hemaima?'

'I did. Good, too. I been feeling a bit sick lately, I needed something salty.'

'No good to go without fresh sea food too long,' Mutu said. 'That's the trouble way inland here. These the first mussels we seen... about a year, I suppose.'

Hinemoa called, 'Show Dad the letter, Mum.'

Polly sprang up. 'Letter today from the Land Court.'

'Eh! Where's it?'

'It's there! You think we hiding it?'

'I don't mind you hiding my bills, you can do what you like with those things. But my *good* mail, you have to give it to me when I come in.'

'I wasn't hiding it, man!'

'Well, tell me what's it say.'

'I can't read it too good. They got very flash language, those Land Court fellows. Get Hinemoa to read it.'

'Hine!'

'Coming!' The girl strolled into the room, looking bored. 'What now?'

'Read that letter to your father!' Polly commanded.

'I read it once.'

'Well, read it again.'

'Can't you tell him what's in it?'

'Do as you're told!'

'All right....' She shrugged, and took a long envelope from behind the tea tin on the mantelpiece. She unfolded the letter.

'Mister Mutu Samuel. House five, Turama Timber Company, Turama Junction. Dear Sir. We are in receipt of your letter of the twenty-fifth June....'

'They must think a man is silly, don't know when he write his own letter,' Mutu said.

'...and have to advise that our records show that there is land registered in your name in the Matiti district as described.'

'That means you got land there all right,' Hemaima said.

'Beauty, eh! We got some land!'

Hinemoa went on: 'Investigations are now being conducted by the Search Officer with a view to establishing the extent, location and monetary value of same. You will be advised in due course. As requested, we shall also investigate the holdings of Mister Hohepa Teihoterangi Tuki. Yours faithfully.'

'That means they know you got land but they don't know where it is or how much of it or what it's worth,' Hemaima explained. 'I think Joe got some too or they wouldn't say they going to go into it. They going to have a good look and find out.'

'How long that going to take?'

'It doesn't say in the letter,' Hinemoa said.

'It might take years,' said Polly.

'That last part means they're going to write to you again when they find out all about it,' Hinemoa said, folding the letter up.

Mutu toyed with the mussels. 'You think I ought to take a day off, go through on the bus and see that fellow wrote the letter?'

'That won't do no good,' Polly said. 'You don't know any more about it than he does. Probly less.'

'He might want to know the names of all the different ones, way back.'

'You don't know them yourself! You don't even know your own *whakapapa!*'

'I do!' Mutu pondered, hurt. 'I know a lot, anyway. Might surprise you just how many I *do* know. Make it easier for that fellow if he got someone there to help him find his way through all the different *hapus.*'

'They know!' said Polly. 'They got it all written down, they look it up. This one and that one, owned this piece and that piece. They got it all written down.'

Mutu opened a mussel and leaned back in his chair, sucking. 'Anyway, we got some land. That's the main thing!'

'We have to wait now till they write to us,' Polly said.

'Then we go to town!' Hemaima whooped. 'Get a keg, an eighteen!

'Crayfish supper!'

'Boy!' Mutu grinned. 'That's going to be a night to give them something to moan about!'

III

Hinemoa got a lift from the turn-off to the shops on the back of Johnny Herewini's motor-bike and stood talking with him at the corner until she saw one of the high school teachers coming along the road. 'See you later,' she said, and walked with great nonchalance past the teacher into the post office.

She recognized the letter and scuttled out. 'Johnny! Johnny! Run me home, quick!'

At the turn-off she rushed up the gravel path calling 'Mum! Mum! The letter's here!'

Polly thrust her head through the kitchen window. 'Give it here, quick!' She peered at the printing in the corner. 'Yes, that's the Land Court writings on the outside. Willie!'

Willie was sitting on the doorstep chiselling the end of a piece of four-by-two into the bow of a boat. 'Yeh?'

'Run to the mill, get your father and Uncle Joe, quick! Tell them the letter's here, to come straight home.

'The whistle hasn't gone yet.'

'Nemmine the whistle! Off you go! Run your fastest!'

'Right!' Willie sprang over the back fence and raced across the paddock towards the mill.

'Hine, run next door and. get Hemaima. No...hold on...I'll call her.' She went through to the end bedroom, opened the window, and called, 'Hemaima! *Haere mai kia tere!*'

They could hear Jackie bawling and screaming, 'Mum! Mum!'

The window opened, 'Yes? Shut up, Jackie! You want a smack? You calling me, Polly?'

'Come over, quick! The letter's here!'

'Ehoa! Hold on a minute!'

Polly and Hinemoa stood in the kitchen looking at the letter.

'You think Willie take long to get to the mill, Hine?'

'He should be there by now. I heard Dad say they'd be working outside today.'

Hemaima padded in, feet bare, holding Jackie over her shoulder. 'Boy! you make me move! Jackie, I don't know what's wrong with him, he's been wanting me to hold him all day.'

'Here's our letter!'

'Let me see!' Hemaima felt its fatness, held it up to the light. 'We open it, eh?'

'No fear! Mutu get wild! We wait for them. Willie's gone for them, shouldn't be long.'

Heavy footsteps boomed in the porch and Mutu burst through the door, sweating. 'Where's this letter, eh? Where's it?'

Joe collapsed puffing on the couch. 'Boy! the coach see me coming across that paddock, he put me out on the wing next Saturday, I think.'

Mutu opened the envelope and unfolded the stiff grey pages. 'Here, Hine, you read it. I can't get my tongue round all them big words.'

Hinemoa took it, her hands trembling. 'Mister Mutu Samuel....'

'You can miss all that stuff out. Get to the land part.'

'Hold on, then...have to advise as follows...let me see...lot of funny stuff here, they've got it all spread out cross the page. File No. 632/KW...Mutu Tamahere Samuel...Parish of Hoe-O-Matiti... Plan No. 8435...approximate number of owners, ninety-four... your share one point five.'

'They mess about a fair bit,' Joe said.

'How much land is it?' Mutu demanded. 'Does he tell you that?'

'They've got it here now...a total of two-and-a-half perches.'

'What's that perches?' Polly asked. 'They talking about a fowlhouse?'

Hinemoa looked at her condescendingly, turning down her lips. 'That's form three stuff,' she said. 'A perch is a measure, about thirty square yards, I think.'

'How many perches he say?' Mutu asked.

'Two and a half.'

Mutu shook his head, mumbling. 'That's to say ...sixty...seventy...five...say seventy-five square yards. I wonder how many feet?'

Hinemoa said: 'It says here, to a total value of seven shillings and sixpence.'

There was silence for ten seconds. They looked at the floor.

'Seven and six,' Polly whispered.

Mutu muttered to himself, 'From the goal line halfway to the twenty-five, say...'

Joe began to laugh. He clasped his thighs and threw his head back, roaring louder, his tight paunch jigging. He coughed, showering spit, and slackened into giggles.

Mutu eyed him without smiling. 'What you laughing at, man?'

Joe shouted: 'I got more than that between my toes!'

Mutu grinned. 'All right, then, See how much *you* got!'

Joe, gulping breath, waved his hand: 'Read it, Hine.'

'They've got it on a separate sheet. The property of Mister Hohepa Teihoterangi Tuki....'

'Never mind that lot number and the rest of it.'

'File...share...owners...Here we are: a total of nine perches ...total unimproved value of one pound two shillings.'

There was silence. Joe's mouth grew firm.

'*Pai kare!*' he whispered.

Mutu looked at him with profound amusement. 'Come on!' he invited. 'Laugh now!'

'*Pai kare!*' Joe said.

Polly was quietly sobbing, dabbing her eyes with her apron. Hemaima, bewildered, stroked Jackie's hair.

'That's to say,' said Mutu, 'that's to say yours and mine together be about the size of the tennis court.'

'Big enough to bury us in,' Joe said.

'*Ka tika tau!*'

'What about all that timber?' Hemaima asked.

'I spose there's a fence going over it,' said Joe. 'Old Paikea must be talking about the battens in the fence, I think.'

Hinemoa said: 'They've got the man's name here at the end. The Search Officer.'

'He have to search bloody hard to find that lot!' Mutu roared. They laughed.

Mutu turned to Polly. 'What you blubbering there for, woman? Where's those jars?'

'What jars?'

'What jars you think? Half-gallon flagons, two of them, mine.'

'In the washhouse.'

Mutu took a deep breath and drew himself up straight. 'Hine.

he commanded, 'put that letter away. Go to the washhouse, give them jars a good rinse-out, put them in the kit. Use cold water. I don't want you to crack them.'

'Willie can do it. . . .'

'Do as you're told!'

She flounced out.

Joe grinned. 'We got nearly thirty bob we never had before, Mutu.'

'Ae. We ought to buy an art union ticket, something. We might do some good. Come on, Joe.'

'Where you fellows going?' Hemaima asked.

'Where do you think!' Joe snapped.

Mutu shouted, 'Hurry up with those jars, Hine!'

'They're ready!'

'Come on, then, Joe.'

'Don't you fellows be long!' Hemaima said, Jackie started to cry. 'Shut up, Jackie! You want a good hard smack?'

Polly had dried her face and pushed her hair back. She called, 'Willie! Go and cut the wood!'

'I cut it!' the boy snarled. He had gone back to working on the four-by-two.

'Cut some more, then. I want to do the washing tomorrow.'

Mutu and Joe had turned from the gravel path into the main road. Polly put her head through the window and called, 'Mutu! Send one of them jars back in the taxi! For us?'

He looked back over his shoulder without stopping. 'What for? We won't be long.'

'See that you come straight home, then!'

'Bring us an ice block, Dad,' Willie called from the wood heap.

MAURICE GEE   **The Losers**
(*b.* 1931)

Dinner was over at the Commercial Hotel and the racing people were busy discussing prospects for the final day. The first day's rac-

ing had been interesting; some long shots had come home, and a
few among the crowd in the lounge were conscious as they talked
of fatter, heavier wallets hanging in their inside pockets. Of these
the happiest was probably Lewis Betham who had, that day, been
given several tips by trainers. The tips had been good ones, but it
would not have mattered if they had been bad. The great thing was
that trainers had come up and called him by his first name and told
him what to back. He thought he had never been so happy, and he
told his wife again how the best of these great moments had come
about.

'He said to me: "Lew, that horse of mine, Torrid, should run a
good one, might be worth a small bet." He's a cunning little rooster,
but he's straight as they come, so I just said to him: "Thanks, Arnold"—I call him Arnold—and I gave him a wink. He knew the
information wouldn't go any further. See? I didn't have to tell him.
And then Jack O'Neill came up and said: "Do you know anything,
Arnold?" and he said: "No, this is a tough one, Jack. They all seem
to have a show." He's cunning all right. But he is straight, straight as
a die. He'd never put you wrong. So I banged a fiver on its nose.
Eleven pound it paid, eleven pound.'

Mrs. Betham said: 'Yes, dear. Eleven pounds eleven and six.'
She sipped her coffee and watched the people in the lounge. She
was bored. Lew hadn't introduced her to anyone and she wished
she could go out to the pictures, anywhere to get away from the
ceaseless jabber of horse names. None of them meant anything to
her. She realized how far apart she and Lew had grown. If someone
came up and murmured Torrid in her ear she would just stare at
him in amazement. But this whispering of names was the only
meaning Lew seemed to demand from life these days. He had
always dreamed of owning a horse and she had not opposed him.
She had discovered too late he was entering a world with values of
its own, a world with aristocracy and commoners, brahmans and
untouchables. He, new brahman, was determined to observe all
its proprieties. And of course he would receive its rewards.

Lew's horse, Bronze Idol, a two-year-old, was having its third start
in the Juvenile Handicap tomorrow. It would be one of the favourites
after running a fifth and a third. Lew was sure the horse would win
and his trainer had told him to have a solid bet. He was tasting his
triumph already. He excused himself and sent into the house-bar
to talk to Arnold. He wanted now to give a tip in return for the one
he had got. Arnold would know the horse was going to win, but that
was beside the point.

Mrs. Betham watched him go, then looked round the lounge.

This place, she thought, was the same as the other racing hotels she'd been in. There were the same pursy people saying the same things. There were the same faint smells of lino and hops, vinegar and disinfectant. And Phar Lap, glossy and immaculate, was on the wall between lesser Carbine and Kindergarten. The Queen, richly framed, watched them from another wall, with that faint unbending smile the poor girl had to wear. How her lips must ache.

Duties, thought Mrs. Betham, we all have duties.

Hers, as wife, was to accompany Lew on these trips. To wear the furs he bought her and be sweet and receptive and unexceptional. Surprising what a hard job that was at times. She yawned and looked for the clock, and found it at length behind her, over the camouflaged fireplace, over the polished leaves of the palm in the green-painted barrel. With straight dutiful hands it gave the time as ten past eight. She yawned again. Too late for the pictures, too early to go to bed. She prepared her mind for another hour of boredom.

There were a dozen or so men in the bar but only two women. Lew recognized one of these immediately: Mrs. Benjamin, the owner, widow of a hotel man. She was sitting at a small table sipping a drink that appeared to be gin. The hand holding the glass sparkled with rings. Between sips she talked in a loud voice to her brother, Charlie Becket, who trained her horse. Arnold, wiry, tanned, and deferential, was also at the table.

Arnold saw Lew and jerked his head. Lew went over, noticing Mrs. Benjamin's lips form his name to Charlie Becket as he approached. When he had been introduced he sat down.

Mrs. Benjamin said: 'You're the Betham who owns that little colt, aren't you?' Whats the name of that horse, Charlie?'

'Bronze Idol,' said Charlie Becket. 'Should go well tomorrow.'

Lew nodded and narrowed his eyes. 'We've got a starter's chance,' he said.

Arnold said: 'Well-bred colt. You've got the filly in the same race, Mrs. Benjamin.'

'Ah, my hobby', cried Mrs. Benjamin. 'I bred that filly myself. If I can make something of her I'm never going to take advice from anyone again.'

'She should go a good race,' said Arnold.

As they talked Lew watched Mrs. Benjamin. She was overpowdered, absurdly blue-rinsed; her nose was flat, with square boxy nostrils, and her eyelids glistened as though coated with vaseline. He'd seen all this before, and refused to see it. This was not what he wanted. He wanted the legend. He remembered some of the stories he'd heard about her. It was said she had a cocktail bar built into the back of her car, and the mark of entry to her select group was to be invited for a drink.

Perhaps, thought Lew, perhaps tomorrow. He found himself wanting to mention the bar.

It was said she carried a wad of notes in her purse for charitable purposes connected with racing. Nobody had ever seen the wad, nobody had seen her pay out, but there were stories of failed trainers mysteriously re-entering business, always after being noticed in conversation with Mrs. Benjamin. Lew did not believe these stories. but he felt it was more important for them to exist than for them to be true.

Mrs. Benjamin said: 'And Bronze Idol is your first venture, Mr. Betham?'

Lew told her of his lifelong ambition to own a horse. He kept his voice casual and tried to suggest that he was one of those who would do well at racing without having to do well. He was trying to make it a paying sport.

Charlie Becket twisted his mouth. He spoke about Bronze Idol and said the horse was very promising. Lew said it was still a bit green; tomorrow's race was in the nature of an 'educational gallop'. He saw Charlie Becket didn't believe him, and was flattered.

Mrs. Benjamin interrupted the conversation to ask Charlie if he would like another drink. Lew understood that the question was really a request. Her own glass was empty while Charlie's was still half full. He was about to say: 'Let me, Mrs. Benjamin,' and take her glass, when he realized it might be wiser to pretend he hadn't understood. He must not appear over-anxious. And his knowledge of women told him Mrs. Benjamin was not of the type that liked to be easily read. Perhaps when she brought her request a little more into the open he might make the offer....

But Charlie gulped his drink and stood up. He had a broad face, a broad white nose, and squinting eyes that looked everything over with cold appraisal—an expression, Lew thought, that should have been saved for the horses. Lew wondered if it was true that at training gallops Charlie always carried two stop-watches, one for other people, showing whatever time he wanted them to see, and one he looked at later on, all by himself. Of course, he thought, watching the eyes, of course it's true. I wish he was training my horse.

Charlie said: 'Don't feel like drinking right now. Come on. I'll take you for that drive.'

Mrs. Benjamin had barely opened her mouth to protest when he added shortly: 'It was your idea, you know.'

She said: 'Oh, Charlie, why have you got such a good memory?' but she stood up and smiled at Lew and Arnold and said: 'Excuse us.' Charlie nodded and the pair left the bar. The eyes in the steam-rollered fox head on Mrs. Benjamin's shoulders glittered back almost sardonically.

Arnold sucked his lips into a tight smile, and nodded in a way that showed he was pleased.

'Charlie must be mad about something,' he said. 'He doesn't often turn on a performance like that in public.'

'So Charlie's the boss,' said Lew softly.

'Always has been. It just suits him to let her play up to things the way she does. All the horses she's got, they might just as well be-long to him. Even this filly of hers—that'll only win when he wants it to.'

Lew nodded and tried to look as if he understood. It was a shock to have Mrs. Benjamin, the legendary figure, cut down to this size. But he experienced also a thrill of pleasure that the was one of the few who knew how things really were. It meant he was accepted. He was one of those Charlie Becket didn't pretend to.

'Good thing too,' Arnold was saying, 'Most of these women get too big for their boots if they start doing well. And hard. My God, that one, she's sweet as pie on the surface but you scratch that and see what you find. She's got one idea, and that's money—grab hold of it, stack it away, that's how her mind works. Don't you believe these yarns about her giving any of it away. If there's one thing you can be sure of it's nothing gets out of that little black purse of hers once she's got it in.'

Lew nodded and said: 'I knew they were just yarns, of course.'

'There's been some fine women in the racing game,' said Arnold. 'But most of 'em go wrong somehow. Look'—he jerked his head—'you take Connie Reynolds over there.'

Lew looked to a corner of the room where a young blonde wo-man with a heavy figure was arguing with a group of men.

'You've heard about Connie?'

Lew shook his head reluctantly.

'Christ, man, she's been banged by every jock from North Cape to the Bluff. And now, believe it or not, she's got herself engaged to Stanley John Edward Philpott. You've heard of him?'

'I've heard the name,' lied Lew.

'Stanley John Edward Philpott,' said Arnold, and he swept a hand, palm down, between them. For a moment Lew wondered what racing sign this was, then understood it was a personal one of Arnold's, meaning the man was no good.

'I could tell you a few stories about him. Could tell you some about Connie too.' Arnold smiled, and the smile deepened, and Lew leaned forward, breathing softly, waiting for the stories, feeling fulfilled and very, very happy.

At half past eight Connie Reynolds left the men in the house-bar corner and went into the lounge. She left abruptly after one of them had made an insinuating remark about her engagement. He said it wasn't fair to the rest of them to take herself out of circulation. As she went towards the door she felt she was behaving as she'd always wanted to behave. She was simply walking out on them. She glanced at the ring on her finger: pride and anger were two of the luxuries she could now afford. And the freedom of not having to please made her for a moment see Stan in the role of champion and liberator, riding to slay the dragon and unchain the maiden. But this image, the unreal figures springing on her from the white delicately haunted innocence she had left long ago, forced her into a hurried retreat, and, 'Maiden?' she said, shrugging and giggling, 'that's a laugh.' And Stan as a knight on a white charger, poor battered old Stanley, who had strength only to assert now and then that one day he'd get his own back on all the bloody poohbahs, just you wait and see if he didn't? No, nothing had really changed, except that she was walking out on them, that and the fact that she didn't care if she had drunk too much whisky. She didn't have to care any more.

Mrs. Betham saw Connie come through the door and say something to herself and giggle.

The poor girl's drunk, she thought, and she looked round for the dark tubby little man who'd been with her at dinner. There weren't many people in the lounge. Most had gone out or into the bar. She remembered that the man had gone upstairs with friends some time ago, and she half rose and beckoned the girl.

'If you're looking for your husband,' said Mrs. Betham, 'he's gone upstairs.'

'Connie stopped in front of her. 'He isn't my husband,' she said. 'he's my boy friend.'

'Fiancé,' she corrected. She sat down in a chair facing Mrs. Betham. She saw the woman smiling at her and thought she looked kind.

'Do you believe in love?' asked Connie.

Mrs. Betham could not decide whether the girl was serious. She was a little drunk, obviously, but drunk people often talked of things they managed to keep hidden at other times, the things that really troubled them.

'You know, a man and a woman, to have an' to hold, an' all that?'
'Yes, I do,' said Mrs. Betham.

'Well, I was hoping you'd say no, 'cause I don't. An' I don't
think it's passed me by 'cause I've had my eyes wide open all the
time an' I haven't seen anything that looks the least bit like it.'

Mrs. Betham thought of several clever things to say, but she didn't
say any of them. 'Would you like me to try and find him for you?'
she asked.

Connie said: 'No, he'll keep. And you can bet your life he's not
worrying about what's happened to me. Still I'm used to looking
after myself. I shouldn't kid myself Stan's going to take over just
because I got a ring on my finger.'

'You know, dear,' said Mrs. Betham, 'these aren't the sort of things
you should be saying to a stranger.'

'You aren't a stranger. You're the wife of the man who owns
Bronze Idol. Stan told me. Stan's got a horse in the same race.
Royal Return. You heard of Royal Return?'

Mrs. Betham shook her head.

'Well, don't ask me if it's got a chance because it isn't forward
enough. That's what I been told to say.'

Mrs. Betham laughed. 'And my instructions are to say that I
don't know anything at all. Haven't we been well trained?'

Connie said: 'Yeah, but not as well as the horses. My God, I'd
love to be groomed, just stroked an' patted an' brushed that way.
Any man who treated me like that would have me for life. But I
haven't got a chance. I'm just an old work horse, the sort that gets
knocked around. The day'll come I'll be sold for lion's meat.'

'My dear, you sound very bitter.'

'You know why I'm getting married?' said Connie. She put a
Mrs. Betham's knee. 'I'm getting married 'cause I'm tired an' I want
a rest. Is that a good enough reason?'

'I'll find your fiancé,' said Mrs. Betham. But she couldn't get up
while the hand was on her knee.

'I want to know is that a good enough reason.'

Mrs. Betham realized the girl was serious.

'Yes, dear,' she said. 'I think that's a very good reason.'

Connie thought for a moment, her mouth open and twisted to one
side, eyes gazing at the Queen on the wall.

'And what's the way to be happy, then?' she asked.

'Why... to be happy,' said Mrs. Betham, but she could find no
answer. 'I suppose each one's got to put the other first,' she said
lamely.

'No,' said Connie, her eyes bright and questioning, 'I don't mean him, I mean me, the way for me to be happy.'

Mrs. Betham knew she should say: My dear, I think you'd better not get married at all, but instead she said, with sudden sharpness: 'You've got to make sure he needs you more than you need him. That's the only way I know.'

She forgot Connie and thought of herself and Lew. After twenty-five years the roles had been reversed. Now she didn't need him any more and so she couldn't be hurt. But over the years he had grown to need her, she was the faithful wife, part of his sense of rightness. Without her his world would crumble. And she thought, so I'm still a prisoner really, just the way I always was. But now it doesn't mean anything either. It's just one of the things that is.

She turned back to Connie. The girl was almost in tears.

'Well, then,' said Connie. 'it's all wrong. It isn't Stan who needs me it's me who needs him, because I'm tired and I've got to stop, just stop, you see, and be still and let things go past me for a while. And Stan had to have some money to buy the horse, so I gave it to him and he's got to marry me.'

Mrs. Betham tried to speak, but the girl said fiercely: 'It doesn't matter if he needs me. That isn't important at all.'

'No, of course, dear,' said Mrs. Betham, trying to soothe her. 'As long as you both put each other first. That's the main thing.'

But Connie jumped up and ran from the room. Mrs. Betham wondered if she should follow, then decided against it. She couldn't think of any advice to give if she did catch the girl. She could only tell the truth again, as she knew it. She wasn't the sweet fairy-godmother type to heal with a sunny smile.

After a while she took a magazine from the rack under the coffee-table and opened it at random. *Plump Correspondent Puts In Cheery Word For The Not So Slim*, she read.

She smiled wrily.

Not So Slim. Why couldn't that be the most serious affliction? A world made happy by dieting and menthoids.

She put the magazine aside and looked round the room. The glossy horses posed, the slim Queen smiled down, and over the fireplace the clock said that at last it was late enough to go to bed.

She yawned and went up the stairs, thinking about Connie, and the impossibility of ever helping any body.

Stan Philpott was playing poker in the room of Jeff Milden, an ex-bookie and small-business man who had failed to survive tax investigations and a heavy fine. He now worked in a factory, where several sly gambling ventures had shown disappointingly small returns, a fact he put down to working-class prejudice against an ex-employer. The truth was that, irrespective of class, nobody he had ever known had really liked him. He was aware of this only in a vague uncomprehending way, and tonight he was directing most of his energy to finding other reasons for his guests' preoccupation. He supposed Joe Elliot the trainer was worried about money or his horses, whereas Joe was really worried about having a stable boy who blushed and giggled whenever he was reprimanded and cried when threatened with being sent home. He supposed Stan Philpott was worried about money and Royal Return. In this he was right. The tremendous complex of preparation, bravado, fear, assessment of chance and luck, which had driven Stan frantic for weeks past had reduced itself on the eve of the event to an urgent knowledge of necessity: Royal Return must win tomorrow or he was finished. It was as simple as that. He, Stanley John Edward Philpott, was finished.

Fingering his cards he told himself that if the horse didn't win there was only one way left to get some money, and that was a way he could never take. He tried to read in the hand he held a sign that he should never even have to consider it. The hand was poor; he threw it aside and watched the others bet.

'Can't seem to get one tonight,' he muttered, and Jeff Milden, pulling in winnings with one hand, pushed the cards towards him with the other, saying:

'Come on, Stan. Stop worrying about that donkey of yours. Deal yourself a good one.'

Stan treated this as an invitation to talk. As he shuffled the cards he said: 'You know, it's that bloody thing of Becket's I'm scared of.' So that he might talk about Royal Return he had told the others to back the horse tomorrow, but had suggested enough uncertainty about winning to make sure they wouldn't.

Joe Elliot shook his head and said with an air of sad wisdom: 'Don't hope for too much, Stan.'

'If there's one bastard who could beat me it's Becket. He's got it in for me.' Stan continued to shuffle though Jeff Milden was showing impatience.

'I'm one up on Becket, and I don't reckon he's going to rest till he gets it back on me.'

'Christ, Stan, that happened years ago,' said Jeff. He snapped his fingers for the cards. But Joe was tired of playing. He asked to hear the story.

Stan smiled, recalling his victory, then began with practised brevity: 'Was when I was riding over the sticks. Becket was just beginning to make his way then. He had a pretty good hurdler called Traveller's Joy. I used to ride it in all its starts so I knew when it was right. We waited, see, we got everything just like we wanted it, an' I said to Becket, right, this is it. So he pulls me aside in that sneaky way he's got an' says, I've got twenty on for you. So then it's up to me, and sure enough I kick that thing home. And then do you think I can find Becket. I chased him all over the bloody course. After a while I give up, and I take a tumble to what's happening. I'm getting the bum's rush. And sure enough next time this horse starts there's another jock up. So I get cunning, see. I think out a little scheme to put Mr. Becket where he belongs. I know he thinks the horse is going to win again, an' I think so too, so I decide to do something about it. Becket's got some kid up, and that's a mistake he wouldn't make now, so just before the race I go round and make myself known to this kid, an' I say, Listen, kid, I've ridden this horse lots of times an' I know how he likes to be rode, an' I tell this kid he's got to be held in at the jumps. Take him in tight, I say, he's got to be steady, an the kid thinks I'm being decent an' he says, Gee, thanks, Mr. Philpott, or words to that effect. Well, this horse Traveller's Joy is a real jumper, he likes to stretch right out, so at the first fence the kid takes him in on a tight rein and gets jerked clean over the bloody horse's head, an' I look round an' see Becket standing there with his face all red an' I spit on the ground an' say, That's for you, bastard, an' he looks at me, an' I reckon he'll be asking that kid some pretty pertinent questions when he gets hold of him.'

'When the kid gets out of hospital,' said Jeff. 'Come on, deal 'em round.'

Joe Elliot said nothing. Stan hadn't enjoyed the story, either. Surprisingly he had lost heart for it as he went along and the climax hadn't been convincing. He said, in a puzzled voice: 'That bloody Becket.'

The telling of the story hadn't changed Becket; he'd stood through it hard and aloof, clothed in success; and Stan saw that the stories a hundred Philpotts could tell wouldn't change a thing about him, wouldn't draw them up or him down in any way that mattered. There was no way to attack him.

Stan thought, It's only the poor bastards who don't like themselves much that you can get at. A man's only piddling in his own boot if he tries with Becket and the rest of them poohbahs.

He was so shaken by this that he wanted to get off alone somewhere so that he could cry out or swear or beat the wall, break something to prove himself real. He stood up and left the room. There even Joe Elliot's silence, the familiarity of a has-been like

Milden, were working for Charlie Becket.

He slammed the door behind him and went along the passage. He was angry that his feet made no sound on the carpet, and when he came to his room he slammed that door too.

'Stan?' said a voice from the bed. It was a wet husky voice with a little ridge of panic in it, and for a second Stan didn't recognize it.

'Connie,' he said, and turned on the light.

She was lying on the bed fully clothed except for her shoes. One shoe was on the floor, the other balanced on the edge of the cover-let. This was so typical of her, of what he called her sloppiness, the way she let her money, her time, even her feelings dribble away, the way she dressed and undressed, and spoke and ate, that he broke into a rage. Becket, grey-suited and binoculared, seemed to stand beside him reproaching him with this blowzy fifth-hand woman. He entered a grey dizzying whirl made up of all he had never won and never achieved, a past of loss and failure, of small grimy winnings, a past of cheap beds and dirty sheets and bad food, of cards, smoky rooms, overflowing ashtrays, of women you could only want when you were drunk, of scabby horses, pulled horses, falls, broken bones, stewards' committees and lies, a past of borrowing and for-getting to pay back, of bludging and cheating and doping, a past of asserting your worth and greeting your winnings with a bull's roar so that you could believe in them, a past of noise and dirt and slipping lower and lower until a frayed collar and a three-day growth and a fifth-hand woman were part of you you weren't even conscious of. All these ran out in words he had never known he could use and broke against the hard withdrawn figure of Becket and made the woman on the bed curl and shrink and turn sobbing into the blankets until she was just tangled yellow hair and a shaking back. And these the hair and back, were all Stan saw as he freed himself at length from the grey clinging fragments of his past.

He went slowly to the bed.

'Connie?'

He sat down and put a hand on her shoulder.

'Connie, I'm sorry. I didn't mean it.'

He sat stroking her shoulder. In a few moments she was quiet. He turned out the light and lay down with her. His feet knocked her balancing shoe to the floor. She gave a small start that brought her body more firmly against his. After a while she said: 'Stan?'

'Yes, Connie?'

She turned suddenly and they lay close together, holding each other.

'Tell me it's going to be all right.'

'It'll be all right. Don't worry about it.'

'Can we get married soon, Stan?'

'Don't you worry. We'll get married. Stanley's got it all figured out.'

It was the first time, he realized, that he'd ever been with her and talked quietly, held her like this and not wanted her. He felt her going to sleep, and soon he heard her gentle snoring; and this sound that she always refused to believe she made, brought him even closer to her, made him realize how helpless she was.

Yes, he thought, yes, it'll be all right. As long as the horse wins. It'll be all right. He stroked her hair as she slept, then carefully drew away and found his coat and laid it over her softly so that she wouldn't wake.

II

Charlie Becket walked from the saddling paddock to the jockey's room. By the time he was there he had the instructions clear in his mind. The filly looked good, but she wasn't quite ready yet—and there was too much money on her. A poor race, a run home in the ruck, would lengthen her price for the next start. He'd get good money off her, but not today.

He beckoned the jockey and spoke to him in the corridor. The little man nodded thoughtfully then went back into the room to smoke. The instructions were simple. He'd ridden work on the horse and knew her well. She always went wide at the turn. He wasn't to check her; let her dive out, pretend to fight her, make her look green. It was a simple job—if you were a good jockey, a top jockey. He smiled and drew deeply on the cigarette and thought how much he'd tell Becket to get on the big race for him. There was a sure win there.

Charlie went back to the stand and smiled as he climbed the steps. Betty was looking at him anxiously, like a grandmother fox in her furs. She was waiting to be told what to bet. She must bet on her dear little filly. Twenty quid he'd tell her. It would teach her a lesson to lose.

He took the money and went to the tote. Bronze Idol was surprisingly long. A tenner each way would net him sixty. And a little bit on Philpott's horse. There was sly work going on there. He placed the bets and went to stand beside the judge's box. He liked to be alone. A quarter hour without Betty twitching at his sleeve was something to be valued.

At the saddling paddock Stan had Royal Return ready. The

horse seemed jaded and was slightly shin-sore. He shouldn't even
be in work with the tracks so hard, but Stan told himself not to
worry. He aimed his habitual punch of affection at the horse's ribs
and murmured: 'It's over to you, you goori.' Royal Return responded by ambling in a circle. Stan placed his mouth beside its ear
and pretended to whisper. The smell of the dope had gone. He
grinned as though at his clowning and led the horse past Connie
on the fence and into the birdcage. Everything was as right as he
could make. It was over to Lady Luck now. And as he walked Royal
Return round and round and saw the white silks of the jockeys
moving in the corridor he began to sweat. This formal part of the
business had always made him nervous. He felt shabby on the green
lawn, and was made to realize how much he had lost, how much
he had to win back, and he tried not to think of the things he still
had to lose. It was over to Lady Luck—she owned him for a lifetime of losses.

Connie had come to the birdcage fence and was watching the
horses circle. Presently the first jockeys came out and mounted, and
she wondered how they managed to look so serious. Perhaps just
getting into those colours and looking neat and clean made the
difference. One of the first things she'd learned about men was that
they were horribly vain. But knowing things like that didn't seem
to help women—or rather, not her sort of woman. She'd read stories
about the siren type who could charm men to them and play them
like harps, and she'd tried to be the siren type herself but it hadn't
worked. It had failed so badly that now it was all she could do to
hold even Stan who, as far as she knew, had never been wanted
by another woman, anyway. He looked rather grimy out there
among the glossy horses and bright little jockeys. He didn't compare
very well with all those stewards and owners and trainers under the
members' stand verandah, with Mr. Betham for instance. Betham
was rather red-faced, but very handsome in his suit and Stetson
and fancy shoes, very prosperous and distinguished looking. She'd
tried to catch men like that and once or twice had actually thought
she'd succeeded. But she couldn't hold them and soon she discovered
that they'd caught her. They'd tossed her back like an eel from a
slimy creek.

She wondered what it was that made the difference. Was it clothes,
or money, or just not having to worry about so much? She looked
from Betham to Stan. Perhaps somehow all three of those put together. But Stan at least was real, you knew where the real part of
him began and where it ended. That was something you'd probably
never find out about Betham.

She watched as Stan talked to his jockey and helped him mount. Then Stan went off somewhere and the horse was on its own. Everything was naked and simple now. The future was that horse out there and a little Maori jockey in red and white silk. This was somehow a point, an end, the top of a hill or something like that, but there was no way of seeing how you'd got to it and no way of going back. You couldn't even see how you'd started on the way. Perhaps it had begun back there at school. You liked some things and you didn't like others, You did a hundred thousand little things and you didn't do the hundred thousand others you might have done. Then some time after you understood that you'd really been making a great big simple choice. What was her choice? Slut, race-course bag. Once she'd thought she might be a model. But all the little things she'd done had made her a slut. She'd wanted so much to enjoy herself.

There should be some way of letting people know what they were doing. It was all so serious. Every little thing done was so serious.

A voice beside her said: 'They're really rather beautiful, aren't they'?

She turned and saw Mrs. Betham there. Mrs. Betham nodded admiringly at the horses.

'Yes,' said Connie.

Watching the horses in the birdcage was the only thing Mrs. Betham enjoyed at the races. They were so clean and so polished looking, so sleek and yet so powerful. They seemed to dominate the men, and she wondered how the jockeys ever found courage to climb up on their backs. Most of the jockeys were only boys. Yet they sat there so unconcernedly—some of them even chewed gum. There was a Maori boy on number eleven who looked like a trained chimpanzee, but the jockey on her husband's horse was quite old and looked rather tired. She felt sorry for him and wondered how on earth he'd survive if the horse fell over. He looked consumptive; the purple and orange colours didn't suit him at all.

'Which one is yours dear?' she asked Connie.

Connie pointed to the one with the Maori on and Mrs. Betham said: 'He looks rather nice.' But the horse that had really taken her fancy was a little black one. It moved daintily, prancing sideways, then going backwards with tiny mincing steps. She was annoyed that the effect was spoiled by the dull moon-faced jockey sitting hunched on its back. The horse was definitely superior. She would have liked to turn it loose in the hills and see it gallop away along the skyline.

Odalisque, she read. *bl. f. Owner Mrs. E. Benjamin. Trainer C. F.*

Becket. She was pleased it was a filly (smiled that she hadn't noticed) and that a woman owned it, and she made a mental note to look up odalisque in the dictionary when she got home.

The first horses went out for their preliminaries and a bell began to ring over at the totalisator. The horses came back down the track, some galloping, others just cantering. Mrs. Betham thought again there was something really graceful and exciting about it all. The worms in the apple were the people. There were queues of them still stretched out at the totalisator scrabbling away at their money.

Connie said she was going round to the hill and Mrs. Betham asked if she could come too. Lew would want to be with the trainer for this race. They went round the back of the stand, past the refreshment tents and the smelly bar where men were gulping down their last drinks. Mrs. Betham saw the man who was Connie's fiance come out and hurry into the crowd wiping his mouth. Before she could point him out he had disappeared in front of taller people. She realized then how short he was; and he seemed some shades darker too, but perhaps that was due to his old-fashioned navy-blue suit.

The stream of people moved on and they moved with it until they found a place halfway down the hill. The horses were at the five furlong start when they arrived. The race would soon begin.

'I hope one of us wins,' said Mrs. Betham. She was finding it embarrassing to be with Connie. She couldn't get the girl to talk. She decided that if there were things on her mind it would be kinder to keep quiet. She tried to concentrate on the horses, but couldn't pick any of them out, and she knew she'd have to listen to the course announcer to find out what happened. And she'd have to listen carefully. It was one of those short races that was over almost as soon as it started.

'Don't you wish you had binoculars?' she remarked wistfully, thinking of Lew's expensive pair. There was no reply, and she turned rather annoyed now, and saw that Connie was staring away down an alley in the crowd. At the end of it was the man in the navy suit, her fiancé. Mrs. Betham could see that their eyes were meeting.

'Your fiancé,' she said.'Why doesn't he come up?'

The man seemed to be trying to say something, though he was too far away for them to hear; he smiled, with a small twist of his mouth, and lifted his fingers in a V sign, Churchill's way, rather pathetically she thought. Then he moved to one side so they couldn't see him any more.

'He should have come up,' said Mrs. Betham.

Connie began to stare at the horses again. Her face seemed thinner and more bony. 'Get them started,' she said. She moved a few steps away.

Mrs. Betham shrugged and told herself not to be angry. Connie was perhaps not so ungracious as she seemed—the race must mean a lot to her. For that reason she hoped Royal Return would win, if Lew's horse didn't.

No, she thought, no, I hope it beats Lew's horse. They probably need the money more than we do.

The announcer's voice blared into her thoughts. 'The field is lining up for the start of the Juvenile Handicap.' He mentioned the horses that were giving trouble. One of them was Royal Return. But soon they were all in line and she saw the heave of brown and heard the crowd rumble as they started. She still couldn't pick out any of the horses.

'Bronze Idol has made a good beginning and so has Odalisque.' Then there was a list of names with Royal Return in the middle. She wondered how the announcer picked them out. She couldn't see any horse clearly. They were all melted together, and their legs flickering under the rail made them look like a centipede.

'As they come round past the three furlong peg it's Bronze Idol a length clear of Samba with Odalisque next on the rails on the inside of Conformist. A length back to Song and Dance getting a trail, a length to Sir Bonny.'

The next time he went through them she counted and found that Royal Return was eighth. Bronze Idol was still a length clear of the field. Lew would be getting excited.

At the turn it was the same except that she was pleased to hear Royal Return had ranged up on the outside of Conformist. Then the horses came into the straight and they seemed to explode. They spread out right across it. She thought this was normal, but the announcer was excited and said Odalisque had run wide and had carried out two or three others and Bronze Idol was holding on a length clear of Samba. She didn't hear Royal Return's name. But she was excited herself now. She could see Bronze Idol looking really beautiful, heaving along with his head out straight and his tail flowing and his body slippery with sunlight as the muscles moved; the little consumptive jockey was crouched very low on his back, not using the whip. They were past too quickly for her. She would have loved to see them going on like that for ever.

Above the roar of the crowd the announcer said Bronze Idol was winning as he liked. She was pleased for Lew's sake, and, she admitted, a little bit for her own too. It had been very exciting.

Then she remembered Royal Return. It hadn't been mentioned after the corner. The girl would be disappointed.

She looked round to find her. But Connie hadn't waited for the finish. She had seen Royal Return go out at the straight entrance, and had turned and gone back through the crowd. She had broken past the red paralysed faces of people staring stupidly away at something they didn't know was already over.

III

Mrs. Benjamin wanted to stay the night at the Commercial Hotel but Charlie Becket insisted on going home. Finally, after he had threatened to leave her behind, she agreed. and a few minutes before nine o'clock they left town and set off along the Auckland highway. It was a fine night, mild and cloudless. The stars were very bright.

They drove for some time in silence, then Mrs. Benjamin began to complain about the meeting. There hadn't been anyone interesting there. All her friends were dying or losing interest.

'Common thing with old people,' said Charlie, hoping to quiet her.

But she seized on the statement and began to worry it with persistent whining energy and he knew she was working to the complaint that nobody cared about her any more. He broke abruptly into her talk, saying: 'That filly isn't right yet. You've been making me push her too fast.'

She grasped this subject eagerly. 'Oh, Charlie, I know she'll be all right. I've never seen a horse I liked better.'

'She over-reaches,' said Charlie. 'Cut herself one day, you see.'

'But I can't afford to lose twenty pounds on her,' she continued. 'Why did you tell me she was going to win?'

'Because I thought she was,' said Charlie. 'It's not my fault if the jockey can't ride her. I'll get someone different next time.' He smiled remembering how perfectly Armstrong had let go on the corner. A good jockey, a good man to have, even if he was expensive.

Mrs. Benjamin sighed.

'She looked as if she was going to go down, pushing those big horses right out. She's so tiny.'

Charlie said: 'Yeah, funny thing happened about that too.'

He told her how after the race, when he'd been talking to Betham, Philpott had come up and accused him of sabotaging Royal Return.

'I told him I'd hardly do that when I had a few quid on it myself, and that seemed to make him worse. I've never seen anyone sweat so much or look so mad. He'd have stuck a knife into me if he'd had one. He's got a kink I reckon. He'll end up in the nuthouse.'

'What happened?' said Mrs. Benjamin.

'He followed me all over the course until I had to tell him to clear out or I'd call a cop.'

'What did he do?'

'He cleared out. They're all the same these brokendown jocks. Yellow. No guts. That's why they don't last.'

'But he was a good jockey once.'

'Plenty of good jockeys. They're a dime a dozen. Plenty of good horses too. What I'm interested in is good prices.'

'Sometimes you're just too hard. Charlie,'

Charlie said: 'We're not here to make friends.' It was his favourite saying and it never failed to please him. He drove on smiling, and Mrs. Benjamin lay back stiffly in her corner and tried to sleep.

After a time she said wearily: 'It was a boring meeting. I didn't meet anyone I liked.'

Charlie grunted.

A little later she said: 'That Betham man is rather nice.'

'Got a good horse' said Charlie.

'It's a pity his wife's such a mousy thing.'

'Anyway,' she said, 'I took him out for a drink.'

'You drink too much,' said Charlie.

They wound down a long hill. The lights ran off down gullies and over creeks and paddocks. Charlie fought the car, making it squeal in a way that pleased him.

They came to a level section of road. It ran for a mile without a curve and then went sharply left. Just round the corner the headlamps picked out two cars and a group of people standing at the back of a horse-float. The tail of the float was down and men were clustered in its mouth, white and yellow in a glare of light.

Charlie drove past slowly.

'Horse is probably down,' he said.

Then, as Mrs. Benjamin said: 'Let's stop, Charlie,' he saw that the float was coupled to a big pre-war Oldsmobile.

'Philpott,' he said. He increased speed.

'But, Charlie, I want to see what's happened.'

Charlie didn't answer. He changed into top gear. Soon the speedometer reached sixty again.

'There are plenty of people there to help. Joe Elliot was there. He'll know what to do.'

'Charlie, why can't you do what I want to, just for once?'

But again Charlie didn't answer. A hundred yards ahead the lights had picked up the figure of a woman walking at the side of the road. She was going their way but she didn't look round as they approached or make any signal. The car sped past.

'It's Connie. Connie Reynolds. Stop, Charlie.' Mrs. Benjamin was peering back.

'Charlie, *stop*.'

'Charl*ie-ie*.'

'I don't feel like it,' he said. The speedometer kept level at sixty.

For a while Mrs. Benjamin sulked in her corner. She didn't see why she couldn't know what was happening. Then she grew morbid. She was old—she wondered how many more pleasures she was to be allowed. Perhaps she couldn't afford to lose this one.

Charlie said: 'For God's sake don't start the waterworks.'

Mrs. Benjamin had not been going to cry but she allowed herself two or three tears and held her handerkchief to her eyes. Then she rearranged herself fussily in her seat, grumbled a little about its hardness, and watched the road in an effort to stay awake. Her frequent desire to sleep had worried her lately. But this time she found reason for it in the motion of the car. She closed her eyes and let her mouth loosen comfortably. Her body sagged a little and she felt a settling lurch in her bowels. Her hands turned in her lap until the palms faced upwards.

She slept, as heavily as a child, and soon Charlie Becket put out a hand and tipped her against the door. He did not want her falling over him as he drove.

Connie had not found Stan until two races after the Juvenile Handicap. She knew at once he'd been drinking, but believed him when he said he wouldn't drink any more. He was determined to win back everything and he asked for money. She gave him the few pounds she had, keeping only enough for petrol to get home on. The hotel bills could be paid by cheque and though the cheque would bounce that was a worry for another day. Now the only thing that mattered was to keep Stan from doing anything crazy. He went off and she sat down shakily on a seat. She had never seen him looking so bad. His face was always blue-bristled by mid-afternoon, but now the skin under the bristles seemed more yellow than white, and his eyes were blood-shot, the lids scraped looking and salty. She wanted desperately to help him; and she wondered what was wrong with her, as a woman, that the only way she could help was by giving him money.

After the sixth race he came to her again. He had won a little, enough to bet more solidly with. But after the seventh race he did not come. That would mean he had lost. She went to sit in the car. From there she heard the course announcer describe the last race. A horse called Manalive won. She had never heard Stan speak of it, and it paid only a few pounds.

Most of the traffic had gone by the time he came. He told her
he'd won twenty pounds on a place bet in the eighth. They drove
out of the course without picking up the float. He said there was
a card game he wanted to get to. His voice was rough and urgent,
and impersonal, not directed at her.

'But, Stan,' cried Connie, 'you can't win enough on a card game.'
She didn't know what she meant by enough, but the word frightened
her, it seemed so full of things that might happen, it uncovered
years that might go any way at all.

'I can win something ,' said Stan savagely. 'I can win enough so
I won't have to...' He too used the word and then didn't finish
the sentence: she was more frightened; it was almost as if she had
to open a door knowing there might be something terrible behind
it. She wanted to put everything farther off.

'Stan, don't let's talk about it. Just drive.'

The card game was in a shabby house down by the harbour. She
could see the sad battered hulk of a scow sunk lower than the
wharf it was moored to, and over beyond a spit of land three sleek
launches in front of a white-sand beach. It seemed they were only
lazing, it seemed they could fly away out of the harbour at any
moment they chose.

She waited two hours without any tea. The launches slowly faded
into the dusk. Then Stan came.

He had lost.

He made her go to a restaurant and went to get the horse. He was
gone for a long time. When he came back she tried to buy him some
food but he said he wasn't hungry. He wanted to get on the road.

They were some miles out of town when she remembered their
bags at the hotel. He said quickly: 'We can't go back for them now.'

She argued. They were hardly out of town. It would take only a
minute.

'We can't go back.' He shouted, and behind the anger in his
voice there was despair, a drawing out of the 'can't' so that she
knew he had done something that was frightening him.

'Stan, you haven't...?' But he began again before she could
finish the question.

'What are you talking about? What do you mean, haven't? I just
say we're too far out of town and you start thinking all sorts of
things.'

She knew then he had done something back there. For a moment
she even wondered if anyone was chasing them, and she looked at
the petrol gauge. But the gauge showed the tank was almost full.

That, in its simplicity, shocked her terribly, and she said under her breath: Stan, what's happened, what's happened? Stan never bought petrol. It was one of the things he always had to be reminded of. Yet today, after that race, he had remembered.

Now as they drove on she grew more aware of the float, and she thought, That's the trouble, that's what causes all the trouble, we're tied to these horses and we can't get away. We're like servants or slaves.

Why couldn't Stan get another job? Why did he have to do things they had to run away from? Why couldn't he go out to work every day, to an ordinary job, like other men? Everything was so complicated. Why couldn't it be simple, as clean and white as that beach and those launches?

The float dragged heavily, lifting the front of the car in a way that gave her almost a feeling of lightheadedness. In this slight dizziness she knew she must speak of the marriage. She must have that chance, the chance for something different even if she couldn't make it just the quiet and rest she wanted.

She said, hesitating: 'Stan, do you—remember last night?'

He broke out again.

'I said I'd marry you, didn't I? What more do you want me to say? I won't break my promise. That's one of the things I don't do.'

'Stan, why can't you—I mean, you could sell the horse, and then get a job.'

'Sell the horse,' he said, and now he spoke softly, as though not thinking of what he was saying.

'He ran a good race today. He was going well until the turn and that wasn't his fault. Somebody would buy him.'

'He's a mongrel,' said Stan. 'He was so full of dope he could hardly breathe. Without it he wouldn't have got to the barrier.'

His hands were light on the wheel so he could feel it move and jump .The float was swaying as they wound down a long hill.

Connie began to speak again, but she stopped when she realized he wasn't taking any notice. He seemed to be listening. And then, from the way he was driving, she saw he was aware of the float.

'Is something wrong, Stan?'

He turned on her irritably.

'What do you mean, wrong?'

'Back there, in the float.'

'What could be wrong? God damn it you say some stupid things.'

The car sagged heavily into the road at the foot of the hill and she heard a faint whinnying scream from the horse, and then a scraping sound that lasted only a second. She looked at Stan quickly.

'Excitable—excitable horse. Doesn't like bumps,' Stan jerked out, and he tried to smile at her.

They came to a straight level stretch of road and he began to drive faster. His hands were white on the wheel. He was sweating, and the float was rattling louder than it ever had before.

'Stan, have you done something to the horse? Is he down?'

Then Stan seemed to go crazy. He began to sway the car over the road; the float lurched and dragged, and the horse screamed again.

'Mongrel, bloody mongrel,' he groaned. He ran the car halfway over the broken edge of the road. It bucked and jolted along; stones rattled against the mudguards and thumped on the chassis and on the bottom of the float.

'Mongrel,' he shouted.

Connie was screaming at him and tearing at his arms, almost running the car off the road. Then she turned from him and opened her door. Grass and bracken whipped on the metal. She looked back but could see only the yellow half-lit face of the float, so close it seemed to overhang and threaten.

'Stan, for God's sake stop.'

There was no sound from the horse.

'Stan', she screamed. She tugged at his arm again and the car jumped to the middle of the road. The open door beat once, like a broken wing.

'Stan.' She fell against him. She was crying, uselessly beating his shoulder with her fist.

At last they came to a corner and he slowed to take it. He said, the first word coming on the rush of a long-held breath: 'All right, we'll stop, but nothing's wrong. Excitable, that's all. Just might have got himself down.'

She had time only to half realize the weakness of his pretence before the car stopped and she was out and back at the float. He followed slowly.

The horse was moaning.

'Christ,' said Stan, but his voice was flat. He pulled her away from the locks and lowered the ramp.

Royal Return was down. At first she could not make out how he was lying. Then she saw that his chest was on the floor and his body was twisted left and right from it, the hind quarters turned one way and raised so she could see a leg that dug spasmodically at the straw (like a chicken's, she thought, and the unnatural likeness struck a sort of terror into her), head and neck turned the other, the neck forced by the wall to an erectness that had dug a great pit in the horse's shoulders. One eye was towards her, but not seeing—it was held in a desperate steadiness just above agony.

'Get the torch,' said Stan.

'Oh God.' Connie moved away from him. 'God. Stan. You *did* it.'

'Get the torch,' he repeated dully.

She stopped at the roadside grass. 'You *did* it.'

'Connie, I . . .'

'You *did*, Stan.'

Connie, it was for you. Don't you see?'

She turned abruptly at that and stumbled down the road.

'Connie, don't go away.'

She made no anwser.

'Connie.'

Soon she was out of sight.

After a while Stan went to the car himself and got the torch. He went down on his knees and looked underneath the float; and stood up immediately, leaving the torch on the ground. He moved to the roadside and sat down in grass with his feet in a gutter. Soon he began to retch. He didn't notice that another car had stopped and other people were climbing into the float, but he heard the horse scream, and he felt himself travelling back with terrible urgency to times and places where there had not been even the smallest beginning of things like this. He was riding back to salute the judge after his first win, a tiny apprentice in gold and green on a chestnut colt with a white blaze. It was a sunny day and people were clapping.

But then Joe Elliot and another man pulled him to his feet and started asking questions. All he could answer, with his face in his hands, was: 'I'm sick, I'm sick.'

They threw him back into the grass.

The Bethams left the hotel shortly after Mrs. Benjamin and Charlie Becket. Mrs. Betham wondered if Lew had taken so long over his last drink in order to drive back to Auckland behind them. His pleasures, it seemed, were becoming increasingly simple; but in spite of that she had to admit they seemed to satisfy him as nothing had done before—as she herself had never done: he spoke of Bronze Idol with an enthusiasm he had never displayed for her. In thinking this she was frightened. She did not want her memories attacked, she did not want them involved in this business at all. The present must not be allowed to war on the past. That must be kept intact. She wondered then what this past really was. Just a few short years after all—the slump years, when they had lived on porridge and rice and turnips in a tin shed that filled with smoke from a fire that couldn't warm it. How could those be the happy years? And yet she thought of them as a sort of Golden Age. Lew and she had been together in a way that could never be broken, not letting the outside touch them at all. Or was it, she wondered, just that memory ran the good things together, creating a closeness that had never really existed? It had all happened so long ago. Yet in spite of her doubts those years would continue to live.

It was a sort of Golden Age, she thought, and now's the depression, when we've got everything we want.

She began to study Lew. He was concentrating on his driving, trying to catch Charlie Becket.

Perhaps the immortals are equipped with faster cars, she thought. Or perhaps their cars have wings and can fly while ours remain earthbound. Her amusement was brief. She seemed suddenly to be driving with someone she knew only slightly. The face was familiar, but the intentness was created by an ambition she could never understand.

Lew seemed to sense her mood. 'What are you so quiet about?' he said.

She could tell by his voice he expected her to complain about something.

I should, she thought, but it wouldn't do any good.

'Nothing,' she said.

'Haven't you enjoyed yourself?'

'Yes,' she said.

'Well, what is it then? You don't seem very excited. Don't you realize some people own dozens of horses before they get a winner?'

'Yes, dear. And you've done it first time. That's very clever of you.'

The sarcasm had come in spite of her. She had now to listen to a lecture about her lack of wifely enthusiasm, her inability to enjoy herself as other women did.

'I don't understand you,' he finished. 'I do everything I can to make you happy.'

She had many answers to that but he had heard them all and not been impressed. So she sat watching the dark bush, trying to see into it, imagining some primitive settlement deep in there, a place where life was simple and people had time to know and like each other. But the headlamps never rested on anything for long. Her mind couldn't settle. Lew was driving too fast. There was a car going down the hill ahead of them, disappearing round a new corner every time they caught sight of it. He was trying to get closer to see if it was Charlie Becket's.

On the flat at the foot of the hill they saw it wasn't and Lew seemed to lose heart. He drove more slowly.

'I think I'll stop and have a whisky,' he said.

Just then they went round a corner and saw what looked to be an accident. Two cars were pulled up behind a horse-float and a third was in front of it. There were some men at the mouth of the float and two inside. They couldn't see the horse.

Lew went past slowly and pulled in at the front of the line. He told Mrs. Betham to wait where she was and went back to the float. He was gone for perhaps five minutes.

Mrs. Betham would have liked to see what was happening, but she thought if the horse was sick or hurt she'd only be in the way. Besides, she hated to seem curious. But she did notice two rather strange things: this was horse business and Charlie Becket hadn't stopped, and back beside the float a man was sitting in the grass. He was very still. At first she thought he was a small tree or a clump of bracken. Then the shape became clearer. He was bent forward with his arms across his knees, his face in the arms. Nobody was taking any notice of him, although the way he was sitting made him appear lonely and in need of comfort. She felt she should go along and see if there was anything she could do.

When Lew came back she said: 'Who's that man sitting in the grass?'

'Philpott,' he said. It was not so much an answer to her question as something he was saying to himself. Then he swore, using a word he'd never used in front of her before.

'What's happened, Lew?' she asked nervously.

Lew was pouring himself a whisky. When he'd drunk it he looked at her and said: 'He's just butchered his horse.'

'Butchered it. You mean he's killed it?'

He shook his head and she saw his eyes fill with tears. 'It's not dead yet,' he said. 'They've gone to get a gun to shoot it.'

She couldn't understand, but she listened as Lew told her what had happened. Philpott had loosened the boards at the front of the float so the horse's legs had broken through when the car hit a bump.

'They must have been trailing along the road for miles. They're almost torn off. Just hanging in tatters. You can see bits of bones.'

Lew poured himself another drink. His hands were shaking and whisky slopped on his trousers.

Mrs. Betham was saying to herself: But that's awful, how could he, how could a person do a thing like that?—but she couldn't say it aloud. Nothing was adequate as she pictured the tattered legs and the pieces of bone.

'But, Lew...' she said.

'He did it for the insurance,' said Lew. 'You knew horses were insured, didn't you?'

'There are people who could do a thing like that for money!' she said.

'For money.' Lew threw the whisky bottle into the glove-box.

'I hope he gets ten years,' he said. 'If I was the judge I'd order a flogging.'

'What about the girl?' said Mrs. Betham. 'Was she in it?'

'His girl? Connie Reynolds? No, she wasn't there. How do you know her?'

'I saw her on the racecourse today,' said Mrs. Betham

Lew grunted. His mind was still on the horse. Mrs. Betham, too, was unable to keep her mind from returning to the horrible picture he had painted. She had had a moment's relief when she heard that Connie wasn't involved, but then she turned and looked again at the figure in the grass. It was motionless, in a hunched cowering attitude.

It's too late for him to be sorry, she thought. And her loathing increased. But strangely it changed so that it was not so much for him as for what had been done. He seemed now to exist outside the act. The act was unimaginable, but he was there, part of the horror he had brought into existence, the only part of it she could really see.

She knew that soon she would feel sorry for him, and she told herself it wasn't right to have that much pity. It was dangerous to forgive too much. There must be things that could never be forgiven, and surely this...

The tattered legs and pieces of bone...

No, that could never be forgiven.

Lew had started the car and they were moving again. He drove without talking, and she was glad, though she expected him to break out at any minute. Her mind was calmer now, and she was trying to convince herself a person couldn't do a thing like that for money. There must be other reasons.

No, she thought, it's not just the money. That's too simple. It's everything money means. You can't blame a person for failing to survive that. And yet you can't forgive. Here I am trying to forgive.

But as she thought of the horse with its legs torn off, and the man sitting on the grass, both seemed equally terrible mutilations, the one as pitiable as the other.

'There's his girl now,' said Lew. He didn't slow down and they flashed by almost before Mrs. Betham saw her.

'Stop, Lew. We'll pick her up.'

'After what happened back there?' said Lew.

But she argued with him and made him stop and back up to the girl. He was angry, but knew she was determined to have her way. He showed his disapproval by not looking round or speaking as Connie got into the back seat.

Then, as he drove on and heard his wife explaining that they knew what had happened and heard the girl break into long scratching sobs, he was seized with an almost physical revulsion. He felt he wanted to be sick. The girl and the crying, and Philpott and the horse, were a sort of disease; he felt unclean having her in the car. There must be ways of avoiding things like this, ways of getting about so that you never saw them.

God why can't things be perfect, he thought.

He heard the girl say: 'I don't know what to do. I don't know.'

'Then wait,' said his wife. 'Just don't do anything. You'll find out what's right.'

A little later Connie said: 'I want to go back, but I *can't*.'

'Just wait,' said his wife, 'Don't think of anything.'

He recognized her 'soothing' voice. It made him jealous when she used it for anyone but him, and he stabbed savagely with his foot to dip for an oncoming car.

The girl said, still crying: 'This is the first time probably he's ever really needed me—and I can't go.'

'Shh,' said Mrs. Betham.

But Connie had not been talking to her, and hadn't listened. In a few moments she stopped crying.

'He said he did it for me,' she whispered. She gave a little moan.

'Shh. Don't think,' said Mrs. Betham.

'So really—really...' She stopped and seemed to talk to herself, and almost cry again.

'So really—it's as much my fault as his.'

'No. Don't even begin to think that,' said Mrs. Betham. She tried to take Connie's hand but the back of the seat made it awkward for her and Connie made no move to help. So she rested her arm along the seat-back with her fingers brushing the sleeve of Lew's coat, and smiled kindly at the girl, wishing there was something she could give her, something she could do: the dead paws of the fur, dangling over her arm, were no more useless than she was.

Later, when they thought she was sleeping, Connie leaned forward and said: 'Stop please. I want to get out.'

Lew stopped quickly. His wife leaned back and put a hand on

Connie's arm. 'What are you going to do?'

'I don't know,' said Connie.

She opened the door, got out clumsily, closed it, and came to Mrs. Betham's window to say something. Lew couldn't hear for the noise of the engine, and didn't want to hear. He thought her face was yellow and ugly; he wanted to get away.

The car began to move again; Mrs. Betham said nothing. She watched until the girl was lost in the darkness. Then she leaned against her door with her cheek against the cold window.

Lew let a little time pass. He said: 'You want to save the Good Samaritan act for somebody worth while. I could tell you stories about that girl.'

'I don't want to hear,' said Mrs. Betham.

He shrugged and drove on. He was happy now that Connie was gone.

Soon he saw a tail-light shining in the darkness ahead, and he increased speed, wondering if at last he had caught up with Charlie Becket.

MAURICE SHADBOLT   # The People Before
(*b.* 1932)

I

My father took on that farm not long after he came back from the first war. It was pretty well the last farm up the river. Behind our farm, and up the river, there was all kind of wild country. Scrub and jagged black stumps on the hills, bush in gullies where fire hadn't reached; hills and more hills, deep valleys with caves and twisting rivers, and mountains white with winter in the distance. We had the last piece of really flat land up the river. It wasn't the first farm my father'd taken on—and it certainly wasn't to be the last—but it was the most remote. He always said that was why he'd got the place for a song. This puzzled me as a child. For I'd heard, of course, of having to sing for your supper. I wondered what words, to what tune, he was obliged to sing for the farm; and where, and why? Had he travelled up the river, singing a strange song, charming his way into possession of the land? It always perplexed me.

And it perplexed me because there wasn't much room for singing in my father's life. I can't remember ever having heard him sing. There was room for plodding his paddocks in all weathers, milking cows and sending cream down river to the dairy factory, and cursing the bloody government; there was room in his life for all these things and more, but not for singing.

In time, of course, I understood that he only meant he'd bought the place cheaply. Cheaply meant for a song. I couldn't, even then, quite make the connexion. It remained for a long while one of those adult mysteries. And it was no use puzzling over it, no use asking my father for a more coherent explanation:

'Don't be difficult,' he'd say. 'Don't ask so many damn questions. Life's difficult enough, boy, without all your damn questions.'

He didn't mean to be unkind; it was just his way. His life was committed to winning order from wilderness. Questions were a disorderly intrusion, like gorse or weed springing up on good pasture. The best way was to hack them down, grub out the roots, before they could spread. And in the same way as he checked incipient anarchy on his land he hoped, perhaps, to check it in his son.

By that time I was old enough to understand a good many of the things that were to be understood. One of them, for example, was that we weren't the first people on that particular stretch of land. Thirty or forty years before, when white men first came into our part of the country, it was mostly forest. Those first people fired the forest, right back into the hills, and ran sheep. The sheep grazed not only the flat, but the hills which rose sharply behind our farm; the hills which, in our time, had become stubbly with manuka and fern. The flatland had been pretty much scrub too, the day my father first saw it; and the original people had been gone twenty years— they'd given up, or been ruined by the land; we never quite knew the story. The farmhouse stood derelict among the returning wilderness.

Well, my father saw right away that the land—the flat land—was a reasonable proposition for a dairy farm. There was a new launch service down to the nearest dairy factory, in the township ten miles away; only in the event of flood, or a launch breakdown, would he have to dispose of his cream by carrying it on a sledge across country, three miles, to the nearest road.

So he moved in, cleared the scrub, sowed new grass, and brought in cows. Strictly speaking, the hills at the back of the farm were his too, but he had no use for them. They made good shelter from the westerlies. Otherwise he never gave the hills a thought, since he had all the land he could safely manage; he roamed across them after wild pig, and that was about all. There were bones up there, scattered skeletons of lost sheep, in and about the scrub and burnt stumps.

Everything went well; he had the place almost paid off by the time of the depression. 'I never looked back, those years,' he said long afterwards. It was characteristic of him not to look back. He was not interested in who had the farm before him. He had never troubled to inquire. So far as he was concerned, history only began the day he first set foot on the land. It was his, by sweat and legal title: that was all that mattered. That was all that could matter.

He had two boys; I was the eldest son. 'You and Jim will take this place over one day,' he often told me. 'You'll run it when I get tired.'

But he didn't look like getting tired. He wasn't a big man, but he was wiry and thin with a lean face and cool blue eyes; he was one of those people who can't keep still. When neighbours called he couldn't ever keep comfortable in a chair, just sitting and sipping tea, but had to start walking them round the farm—or at least the male neighbours—pointing out things here and there. Usually work he'd done, improvements he'd made: the new milking-shed, the new water-pump on the river. He didn't strut or boast, though; he just pointed them out quietly, these jobs well done. He wanted others to share his satisfaction. There was talk of electricity coming through to the farm, the telephone; a road up the river was scheduled. It would all put the value of the property up. The risk he'd taken on the remote and abandoned land seemed justified in every way.

He didn't ever look like getting tired. It was as if he'd been wound up years before, like something clockwork, and set going: first fighting in the war, then fighting with the land; now most of the fighting was done, he sometimes found it quite an effort to keep busy. He never took a holiday. There was talk of taking a holiday, one winter when the cows dried off; talk of us all going down to the sea, and leaving a neighbour to look after the place. But I don't think he could have trusted anyone to look after his land, not even for a week or two in winter when the cows were dried off. Perhaps, when Jim and I were grown, it would be different. But not until. He always found some reason for us not to get away. Like our schooling.

'I don't want to interfere with their schooling,' he said once. 'They only get it once in their lives. And they might as well get it while they can. I didn't get much. And, by God, I regret it now. I don't know

much, and I might have got along all right, but I might have got
along a damn sight better if I'd had more schooling. And I'm not
going to interfere with theirs by carting them off for a holiday in
the middle of the year.'

Yet even then I wondered if he meant a word of it, if he really
wasn't just saying that for something to say. He was wrangling at
the time with my mother, who held opinions on a dwindling number
of subjects. She never surrendered any of these opinions, exactly;
she just kept them more and more to herself until, presumably, they
lapsed quietly and died. As she herself, much later, was to lapse
quietly from life, without much complaint.

For if he'd really been concerned about our schooling, he might
have been more concerned about the way we fell asleep in afternoon
classes. Not that we were the only ones. Others started getting
pretty ragged in the afternoons too. A lot of us had been up helping
our fathers since early in the morning. Jim and I were up at half-
past four most mornings to help with the milking and working the
separators. My father increased his herd year after year, right up to
the depression. After school we rode home just in time for the evening milking. And by the time we finished it was getting dark; in
winter it was dark by the time we were half-way through the herd.

I sometimes worried about Jim looking worn in the evenings,
and I often chased him off inside before milking was finished. I
thought Jim needed looking after; he wasn't anywhere near as big
as me. I'd hear him scamper off to the house, and then I'd set about
stripping the cows he had left. Father sometimes complained.

'You'll make that brother of yours a softy,' he said. 'The boy's
got to learn what work means.'

'Jim's all right,' I answered. 'He's not a softy. He's just not very
big. That's all.'

He detested softies, even the accomplices of softies. My mother,
in a way, was such an accomplice. She'd never been keen about
first me, then Jim, helping with work on the farm. But my father
said he couldn't afford to hire a man to help with the herd. And
he certainly couldn't manage by himself, without Jim and me.

'Besides,' he said, 'my Dad and me used to milk two hundred
cows'—sometimes, when he became heated, the number rose to
three hundred—'when I was eight years old. And thin as a rake too,
I was. Eight years old and thin as a rake. It didn't do me no harm.
You boys don't know what work is, let me tell you.'

So there all argument finished. My mother kept one more opinion
to herself.

And I suppose that, when I chased Jim off inside, I was only taking my mother's side in the argument—and was only another accomplice of softies. Anyway, it would give me a good feeling afterwards—despite anything my father would have to say—when we tramped back to the house, through the night smelling of frost or rain, to find Jim sitting up at the table beside my mother while she ladled out soup under the warm yellow lamplight. He looked as if he belonged there, beside her; and she always looked, at those times, a little triumphant. Her look seemed to say that one child of hers, at least, was going to be saved from the muck of the cowshed. And I suppose that was the beginning of how Jim became his mother's boy.

I remained my father's. I wouldn't have exchanged him for another father. I liked seeing him with people, a man among men. This happened on winter Saturdays when we rode to the township for the football. We usually left Jim behind to look after my mother. We tethered our horses near the football field and went off to join the crowd. Football was one of the few things which interested my father outside the farm. He'd been a fine rugby forward in his day and people respected what he had to say about the game. He could out-argue most people; probably out-fight them too, if it ever came to that. He often talked about the fights he'd had when young. For he'd done a bit of boxing too, only he couldn't spare the time from his father's farm to train properly. He knocked me down once, with his bare fists, in the cowshed; and I was careful never to let it happen again. I just kept my head down for days afterwards, so that he wouldn't see the bruises on my face or the swelling round my eye.

At the football he barracked with the best of them in the thick of the crowd. Sometimes he called out when the rest of the crowd was silent and tense; he could be very sarcastic about poor players, softies who were afraid to tackle properly.

After the game he often called in, on the way home, to have a few beers with friends in the township's sly-grog shop—we didn't have a proper pub in the township—while I looked after the horses outside. Usually he'd find time, while he gossiped with friends, to bring me out a glass of lemonade. At times it could be very cold out there, holding the horses while the winter wind swept round, but it would be nice to know that I was remembered. When he finished we rode home together for a late milking. He would grow talkative, as we cantered towards dark, and even give me the impression he was glad of my company. He told me about the time he was young, what the world looked like when he was my age. His father was a sharemilker, travelling from place to place; that is, he owned no land of his own and did other people's work.

'So I made up my mind, boy,' he told me as we rode along together, 'I made up my mind I'd never be like that. I'd bend my head
to no man. And you know what the secret of that is, boy? Land.
Land of your own. You're independent, boy. You can say no to
the world. That's if you got your own little kingdom. I reckon it was
what kept me alive, down there on the beach at Gallipoli, knowing
I'd have some land I could call my own.' This final declaration
seemed to dismay him for some reason or other, perhaps because
he feared he'd given too much of himself away. So he added half-
apologetically, 'I had to think of something, you know, while all
that shooting was going on. They say it's best to fix your mind on
something if you don't want to be afraid. That's what I fixed my
mind on, anyhow. Maybe it did keep me alive.'

In late winter or spring we sometimes arrived back, on Saturdays,
to see the last trembling light of sunset fade from the hills and land.
We'd canter along a straight stretch, coast up a rise, rein in the horses,
and there it was—his green kingdom, his tight tamed acres beneath the hills and beside the river, a thick spread of fenced grass
from the dark fringe of hillscrub down to the ragged willows above
the water. And at the centre was his castle, the farmhouse, with
the sheds scattered round, and the pine trees.

Reining in on that rise, I knew, gave him a good feeling. It would
also be the time when he remembered all the jobs he'd neglected,
all the work he should have done instead of going to the football.
His conscience would keep him busy all day Sunday.

At times he wondered—it was a conversation out loud with himself—why he didn't sell up and buy another place. There were, after
all, more comfortable farms, in more convenient locations nearer
towns or cities. 'I've built this place up from nothing.' he said, 'I've
made it pay, and pay well. I've made this land worth something.
I could sell out for a packet. Why don't I?'

He never really—in my presence anyway—offered himself a
convincing explanation. Why didn't he? He'd hardly have said he
loved the land: love, in any case, would have been an extravagance.
Part of whatever it was, I suppose, was the knowledge that he'd
built where someone else had failed; part was that he'd given too
much of himself there, to be really free anywhere else. It wouldn't
be the same, walking on to another successful farm, a going concern,
everything in order. No, this place—this land from the river back
up to the hills—was his. In a sense it had only ever been his. That
was why he felt so secure.

If Sunday was often the day when he worked hardest, it was also the best day for Jim and me, our free day. After morning milking, and breakfast, we did more or less what we liked. In summer we swam down under the river-willows; we also had a canoe tied there and sometimes we paddled up-river, under great limestone bluffs shaggy with toi toi, into country which grew wilder and wilder. There were huge bearded caves in the bush above the water which we explored from time to time. There were also big eels to be fished from the pools of the river.

As he grew older Jim turned more into himself, and became still quieter. You could never guess exactly what he was thinking. It wasn't that he didn't enjoy life; he just had his own way of enjoying it. He didn't like being with his father, as I did; I don't even know that he always enjoyed being with me. He just tagged along with me: we were, after all, brothers. When I was old enough, my father presented me with a ·22 rifle; Jim never showed great enthusiasm for shooting. He came along with me, all right, but he never seemed interested in the rabbits or wild goat I shot, or just missed. He wandered around the hills, way behind me, entertaining himself and collecting things. He gathered leaves, and tried to identify the plants from which the leaves came. He also collected stones, those of some interesting shape or texture; he had a big collection of stones. He tramped along, in his slow, quiet way, poking into everything, adding to his collections. He wasn't too slow and quiet at school, though; he was faster than most of us with an answer. He borrowed books from the teacher, and took them home. So in time he became even smarter with his answers. I grew to accept his difference from most people. It didn't disturb me particularly: on the farm he was still quiet, small Jim. He was never too busy with his books to come along with me on Sundays.

There was a night when Jim was going through some new stones he'd gathered. Usually, in the house, my father didn't take much notice of Jim, his reading or his hobbies. He'd fought a losing battle for Jim, through the years, and now accepted his defeat. Jim still helped us with the herd, night and morning, but in the house he was ignored. But this night my father went across to the table and picked up a couple of the new stones. They were greenish, both the same triangular shape.

'Where'd you get these?' he asked.

Jim thought for a moment; he seemed pleased by the interest taken in him. 'One was back in the hills,' he said. 'The other was in a cave up the river. I just picked them up.'

'You mean you didn't find them together?'

'No,' Jim said.

'Funny,' my father said. 'They look like greenstone. I seen some greenstone once. A joker found it, picked it up in the bush. Jade. it is; same thing. This joker sold it in the city for a packet. Maori stuff. Some people'll buy anything.'

We all crossed to the table and looked down at the greenish stone. Jim's eyes were bright with excitment.

'You mean these used to belong to the Maoris?' he said. 'These stones?'

'Must have,' my father said. 'Greenstone doesn't come natural round here. You look it up in your books and you'll see. Comes from way down south, near the mountains and glaciers. Had to come up here all the way by canoe. They used to fight about greenstone once.' He paused and looked at the stones again. 'Yes,' he added. 'I reckon that's greenstone, all right. You never know, might be some money in that stuff.'

Money was a very important subject in our house at that time. It was in a lot of households, since that time was the depression. In the cities they were marching in the streets and breaking shop windows. Here on the farm it wasn't anywhere near so dramatic. The grass looked much the same as it had always looked; so did the hills and river. All that had happened, really, was that the farm had lost its value. Prices had fallen; my father sometimes wondered if it was worth while sending cream to the factory. Some of the people on poorer land, down the river, had walked off their properties. Everything was tighter. We had to do without new clothes, and there wasn't much variety in our eating. We ran a bigger garden, and my father went out more frequently shooting wild pig for meat. He had nothing but contempt for the noisy people in the city, the idlers and wasters who preferred to go shouting in the streets rather than fetch a square meal for their families, as he did with his rifle. He thought they, in some way, were to blame for the failure of things. Even so, he became gripped by the idea that he might have failed himself, somehow; he tried to talk himself out of this idea—in my presence —but without much success. Now he had the land solid beneath his feet, owned it entirely, it wasn't much help at all. If it wasn't for our garden and the wild pig we might starve. The land didn't bring him any money; he might even have to leave it. He had failed, perhaps much as the land's former owners had failed; why? He might have answered the question for himself satisfactorily, while he grubbed away at the scrub encroaching on our pasture; but I doubt it.

'Yes,' he said. 'Might be some money in that stuff.'

But Jim didn't seem to hear, or understand. His eyes were still bright. 'That means there must have been Marois here in the old days,' he said.

'I suppose there must have,' my father agreed. He didn't seem much interested. Maoris were Maoris. There weren't many around our part of the river; they were mostly down towards the coast. (Shortly after this, Jim did some research and told me the reason why. It turned out that the land about our part of the river had been confiscated from them after the Maoris wars.) 'They were most places, weren't they?' he added.

'Yes,' Jim said. 'But I mean they must have been here. On our place.'

'Well, yes. They could of been. Like I said, they were most places.' It didn't seem to register as particularly important. He picked up the greenstone again. 'We ought to find out about this,' he continued. 'There might be a bit of money in it.'

Later Jim took the stones to school and had them identified as Maori adzes. My father said once again that perhaps there was money in them. But the thing was, where to find a buyer? It mightn't be as easy as it used to be. So somehow it was all forgotten. Jim kept the adzes.

Jim and I did try to find again that cave in which he had picked up an adze. We found a lot of caves, but none of them seemed the right one. Anyway we didn't pick up another adze. We did wander down one long dripping cave, striking matches, and in the dark I tripped on something. I struck another match and saw some brownish-looking bones.' 'A sheep,' I said. 'It must have come in here and got lost.'

Jim was silent; I wondered why. Then I saw he wasn't looking at the bones, but at a human skull propped on a ledge of the cave. It just sat there sightless, shadows dancing in its sockets.

We got out of that cave quickly. We didn't even talk about it when we reached home. On the whole I preferred going out with my ·22 after rabbits.

II

It was near the end of the depression. But we didn't know that then, of course. It might have been just the beginning, for all we knew. My father didn't have as much interest in finishing jobs as he used to have. He tired easily. He'd given his best to the land, and yet his best still wasn't good enough. There wasn't much sense in anything and his dash was done. He kept going out of habit.

I'd been pulled out of school to help with the farm. Jim still more or less went to school. I say more or less because he went irregularly. This was because of sickness. Once he was away in hospital two months. And of course it cost money; my father said we were to blame, we who allowed Jim to become soft and sickly. But the doctor thought otherwise; he thought Jim had been worked hard enough already. And when Jim returned to the farm he no longer helped with the herd. And this was why I had to leave school: if he couldn't have both of us working with him part-time, my father wanted one full-time. Jim was entirely surrendered at last, to the house and his books, to school and my mother. I didn't mind working on the farm all day, with my father; it was, after all, what I'd always wanted. All the same, I would have been happier if he had been: his doubts about himself, more and more frequently expressed, disturbed me. It wasn't like my father at all. He was convinced now he'd done the wrong thing, somewhere. He went back through the years, levering each year up like a stone, to see what lay beneath; he never seemed to find anything. It was worst of all in winter, when the land looked bleak, the hills were grey with low cloud, and the rain swirled out of the sky. All life vanished from this face and I knew he detested everything: the land which had promised him independence was now only a muddy snare; he was bogged here, between hills and river, and couldn't escape. He had no pride left in him for the place. If he could have got a price for the farm he would have gone. But there was no longer any question of a price. He could walk off if he liked. Only the bush would claim it back.

It was my mother who told us there were people coming. She had taken the telephone message while we were out of the house, and Jim was at the school.

'Who are they?' my father said.

'I couldn't understand very well. It was a bad connexion. I think they said they were the people who were here before.'

'The people who were here before? What the hell do they want here?' His eyes became suspicious under his frown.

'I think they said they just wanted to have a look around.'

'What the hell do they want here?' my father, repeated baffled. 'Nothing for them to see. This farm's not like it was when they were here. Everything's different. I've made a lot of changes. They wouldn't know the place. What do they want to come back for?'

'Well,' my mother sighed, 'I'm sure I don't know.'

'Perhaps they want to buy it,' he said abruptly; the words seemed simultaneous with his thought, and he stiffened with astonishment.

'By God, yes. They might want to buy the place back again. I hadn't thought of that. Wouldn't that be a joke? I'd sell, all right—for just about as much as I paid for the place. I tell you, I'd let it go for a song, for a bloody song. They're welcome.'

'But where would we go?' she said, alarmed.

'Somewhere,' he said. 'Somewhere new. Anywhere.'

'But there's nowhere,' she protested. 'Nowhere any better. You know that.'

'And there's nowhere any worse,' he answered. 'I'd start again somewhere. Make a better go of things.'

'You're too old to start again,' my mother observed softly.

There was a silence. And in the silence I knew that what my mother said was true. We all knew it was true.

'So we just stay here,' he said. 'And rot. Is that it?' But he really wished to change the subject. 'When are these people coming?'

'Tomorrow, I think. They're staying the night down in the township. Then they're coming up by launch.'

'They didn't say why they were interested in the place?

'No. And they certainly didn't say they wanted to buy it. You might as well get that straight now. They said they just wanted a look around.'

'I don't get it. I just don't get it. If I walked off this place I wouldn't ever want to see it again.'

'Perhaps they're different,' my mother said. 'Perhaps they've got happy memories of this place.'

'Perhaps they have. God knows.'

It was early summer, with warm lengthening days. That sunny Saturday morning I loitered about the house with Jim, waiting for the people to arrive. Eventually, as the sun climbed higher in the sky, I grew impatient and went across the paddocks to help my father. We were working together when we heard the sound of the launch coming up the river.

'That's them,' he said briefly. He dropped his slasher for a moment, and spat on his hands. Then he took up the slasher again and chopped into a new patch of unruly gorse.

I was perplexed. 'Well,' I said, 'aren't you going down to meet them?'

'I'll see them soon enough. Don't worry.' He seemed to be conducting an argument with himself as he hacked into the gorse. 'I'm in no hurry. No, I'm in no hurry to see them.'

I just kept silent beside him.

'Who are they, anyway?' he went on. 'What do they want to come traipsing round my property for? They've got a bloody cheek.'

The sound of the launch grew. It was probably travelling round the last bend in the river now, past the swamp of raupo, and banks prickly with flax and toi toi. They were almost at the farm. Still chopping jerkily, my father tried to conceal his unease.

'What do they want?' he asked for the last time. 'By God, if they've come to gloat, they've got another think coming. I've made something decent out of this place, and I don't care who knows it.'

He had tried everything in his mind and it was no use: he was empty of explanation. Now we could see the launch white on the gleaming river. It was coasting up to the bank. We could also see people clustered on board.

'Looks like a few of them,' I observed. If I could have done so without upsetting my father, I would have run down to meet the launch, eager with curiosity. But I kept my distance until he finished arguing with himself.

'Well,' he said, as if he'd never suggested otherwise, 'we'd better go down to meet them, now they're here.' He dug his slasher into the earth and began to stalk off down to the river. I followed him. His quick strides soon took him well ahead of me; I had to run to keep up.

Then we had our surprise. My father's step faltered; I blundered up alongside him. We saw the people climbing off the launch. And we saw who they were, at last, My father stopped perfectly still and silent. They were Maoris. We were still a hundred yards or more away, but there was no mistaking their clothing and colour. They were Maoris, all right.

'There's something wrong somewhere,' he said at last. 'It doesn't make sense. No Maori ever owned this place. I'd have known. Who the hell do think they are, coming here?'

I couldn't answer him. He strode on down to the river. There were young men, and two old women with black head-scarves. And last of all there was something the young men carried. As we drew nearer we saw it was an old man in a rough litter. The whole party of them fussed over making the old man comfortable. The old women, particularly; they had tattoos on their chins and wore sharktooth necklaces. They straightened the old man's blankets and fixed the pillow behind his head. He had a sunken, withered face and he didn't look so much sick, as tired. His eyes were only half-open as every one fussed around. It looked as if it were a great effort to keep them that much open. His hair was mostly grey, and his dry flesh sagged in thin folds about his ancient neck. I reckened that he must have been near enough to a hundred years old. The young men talked quickly among themselves as they saw my father approaching. One came forward, apparently as spokesman. He looked about the oldest of them, perhaps thirty. He had a fat, shiny face.

'Here,' said my father. 'What's all this about?' I knew his opinion of Maoris: they were lazy, drank too much, and caused trouble. They just rode on the backs of the men on the land, like the loafers in the cities. He always said we were lucky there were so few in our district. 'What do you people think you're doing here?' he demanded.

'We rang up yesterday,' the spokesman said. 'We told your missus we might be coming today.'

'I don't know about that. She said someone else was coming. The people who were here before.'

'Well,' said the young man, smiling. 'We were the people before.'

'I don't get you. You trying to tell me you owned this place?'

'That's right. We owned all the land round this end of the river. Our tribe.'

'That must have been a hell of a long time ago.'

'Yes,' agreed the stranger. 'A long time.' He was pleasantly spoken and patient. His round face, which I could imagine looking jolly, was very solemn just then.

I looked around and saw my mother and Jim coming slowly down from the house.

'I still don't get it,' my father said. 'What do you want?'

'We just want to go across your land, if that's all right. Look, we better introduce ourselves. My name is Tom Taikaka. And this—'

My father was lost in a confusion of introductions. But he still didn't shake anyone's hand. He just stood his ground, aloof and faintly hostile. Finally there was the old man. He looked as though he had gone to sleep again.

'You see he's old,' Tom explained. 'And has not so long to live. He is the last great man of our tribe, the oldest. He wishes to see again where he was born. The land over which his father was chief. He wishes to see this before his spirit departs for Rerengawairua.'

By this time my mother and Jim had joined us, They were as confused as we were.

'You mean you've come just to—' my father began.

'We've come a long way,' Tom said. 'Nearly a hundred miles, from up the coast. That's where we live now.'

'All this way. Just so—'

'Yes,' Tom said. 'That's right.'

'Well,' said my father. 'What do you know? What do you know about that?' Baffled, he looked at me, at my mother, and even finally at Jim. None of us had anything to say.

'I hope we're not troubling you,' Tom said politely. 'We don't
want to be any trouble. We just want to go across your land, if that's
all right. We got our own tucker and everything.'

We saw this was true. The two old women had large flax of food.

'No liquor?' my father said suspiciously. 'I don't want any drinking round my place.'

'No,' Tom replied. His face was still patient. 'No liquor. We don't
plan on any drinking.'

The other young men shyly agreed in the background. It was not,
they seemed to say, an occasion for drinking.

'Well,' said my father stiffly, 'I suppose it's all right. Where are
you going to take him?' He nodded towards the old sleeping man.

'Just across your land. And up to the old *pa*.'

'I didn't know there used to be any *pa* round here.'

'Well,' said Tom. 'It used to be up there.' He pointed out the
largest hill behind our farm, one that stood well apart and above
the others. We called it Craggy Hill, because of limestone outcrops.
Its flanks and summit were patchy with tall scrub. We seldom went
near it, except perhaps when out shooting; then we circled its steep
slopes rather than climbed it, 'You'd see the terraces,' Tom said,
'if it wasn't for the scrub It's all hidden now.'

Now my father looked strangely at Tom. 'Hey,' he said, 'You
sure you aren't having me on? How come you know that hill straight
off? You ever been here before?'

'No,' Tom said. His face shone as he sweated with the effort of
trying to explain everything. 'I never been here before. I never been
in this part of the country before.'

'Then how do you know that's the hill, eh?'

'Because,' Tom said simply, 'the old men told me. They described
it so well I could find the place blindfold. All the stories of our
tribe are connected with that hill. That's where we lived, up there,
for hundreds of years.'

'Well, I'll be damned. What do you know about that?' My father
blinked, and looked up at the hill again. 'Just up there, eh? And for
hundreds of years.'

'That's right.'

'And I never knew. Well, I'll be damned.'

'There's lots of stories about that hill,' Tom said. 'And a lot of
battles fought round here. Over your place.'

'Right over my land?'

'That's right. Up and down here, along the river.'

My father was so astonished he forgot to be aloof. He was trying to fit everything into his mind at once—the hill where they'd lived hundreds of years, the battles fought across his land—and it was too much.

'The war canoes would come up here,' Tom went on. 'I reckon they'd drag them up somewhere here'— he indicated the grassy bank on which we were standing—'in the night, and go on up to attack the *pa* before sunrise. That's if we hadn't sprung a trap for them down here. There'd be a lot of blood soaked into this soil.' He kicked at the earth beneath our feet. 'We had to fight a long while to keep this land here, a lot of battles. Until there was a day when it was no use fighting any more. That was when we left.'

We knew, without him having to say it, what he meant. He meant the day when the European took the land. So we all stood quietly for a moment. Then my mother spoke.

'You'd better come up to the house,' she said. 'I'll make you all a cup of tea.'

A cup of tea was her solution to most problems.

We went up to the house slowly. The young men followed behind, carrying the litter. They put the old man in the shade of a tree, outside the house. Since it seemed the best thing to do, we all sat around him; there wouldn't have been room for everyone in our small kitchen anyway. We waited for my mother to bring out the tea.

Then the old man woke. He seemed to shiver, his eyes opened wide, and he said something in Maori. 'He wonders where he is,' Tom explained. He turned back to the old man and spoke in Maori.

He gestured, he pointed. Then the old man knew. We all saw it the moment the old man knew. It was as if we were all willing him towards that moment of knowledge. He quivered and tried to lift himself weakly; the old women rushed forward to help him. His eyes had a faint glitter as he looked up to the place we called Craggy Hill. He did not see us, the house, or anything else. Some more Maori words escaped him in a long, sighing rush. *'Te Wahiokoahoki,'* he said.

'It is the name,' Tom said, repeating it. 'The name of the place.'

The old man lay back against the women, but his eyes were still bright and trembling. They seemed to have a life independent of his wrinkled flesh. Then the lids came down, and they were gone again. We could all relax.

'Te Wahiokoahoki,'' Tom said. 'It means the place of happy return. It got the name when we returned there after our victories against other tribes.'

My father nodded. 'Well, I'll be damned,' he said. 'That place there. And I never knew.' He appeared quite affable now.

My mother brought out tea. The hot cups passed from hand to hand, steaming and sweet.

'But not so happy now, eh?' Tom said. 'Not for us.'

'No. I don't suppose so.'

Tom nodded towards the old man. 'I reckon he was just about the last child born up there. Before we had to leave. Soon there'll be nobody left who lived there. That's why they wanted young men to come back. So we'd remember too.'

Jim went into the house and soon returned. I saw he carried the greenstone adzes he'd found. He approached Tom shyly.

'I think these are really yours,' he said, the words an effort.

Tom turned the adzes over in his hand. Jim had polished them until they were a vivid green. 'Where'd you get these, eh?' he asked.

Jim explained how and where'd he found them. 'I think they're really yours,' he repeated.

There was a brief silence. Jim stood with his eyes downcast, his treasure surrendered. My father watched anxiously; he plainly thought Jim a fool.

'You see,' Jim added apologetically, 'I didn't think they really belonged to anyone. That's why I kept them.'

'Well,' Tom said, embarrassed. 'That's real nice of you. Real nice of you, son. But you better keep them, eh? They're yours now. You find, you keep. We got no claims here any more. This is your father's land now.'

Then it was my father who seemed embarrassed. 'Leave me out of this,' he said sharply. 'You two settle it between you. It's none of my business.'

'I think you better keep them all the same,' Tom said to Jim.

Jim was glad to keep the greenstone, yet a little hurt by rejection of his gift. He received the adzes back silently.

'I tell you what,' Tom went on cheerfully, 'You ever find another one, you send it to me, eh? Like a present. But you keep those two.'

'All right,' Jim answered, clutching the adzes. He seemed much happier. 'I promise if I find any more, I'll send them to you.'

'Fair enough,' Tom smiled, his face jolly. Yet I could see that he too really wanted the greenstone.

After a while they got up to leave. They made the old man comfortable again and lifted him. 'We'll see you again tomorrow,' Tom said. 'The launch will be back to pick us up.'

'Tomorrow?' my father said. It hadn't occurred to him that they might be staying overnight on his land.

'We'll make ourselves a bit of a camp up there tonight,' Tom said,

pointing to Craggy Hill. 'We ought to be comfortable up there.
Like home, eh?' The jest fell mildly from his lips.

'Well, I suppose that's all right.' My father didn't know quite what
to say. 'Nothing you want?'

'No,' Tom said. 'We got all we want, thanks. We'll be all right.
We got ourselves. That's the important thing, eh?'

We watched them move away, the women followed by the young
men with the litter. Tom went last, Jim trotting along beside him.
They seemed, since the business of the greenstone, to have made
friends quickly. Tom appeared to be telling Jim a story.

I thought for a moment that my father might call Jim back. But
he didn't. He let him go.

The old women now, I noticed, carried green foliage. They beat
it about them as they walked across our paddocks and up towards
Craggy Hill; they were chanting or singing, and their wailing sound
came back to us. Their figures grew smaller with distance. Soon they
were clear of the paddocks and beginning to climb.

My father thumbed back his hat and rubbed a handkerchief
across his brow. 'Well, I'll be damned,' he said.

*   *   *

We sat together on the porch that evening, as we often did in summer after milking and our meal. Yet that evening was very different
from any other. The sun had set, and in the dusk we saw faint smoke
rising from their campfire on Craggy Hill, the place of happy return. Sometimes I thought I heard the wailing sound of the women
again, but I couldn't quite be sure.

What were they doing up there, what did they hope to find? We
both wondered and puzzled, yet didn't speak to each other.

Jim had returned long before, with stories. It seemed he had
learned, one way and another, just about all there was to be learned
about the tribe that had once lived on Craggy Hill. At the dinner
table he told the stories breathlessly. My father affected to be not
much interested; and so, my father's son, did I. Yet we listened,
all the same.

'Then there was the first musket,' Jim said. 'The first musket in
this part of the country. Someone bought it from a trader down
south and carried it back to the *pa*. Another tribe, one of their old
enemies, came seeking *utu—utu* means revenge—for something that
had been done to them the year before. And when they started
climbing up the hill they were knocked off, one by one, with the
musket. They'd never seen anything like it before. So the chief of the

tribe on Craggy Hill made a sign of peace and called up his enemies.
It wasn't a fair fight, he said, only one tribe with a musket. So
he'd let his enemies have the musket for a while. They would have
turns with the musket, each tribe. He taught the other tribe how to
fire and point the musket. Then they separated and started the battle
again. And the next man to be killed by the musket was the chief's
eldest son. That was the old man's uncle—the old man who was
here today.'

'Well, I don't know', said my father. 'Sounds bloody queer to me.
That's no way to fight a battle.'

'That's the way they fought,' Jim maintained.

So we left Jim, Still telling stories to my mother, and went out
on the porch.

The evening thickened. Soon the smoke of the campfire was lost.
The hills grew dark against the pale sky. And at last my father, looking up at the largest hill of all, spoke softly.

'I suppose a man's a fool,' he said. 'I should never have let that
land go. Shouldn't ever have let it go back to scrub. I could of run
a few sheep up there. But I just let it go. Perhaps I'll burn it off one
day, run a few sheep. Sheep might pay better too, the way things
are now.'

But it wasn't somehow, quite what I expected him to say. I suppose
he was trying to make sense of things in his own fashion.

III

They came down off Craggy Hill the next day. The launch had been
waiting for them in the river some time.

When we saw the cluster of tiny figures, moving at a fair pace
down the hills, we sensed there was something wrong. Then, as they
drew nearer, approaching us across the paddocks, we saw what was
wrong. There was no litter, no old man. They all walked freely,
separately. They were no longer burdened.

Astonished, my father strode up to Tom. 'Where is he?' he demanded.

'We left him back up there,' Tom said. He smiled sadly and I had
a queer feeling that I knew exactly what he would say.

'Left him up there?'

'He died last night, or this morning. When we went to wake him
he was cold. So we left him up there. That's where he wanted to be.'

'You can't do that,' my father protested. 'You can't just leave
a dead man like that. Leave him anywhere. And, besides, it's my
land you're leaving him on.'

'Yes,' Tom said. 'Your land.'

'Don't you understand? You can't just leave dead people around. Not like that.'

'But we didn't just leave him around. We didn't just leave him anywhere. We made him all safe and comfortable. He's all right. You needn't worry.'

'Christ, man,' my father said. 'Don't you see?'

But he might have been asking a blind man to see. Tom just smiled patiently and said not to worry. Also he said they'd better be catching the launch. They had a long way to go home, a tiring journey ahead.

And as he walked off, my father still arguing beside him, the old women clashed their dry greenery, wailing, and their shark-tooth necklaces danced under their heaving throats.

In a little while the launch went noisily off down the river. My father stood on the bank, still yelling after them. When he returned to the house, his voice was hoarse.

He had a police party out, a health officer too. They scoured the hills, and most of the caves they could find. They discovered no trace of a burial, nor did they find anything in the caves. At one stage someone foolishly suggested we might have imagined it all. So my father produced the launchman and people from the township as witnesses to the fact that an old Maori, dying, had actually been brought to our farm.

That convinced them. But it didn't take them anywhere near finding the body. They traced the remnants of the tribe, living up the coast, and found that indeed an old man of the tribe was missing. No one denied that there had been a visit to our farm. But they maintained that they knew nothing about a body. The old man, they said, had just wandered off into the bush; they hadn't found him again.

He might, they added, even still be alive. Just to be on the safe side, in case there was any truth in their story, the police put the old man on the missing persons register, for all the good that might have done.

But we knew. We knew every night we looked up at the hills that he was there, somewhere.

So he was still alive, in a way. Certainly it was a long time before he let us alone.

And by then my father had lost all taste for the farm. It seemed the land itself had heaped some final indignity upon him, made a fool of him. He never talked again, anyway, about running sheep on the hills.

When butter prices rose and land values improved, a year or two afterwards, he had no hesitation in selling out. We shifted into another part of the country entirely, for a year or two, and then into another. Finally we found ourselves milking a small herd for town supply, not far from the city. We're still on that farm, though there's talk of the place being purchased soon for a city sub-division. We think we might sell, but we'll face the issue when it arises.

Now and then Jim comes to see us, smart in a city suit, a lecturer at the university. My father always found it difficult to talk to Jim, and very often now he goes off to bed and leaves us to it. One thing I must say about Jim: he has no objection to helping with the milking. He insists that he enjoys it; perhaps he does. It's all flatland round our present farm, with one farm much like another, green grass and square farmhouses and pine shelter belts, and it's not exactly the place to sit out on a summer evening and watch shadows gathering on the hills. Because there aren't hills within sight; or shadows either, for that matter. It's all very tame and quiet, apart from cars speeding on the highway.

I get on reasonably well with Jim. We read much the same books, have much the same opinions on a great many subjects. The city hasn't made a great deal of difference to him. We're both married, with young families. We also have something else in common: we were both in the war, fighting in the desert. One evening after milking, when we stood smoking and yarning in the cool, I remembered something and decided I might put a question to Jim.

'You know,' I began, 'they say it's best, when you're under fire in the war, to fix your mind on something remote. So you won't be afraid. I remember Dad telling me that. I used to try. But it never seemed any good. I couldn't think of anything. I was still as scared as hell.'

'I was too. Who wasn't?'

'But, I mean, did you ever think of anything?'

'Funny thing,' he said. 'Now I come to think of it, I did. I thought of the old place—you know, the old place by the river. Where,' he added, and his face puckered into a grin, 'where they buried that old Maori. And where I found those greenstones. I've still got it at home, you know, up on the mantelpiece. I seem to remember trying to give it away once, to those Maoris. Now I'm glad I didn't. It's my only souvenir from there, the only thing that makes that place still live for me.' He paused. 'Well, anyway, that's what I thought about. That old place of ours.'

I had a sharp pain. I felt the dismay of a long-distance runner who, coasting confidently to victory, imagining himself well ahead of the field, finds himself overtaken and the tape snapped at the very moment he leans forward to breast it. For one black moment it seemed I had been robbed of something which was rightfully mine.

I don't think I'll ever forgive him.

C. K. STEAD   **A Fitting Tribute**
(*b.* 1932)

I don't ask you to believe me when I say I knew Julian Harp, but I ask you to give me a hearing because in every detail the story I'm going to tell is gospel true. I've tried to tell it before. After Julian's flight I even got a reporter along to the house and he wrote me up as 'just another hysterical young woman claiming to have known the National Hero'. That was a year or more ago and I haven't mentioned Julian Harp since.

What reason can a person have for telling a story that she knows won't be believed? I have two: a cross-grained magistrate and a statue. You might have heard about the case in Auckland in which a woman, a shopkeeper in court for trading without a licence, happened to say in evidence that Julian Harp had once come into her shop and bought one of those periscopes short people use for seeing over the heads of a crowd. The magistrate asked her to please keep calm and stick to the truth. Then he called for a psychiatrist's report because he said she was obviously a born liar. Next day, which happened to be the anniversary of Julian's flight he sentenced her to a month in jail and the *Herald* published an editorial saying No one knew Julian Harp. Julian Harp knew no one. A privileged few watched his moment of glory; but he died as he had lived, a Man Alone....

Of course if the woman hadn't mentioned Julian Harp she might have got away with a fine. But she insisted she remembered his name because he asked her to keep the periscope aside until he had money to pay for it. And she said he wore his hair down around his shoulders. That was unthinkable!

When I read about that case I knew what no one else could know, that the woman was telling the truth. But it was the statue that really persuaded me it was time I tried to write down the facts. I was walking in the Domain pushing my baby Christopher in his pram. Some workmen were digging on the slope among those trees between the main gates and the pavilion and what pulled me up was that they were working right on the spot where Julian first got the idea for his wings. Then a truck arrived with a winch and a great slab of polished granite and in no time all the workmen were round it swearing at one another and pulling and pushing at the chains until the stone was lowered into the hole. I thought why do they want a great ugly slab of graveyard stone there of all places? I didn't know I had asked it aloud, but one of the workmen turned and said it was for the new statue. The statue was to go on top of it. What new statue? The statue of Julian Harp of course. The one donated by the Bank of New Zealand. *The statue of Julian Harp*! You can imagine how I felt. I sat down on a bench and took Christopher out of his pram and rocked him backwards and forwards and thought how extraordinary! Miraculous! That after all the arguments in the newspapers about a site, not to mention the wrangling about whether the statue should be modern or old fashioned, they had at last landed it by accident plonk on the spot where Julian thought of his solution to the problem of engineless flight.

I sat there rocking my baby while he held on to my nose with one hand and hit me around the head with the other, and all the time I was thinking, I might even have been saying it aloud, what have I got to lose? I must tell someone. If they laugh at me, too bad. At least I will have tried. And besides, I owe it to Christopher to let everyone know the solemn truth that he is the son of Julian Harp. By the time I had wheeled the pram back through the Domain I was ready to start by telling Vega but when I saw her there in the kitchen cutting up beans for dinner and looking all straggly and cross I knew I oughtn't to tell anyone until I had the whole story sorted out in my head and perhaps written down.

I should explain before I go any further that Vega is a sort of awful necessity in my life. Before Christopher was born I had to give up work and I didn't know how I was going to pay the rent. I want to stay on in the house I lived in with Julian, because although everyone says he is dead no one knows for certain that he is. I wasn't planning to sit around expecting him, but I had to keep in mind that if he did come back the house would be the only place he would know to look for me. The house and Gomeo's coffee bar. So when someone advertised in the *Auckland Star* that she was a respectable middle-aged female clerk wanting board, I took her in; and now there are the three of us, Christopher and Vega and me, sharing the little two-storeyed wooden house with three rooms upstairs and two down that sits a yard from the footpath in Kendall Road on the Eastern edge of the Domain. Vega isn't a great companion or anything. She hasn't much to say—except in her sleep; and then although she goes on for hours at a time it isn't in English or any other language. But when I was ready to start work again at Gomeo's I discovered I had been lucky to find her. I needed someone in the house at night to watch over Christopher, and when I mentioned it to Vega she said in her flat voice I could stop worrying about it because hadn't I noticed she never went out at night. She was afraid of the dark! Then she told me she was named after a star we don't often see in the Southern Hemisphere; and she made a noise that sounded like a laugh and said had I ever heard of a star going out at night.

All the time I was feeding Christopher that evening after seeing the workmen in the Domain I kept thinking about the statue and how wrong it would be if no one ever knew that Julian had a son. So when Christopher was asleep and I was helping Vega serve the dinner I asked her whether she thought Julian Harp might have had a family. She said no. I asked her what she thought would happen if someone claimed to be the mother of Julian's child. She said she didn't know, but she did know there was a good deal too much money being spent on a statue that made him look like nothing she'd ever seen and that kind of sculpture was a pretty disgusting way to honour a man who had given his life. I said but leaving aside the statue what would she think if a girl in Auckland claimed to be the mother of his child, Vega said she thought some of the little minxes had claimed that already, out for all they could get, but she didn't think Julian Harp would have been the marrying kind. She said she imagined him like Lawrence of Arabia, married to an idea. When I said I hadn't mentioned marriage but only paternity she said there was no need to be obscene.

I gave up at that and I didn't have time to think about Julian for the rest of the evening until it was quite late and something happened at the coffee bar that made me remember my first meeting with him. I was bending over one of the tables when Gomeo came out of the kitchen and put his hand on my buttocks and said in a sort of stage whisper you could hear all over the shop that tonight he'd gotta have me or that's the end. The sack. Finish. I said nothing and went to wipe down another table but he followed me and said in the same whisper well was it yes or no. So I swung round and said no, no, no— and each time I said it I pushed the wet cloth in his face until he had backed all the way into the kitchen. By now the people in the shop were waiting to hear me get the sack but Gomeo only said one day I would really make him mad and my God that would be the finish of us both.

You might wonder why that should remind me of Julian. It's because Gomeo threatens to sack me and for the same reason nearly every time there's a full moon and it was after one of his more spectacular performances I first talked to Julian. Julian was in the shop and like everyone else he took it all seriously and thought I had lost my job. So when I had finished pushing Gomeo back into the kitchen where he belongs Julian asked could he help me find a new job and he said he would even be willing to hit Gomeo for me if I thought it would help. I had to explain that Gomeo isn't quite one hundred per cent and he doesn't mean what he says. But you have to pretend he means it and fight him off. If you just laughed at him, or if you said yes you'd like to go to bed with him, you would be out on the pavement in five minutes, because Gomeo only wants the big drama, nothing real. I explained all this to Julian and he looked relieved but then he said he was sorry because now there wasn't any excuse to invite me to his bed sitter after I finished work. When I looked at his face I could see he meant just what he said so I asked him did he have to have an excuse.

And thinking of Julian's face reminds me I ought to say something about his appearance because reading about him in the papers will have given you a wrong picture of him. It's well known there's only one photograph of Julian, the one taken by a schoolgirl with a box camera just before he took off. His face is slightly obscured by the crash helmet he's just going to put on and the camera hasn't been properly focused. So all the local Annigonis have got to work and done what they call impressions of him and I can tell you quite honestly the more praise the picture gets the less it looks like Julian. They all dress him up in tidy clothes and cut his hair short and some of them have even put him in a suit and tie and stuck his hair down with Brylcreem. Well if it's important to you that your local hero should look like a young army officer I'm sorry but the fact is when I first knew Julian he was one of the most disreputable looking men I had seen. His clothes never seemed to fit or match and he never went near a barber. Every now and then he would reach round to the back and sides of his head and snip off bits of hair with a pair of scissors but that was all. I think he had given up shaving altogether at the time but he didn't have the kind of growth to make a beard so he was what you might call half way between clean-shaven and bearded. He wore a rather tattered raincoat done right up to the neck, and at midnight when I finished work and he took me to a teen club under the street where you could twist and stomp he kept it on and buttoned up until I began to wonder whether he had a shirt underneath.

I hadn't turned eighteen then but I was older than most of the others in the teen club and Julian was probably twenty-two or three so I felt embarrassed especially because Julian looked such a clown. When we arrived we sat at a table and didn't dance until one of the the kids called out Hey Jesus can't you dance? and several others laughed and jeered. Julian laughed too and clapped in a spastic kind of way and looked all round like a maniac as if he couldn't see who they were jeering at and then he got up without me and drifted backwards into the middle of the dancers and began to jerk and twist and stamp and roll in time to the music. Julian could certainly dance and in no time they had all stopped and made a circle round him clapping and shouting and urging him on until the sweat was pouring off him. He had to break out of the circle and make his way back to our table waving one hand behind him while they all shouted for more.

After that we drank coffee and danced and talked but you couldn't have much of a conversation above the noise of electric guitars and when we came out at 2 a.m. I felt wide awake and not very keen to go back to my bed sitter. Julian said I should come to his and I went. We walked up Grey's Avenue under the trees and then between two buildings and through an alley that came out at the back of the house where Julian had a room. I followed him up a narrow outside stairway right to the top of the building and through french doors off a creaky verandah. He threw up a sash window and we sat getting our breath back looking out over a cluster of old wooden houses like the one we were in and the new modern buildings beyond and the harbour and the bridge. Julian said the nice thing about coming back to Auckland after being away was the old wooden houses. I had thought that was what people coming back complained about, a town where nothing looked solid, but Julian said it was as if people lived in lanterns. He liked the harbour too and the bridge and everything he looked at and I found that unusual because the people who came into Gomeo's were forever arguing about which buildings in Auckland were any good and which were not and nobody was ever enthusiastic about anything, least of all those like Julian who had been away overseas.

Julian said he liked living right in the busy part of the city and he liked to be up high. He had worked as a window cleaner on the A.M.P. building in Sydney and as a waiter in the Penn Top of the

Statler Hilton in New York. And before coming back to Auckland he had driven a glass elevator that ran up and down the face of a hotel at the top of Nob Hill in San Francisco looking out over the harbour and the Golden Gate Bridge and the Bay. He said that was the best job he had ever had and he was willing to make a career of it but they made the elevator automatic to save the expense of an operator. Julian offered to run it for nothing and live off whatever tips he could get from sightseers, and when the hotel managers refused he still spent hours of every day going up and down as a member of the public until it was decided he was making a nuisance of himself and he was told not to come into the building again. A week or so later when he tried to slip in wearing dark glasses someone called the police and Julian decided it was time to leave San Francisco.

We sat without any light drinking and talking or rather Julian talking and me listening and I remember being surprised when I noticed the wine bottle was half empty and I could see the colour of the heavy velvet cloth it stood on was not black but dark red. It had got light and still I didn't feel tired. Julian said he would make us some breakfast and while he cut bread and toasted it I had a chance to look around at his things, and especially at a big old desk that had taken my eye. It was half way down the room facing one wall and it was covered with a strange collection of letters, newspaper clippings, stationery, bottles of ink of all different colours and makes, every kind of pen from a quill to a Parker, and three typewriters. Pinned to the wall above the desk there was a huge chart, but before I could begin to read it Julian saw me looking at it and called me over to help him make the breakfast.

I got to know that chart well later on because it was the nerve centre of what Julian called his Subvert the Press Campaign. On it were the names and addresses of all the people Julian had invented to write letters to the editor, then a series of numbers which showed the colour of ink each one used, the type of notepaper, and the kind of pen—or t^1, t^2, or t^3 if one of the typewriters was used; then examples of their scripts and signatures and details about their opinions and prejudices. Each name had stars beside it to show the number of letters published, and the letters themselves hung in bulldog clips at the end of each horizontal section. It had come to Julian that a newspaper really prefers letters signed with pseudonyms because it can pick and choose among them and print the opinions it likes but within reason it has to print all the signed letters that come in. So the idea of his Subvert the Press Campaign was very very gradually to introduce a whole new group of letter writers who all signed their names. They had to be all different types and live in different parts of town so the paper wouldn't suspect what was going on; but as Julian explained to me later, once he had established his group he could concentrate them suddenly on one issue and create a controversy. He called them his Secret Weapon because he said only a small group of people reads the editorials but everyone reads the correspondence columns.

But when it was put to the test and Julian decided to bring the Government down (I think it was over the cancellation of the Lyttleton scaffolding factory and the issue of extra import licences; the Secret Weapon misfired. He sent letter after letter. not only to the *Herald* and the *Star* but all over the country and soon there was a raging controversy. But he wrote his letters in a sort of daze, almost as if voices were telling him what to write, and what each letter said seemed to depend on the person supposed to be writing it instead of depending on what Julian himself really wanted to say. In the end his letter writers said as many different things as it was possible to say about the cancellation of the contract and when Parliament assembled for the special debate not only the Opposition members but the Government ones as well were armed with clippings of letters Julian had written. That was a great disappointment for Julian. He lost faith in his Secret Weapon and when I tried to get him going again he said what was the use of secretly taking over the correspondence column of a newspaper if when you succeeded it looked exactly the same as it looked before.

But it wasn't until I knew Julian well that he let me into the secret about his letters. That first morning he called me away to help with the breakfast before I had got more than a quick glance over the desk and when I thought about the chart afterwards all I could guess was that he might be the ringleader of a secret society of anarchists, or even a criminal.

We sat at the big sash window eating breakfast and watching the sun hitting off the water on to the white weatherboards and listening to pop songs and the ads on 1ZB. Julian sang some of the hits and we did some twisting and while the ads were on we finished off the wine. Julian told me the Seraphs were his favourite pop singers and that was weeks before anyone else was talking about them or voting them on to the Top Twenty. I often thought about that when Julian got to be famous and the Seraphs were at the top of the Hit Parade with 'Harp's in Heaven Now'. And when the N.Z.B.C. banned the song because they said it wasn't a fitting tribute to the national hero I felt like writing some letters to the editor myself.

It must have been eleven o'clock before I left to go home that

morning and I left in a bad temper partly because I hadn't had any
sleep I suppose but partly because Julian had stretched out on his
divan and gone to sleep and left me to find my own way out. He
hadn't said goodbye or anything about seeing me again and when
I thought about it I didn't even know his second name and he didn't
know mine.

I slept all that afternoon and had a ravioli at Gomeo's before
starting work and I spent a miserable evening watching out for
Julian to come in. It wasn't that I had any romantic feelings about
him, the sort I might have had in those days about one of those
good looking boys in elastic sided boots and tapered trousers. But
I had a picture fixed in my head of Julian with his straggly hair and
mottled blue eyes going up and up in that glass elevator like a saint
on a cloud, and I kept looking for him to come into Gomeo's as if
it would be almost a relief to see just the ordinary Julian instead of
the Julian in my head.

He didn't come of course because he was busy writing his letters
to the newspapers, but I wasn't to know that. The next day was
Sunday and I spent the afternoon wandering around the lower slopes
of the Domain among the trees—in fact it must have been somewhere near where they've built the Interdenominational Harp
Memorial Chapel. I was feeling angry with Julian and I
started to think I might get back at him by ringing the police and
telling them he was a dangerous Communist. I probably would
have done it too but I didn't know his address exactly and I only
knew his Christian name.

I still go for walks down there, with Christopher in the pram,
and sometimes I sit inside the chapel and look out at the trees
through all that tinted glass. People who come into Gomeo's say it's
bad architecture but I like it whatever kind of architecture it is and
sometimes I think I can get some idea in there of how Julian felt in
the glass elevator. I've had a special interest in the chapel right from
the start because Vega belongs to the Open Pentecostal Baptists and
her church contributed a lot of money to the building. She told me
about all the fighting that went on at first and how the Anglicans
tried to get the Catholics in because of the Ecumenical thing. She
said they nearly succeeded but then a Catholic priest testified to
having seen Julian cross himself shortly before he put on his wings
and the Catholics decided to put up a memorial of their own. Vega
said it was nonsense, Julian Harp couldn't have been a Catholic,
and I agreed with her because I know he wasn't anything except
that he used to call himself a High Church Agnostic and an occasional Zen Buddy. Of course Vega was really pleased to have the Catho-

lics out of the scheme and so were a lot of other people even though
it meant raising a lot more money. Vega said it was better raising
extra money than having the Catholics smelling out the place with
incense.

It must have been nearly a week went by before Julian came into
Gomeo's again and when I saw what a scraggy looking thing he was
I wondered why I had given him a second thought. I ignored him
quite successfully for half an hour but when he asked me to come
to his bed sitter after I finished work I went and the next night he
came to mine and before long it seemed uneconomical paying two
rents. We more or less agreed we would take a flat together but
weeks passed and Julian did nothing about it. By now he had told
me about his Subvert the Press Campaign and I knew how busy he
was so I decided to find us a flat myself and surprise him with it.
I answered probably twenty ads before I got one at Herne Bay at a
good rent with a fridge and the bathroom shared with only one
other couple. I paid a week's rent in advance and when Julian came
into Gomeo's and asked for a spaghetti I brought him a clean
plate with the key on it wrapped in a note giving the address of the
flat and saying if Mr. Julian Harp would go to the above address
he would find his new home and in the fridge a special shrimp salad
all for him. I watched him from behind the espresso machine. Instead of looking pleased he frowned and screwed up the note and
called me over and said he wanted a spaghetti. I didn't know what
to do so I brought him what he asked for and he ate it and went out.
When I finished work I went to his bed sitter to explain about the
flat. He wouldn't even go with me to look at it because he said anywhere you had to take a bus to get to was the suburbs and he
wasn't going to live in the suburbs.

I decided I wouldn't have anything more to do with him. I knew
he was friendly with a Raratongan girl who was a stripper in a place
in Karangahape Road and I thought he was possibly just amusing
himself with me while she did a three month sentence she had got
for obscene exposure. A few days later when he came into Gomeo's
and said he had found a flat in Grafton for us I brought him a plate
of spaghetti he hadn't asked for and when I finished work I went
out by the back door of the shop and left him waiting for me at the
front. The next evening and the next I refused even to talk to him.
I was quite determined. But then he stopped coming to Gomeo's
and began to send me letters, not letters from him but from his
people who wrote to the newspapers. Every letter looked different
from the one before and told me something different. Some told me
Julian Harp ought to be hanged or flogged and I was right to have

nothing to do with him. Others said he was basically good but he
needed my help if he was going to be reformed. One said there was
nothing wrong with him, it was only his mind that was disordered.
One told me in strictest confidence that J. Harp was too good for
this world and would shortly depart for another. They were really
quite funny in a way that made it silly to stay angry about the flat,
so when he had run through his whole list of letter writers I went
round to his place and knocked and when he came to the door I
said I had come to sing the Candy Roll Blues with him. It wasn't
long after that we took the little two storeyed house in Kendall
Road, the one I'm in now with Christopher and Vega.

The first few months we spent there Julian wasn't easy to live with.
He liked the house well enough and especially the look of it from
the outside. He used to cross the street sometimes early in the morning and sit on a little canvas stool and stare at the house. He said
if you looked long enough you would see all the dead people who
had once lived there going about doing the things they had always
done. But I soon discovered he was missing the view he had from
his bed sitter of the city and the harbour, and if I woke and he wasn't
down in the street he was most likely getting the view from the steps
in front of the museum. I used to walk up there often to call him for
breakfast or lunch and I would find him standing on the steps above
the cenotaph staring down at the ships and the cranes or more often
straight out across the water beyond the North Shore and the Gulf
and Rangitoto.

We had lots of arguments during those first couple of months.
I used to lose my temper and walk up and down the kitchen shout-
ting every mean thing I could think of until I ran out of breath and
if I was still angry I would throw things at him. Julian couldn't
talk nearly as fast but he didn't waste words like I did, every one
was barbed, so we came out pretty nearly even. But Julian caused
most of the fights and I used to make him admit that. It was because
he didn't have anything better to do. His Subvert the Press Campaign had ended in a way he hadn't meant it should and now there
didn't seem to be anything especially needing to be done. He took
a job for a while as an orderly in the hospital because the money
he had brought back from America was beginning to run out but
when they put him on duty in the morgue he left because he said
he didn't like seeing the soles of people's feet.

It was Anzac Day the year before his flight that Julian first thought
of making himself a set of wings. In the morning there were the
usual parades, and the servicemen and bands marched up Kendall
Road on their way to the cenotaph. Julian wasn't patriotic. He

couldn't remember any more about the war than I can. But he liked crowds and noise so he tied our table cloth to the broom handle and waved it out of the upstairs window over the marchers until a man with shiny black shoes and a lot of medals on a square suit stopped and shouted what did he think he was up to waving a red flag over the Anzac parade. Julian said it wasn't a red flag it was a table cloth and that made the man angrier. He shouted and shook his fist and a crowd gathered. When the Governor-General's car arrived on its way to the cenotaph it was held up at the corner. By this time Julian was making a speech from the window. He was leaning out so far I could only see the bottom half of him and I couldn't hear much of what he was saying but I did hear him shout

> Shoot if you must this old grey head
> But spare my table cloth she said.

Then the police arrived and began clearing a path for the Governor-General's Rolls and I persuaded Julian to come in and close the window.

By now he was in a mood for Anzac celebrations and we followed the crowd up to the cenotaph and listened to the speeches and sang the hymns. After the service we wandered about in the Domain. Julain kept chanting Gallipoli, El Alamein, Minqar Qaim, Tobruk, Cassino and all the other places the Governor-General had talked about in his speech until I got sick of hearing them and I turned up my transistor to drown him out. He wandered away from me across the football fields and kept frightening a flock of sea gulls into the air every time they came down. When he came back to where I was sitting he was quiet and rather solemn. We walked on and it was then we came to the place where the workmen are putting in the statue and right on that spot Julian stopped and stared in front of him and began slowly waving one arm up and down at his side. I asked him what was the matter and he said quick come and have a look at this and he ran down the slope and lay flat on his stomach on one of those park benches that have no backs and began flapping his arms. When I got down to the bench he asked me did his arms look anything like a bird's wings. I said no but when he asked me why I couldn't think of the answer. Then he turned over on his back and began flapping his arms again and asked me did they look anything like a bird's wing now. At first I said no but when I looked properly I had to admit they did. His forearms were moving up and down almost parallel with his body and the part of his arms from the shoulders to the elbows stayed out at right angles from him. So I said yes they did look more like a bird's wings now because a bird's wings bent forward to the elbows and then back along the body and that was why his arms hadn't looked like wings when he lay on his stomach. As soon as I said that he jumped up and kissed me on both cheeks and said I was a bright girl, I had seen the point, he would have to fly upside down.

It wasn't long before I began to notice sketches of wings lying about the house and soon there were little models in balsa wood and paper. One of the things that annoy me every time I read about Julian's flight is that it's not treated as a proper scientific achievement. People talk as if he flew by magic or just willed himself to stay in the air. They seem to think if no one in human history, not even Leonardo da Vinci, could make wings that would carry a man, Julian Harp can't have been human or his flight must have been a miracle. And now Vega tells me there's a new sect called the Harpists and they believe Julian wasn't a man but an angel sent down as a sign that God has chosen New Zealand for the Second Coming. I've even wondered whether Vega doesn't half believe what the Harpists say and it won't surprise me at all if she leaves the Open Pentecostals and joins them.

Gradually I learned a lot about the wings becauses designing them and building the six or seven sets he did before he got what he wanted spread over all that winter and most of the following summer, and once Julian had admitted what he was doing he was willing to explain all the stages to me. I don't suppose I understood properly very much of what he told me because I haven't a scientific sort of brain but I do remember the number $1 \cdot 17$ which had something to do with the amount of extra energy you needed to get a heavier weight into the air. And also $\cdot 75$ which I think proved that animals as big as man could fly if they used their energy properly but animals that weighed more than 350 pounds, like cows and horses, couldn't, not even in theory. But the main thing I remember, because Julian said it so often, was that everyone who had tried to fly, including Leonardo da Vinci, had made problems instead of solving them by adding unnecessarily to the weight they had to get into the air. The solution to the problem Julian used to say was not to build yourself a machine. It was simply to make yourself wings and use them like a bird. But you could only do that by making your arm approximate to the structure of a bird's wing—that was what he said—and that meant flying upside down. Once you imagined yourself flying upside down it became obvious your legs were no longer legs but the bird's tail, and that mean the gap between the legs had to be filled in by a triangle of fabric. In theory your legs ought then to grow out of the middle of your back, about where your kidneys are, and that of course was one of Julian's biggest problems—how he was to take off lying flat on his back.

But his first problem and it was the one that nearly made him give up the whole project was finding the right materials for the framework. He must have experimented with twenty different kinds of wood and I was for ever cleaning up shavings off the floor. but they were all either too brittle or too heavy or too inflexible. Then I think he got interested in a composition that was used to make frames for people's glasses but you would have needed to be a millionaire to pay for it in large amounts. It was the same with half a dozen other materials, they were light enough and strong enough but too expensive.

By the middle of that winter Julian was ready to give up and go to work. It was certainly difficult the two of us living off what I earned at Gomeo's and paying the rent but Julian was so happy working on his wings even when he was in despair about them I said he must keep going at least until he had given his theory a proper trial. It was about this time he decided nothing but the most expensive materials would do and he wasted weeks thinking up schemes to make money instead of thinking how to make his wings.

It must have been June or early July he hit on a solution. He had gone to Sir Robert Kerridge's office, the millionaire who has a big new building in Queen Street, and offered to take off from the building as a publicity stunt if K. O. would put up the money for making the wings, but he hadn't got very far because the typists and clerks mistook him for a student and he was shown out of the building without seeing Sir Robert. It had begun to rain heavily and Julian had no coat and no bus fare and he walked all the way back to Kendall Road that day with nothing to keep him dry but a battered old umbrella with a broken catch and a match stick wedged in it to keep it open. When he got home he couldn't get the match out and he had to leave the umbrella outside in our little concrete yard. He was standing at the kitchen window staring out and I didn't ask him about his idea of taking off from the Kerridge building because I could see it hadn't been a success when suddenly the match must have come out and the umbrella sprang shut so fast it took off and landed on the other side of our six-foot paling fence. I could see Julian was very angry by now because he walked slowly into the neighbour's yard and back with the umbrella and slowly into the shed and out again with the axe and quite deliberately with the rain pouring down on his back he chopped the umbrella to pieces. I went into the other room to give him time to cool off and when I came back ten minutes or so later he was sitting quite still on one of our kitchen chairs with the water running off him into pools on the floor and held up in front of him between the thumb and the forefinger of his right hand was a single steel strut from the framework of the umbrella. He seemed to be smiling at it and talking to it and even I could see what a perfect answer it was, light, thin, strong, flexible, with even an extra strut hinged to the main one.

Julian was impatient how to get on but he needed a lot of umbrellas because his wings were to be large and working by trial and error a lot of struts would be wasted. We couldn't afford to buy umbrellas and in two days searching around rubbish tips he found only three, all of them damaged by rust. The next morning he was gone when I woke and when I walked up to the museum steps where he was standing staring out across the harbour he said we would have to steal every umbrella we could lay our hands on. So that afternoon and every afternoon it rained during the next few weeks I left Julian at home working and I went to some place like the post office or the museum or the art gallery and came away with somebody's umbrella. It was easy enough when Julian wanted women's umbrellas but when he wanted the heavier struts I always felt nervous walking away with a man's. Occasionally there were umbrellas left at Gomeo's in the evenings and I took these home as well. Soon the spare room upstairs, the one Vega sleeps in now, was crammed with all kinds and I got expert at following a person carrying the particular make Julian needed and waiting until a chance came to steal it. I still have a special feeling about umbrellas and sometimes even now I steal one just because it reinmds me of how exciting it was when Julian was getting near to finishing his final set of wings. I even stole one at the town hall on the night of the National Orchestra concert when that poet read the ode the Government commissioned him to write about Julian and the Orchestra played a piece called Tone Poem: J...H...by a localcomposer.

I should mention that all the time this was going on Julian was in strict training for his flight. I used to tell him he was overdoing it and that he didn't need to train so hard. because to be honest I always felt embarrassed in the afternoons sitting on the bank watching him panting around the Domain track in sandshoes and baggy white shorts while Halberg and Snell and all those other Auckland Olympic champions went flying past him. But Julian insisted that success didn't only depend on making a set of wings that would work. It depended on having enough stamina left to keep using them after the first big effort of getting into the air. The flight he said would be like running a mile straight after a 220 yard sprint and that was what he used to do during his track training. He had put himself on a modified Lydiard schedule and apart from the sharpening up work on the track he kept up a steady fifty miles jogging a week. There were also special arm exercises for strength and co-ordination and he spent at least ten minutes morning and evening lying flat on his back on the ironing board flapping his arms and holding a ten ounce sinker in each hand. Julian was no athlete but he was determined and after six months in training he began to get that scrawny haggard look Lydiard world champions get when they reach a peak. It wasn't any surprise to me when he timed himself over the half mile and found he was running within a second of the New Zealand women's record.

By now the framework for the final set of wings was built and ready to be covered with fabric and there were only a few struts still to be welded in to the back and leg supports. Julian had bought a periscope too and attached it to the crash helmet so he could hold his position steady, flat on his back, and still see ahead in the direction of his flight. Everything seemed to be accounted for except there was still no anwser to the problem of how he was to take off lying on his back. He needed a run to get started but he could hardly run backwards and jump into the air. He considered jumping off something but that seemed unnecessarily dangerous and besides he thought it would be important to hold his horizontal position right from the start and that meant a smooth take-off not a wild jump.

I suppose I won't be believed when I say this but if it hadn't been for an idea that came to me one morning while I was watching Julian lying on his back flapping on the ironing board he would probably have had to risk jumping off a building. It came to me right out of the blue that if the ironing board had wheels and Julian was wearing his wings he would shoot along the ground faster and faster until he took off and left the ironing board behind. I don't think I realized what a good idea it was until I said it aloud and Julian stopped flapping and stared at me for I don't know how many seconds with his arms out wide still holding the ten ounce sinkers and then he said very loudly my God why didn't I think of that. The next moment he was gone, clattering up the stairs, and then he was down again kissing me and saying I was the brightest little bugger this side of Bethlehem and for the rest of the day he got nothing done or nothing that has anything to do with his flight. Of course Julian dropped the idea of actually putting wheels on the ironing board, and the take-off vehicle he did use is the only publicly owned relic of his flight. I find it strange when I go to the museum sometimes and see a group of people standing behind a velvet cord staring at it and reading a notice saying this tubular steel chromium plated folding

vehicle on 6″ wheels was constructed by the late Julian Harp and
used during the commencement of his historic flight. It puzzles me
why no one ever says good heavens that's one of those things undertakers use to wheel coffins on, because that's what it is. Julian had
seen undertakers using them—church trucks they call them—when
he was working in the hospital morgue, and when I suggested putting
wheels on the ironing board he immediately thought how much
better a church truck would be. I don't know where he got the one
he used but I think he must have raided the morgue or an undertaker's chapel at night because one morning I came down to breakfast and there it was gleaming in the middle of the kitchen like a
Christmas present.

If I'm going to tell the whole story of the flight and tell it truth-
fully I might as well come straight out with it and say Julian didn't
get any help or encouragement from the organizers of that day's
gymkhana. It makes me very angry the way it's always written
about as if the whole programme was built around Julian's flight,
and the way everyone who was there, Vega for example, talks as if
she went only to see that part of the programme and even tells you
she had a feeling Julian Harp would succeed. Up in the museum
under glass that's supposed to be protected by the most efficient
burglar alarm system in the Southern Hemisphere they show you
the form Julian had to fill in when he asked the gymkhana organizers to put him on the programme. They don't tell you he had to
call on them six or seven times before he got them to agree. Even
then I don't think he would have succeeded if he hadn't revived two
of his letter writers and had them send letters to the *Herald*, one
saying he had seen an albatross flying in the Domain and another,
a woman, saying she didn't think it was an albatross, it looked remarkably like a man.

Then you find there's a lot of fuss made by some people about
the fact the Governor-General was there and how wonderful it is
that the Queen's representative went in person to see Julian Harp
try his wings. The truth is the Governor-General was there because
the gymkhana was sponsored jointly by the fund-raising committees
of the Blind Institute and the Crippled Children's Society and he
agreed as their patron to present the prizes for the main event of
the day. And in case like everyone else I talk to you have forgotten
what the main event was and allowed yourself to think it was
Julian Harp's flight, let me just add that it was an attempt on the
unofficial world record for the one thousand yards on grass. In fact
Julian had to sit round while the mayor made his speech, a pole-
sitting contest was officially started, twelve teams of marching girls

representing all the grades competed, the brass and highland bands held their march past, and the police motor cycle division put on a display of trick riding. And when he did try to begin his event at the time given on the programme he was stopped because the long jump was in progress.

Of course now it's different. It's different partly because Julian succeeded, partly because he's supposed to be dead and everyone likes a dead hero better than a live one, but mostly because he made us famous overseas, and when all those reporters came pouring into the country panting to know about the man who had succeeded where men throughout history had failed—that was what they said —everyone began to pretend New Zealand had been behind him on the day. People started to talk about him in the same breath as Snell and Hillary and Don Clark, and then in no time he was up with Lord Rutherford and Katherine Mansfield and now he seems to be ahead of them and there's a sort of religious feeling starts up every time his name is mentioned.

There's nothing to get heated about, I know, but when I hear the Prime Minister (Our Beloved Leader, Julian used to call him) on the radio urging the youth of the nation to aim high like Harp I can't help remembering Julian so nervous that morning about appearing in public he even cleaned his shoes and with me just as nervous the only person there to give him any help or encouragement. And then when we got to the Domain Julian was told he couldn't have an assistant with him because the field was already too cluttered with officials and sportsmen, so there he was crouching down in front of the pavilion with his shiny coffin carrier and his scarlet wings for hour after hour waiting his turn while I sat on the far bank knowing there wasn't a thing more I could do for him. We were nervous partly because he hadn't given the wings a full test and partly because he had tested them enough to know they would carry him. They couldn't be tested in broad daylight and remain a secret, so Julian had to be satisfied with a trial late one night. I remember it almost as clearly as the day of the flight, Julian's church truck speeding across the grass getting faster and faster until I could just see the wings, black they looked in the dark, lift him clear of it. Each time he was airborne he let himself drop back on to the truck because he didn't trust his vision through the periscope at night and he was afraid of colliding with overhead wires. But there was enough for us both to know what he could do and to put me in a terrible state of nerves that afternoon watching the marching girls and the bands and waiting for Julian to get his chance.

Everyone knows what happened when that chance came. I don't

think many people saw him climb on to his truck and lie down and the few around me who were watching were saying look at this madman, he thinks he's Yuri Gagarin. But by the time the little truck and the scarlet wings were shooting full speed across the grass everyone was looking, and when somebody shouted over the loud speakers look at the wheels and the whole crowd saw the truck was rolling free there was a tremendous cheer. There was a gasp when he cleared the trees at the far end of the ground and then as he veered away towards the museum with those scarlet wings beating and beating perfectly evenly something got into the crowd and it forgot all about the athletic events and surged over the track and up the slope through the grove of trees by the cricket scoreboard, then down into the hollow of the playing fields and up again towards the museum. I would have followed Julian of course but I didn't have to make up my mind to follow. I was one of the crowd now and I was swept along with it running and tripping with my eyes all the time on Julian like a vision of a heavenly angel rising on those wings made out of hundreds of stolen bits and pieces. He rose a little higher with each stroke of his wings and even when he seemed to try for a moment to come down and almost went into a spin I didn't understand what was happening. I didn't think about whether he intended to go on climbing like that I was so completely absorbed in the look of it, the wings opening and the sunlight striking through the fabric showing the pattern of the struts, and then closing and lifting the tiny figure of Julian another wing-beat up and out and and away from us. I had stopped with the crowd on the slopes in front of the museum and Julian must have crossed the harbour and crossed the North Shore between Mt. Victoria and North Head and got well out over the Hauraki Gulf towards Rangitoto before it came to me and it came quite calmy as if someone outside me was explaining to me that I was seeing the last of him. I don't know any more than anyone else whether it was a fault in the wings or whether flying put Julian into some kind of trance he couldn't break or whether he just had somewhere to go, but it seemed as you watched him that once he began to climb there was no way to go but higher and further until his energy was used up. I stood there with everyone else watching him get smaller and smaller until we were only catching flashes of colour and losing them again and finally there was nothing to see and we all went on standing there for I don't know how long, until tea time anyway.

After that I was ill and I lay in a bed in hospital for ten days without saying a word seeing Julian's wings opening and closing above me until I was sick of the sight of them and all through the day hearing people talking about him and reading bits out of the newspapers about him. By the time I began to feel better he was famous and I remember when a doctor came to see me and explained I was pregnant and asked who the father was I said Julian Harp and I heard him say to the sister she needs rest and quiet. Soon I learned to say nothing about Julian. He belongs to the public and the public makes what it likes of him. But if you ever came out of a building and found your umbrella missing you might like to believe my story because it may mean you contributed a strut to the wings that carried him aloft.

ALEXANDER GUYAN
(*b.* 1933)

An Opinion of the Ballet

Finally there it was. Even while we were engaged, no, before then, perhaps from the first moment I met her, I sensed something of it. Then it was a certain look in her eyes, or a gesture. I sensed it, but was blind to it; incapable in love.

After we were married it appeared more in the open. Not directly afterwards of course; during our honeymoon, and for the first few weeks in our new home, we were blissfully happy together. Perhaps that was the reason, the fact that we were really together then, with no one else to talk to, or talk about.

Like every other newly married couple we knew, we were paying our home off. I'd managed to save a fair deposit, and we were able to keep the car, and we had managed to buy some good furniture. We even had a little in the bank. We certainly weren't rich, but then we weren't poor either. And the fact that all our friends were in much the same boat seemed to me to be a kind of security. I mentioned this to Pam one day.

'What I mean is that as it seems to be working out well enough for the others, I can't see how it won't for us.'

I knew right away that I had said the wrong thing. She started at me with that slow look she has, as if she is examining everything I have said before she gives a definite reply.

'Don't you think it would be fun', she said. 'if they came and took the 'fridge back because we couldn't keep up the payments?'

She didn't sound angry, only cold. 'Fun?' I said.

'Yes. Like what happened to the Marsdens.'

'That was two years ago', I snapped, 'and they are over all that now. They struck a sticky patch. *Practically* everyone has forgotten about it?'

'And has *practically* everyone forgiven them for it?'

'Do you have to be so quarrelsome?' I asked feeling frightened.

'No, I don't have to be. I'm not really. I was only joking. Do forget about it.'

She wasn't joking, and I didn't forget about it.

Some weeks afterwards we were invited to a party at the Browns. We have both known Jennifer and Cliff Brown for years; I went to school with Cliff—he has a pretty secure job with a petrol company—and we have always been close friends.

Pam didn't want to go.

'Well it's too late to pull out now,' I said.

'You could ring them and say that I have a headache.'

I felt a bubble of annoyance burst inside me. 'But why?'

'I just can't be bothered, and—', she paused, glaring at me, '—I detest Jennifer Brown.'

'Well, that's new to me,' I said.

'That b-bloody accent. A damned nurse, emptying bed pans, marries a clerk, and she develops an accent like that.'

'She—'

'It's all such a bloody pose.'

'There's no need to swear.'

'Oh to hell with you', she said, and began to cry.

Pam swears quite a lot, especially when she is angry, and I don't like it. Not that I mind women swearing, a little that is. They don't do it properly anyway, and I think that is what makes it sound so, if not attractive, amusing. They are so obviously conscious that they are doing it. But in Pam's case that isn't so. So is quite unconscious that she is doing it, as if it was the most natural thing in the world.

Surprisingly enough we went to the party, because later when she had cooled down, and said she was sorry, she insisted that we go. I watched her closely during the evening and she certainly seemed to be enjoying herself, laughing and talking with everyone, and getting slightly tipsy.

But again it could not be forgotten. I was conscious now of what I sensed to be a feeling of rebellion in her. It wasn't always as ob-

vious as it had been on the eve of the Brown's party, but it was there
just the same: a gesture of irritation at something quite trivial, a
completely uninterested attitude towards anything that concerned
our friends, a calculated absentmindedness as if she was thinking
about something that wasn't pleasant, and that I did not know
anything about.

She refused to admit that there was something wrong, insisted
in fact that she was perfectly happy, which merely made me more
certain that she wasn't .The only consolation I had was that nothing
of her queer behaviour was ever apparent in public, and even that
did not remain so for long.

When a well-known ballet company came to town for a brief season Pam and I were invited to join a group of our friends who were
all going together one evening. Pam seemed keen, which surprised
me. I didn't especially want to go, but then neither did any of the
men. The women were very excited about it.

There were four couples including Pam and me. I don't know if
the ballet was any good, but during the interval the women went into
raptures about it. Bill Cummings—he has a fairly good position in
insurance—spoke for the rest of the men when he laughingly admitted that he wasn't much up on the ballet. Not that anyone minded
that, because after all men aren't supposed to know much about it.

Pam was quiet, but I wasn't worried about that. She had seemed
so keen on the evening, and the other women were so insistent that
the ballet was good, that I presumed she was enjoying herself.
Then suddenly, filling up one of those silences that occur inside a
maze of conversation, she spoke.

'I hate the ballet,' she said.

I think it was the most painful few seconds of my life. Yet on the
surface nothing very terrible happened: there was another brief
silence, and then someone said something that changed the subject,
and everyone joined in trying to cover up. But she had said it and
that could not be covered up, nor could the way she had said it:
as if she were cursing everyone for being fools.

I don't understand it. What is she trying to do? Does she have
no sense of responsibility! How can I ever introduce a business
acquaintance into my home when I don't know how she will behave?
Even if she does hate the ballet, does she have to say so, and in that
manner? What is it that she is fighting? I don't know.

MARILYN DUCKWORTH
(*b.* 1935)

Loops of her Hair

There was once a woman with a low slung bust like a half filled shopping bag, who came to live in Woolton. Woolton is a slick New Zealand suburb with lawns and hedges polished by the sun until it resembles an array of bridal gifts—unused, unusable. The woman, Mrs. Doubleday, could arrange flowers artistically, whip up an excellent zabaglione, talk books—even New Zealand books—and say without hesitation what was dreadful in art and home decoration. She only practised these things when anyone was watching, but people usually were because she saw to that as well. Women friends who called on her in the sunny afternoons were served mint julep or passionfruit cocktails with glass straws. There was a piano in the windowed lounge which she had bought some years ago for her son.

Her son neglected to become a genius. He played 'Underneath the Lamplight's Glitter' with one hand, and then stopped. He was a sad young man with perpetual tears in his eyes, but who had never once sobbed, never laughed, and only occasionally sneezed. There was a still dignity about his face, his shoulders, his feet. The rest of him went unnoticed. Nobody ever remembered the colour of his eyes, the size of his hands, or what trousers he had worn with his reefer jacket.

One afternoon Mrs. Doubleday and Jeremy, her son, went walking in the town belt which lay behind Woolton. Under the pinetrees they sat down to unscrew the thermos flasks—hot beef soups, liquidized bananas and cream, iced fruit cocktail. When they had sipped and supped they looked up toward their suburb and noticed something terrible.

'Oh, I feel sick,' Mrs. Doubleday gulped, lying back on the tartan rug and placing a hand across her eyes. Her shopping bag bosom divided over her ribs, while her soft chins multiplied. But Jeremy didn't cover his eyes. He only shaded them from the glare, stared at what she had seen and smiled faintly.

Directly behind the hill at the back of their house were several decaying crooked bungalows, drooping on their piles, and so close together they threatened to lean on one another's shoulders.

Their windows winked lewdly and lopsidedly and the backyards were obscenely exposed. The wash-houses and toolsheds were even grubbier than the houses themselves and jostled a variety of faded colours against the hill. One particular house was larger than the rest, having several stories. It was a peeled, blackened, red weatherboard creature, sprawling like a heavy rooted tree.

'What is it?' Mrs. Doubleday mouthed, peeping under her hand. 'Find me the field glasses, Jeremy.'

'I think it's a boarding house,' he told her.

'You mean you *knew* it was there? You haven't *been* there?'

'Not particularly,' Jeremy said.

'Not particularly? What can that mean?' Mrs. Doubleday looked at him with new doubt. Jeremy had often failed her but never in this way of holding something unexpected.

'I think I went past there once when the bus took me too far. It has a notice outside—Avocado Guest House or something. And it's pink in the front.'

'Pink? But that's *wrong*. How is it you never mentioned this pink boarding house? You mean people actually pay good money to stay in a pink boarding house with a yard full of washing and cabbages? Jeremy, I'm still waiting for those glasses.' She held out her ringed hand impatiently.

Through the field glasses there was more to be seen. A slim dark figure in a too long frock was hanging a shirt on a coat hanger and pegging it to the line.

'Whoops!' exclaimed Mrs. Doubleday, as the wind took the garment and nearly whipped it away. But she quickly recovered herself to add: 'My gracious goodness, it looks like Sue May.'

Sue May was the young Indian girl who delivered their vegetables from the Indian fruit shop every Saturday morning. She used a boy's trolley on wheels to carry out this task and stood at the back door, shyly wiping her dark hands in her dress, while Mrs. Doubleday checked off the list—beetroot, Chinese gooseberries, passion fruit, tree tomatoes—and finally dismissed the girl, patting the curlers in her Saturday morning hair before going back to her electric dryer.

'It is Sue May,' Jeremy agreed, with a strange excitement in his voice.

Mrs. Doubleday had to prise the field glasses back from his grip.

'Oh well,' she said. 'That explains it. If they're *that* kind of people.'

Jeremy looked disappointed that the excitment was over. He had noticed recently that it gave him an odd feeling of pleasure to see his mother upset or put out. Her original horror on seeing the grubby bungalows had given him a pang of pure delight.

The following Saturday morning Sue May delivered the vegetables. Jeremy was waiting in the upstairs sunporch for the rattle of the burdened little wheels. He looked down on the girl's shining head as she passed beneath him, and a curious gay smile shadowed his blank face.

His mother seemed to have forgotten the incident of the thermos picnic for she checked the list in her usual absentminded fashion. In fact she was even more preoccupied than was her habit. she had a cavity in a front tooth and was trying to make up her mind whether to have it capped or filled with gold. She tumbled the vegetables carelessly into the rack and selected beetroot at random to cook for lunch. She was to make an aspic.

The morning passed and the beetroot simmered—an ugly smell in such a dainty kitchen. She was removing the cooled red knobs from their liquor when Jeremy came into the kitchen for his glass of mid-morning lemon tea. He seemed oddly bored and discontented with the day.

'What's the matter, darling?' his mother wondered, handling the beetroot carefully and distastefully.

He shrugged with a suggestion of irritation in his expression. 'I'm bored,' he announced heavily.

And then quite suddenly he was no longer bored. Mrs. Doubleday had given a small shriek of horror and lifted an object from the pot on the prongs of her fork. It dangled—a black spidery web, stained with dark red.

'Ooh it's a—oh I believe it's a —*hairnet*!' Mrs. Doubleday shrieked and gave a tiny retch under her white, ringed hand. 'Just think—that greasy hair—that greasy girl—.' She gave a noisier, more unmistakable retch and a moment later she had vomited right there in the kitchen—at Jeremy's feet.

He stepped back, gazing at the mess in mild surprise. Then a slow smile—more like a grin—stretched across his face. He made an odd sound, like a giggle.

'Let me see.' He took the hairnet from the prongs of the fork and examined it in the window light.

'Oh dear, oh dear!' Mrs. Doubleday gasped, whiping her fingers across her brow and avoiding looking at the floor. 'Oh, Jeremy—'.

However Jeremy was occupied. He rinsed the hairnet quickly in the sink and went upstairs to collect his reefer jacket.

'Where are you going, dear?' his mother called to him anxiously as he passed the window.

But 'Don't *bother* me, Mother,' Jeremy chided her and heard the delightful gasp she gave.

He thought he could remember the way to the Avocado Guest House. It wasn't a long walk provided you went in the right direction. When he arrived there it was just as pink as he had thought, but a little bit sootier.

An assortment of children in liquorice all-sorts shirts and plastic sandals were tumbled in disarray on the porch. A basket chair housed a very old woman, her legs encased in lumpy layers of grey stockings. She didn't look up when he stepped over the threshold but creaked out at his back.

'Mind the floor! Slippery.'

'Thank you,' he replied, walking carefully on the shiny porous wood.

The hall wall paper was wrinkled and brown. Queen Elizabeth II sparkled arrestingly at the turn of the stairs. A red slippered woman with a fistful of toilet rolls pushed past him in a crabwise shuffle on the stairway.

'Excuse me,' she muttered. 'In a hurry.'

'That's all right,' he answered her. 'So am I. So am I.'

Next he passed a little twisted man seated on an overstuffed couch on the landing.

'Good morning. How are you today?' Jeremy touched his hat which, however, he found he had neglected to wear.

The man looked at him in distgust and spat in his Khaki handkerchief. 'What do you care how I am? I've been here twenty-five years and nobody's thought to ask me how I am.'

And I suppose you've been sitting thinking about it for twenty-five years, Jeremy thought. You grumpy little man. But what he said was, 'I'm looking for a girl called Sue May. An Indian girl. Could you tell me where to find her?'

'Bound to find her if you keep on looking. She lives here but I couldn't tell you where. Keep walking. But mind the floor. Slippery.'

He found her at the top of the house washing her father's shirt. In the second room her little brothers and sisters had put their dolls to bed all the way around the skirting board. The untidy effect charmed and soothed him. The harsh smell of the yellow soap she scrubbed with excited him.

It was Sue May's hairnet right enough. He fastened it over her raggedy plaited chignon, tucking in one escaping end and then another. Finally he tucked her face under his own and her mouth under his and although she was shy she didn't seem surprised or put out.

It was lunch time the following day when the couple emerged from the house hand in hand. The sun was on the top of the sky and the lunch gong was sounding behind them. Sunday was the one day when lunch was available at the Avocado and the one day when the gong was struck in mid sunlight. The woman in red slippers was no longer in a hurry on Sundays and she struck her gong with a ponderous easy joy.

Mrs. Doubleday, beside herself with doubts for her son, had placed one or two things together in her mind and at this moment was hovering outside the pink guest house. She ducked and rose behind the fence, hid her eyes and peered, sighing. Until the gong sounded. And now to her horror the darkened doorway expels Jeremy and Sue May who walk hand in hand, shoulder to shoulder. The still faced Jeremy is no longer still faced. His cheek bones jut with emotion, his eyes are blackened with tears. He is crying, silently and deeply. He weeps with the easy emotion to be found on public occasions such as death and weddings.

Mrs. Doubleday saw his tears and registered the slow striking of the gong. 'Why is he weeping? My God,' she thought, 'I believe he's caught something dreadful! That's it—he's caught something dreadful!' Instantly the gong became the leper's bell, tolling horror. She clutched her throat and shrieked with dismay.

Jeremy heard her out of his daze, turned his head and saw her out of his new joy. And laughed and laughed and laughed, and went on laughing.